W9-ASW-889

Dear Reader:

In HarperPaperbacks's continuing effort to publish the best romantic fiction at the best value, we have taken the unusual step of pricing nine of our summer Monogram titles at the affordable cost of $3.99. Written by some of the most popular and bestselling romance writers today, these are magical and exciting stories that we hope you will take to your hearts and treasure for a long time.

Open the pages of these wonderful books and give yourself the gift of a reading experience like no other. HarperPaperbacks is delighted to present nine extraordinary novels—at a very attractive price—by favorite authors who can bring the world of love alive for you.

Sincerely,

Carolyn Marino

Carolyn Marino
Editorial Director
HarperPaperbacks

Books by Donna Valentino

Conquered by His Kiss
Mirage
Prairie Knight
Queen of My Heart
*Always in My Heart**

Published by HarperPaperbacks

*coming soon

Harper
Monogram

Queen of My Heart

⊱ DONNA VALENTINO ⊰

HarperPaperbacks
A Division of HarperCollinsPublishers

HarperPaperbacks   *A Division of* HarperCollins*Publishers*
10 East 53rd Street, New York, N.Y. 10022

Cover illustration by Bob Berran

First printing: June 1996

Printed in the United States of America

HarperPaperbacks, HarperMonogram, and colophon are trademarks of HarperCollins*Publishers*

❖ 10 9 8 7 6 5 4 3 2 1

In memory of Albert J. Pinelli — thirty-seven years wasn't nearly enough time. We miss you.

Queen of My Heart

Prologue

Hertford Castle, England, 1538

He had come to this meeting fully prepared to dislike her.

Any twenty-two-year-old man who allowed naught but ambition to lure him into accepting a betrothal to a six-year-old outcast expected to despise the unwanted wench on sight. Particularly when her outrageous insistence upon meeting face-to-face had cost him the chance to join an expedition to the New World.

And yet Dante Alberto Trevani found something endearing about the young girl who sat before him, unsuccessfully struggling with her urge to wriggle. Her thin body quivered with subdued intensity, from the crest of her bowed head to her clasped hands to the cascade of red-gold hair neatly tied back with a frayed blue ribbon.

The girl's name was Elizabeth Tudor—or at least he supposed he could call her by the notorious English king's surname. While Henry VIII had gone to great pains to have the red-headed brat declared illegitimate, he had nonetheless endured a considerable amount of humiliation to arrange this secret betrothal for her.

"You Italians strike me as a rude lot," Elizabeth piped up in flawless French. "My governess explained that I must marry you because your kinswoman made a mockery of my father's marriage proposal, and now you stand there staring at my royal person without first asking leave."

Dante muffled a chuckle. Full-grown villains quailed before his exceptional height, his ominous width, his reputation as Charles V's most ruthless captain of the guard. She, who made scarcely a handful of trouble, dared insult and challenge him. The tiny firebrand might burst into full angry flame if he laughed aloud.

He sought a compliment to soothe her ire. "Your father's messenger did not err when he said I would find you as mature as any forty-year-old. And you are quite correct about one Italian, at least—I am considered a very rude man. Thus I conclude you are an excellent judge of character for such a tiny girl . . . Your Highness."

A smile bloomed on her pinched features, and she flushed at the compliment, at the title she had no right to expect. Such a small effort on his part to provoke such delight on hers. Dante swallowed hard, realizing that Elizabeth's reaction betrayed the same craving for attention that had plagued him until he grew up and accepted the hard ways of the world. When she gained experience, she would not be so easily pleased.

"I have been told that I am quite forward for my age."

She seemed eager to prompt more compliments. Dante obliged, having naught else to offer. "So you are, to speak French so well. I confess I could not converse in English without rousing peals of laughter. I am forever boggled by the proper use of *thee* and *thou* and when one must needs add *-eth* or *-est* to a word."

"Nor do I have a command of your tongue." A frown creased Elizabeth's forehead. "I shall begin studying Italian at once."

"I, too, shall take measures to master English, both written and spoken." After all, a man who hoped to gain power through his bride should learn the language of those he sought to rule. He switched into his rudimentary English, hoping to amuse her. "I swear to master those *thees* and *thous* and *-eths* and *-ests*. I shallest becometh so fluent in thou . . . thy language that people will suspectest I haileth from London."

A girlish giggle rewarded his effort. She stuck out a small hand. He shook it to seal their bargain, feeling uncomfortably like a duplicitous older brother engaged in some childhood conspiracy against his trusting baby sister. She reinforced the notion by curling her hand within his. To his consternation, her hand began to shake.

"My father still has not secured a betrothal for my older sister Mary. And yet he is the one who insisted that you and I meet, so I might decide whether I find you pleasing."

"Then I have your father to blame for costing me the chance to sail to New Spain," Dante remarked. Learning that this enforced meeting had come about at a king's demand did not lessen the sting of knowing that his hero, Francisco Vásquez de Coronado, had sailed to New Spain without him.

"Oh—did you want to go very badly?" At Dante's curt nod, she sighed, and fixed her attention back upon herself, from where Dante suspected it seldom wavered. "My father has never before cared what I think on any matter. Do you suppose . . . do you suppose this means he loves me after all?"

She must have known the answer, for she looked down at her toes as tears began trickling from her eyes.

Dante's heart lurched with pity, and without taking his usual time to weigh the consequences of his action, he abandoned the purely businesslike purpose of the meeting. He scooped Elizabeth up against his chest and cuddled her like the sniffling six-year-old that she was. He patted her back and cursed himself for indulging her with this impulsive, gentle gesture, for it subtly, and irrevocably, altered his feelings toward her.

Cold-hearted bastard he might be, but he knew that after this moment he could never act the husband to a female who would forever be branded a sobbing little girl in his mind.

But marry her he must. Marry her he would—or die trying. Taking Elizabeth Tudor to wife would bring him the status and respect he had coveted all his life. It mattered not whether he exercised his husbandly rights with enthusiasm.

By the time she spoke again, his shirtfront was soaked with her tears. "I have resolved never to give my heart to any man. I will never love you. I hope this does not distress you, Dante."

"Not at all," he admitted as relief flooded through him.

She squirmed out of his embrace and peered up at him. Her cold eyes seemed to shift from gray to black to icy blue and back again. They glinted now with uncommon resolve. "I meant to avoid marriage altogether, but

Father seems so pleased about this betrothal that I feel I must accept it."

He crouched to meet her eye to eye. He'd never known anyone who swept through so many changes of mood. In the space of a hundred heartbeats, he'd gone from soothing a near-baby to speaking to her as he might to an adult.

"Do you understand, Elizabeth, that my cousin Christina did grievously insult your father by refusing his proposal?"

When Henry VIII's third wife, Jane Seymour, died, Henry had commenced the search for a new bride with a bold pronouncement: His new queen must enlarge his importance in the courts of Europe, and she must be a beauty.

Christina, dowager Duchess of Milan, boasted blood ties to Charles V, the Holy Roman Emperor. Her beauty fired Henry's lust. But Christina had rejected Henry's suit and enraged him by reminding all Europe of his second wife's execution: "If I had two heads, I might risk marrying the English king. Having only one, I dare not!"

At any other time Charles would have applauded Henry's humiliation—he had never forgiven Henry for discarding and divorcing Catherine of Aragon, who was Charles's aunt. However, Charles was forming a continental truce to protect Catholic Italy against the Turkish infidel. Desperate for Henry's cooperation, Charles offered to mend the rift between the royal families.

Henry had demanded a marriage, no doubt still cherishing dreams of the lovely Christina. Charles had instead suggested Dante as a husband for Elizabeth, who had been declared illegitimate after the beheading of Anne Boleyn. A bastard for a bastard. Charles and

Henry both agreed that the betrothal must remain a secret throughout the ten-year truce period, to avoid any appearance that Henry's cooperation had been purchased.

"Our fathers are very free with our persons," said Elizabeth.

Dante sensed that behind Elizabeth's young, tear-stained countenance worked a sharp-minded girl who resented being ordered about by her father, the King of England, and his father, the Holy Roman Emperor. A tiny girl who dared express annoyance with the two most powerful men in the world might equally resent a husband taking charge of her life. Dante thought fleetingly that it would suit Elizabeth well if he never returned to enforce their contract. The realization doused any spark of pleasure that might have remained concerning their betrothal.

"Our fathers have no care for our persons," he said. "Our circumstances just happen to suit their needs at the moment."

"It does not seem fair, Dante, that while they pretend to despise us as bastards, they use us for their convenience and prey upon our love for them."

Odd that a six-year-old stranger had so unerringly fastened upon the nature of Dante's relationship with his father.

Over the years father and son had reached a tenuous peace while Dante served in his father's army and gradually earned Charles's respect as a trusted confidante. This betrothal to the Tudor brat proved the extent of Charles's trust, for the truce's failure could plunge Europe into bitter religious war.

And as for its success—well, Henry VIII had but to turn a favorable eye toward Elizabeth. Dante's bride could bring him more lands than he could have found in New Spain, as well as the title, the wealth, and the respect that his stubborn pride refused to accept directly from the father who would not publicly acknowledge him as his son. His instincts cautioned him against admitting such self-serving motives. "My father entrusts me with many sensitive tasks," Dante contented himself with saying.

"Such as becoming betrothed to me, so my father won't be angry at your father anymore."

"Exactly so. This betrothal is very important, considering that you and I are, at present, rather insignificant."

Elizabeth bristled at being called insignificant. "I have always yearned to be important above all else."

Dante knew Elizabeth's story: banished to an outlying estate, ignored by her father, reviled by the English people as the offspring of the notorious Anne Boleyn. Not a soul would miss Elizabeth if she vanished from the face of the earth. Small wonder she hungered for importance. He understood far too well, with the familiarity of one enslaved by the same craving.

"Mayhap you should not accord so much importance to this betrothal, Elizabeth."

"It has already earned my father's approval." Her face glowed with fierce emotion. "To please him, I shall marry you and no other, Dante Alberto Trevani."

Her declaration left him uneasy. Dante had no intention of letting this English prize escape him. Still, it tempted fate to boldly declare that no interference would be tolerated.

"We cannot announce this pledge for ten years. Many things could happen. Why, your father might regret promising you to me and seek another, more important man."

"My father does not interest himself so much in my life. I might earn his regard if I behave very well and do as he wishes."

He bit back further cautions. It did seem unlikely that Henry would ever again trouble himself over her prospects.

And yet he felt a vague disquiet. It seemed prudent to caution Elizabeth that she could not always expect to get her own way, unless she—like him—planned for every contingency. "Some say I am overfond of weighing all options before committing myself to any course. I learned to do so from watching my mother, who might have enjoyed life more had she mastered the skill. She always excused her soft-hearted mistakes by saying, 'Sometimes circumstances force decisions upon us that all but tear out our hearts.' Do not permit yourself fall prey to circumstance, Elizabeth."

"I have been called a very willful and most stubborn female. My heart is impervious. I will never wed any man but you."

He pressed a finger lightly against her lips, but too late to stop her from repeating her vow. Very well. Considering that he intended to put all of his strength and effort into ensuring that their marriage took place, it did seem futile to worry over problems that might never arise.

Childish anxiety twisted her features. "You'll no doubt look just as fierce and frightening as you do now, but I am not a remarkable girl. You might not recognize me in ten years."

Dante knew that all women, regardless of age, sought appreciation of their graces. He took her hand in his and strove to find something memorable about her immature face and form. "Ah, but you have such lovely, deft hands, Elizabeth. And your hair, all gold shot with red. Women the world over will envy you your hair."

"Tudor hair," she said. "My father cannot deny I have his Tudor hair."

Again he felt a tug of pity. "Then I shall always be able to recognize you by your lovely hands and Tudor hair. And what about this bauble?" He touched a bejeweled object that hung on a chain round her neck.

"'Twas my mother's favorite bracelet." Elizabeth caught the object between her fingers, her excitement and pleasure betraying her youth. "Look, Dante, 'tis a turtle! The bracelet is too large for me to wear now, so my governess fashioned it with a longer chain so that I might wear it close to my heart."

It was a lovely thing, solid gold embellished with a green enameled shell and diamond eyes. "I will recognize this too," he said. "Wear it when we meet again."

"I mean to wear it . . ." Her words trailed away as she pressed her lips into a determined line. She leaned close and dropped her voice to a whisper. "I mean to wear it on the day I am crowned Queen of England."

God's blood, but her ambitions dwarfed his own! They might never find love, but they would serve each other well, he and Elizabeth. Two bastards who yearned for what had been denied by the circumstances of their birth.

He smiled. "*Auguri, ragazzina corragia.* It means 'Good luck, brave little girl.' Your first lesson in Italian."

"You will not forget your promise to learn English."

"I will hire a tutor to help with those infernal *thees* and *thous* and *-eths* and *-ests.*" The mild jest elicited a wobbly smile from her, and he vowed that he would never tell her that mercenary intent prompted this promise. She was but a heartbroken, motherless child who yearned for her father's love. A little girl who nurtured hopeless dreams of wearing a turtle bracelet on the day she was crowned ruler over people who would sooner forget her very existence. Her childish illusions would be destroyed soon enough without his adding fuel to the pyre.

The ten-year enforced silence suddenly seemed like a blessed interlude, granting Elizabeth time to mature and Dante time to become accustomed to the idea of marrying a woman who held no appeal for him. A time for peace to flourish throughout Europe—and it *was* gratifying to be temporarily important to this noble cause, if for nothing else. So Dante Trevani kept his deception to himself and did not voice his misgivings aloud as he took his leave of Elizabeth Tudor.

INTERLUDE
Mortlake, England, 1544

John Dee noted with scientific detachment that the fear-inspired shaking of his hand did not reduce its effectiveness in dribbling sand over his freshly inked parchment.

The tremors might, however, interfere with the steadiness required when sealing the important missive with melted wax. 'Twould not do, not at all. Should the wrong person open it and decipher its deliberately cryptic message, John Dee would likely find himself swinging from the end of a rope.

It sat sour upon him to feel such gut-churning trepidation on the very day he'd made his most astounding discovery. Perhaps he misinterpreted his faltering heartbeat, the coppery-tasting dryness in his throat, the distressing necessity to scurry again and again to the stool room. Perhaps 'twas not terror but excitement that prompted these unfortunate bodily discomforts.

"I will read the signs again." Reversion to proper scientific behavior strengthened his spine, and he sat a little straighter, spoke a little louder. "Yes, read the signs again."

Of course, no one could hear his strong declaration or witness his bold action. He would not dare allow anyone, even his most trusted servant, to learn the secret he had discovered.

He peered skyward through the finely wrought sights of his specially built radius astronomicus, the wondrous instrument which enabled him alone to look so closely into the sky's mysteries. He swallowed the gorge that rose at what the heavens revealed, and he consulted his charts to assure himself he had not made a mistake.

No. All was in order. At least on his part.

The same could not be said for the Tudor dynasty. All would die before their time, save one.

Hale, hearty King Harry, beloved prince of the English people, would die so soon that Dee grieved to think on it. Sickly Edward would follow his father to the grave only a few years later, placing pious, pinch-faced Mary upon the throne for a brief time. And then 'twould be Elizabeth's turn. A glorious reign spanning more than four decades, drawing John Dee himself into the splendor, providing . . . providing . . .

Providing Elizabeth never wed. She, the last of Henry's direct descendants, must rule in her own right. With no husband to guide her, no husband to love her, she was destined to die without issue. 'Twas a fearsome price to pay, even for one who yearned for the crown so passionately that the aura of her wanting surrounded her like an unholy halo.

There was but one small matter to resolve to ensure the glory would come about. And John Dee, alone of all men, possessed the knowledge and the means.

The weight of responsibility steadied his hand, and he sealed his letter.

1

Mortlake, England, 1544

He is at it again.

Dante stared at the limp parchment, riveted by those five words written in a crabbed, spidery hand. He had not yet mastered the near-incomprehensible subtleties of spoken English, but he could read this warning that sly old Henry was once more testing Dante's determination to wed Elizabeth.

On at least two other occasions Dante's spies had informed him that Henry was bargaining covertly with powerful men throughout the world, suggesting marriage to his youngest daughter in exchange for Henry's favor, much the same way he'd haggled with Charles. Each time Dante had sent to Henry swift messengers bearing strongly worded reminders of his rights to Elizabeth. Each time Henry's clandestine negotiations sputtered and died like flames starved for the bellows. But Dante harbored no delusions that 'twas his outrage that led to Henry's renewed amiability; only the truce negotiated with Charles held Henry in line.

That truce had crumbled scant months before. No matter. Dante's betrothal remained valid. Elizabeth was yet a child. He felt sure he would be able to enforce the betrothal himself, in good time. And then this letter had arrived, telling him there was no more time.

He is at it again. This time he means to see her wed to another. Come to Mortlake before confronting him. This matter has but one rightful conclusion, which I alone can help you bring about.

Your Friend,
Dr. John Dee

Dante counted few friends in Italy, and none at all in England. Of this Dr. John Dee he knew nothing save that the man knew about Dante's betrothal and that his missive promised assistance in resolving once and for all a situation Dante found intolerable.

Confronting Henry had meant a trip to England, to the king's London residence. Dante had studied the maps and calculated what a detour to Mortlake might cost against the chance that this mysterious Dr. Dee might indeed have some valuable information to impart. He had decided to visit Dee. The worst that could happen was the loss of a few hours.

Dante stood now in Dee's chilly, shadowed parlor. For once he welcomed the way his armor breastplate trapped his body heat. Hunger and bone-deep fatigue held him in thrall, but Dee's ancient servant had offered no refreshment, and Dante was reluctant to take his rest upon the lone settle that had long ago passed beyond mere shabbiness.

A quarter-hour passed, and then another, until all the time Dante had allotted for this venture expired. The grim surroundings and Dee's protracted absence fueled his annoyance. He turned on his heel, berating himself for wasting time pursuing some prank.

He all but crushed the frail wraith that somehow materialized in his path. Cursing aloud, he gripped the man about his shoulders to prevent them both from crashing to the floor.

"I am a seer," the apparition intoned in a voice he probably meant to sound frightening. "I predict that you have just this moment reached the limit of your patience."

"No skill was required for that." Dante snorted his scorn. "Now, out of my way ere I report thee to thy master for playing at sorcery."

"Oh, but I am master here."

"Thou art master?" Dante swallowed hard and peered at the man's face. A close inspection revealed that he wasn't as old as his hunched posture and skeletal thinness made him appear. A long, odorous black robe hung upon him like a sack, and a leather skull cap had been tugged unceremoniously over hair that hung in greasy strands past his shoulders. A verminous-looking beard straggled from his chin. "Thou . . . *thee* art John Dee?"

"Oh, yes." His vigorous nod set his cap's earpieces to flapping. "*Dr.* Dee, if it please you. I predict they will drum me out of Cambridge a few years hence, but they can never take my degree away from me."

Fastidiousness deserted Dante along with the strength in his legs. He lowered himself upon the decaying settle.

Dr. Dee scurried to a draped wall and tugged moldering layers of cloth aside to reveal a shuttered window. He jerked his head toward an ornate mirror and several other objects heaped upon the floor.

"Stand alongside yon magic glass before I let in the sun."

A few streaks of light penetrated cracks in the shutter. The squalid room appeared more disreputable and Dante himself more pitiable for placing himself at Dee's mercy. He heaved himself from the settle. "I will not. I am leaving right now."

"Do not leave unless 'tis your desire to plunge all England into disorder!" The sharp order stunned Dante into stillness, for its commanding note was so at odds with Dee's fantastical appearance. "If you value your life and soul, you will hear what I have to say about my lady Elizabeth's Grace."

"How couldst one such as thee claimest *any* knowledge of England's royal family?" Dante asked.

"Why, because of my close association with Dr. Cheke." Dee looked mildly startled that Dante had not divined this information for himself.

"Dr. Cheke?"

"He tutors young Edward Tudor in Greek and Latin. You do know of Edward—King Henry's son? Dr. Cheke acts as my mentor, and in exchange I provide him with valuable astrological services. We are colleagues."

The colleague of a world-renowned scholar—this filthy, maniacal-looking lunatic? Not even the astrology-mad nobles of his father's court would trust readings cast by this disreputable lout. Dante shifted, fully intending to storm from the room. Dr. Dee lifted a forestalling hand, and Dante found himself oddly incapable of any movement whatsoever.

"I recently cast Edward's horoscope for Dr. Cheke, but I can never show it to him, oh, my, never." Dee's voice lowered to a whisper. He darted a furtive glance around. "I told you I am a seer— my horoscopes predict young Edward will become king!"

"How astonishing," Dante drawled, not the least bit impressed by the prediction that so amazed Dr. Dee. "Just thinkest upon how tongues will wageth over this occurrence—the king's eldest son will himself become king in due course."

"The king's *only* son. Despite his single-minded pursuit of male heirs, Henry will never sire another."

"One is all he needs, especially when that one has survived the perils of childhood."

"Alas, weakness prevails in the Tudor line. They will all topple like dominoes until my lady Elizabeth's Grace commences her glorious forty-five-year reign, ruling in her own right, eclipsing her father in the people's hearts."

The lunatic's ravings hovered dangerously close to treason. "Dee—" Dante began.

"*Dr.* Dee." The man's asperity shifted into shy modesty. "I will be named royal astrologer once she takes the throne. You, sir, with your secret betrothal, are in the way."

There were a hundred corrections ready to tumble from Dante's lips. Such as: Henry VIII was newly and scandalously wed yet again, this time to his sixth wife, and would no doubt produce additional heirs, all more likely than Elizabeth to claim the throne; no woman could rule without a husband to guide her, not for forty-five days, let alone forty-five years; everyone knew that horoscopes and predictions were nothing but superstitious nonsense, and Dante Trevani was the world's worst fool for indulging this madman for as long as he had.

Everything he meant to say died stillborn, crushed by the weight of Dee's words. *You are in the way.* The taunt had dogged him all his life; until this moment he had thought himself inured to its painful thrust.

"Thy letter promised to helpeth me secure Henry's support for my betrothal. That is what I seek."

"I am telling you that you cannot enforce the marriage agreement!" Dee's countenance twisted with horror.

"I can."

"Nay! You must allow me to make you magically disappear!"

Dante's first impulse was to demand the return of his sword so he might drive it through Dee's heart and put a merciful end to his mad existence. And then he considered Dee's "magical" accomplishments: predicting that Dante had tired of cooling his heels and predicting that Henry's acknowledged heir would inherit the throne, both matters as logical as they were inevitable.

He rested his chin against his fist and pretended intense concentration. "Hmm. Mayhap thou shouldst closest thy eyes whilst predicting my disappearance, and I shall be gone by the time thou openest them again."

"You and your rude command of my tongue mock me, sir."

Dante felt a stab of shame for taunting a madman. "What dost thou want of me, Dr. Dee?"

"Listen well before you judge." At Dante's curt nod, he continued. "Elizabeth must never wed. She must rule in her own right. A virgin queen! All that stands between what must be and utter disaster is the vow she made to you: *I will marry you and no other, Dante Alberto Trevani.*"

A chill traveled along Dante's spine. How could Dee know Elizabeth's exact words, unless he had heard them directly from Elizabeth's lips? That meant that the two of them were in league. "So she toldest thee of her childish vow," Dante said.

Dee shook his head. "I have never yet spoken with my lady Elizabeth's Grace, though we will converse often in the future. But that is of no import. You are no doubt worrying that I intend to murder you where you stand."

Dante caught a surprised breath. The possibility that he might die had not entered into his decision to make this side trip. Until that moment he'd viewed Dee with condescending contempt. The mildly offered threat roused his instincts, reminding him that his stubborn pride had led him to make this long journey alone and telling no one where he meant to go. He stood unarmed in a madman's parlor, deep within a country ruled by a king who seemed to rue their long-ago bargain. Not an enviable position for a man who had just been told he stood *in the way . . .*

"Alas, I cannot kill you." True regret lit Dee's eyes, sending a shudder coursing through Dante. "Your death while she is still so young and so far removed from the throne would be the one factor freeing my lady Elizabeth's Grace from her vow. She could then accept another man with a clear conscience."

"Thou canst not think I would willingly steppest aside." Dante spoke harshly, inwardly embarrassed that he had permitted a fool's threats to shake his confidence, even for a moment.

"Nay. I cannot expect you to lightly cast off something most men would sell their souls to achieve." Dee stared at him straight on, and there was no madness whatsoever in his level gaze. "You will forever be what you are right now: a man of no consequence. She will be queen of England, Trevani. The man who weds her could rule at her side as royal consort."

The ambition that forever lived within Dante stirred. Royal consort. Heads would bow toward him the way they did toward his father. His father! Yes, even Charles V would find himself acknowledging his bastard son as his equal. No one, not even the Holy Roman Emperor, would dare fling Dante's illegitimacy in his face—providing Dee's outrageous predictions came about.

Impossible.

Dee's eyes glittered with a satisfaction that hinted he'd somehow read straight into Dante's soul.

"You need only show yourself at court and Elizabeth will feel honor-bound to marry you. Unlike you, she entered into this betrothal in good faith."

Dante swiveled on his heel with a wordless dismissal. Barring his way, though, stood Dee's ancient servant, clutching a stout broomstick, looking for all the world as if he meant to pummel Dante about the head if he dared take another step. Such fright marked the man's face that Dante worried the slightest move on his part would provoke a fatal fit. He threw up his hands in resignation; the servant subsided into a harmless huddle after sending him a relieved smile.

"He could marry another more suitable to his station, master, and remove himself from contention for my lady Elizabeth's hand," the servant suggested.

Dee shook his head. "And Elizabeth might then feel compelled to marry another man just to prove Trevani had not hurt her feelings. Women are notoriously unpredictable over such matters. He must disappear. There is no alternative."

Hearing two fools discuss his future as if they had any say in the matter cleared Dante's head. He would never outlive the jeers if word escaped that he'd been trapped into listening to such drivel between an old man brandishing a broomstick and a lunatic bent upon making him magically disappear.

"So where dost that leave us, Dee, if thou canst neither kill me nor foist a more suitable match upon me?"

"'Tis more than suitability at stake here, but 'tis true you are unfit to honor this betrothal."

"Unfit?" Dante echoed the insult with a deceptive softness that would have warned those who knew him well to reach for their swords. Dee, possessing no such knowledge, prattled on, worsening matters for himself.

"Unfit. The man who dares love a queen cannot pretend to have her interests at heart whilst secretly working toward his own goals. The man who dares love a queen must understand he has nothing to offer that she cannot command, save for his true love. You lack understanding, Trevani. You do not even understand why you desire so desperately the consummation of this betrothal!"

"I thought thou wert a seer." Dante sniffed his scorn at Dee's ravings. "I have ever wanted two things from this betrothal: lands and title. And thou hast only worsened thy cause by predicting such a glorious future for *my bride.*"

Dee ignored Dante's sarcasm. "You think to impress your father by forcing the English king to honor his word."

Dante glared at Dee. "I am a man, not a sniveling youth ruled by the yearning to impress his father. My father valueth my sword arm. I value the gold he sendeth my way in return. I ceased caring years ago whether he hath any affection for me."

"So says your head. Your heart beats a different tune. 'Tis your heart that must learn you are worthy." Dee smiled magnanimously. "This knowledge I shall grant you in exchange for magically disappearing."

Dante fell briefly silent. Many of the things Dee said had struck uncomfortably close to truths Dante avoided acknowledging. He sought to distract Dee's attention from himself.

"I would not be forced to press my suit if Henry were not so obviously determined to see Elizabeth wed. She wishes above all else to please him."

"Alas, poor King Harry will depart this earth ere growing displeased over Elizabeth's indifference toward marriage. I told you—you must disappear. That would serve Elizabeth best."

"By souring her so much on men that she dares never trust another."

"My, but you are a self-important lout to think your disappearance would so affect her." Dee sneered at him. "My lady Elizabeth's Grace will *use* your unexplained absence to her advantage. Believe me, Trevani, she will remain forever grateful to you—so long as you stay out of her life!"

There seemed to Dante little point in continuing this argument; perhaps if he pretended to indulge Dee's fantasies, he could make his escape and get on to the important business of confronting Henry VIII. "Very well, Dee. Makest me magically disappear, but be thou quick about it."

Dee smiled. He dismissed the servant, and when only he and Dante remained in the parlor, he returned to the small pile of objects littering the center of the room. "My radius astronomicus," he said, patting with great satisfaction at an odd-shaped instrument. "I am not at all sure that it is required for this venture, but I do not want to risk failure."

Dante groaned at the rambling explanation. Dee next picked up a mirror and rubbed his elbow across it to remove a smear.

"And this is my magic glass. Quite ancient. Legend says that prolonged exposure to sunlight might shatter it, so we must ration its use very sparingly." He tugged Dante's arm until they both stood in front of the radius astronomicus. Dante resigned himself to being pushed about—anything, if only it would bring an end to this ridiculous meeting.

"Verily, I tirest of waiting, Dr. Dee."

"To the left, one step—there. Now I shall fling open the shutter and let the sunlight reflect off the magic glass. As soon as the beam strikes you, then *pfft*, you will disappear."

Dee's elaborate preparations provoked Dante's curiosity. Dante's men often grumbled that their horses could not fart unless Dante had first determined their positions and what the outcome might be. He had always considered meticulous planning to be the mark of a sound, logical thinker. Dee's obsession with mundane details, however, seemed to mark him as a madman.

"Where shall I findest myself after I, er, disappear?"

"The future, of course."

"Why not the past?" he asked, genuinely interested in knowing whether Dee had considered that option.

Dee gaped at him but offered an explanation that showed he had indeed given that aspect some consideration. "If I sent you to the past, you might leave a secret legacy for Elizabeth to find, and my part in this should be discovered!"

"Aha, so thou intendest to forever deceive thy queen?" Dee paled before the mild jest, and so Dante teased him even more. "Soothly, this striketh me as unfair, Dr. Dee. Thou wilt obtain all thou wantest, whilst Elizabeth and I lose all."

Dr. Dee slanted a queer look at him. "Elizabeth will attain her heart's desire. She craves power and glory above everything—and she will have her place in history, provided you do not force her into a marriage she does not want."

"So I am the only one who standeth to be hurt."

"Hurt? 'Tis a strange word coming from you, Trevani. Your heart has hardened so well over the years that I doubt you will even notice when it stops beating."

Dante prided himself upon the impervious shield he'd erected round his heart. And yet he felt an uncomfortable stirring within him, as if something longed to deny Dee's accusation but lacked the conviction to do so.

Dante's expression must have revealed his inner turmoil, for Dee stared at him with somewhat surprised speculation. "Well, mayhap there is some hope for you after all. Like yourself, I am a man of honor. I would not demand this of you without offering adequate recompense. You will find yourself in a situation that offers everything you could hope to win here."

"A queen, a kingdom to rule, and a place where I am not in the way." Dante meant it as a mockery. Instead, he felt a stab of remorse to know that the best he could hope for was a businesslike marriage with a reluctant bride. He tightened his jaw, willing all such inappropriate thoughts out of his mind.

"Exactly so. Coupled with the healing of your heart. Yours to scorn if your pride blinds you to its true worth. Or yours for the taking—if you dare."

"A challenge, Dee? I warn thee, my strength is formidable, as my enemies have learned to their detriment."

Again Dee studied him with disquieting intensity. "The wounds you will suffer shall not bleed, but will cause greater pain than the loss of life or limb. You have never tested the strength you will need to face these challenges, Trevani."

Dante enjoyed bargaining; it seemed a shame to pass up the chance at it now, no matter that Dee's fancies were all in his head. "Suppose I endure this unearthly pain and triumph over these mysterious challenges? A victor deserveth some spoils."

"Battles of the heart reward the winner with happiness. 'Tis a prize above price."

Dante shook his head. "Nay, Dee. A happy heart holdeth less appeal for me than the notion of hearing my father address me as 'my lord.' Let us make a wager. I will allow thee to try to make me disappear. But if I prove I am fit consort for a queen, I may return here to claim all thou seekest to deny me."

Dee's countenance screwed into lines of worry. "I am not at all sure if that is possible. There is the passage of time to consider. It might pass more quickly there than here, or perhaps more quickly here than there. Why, a day spent in the future might encompass a week, a month, or a year of this time, or—"

"Dee, thou art worse than a grandmother trying to remember where she mislaid her purse."

Dee cast him a reproachful look. "Then mayhap 'tis of no matter to you that Elizabeth could well be an old woman by the time you find your way back. I daresay you will not want to return, regardless."

"Then thou hast naught to fear by agreeing to the wager."

"Oh, very well." Dee pouted for a moment. "Remember this: The mirror will carry you away; the mirror can bring you back."

"The mirror." Dante stared askance at it and had to blink, for it seemed that its surface reflected scudding clouds in a roiling sky—but it couldn't possibly carry such a reflection, for only the narrowest light ray penetrated the shutters.

"Now, do not slouch!" Dee scolded. "Do not forget that the legend says the sun must strike the mirror precisely, and for only a brief time, or it might shatter. I must deflect the sunbeam from the mirror to your head." Dee fumbled at the shutter and threw it open. He clutched the magic glass to his chest and turned toward the sun, angling the mirror and shifting it by small degrees until a brilliant white ray bounced off it and danced madly over the floor toward Dante's feet. Dee squinted and then grimaced as if he were in pain. "It is too bright. I cannot watch any longer. Do not slouch!"

"So thy eyes art closed, Dr. Dee?"

"Yes, yes! Do not move!"

Dante edged toward the door, muffling a chuckle with his hand. He would leave this place now, even if the servant lay in wait on the other side of the door. He would simply bowl him over without regard for his age or his broomstick.

"'Tis terribly bright, Dr. Dee. Shieldest thine eyes for at least a quarter-hour." He would indeed have magically disappeared by the time Dee opened his eyes once more.

The reflected beam skittered wildly and then settled on Dante's face. His hilarity abruptly deserted him. A sizzling commenced in his head, until he could hear nothing but it and the overwhelming thud of his heart.

The shaft of light skewered him right between the brows. Hot. Impossibly hot. The heat stole his breath and fed on it, growing even more intense in warmth and brightness, seeming to pierce his eyes with burning, stabbing agony.

And everything went black.

2

Dante awoke to misery.

His head pounded with an intensity he doubted he could endure for long. Dee's servant must have sneaked up from behind and clouted him in the head with the broomstick after all. His eyes ached and watered from Dr. Dee's devilish experiment, so he kept them squeezed tightly shut, fearing above all else that the burning pain, the brief space of utter blackness that had engulfed him, meant he'd gone blind.

A blind swordsman would have a devil of a time convincing Henry Tudor to stand by his word.

Clackety-clackety. Clackety-clackety.

As if to taunt him, a clanging reminiscent of a thousand swords striking a thousand shields filled his ears. *Clackety-clackety. Clackety-clackety.* But what army of men could strike with such swift rhythmic precision, with such force that the very floor he lay upon vibrated from the sound? The swordsmen never tired, either—the blows continued past counting.

Clackety-clackety. Clackety-clackety. A muted roar enhanced the crashing noise, the way wind whistling between the sheer walls of a mountain pass heightened the din of battle. And then a metallic shriek smote his ears. He could not fathom what it might be, other than the sound of a dungeon door swinging shut upon a blind, unconscious prisoner.

"Nay!"

His denial came out as more of a strangled gasp than a strong challenge, and the never-ending *clackety-clackety* drowned it out even from his own ears. He cursed Dee and cursed himself for becoming so distracted by the wild-eyed sorcerer's ravings. All that nonsense about virgin queens and making him magically disappear into the future had turned Dante careless and led to this humiliating imprisonment. Imprisonment . . . that was an alternative the crafty Dee had failed to mention. A man locked away in a dungeon could not enforce a marriage contract.

Eager as he was to test his vision, Dante thought it might be better to remain blind than to find a chortling jailer mocking his enfeebled state. Still, he forced open his eyes. Soft light illuminated the space around him. Praise God, he could see—but it seemed Dee had stolen his wits in place of his sight, for the scene greeting his eyes made no sense.

Dante expected oozing stone walls; instead, he found himself in a snug little corner where smooth, polished wooden plank walls gleamed in the dim light. No vermin-ridden, moldy straw lay beneath him; instead, heaps of cool, luxurious cloth cradled him with a seductive softness a Turkish pasha might envy. A stack of bound trunks blocked his view to the right, but from what he could see, the room seemed somewhat narrow in proportion to its length. Strangest of all, the entire chamber shivered and shook with motion—but not the familiar jolting of a carriage.

"I will have answers," Dante muttered. He attempted to gain his feet, a task made more difficult with the armored breastplate restricting his upper body. He found himself flung back against the cloth when the *clackety-clackety* vibrated through his legs and stole his balance. Had Dee somehow poisoned him, to cost him control of his body? Very well. He would crawl like a babe if that was the only way to learn what had happened to him.

So, on hands and knees, he edged his way past the trunks. He poked his nose beyond the edge, and what he saw drew him to his full height, with his limbs so locked with amazement that no amount of *clackety-clackety* could ever send him tumbling again.

At the far end of the chamber a woman sat at a table with Dr. Dee's infernal mirror propped against the wall before her. Her slim, deft hands ran a comb through red-gold hair that curled over her shoulders to her waist. Those hands. That Tudor hair. Dee, that ambitious black-garbed madman, had brought Dante face-to-face with Elizabeth Tudor despite all his blathering about ending the betrothal.

But her sideways posture revealed a figure far more buxom than Dante would have expected for a girl of no more than twelve, and to judge by her profile, her young face had matured into a finer, more pleasing aspect than he had dared imagine.

"Elizabeth?" Dante all but croaked like a frog.

"Huh?" Surprise, and a touch of distress, lit her expression as she whipped her head around to face him. She gripped the collar of her loose garment with unconscious modesty. "I wasn't expecting anyone else. Maud told me that I'd finished interviewing all the applicants hours ago."

All the applicants? Dante tightened his jaw. Henry's perfidy must have extended even further than Dante's spies had discovered. *All* the applicants. Did a veritable army of suitors strive for the hand of a girl who had once called herself unremarkable and beyond her father's notice?

But . . . Elizabeth hadn't looked like this six years ago. She'd been little more than a babe in arms six years ago. Had her childlike appearance then been some kind of trick?

"How many . . . applicants . . . have presented themselves to thee?"

She waved one of her slim, lovely hands. "Oh, I don't know. Maud rounded up at least a couple of dozen from those who met the railroad in Santa Fe." She gave a small shrug that caused her hair to shift over her shoulders like molten silk. "They weren't all good candidates. Some of them were married."

At his hiss of disbelief, she nodded solemnly. "I know just what you mean. I don't expect my need of them to last very long, but I didn't feel right about taking them away from their families. You're not running out on a wife and kids, are you?"

"Certainly not!"

"I'm purely amazed that so many men were willing to be considered. I guess it's the money." She cast him a coy glance. "I'm prepared to pay very well for the right service, if you know what I mean."

"Not entirely, my lady." At least, he prayed he did not understand.

She drew back, seemingly startled at his form of address, and he rebuked himself for failing to accord her a royal title in the face of his astonishment. Then she shrugged. "Not all of them were married. Maudie keeps telling me that there's a woman shortage out here, and it seems she's right. Most of the single fellows wanted to make more of this than a simple business arrangement. I guess the fact that I come ready-made with my father's land makes me good wife material, and they sort of lost interest when I convinced them I don't ever intend to marry."

She had remained constant in that regard, at least. He was about to compliment her on her resolve when she spoke again.

"So the job's still open, if you'd like to be considered."

I will marry you and no other, Dante Alberto Trevani. He fancied he could hear the words echo through his mind. He suppressed the urge to remind her of the long-ago vow. He ran the very real risk of asking her to repeat it so that he might revel in the sound of his name called in her new, honey-toned woman's voice.

He could not permit her artless seduction to blind him to the contradictions she presented. With one breath she confirmed Dee's contention that she had no desire to marry. With the next breath she admitted to casting her eye over dozens of eager suitors. And with yet another breath she offered the position to him. 'Twould require the wisdom of a priest to sort through the muddle she created, and he should bend every thought toward that task. Instead he found himself vexed at being lumped with dozens of others, some already married, vying for her hand.

"Hath thy father enlistedest thee in this scheme?"

A slight pause preceded her response. Dante could not tell whether she sought the correct words or whether it took her a moment to decipher his spoken English.

Perhaps he should have said *enlistedeth* instead of *enlistedest*.

"My father? Heavens, no! He wouldn't have approved at all. I came up with this idea all by myself." She smiled and modestly lowered her lashes, apparently quite pleased with herself for thwarting the plans of a king.

Dante caught a flash of emerald fire from her eyes, and it stifled his next question in his breast. He remembered how Elizabeth's eyes had shifted from gray to icy blue to charcoal and back again, with nary a glint of green. Perhaps he could no longer rely upon his memory. This lovely, tempting creature sitting before Dr. Dee's magic glass didn't resemble Elizabeth Tudor in the slightest, except for her hands and her hair—but who else could she be? Perhaps Dee's reflected beam of light had so addled his brains that he could not remember anything aright.

"Go ahead." A shy smile lent a sweet tilt to her lips. "I swear this is as embarrassing for me as it is for you. I guess any man who needs to wear a tin can for a shirt needs the work, so tell me why you're the right man for the job."

Dante glanced down. "Aye, my garments are travel-stained, but they boast the finest weave and are in the latest fashion. Everyone in Europe looketh toward Italy for style." She cocked her head in confusion, and he realized that his armor breastplate hid his embroidered shirt and slash-fronted doublet. He flicked his cape away from his forearm so she could see for herself that no man in England could lay claim to grander puffed sleeves or ruffled wrists.

He'd forgone the codpiece and leg armor while riding, but he knew his long legs looked fine in hose, and his short, belled breeches lent breadth to his narrow hips. His fur-lined velvet cape swirled in the manner only one carrying a broad set of shoulders could manage. He had bedecked his utilitarian but head-protecting metal cabassat with an ostrich feather, and taken care during spells of rain to shelter the downy plume—even now he could feel its soft fullness tickling his neck above his narrow ruff.

He had spent all and a bit more than he could spare upon the finery, knowing he would meet face-to-face with Henry VIII. He had hoped his dazzling appearance might so impress Elizabeth that she would lend her childish support to his demands. It rankled to hear her disparage his best.

"I cannot imagine why my garments give thee pause."

"Well, dressed like that, you remind me of Willy Snell," she said.

Dante had approached his English lessons with the same attention to detail that governed his battle strategy. His studies had included the British peerage, and the name *Snell* did not strike familiar. "Thou tauntest me with a common man's name," he said, oddly disappointed that she should fling his illegitimacy in his face in this manner.

"Willy's anything but common," she said. "He's the best clown that ever worked the Fontanescue Circus, and your outfit's just like the one he wore when he played court jester."

She sat easily upon her stool, with her hands clasped lightly in her lap, and nothing in her demeanor betrayed knowledge that by likening him to a court jester she had dealt him a deadly insult. Or perhaps he had erred in thinking his grasp of her tongue was profound, save for an inadequate grasp of *thous* and *thees* and the rules for tacking an occasional *-est* or *-eth* to the back end of a word. Curse English! Why could it not be like Italian, where word meanings weren't so elusive, and where the rules governing the tongue seldom varied?

At least two of Elizabeth's words—*railroad* and *santafe*—had made no sense to him. But he had understood enough. It did not bode well that she presumed to liken her betrothed to a court jester. Dee must have gained access to her ear and poisoned her mind against Dante's suit. He took several quick steps toward her. "I am a master swordsman, well versed in the difficult art of sword fence. Thou darest to compare me to a fool—"

The balance of his rebuke died in his throat, for his movement had caused a bit of drapery to flutter away from the wall. It revealed a small window, fashioned of glass, and through its transparent protection he saw blurs of blue and brown and green—blurs that soon sorted themselves into sky, rock-strewn earth, and the occasional tree, racing past with a speed that told Dante that the beasts pulling this strange conveyance had taken the bits in their teeth and bolted, no doubt frightened by that hellish *clackety-clackety* that went on without respite.

"By all that be holy, our lives art in danger!" He ran to the window, and his heart dived to his toes when this vantage point revealed the true extent of their helplessness. The conveyance sped so quickly it set his stomach churning to the rhythm of *clackety-clackety*. He pounded against the wall and bellowed toward the ceiling, "Driver! Control thy horses!"

"Say, mister?" Elizabeth's tentative query roused something feral within Dante's breast. She sat calmly, unaware of their danger. He must protect her at all costs.

"Fearest not, Elizabeth. Mayhap the driver hath taken a fit and lost control of his team. I will climbest out and take his place."

"Why do you keep calling me Elizabeth?"

Clackety-clackety all but numbed his ears now that he stood so close to the window. Certainly he had not heard her question aright, but he had no time to ask for a clarification. He pushed and prodded at the window but could not force the glass aside, and then happened to strike against a latch that sent the whole business swinging free.

"Oh, I just closed that window a minute ago on account of the sun beating down on that side. Don't open it! I know it's stuffy in here, but I hate for all that heat and soot to fly in."

He did not see how he would ever squeeze his whole body through the window. "Where be the door?" he yelled.

"Same place it was when you came in." She gestured toward the rear of the chamber, where he'd first found himself in his corner.

He spared a backward glance but saw no rough planked door marring the smooth wood-paneled walls. He stuck his head through the window and swallowed his dismay. Fully a dozen conveyances similar to this one were strung out in front of him, with no straining horses in sight. Yet another dozen followed to the rear, all so close that a man could stand between any two of them and touch both boxlike structures by simply stretching his arms.

Acrid, gritty smoke hung like a pall over them all. Such smoke could drift only from the bowels of hell. And what manner of beasts could pull such a string of carriages, at mind-numbing speed, over near-barren earth as flat as the sea? No earthly creature possessed such unholy strength.

The image of Dr. Dee came unbidden to his mind. Dee had laid him low—he, master swordsman Dante Trevani!—with a mere deflection of light. Perhaps every conveyance in this long string likewise imprisoned one of Elizabeth's secret suitors, and Dr. Dee, bent upon seeing Elizabeth rule as a virgin queen, was employing sorcery to speed them all to their deaths.

"You know, mister, you act like you've never ridden on a train before."

He had no time to spare upon deciphering her chatter, particularly as his most casual analysis spotted a flaw in Dee's evil plan. Elizabeth rode this hellish conveyance, too, so Dee could not take Dante's life without killing her along with him. She had to be in league with Dee—she had claimed full credit for this plan, and she seemed singularly unconcerned over their *clackety-clackety* plunge toward doom.

Perhaps this fearsome moment had been designed to test the bravery of those pledged to Elizabeth's hand. Dee had, after all, warned him to expect an unprecedented challenge to his strengths.

His pulse quickened. Might there be some truth to Dee's fantastical claim that Elizabeth would rule as queen and that only a man of great valor could expect to rule along with her? Royal consort! He imagined the sons of his loins ruling England, accorded the same rights and respect as those granted to the offspring of his father's legitimate get.

"I will not let thee die, my lady, even if I losest mine own life in the bargain," he swore, thinking she could not fail to remark upon his courage.

"Well, that sure is a good point in your favor." She swept a cool, appraising glance over him, one he found exceptionally forward for a maiden to bestow upon a man. "You're big enough, but you do seem a mite jumpy for a stable hand. And maybe a little too . . . fine." An entrancing blush flooded her cheeks, and she glanced away.

"Stable hand!" Outrage made it all but impossible to choke the offensive words through his throat. Then he remembered another bit of English custom that he'd gleaned from his studies. British royalty had created a vast web of honorary positions to ennoble and reward their favorites. Perhaps Elizabeth thought to place him into one of the most coveted positions. "Dost thou meanest 'Master of the Horse,' Elizabeth?"

She shook her head and wagged a reproving finger in Dante's direction. "My name is *not* Elizabeth."

Who could she be but Elizabeth? This too must be part of the ruse, to confound him with insults and lies while judging his suitability.

"I guess it wouldn't hurt for you to call yourself Master of the Horse while you're shoveling out the stalls. I don't care what title you give yourself, but it seems awfully presumptuous of you to call me anything but Miss Carlisle, considering that we just met and that you just might become my employee."

"Em . . . ploy . . . ee." He sounded it out syllable by syllable, as his tutor had taught him.

"Someone who works for me," she offered helpfully. "The train doesn't run all the way into Pleasant Valley, so it seemed like a good idea to bring my horses and wagon. But Maud and I never traveled apart from the circus before, and we didn't realize how hard it is to take care of two horses. That's why I want to hire a stable hand. Just for a week or two, until I decide what I want to do with the land my father gave me."

A metallic squeal shrieked through the car, twin to the sound that had earlier reminded him of a dungeon door slamming shut. So too did her words clang with dreadful finality. Did she think his name, his fidelity, could be *hired* for a fortnight, that he would meekly accept exile once appearance was served? Did she think he would be happy to be that kind of royal consort, a dronelike hireling with no true power or influence, no hope of siring England's future rulers, not even permitted to address his wife by her given name?

Her alliance with Dee must have so warped her womanly heart that she had forgotten all about her long-ago vow, the tender moment when they had shared importance in a noble cause. Dee, the self-proclaimed conjurer, must have ensorcelled her to make her forget it. That was it! Nothing else could explain her transformation from innocent child to evil witch. Nothing else could explain her unnatural maturity, her denial of her identity, the change in the color of her eyes.

"I wouldst never toil so, especially for the likes of thee." His tight-throated anger over Dee's theft of her innocence twisted his words into a snarl.

She took offense. Her delicate form stiffened, and she tilted her chin with imperious wrath. Her eyes narrowed with suspicion. "You never arranged an appointment through Maud, did you? You don't want to be my stable hand. Explain yourself!"

"I dost not think any explanation necessary." He paused deliberately, to lend weight to his accusation. "Witch."

She gasped, and her face drained of color. "You're

. . . you're one of them, aren't you? One of those god-damned sheepmen who want to take over my father's land!"

Dante mulled the meaning of her statement. "Dost thou claim that shepherds holdeth aspirations to wrest the English crown away from Henry VIII and rule England?"

"Huh?"

Perhaps in his astonishment over her revelation he had misspoken. He settled upon a simpler comment. "Thou canst not believe that I might be in league with misguided souls who seek to oust thee from what is rightfully thine."

"Prove you're not," she taunted. "Tell me what the hell you're doing in my private coach."

Dante struggled mightily to summon an explanation for his presence that did not brand him a lunatic. She watched him, which made his task all the more difficult. Her eyes narrowed as if she was mentally ticking off each passing second, until with a little cry of frustration she twisted on her stool. When she whirled back, her eyes brimmed with tears and deadly resolve—and her fist bristled with a cluster of daggers.

He threw his hands back against the wall, flinging his cape away from his sides so she could see he stood unarmed but well protected by his breastplate. Any sensible person would recognize the futility of pitting such tiny knives against armor and would have to consider the possibility that a deflected knife could bounce back and draw blood from the thrower.

Not she.

With quick, lethal precision she hurled the daggers straight at him, so swiftly that it seemed one had scarcely left her fingers before another took its place.

Her skill so astonished him that he could not move—
and perhaps that alone saved his life.

One by one the daggers pierced the fashionably
puffed folds of his fine but travel-stained garments and
skewered Dante Trevani to the wall.

3

"You'll rip that outfit you like so much to shreds if you try to wrench yourself free. And I still have one knife left, so don't try anything funny." Gloriana pointed the last dagger at the intruder's heart, then realized she'd never be able to stab through that metal contraption covering his chest. She angled the knife toward his privates instead. She could tell by the way he jutted his jaw and narrowed his eyes that he respected her skill enough to worry about her new target—and that he noticed how badly her hand trembled.

She edged toward the rear of the car. It took her a good three minutes to get there, open the door that led to her tiny balcony, cross the coupling bridge, and pound with all her might against the door to the stable car. She didn't wait for a response. She knew Maud would hear and skip across the coupling bridge the way she used to cavort along a tightrope. She prayed Maud would come quickly, so the two of them could decide what to do with the oddly dressed man who'd barged into Glory's private car.

She returned to her prisoner, noting the wary, surly way he watched her approach.

"I can see these few minutes of hanging around haven't done much to improve your disposition," she said.

"Fresh-killed game improveth with hanging, not men," he answered.

He held himself rigid as a scarecrow, though Glory had never seen any straw-stuffed figure tax the limits of its sleeves the way this fellow's arms did. The metal vestlike contraption he wore around his chest fit too close to his body for her to aim any daggers near his waist, but she'd pinned a few in the puffy pants ballooning around his hips. She had only herself and her good aim to blame for drawing the cloth so tightly over his lower belly and thighs that the outlines of unmentionable male parts were plain for anyone to see. And his legs! No woman could grow up in a circus without being surrounded by men wearing tights, but never before had she been so aware of the muscular power contained within a male limb.

He looked big enough, strong enough, and angry enough to scare anyone to death—except for the silly feather he'd stuck in his metal hat. It kept bobbing along with the rhythm of the train.

"Dost thou meanest to kill me?"

Though he used a few strange words, she recognized a hint of a familiar accent in the low, rich timbre of his voice. "I'm trying to place your accent. Are you related to the Flying Zambellis? You sort of sound like them, but not quite."

The hint of a smile quirked his lips. "First Willy Snell

and now the Flying Zambellis. It seemeth everything about me remindest thou . . . thee of someone else."

Never again. She felt her face grow warm with the knowledge that each minute she spent in his presence had the distressing effect of blotting other people right out of her mind.

"It's usual to try to find some common ground when you meet a person for the first time."

All trace of his humor vanished. "Thou dost not remember meeting me ere now?"

"I . . . I don't think so." It was possible, though, so she couldn't flat-out deny it. Through the years, Glory had performed before thousands of men. It was part of her job to flirt, to flatter, to distract their attention while she performed her simple illusions. Every once in a while some man would linger on the grounds after the show ended, certain that her act had held a secret invitation. She invariably sent them away, nursing their disappointment that she hadn't even noticed their faces in the crowd.

She studied her prisoner's face: lean and strong with a hint of copper glowing from dark, deep-set eyes. Eyes that betrayed a familiarity with being branded an unwelcome visitor. Proud lips, firm chin, all arranged in an extraordinarily pleasing manner. She couldn't see much of his hair because of his hat, but she suspected it must be brown tipped with bronze, like tiger stripes, to match his brows and facial hair. He wore a mustache, and a slight stubble of beard shadowed his cheeks.

She found herself thanking her guardian angel that he'd been unwilling to take the job. She'd worked around men all her life and knew how they spent every waking moment trying to finagle their way close to women. She could just imagine this fellow innocently asking her to help him shuck off that metal vest, and the next thing she knew, he'd be trying to sneak a little kiss. She could easily picture the stranger bending his head toward hers, those sad, dark-souled eyes mesmerizing her while his lips brushed hers and left the scratch of mustache and bearded cheek against her skin. She could not picture herself taking in the loneliness from his eyes and then pushing him away.

Kissing her stable hand? Good heavens, where had such an outrageous thought sprung from?

"No, I've never met you before," she whispered. "I would have remembered."

"Thou art not Elizabeth."

He spoke with such profound despair that she found herself, just for a moment, wishing that she were the woman he sought. "No."

She caught something in his expression, a brief, flickering panic that he quickly stifled. For a moment he reminded her of a half-tamed tiger bounding from its cage into the performance ring while the audience taunted it and shouted for its death.

"I don't suppose you're a sheepman, are you?"

He shook his head in denial but volunteered no information about himself. Glory guessed that if she found herself skewered to the wall while someone stood in front of her with a knife pointed at her privates, she might not feel like talking, either. She shifted the weapon behind her back. She didn't trust him enough to relinquish the knife. She felt no physical peril, but her whole body tingled with the warning that something about him posed a threat to her peace of mind, a threat that she didn't quite understand.

"My name's Gloriana. Gloriana Carlisle. Most folks call me Glory for short."

"Gloriana." He ignored the nickname and rolled the full version over his tongue. She shivered at the way it sounded, the way he softened the nasal *a*'s into *ah*'s. She felt his gaze dance over her, taking in her unbound hair, her loose wrap, her bare feet. Ordinarily she would have crossed her arms or made some excuse to turn away, for she couldn't abide being stared at when she wasn't working. "Gloriana," he said again, and she realized his attention didn't bother her because he looked at her as Gloriana and not a posturing circus illusionist. "'Tis fitting."

"It's from a poem about an English queen," Gloriana offered impulsively. "All the Carlisle women are named after queens."

Her mother had picked her name from a poem about that long-dead queen and told her that it meant "splendor." Nobody else had ever taken any notice of her name or remarked on whether or not it fit her. Maybe that was why Gloriana felt such a pleasurable melting sensation deep inside. Courtesy demanded that she ask his name in return, but instead she found herself asking, "Who's Elizabeth?"

He grew very still. "She is not important just now. My business is with the whoreson who owneth yon magic glass." He jerked his head toward her dressing table.

"That's *my* mirror."

"Nay, it belongeth to Dr. John Dee, accursed sorcerer."

"The hell it does!" Her voice shook, but with disappointment rather than anger. What was wrong with her, getting so annoyed and even somewhat jealous because her mirror held more attraction for him than she did?

She should just summon the conductor and order him to run this intruder off the train. But then she'd never know why he'd claimed her mirror belonged to a sorcerer. Of all the things he might have said, nothing could have intrigued her more.

She never had liked that mirror. Even though it was foolish of her, she felt uncomfortable around it. She'd occasionally found unfamiliar items near it, and several things she distinctly remembered setting by the mirror had vanished. Mirrors didn't have feelings, of course, but there were times when the darned thing seemed disappointed that she didn't use it to perform real magic instead of the simple illusions that she'd learned from her mother. She'd tried replacing it but hadn't been able to find one that could duplicate its best trick: reflecting sunlight with enough intensity to set objects on fire.

A sorcerer's mirror. It couldn't possibly be true, but it would explain a lot.

Despite all her misgivings about it, she felt bound to defend the object that the Carlisle women had depended upon to keep their bellies full. "That mirror is a bona fide antique. It's been passed from woman to woman in my family for three generations now."

"Thou art descended from Dee?" He gaped at her with the sort of horror-stricken expression that usually marked the faces of those exiting the freak tent. "God's blood, Dee's boasting was not idle. He hath shifted me into the future! Thy hands, thy hair—good God, I pray thee to assure me he did not takest Elizabeth for himself and conjure thee . . . thou from his unholy loins!"

She wanted to take offense at his words but found she couldn't, since at least half of them made no sense to her. "I never heard of your precious Elizabeth or any Dr. John Dee. My father's name was Harry Trask."

"Aha! Harry, Henry—my English tutor saidest those names are one and the same, *Elizabeth*."

"I told you, I am not Elizabeth!"

"Very well. If thou persistest in denying thy identity, explain thy possession of the mirror," he dared her.

Oh, this was too ridiculous—citing the provenance of a family heirloom to placate an intruder standing knifed to her wall. But Gloriana had never been able to resist a dare.

"My grandmother bought the mirror at an auction in England before I was born. Back in 1841. She used it in her act and passed it on to my mother, and now it belongs to me." At some point during her explanation he'd grown deathly pale, which caused a little lurch of trepidation within her. "So there," she finished.

"When thou sayest . . . Dost thou mean the year of our Lord eight . . . eighteen . . . forty-one?"

She nodded. "Almost fifty years ago."

"Almost fifty years ago?"

"Oh, bother, that feather should have given me a clue that you were the fussy type." She made a surreptitious calculation with her fingers. "Forty-seven years ago, since this is 1888."

"1888?" He might have been a parrot, squawking back every word she said, or a jackass by the way he wheezed out the year. Yes, she might have hit on something there, considering how wrong-headed and stubborn he was proving to be. She was smiling at the thought when Maud burst into the car.

"Glory—what on earth?"

One thing Glory admired about Maud Malone was that she could stop like a cat at the merest hint of trouble, with her feet firmly planted and ready to run even if half her body leaned forward like the figure gracing the prow of a Viking ship. It came from years of walking the tightrope, Maud claimed. She was poised like that now, a good ten feet away from the stranger, and was darting quick glances between him and Glory. Since he just stood there looking as stunned as if he'd been shot from a cannon, Glory felt obliged to explain.

"I thought he came to apply for the job."

"Well, I knew you were doing something to turn all those fellas against working for you. I never suspected you'd go this far, though, to scare them off."

"I didn't throw knives at the others," Glory said. "Um, I guess I might have overreacted a tiny little bit with this one because he tried bossing me around and called me names."

"Hmm." Maud inched closer and squinted, though Glory knew it was only habit that made her do it. Nearsightedness had always served her well on the tightrope, Maud said, since she had never been able to see all the way to the ground and couldn't tell how far she might fall. Now that she'd gotten older and her vision had inexplicably sharpened, so that she was now farsighted instead of nearsighted, she couldn't walk the ropes anymore, though she vowed she would again someday. "Maybe you did the right thing. I never saw him before, and I pestered every man on this train to apply for that job. A bunch of lily-livered sluggards, the lot of them. What's his name?"

"I don't know."

"Well, what kind of experience does he have?"

Glory winced. "I never got around to asking him."

"My experiences wouldst confound most men," he said with a morose glower.

"Well, spill the beans, then," said Maud. "Who are you, and what jobs did you hold up to now?"

"Jobs?"

"You know, where did you work?"

He frowned, and then understanding dawned upon his features. "Ah! Of late, I have served in my father's army as captain of the guard. As is fitting, for I, Dante

Alberto Trevani, have forged a fearsome reputation as defender of the realm."

"Huh?"

He seemed to grope for the right words.

"An assassin."

"Oh, my," Gloriana said faintly.

"He's just saying that to impress you," Maud said. "Look at him. He doesn't even have a gunbelt. How does he assassinate people—bend at the waist and ram his victims with that pointy thing that looks like an upside-down acorn on his head?"

"It doesn't matter, he just likes to call himself by fancy titles," said Glory. "He doesn't want to work for me anyway. Called me a witch when I offered him the job."

"Bossing you around and calling you names—acts like he's your husband instead of your hired hand. I don't blame you for knifing him to the wall." Maud issued a lewd cackle and gave him a quick assessment from head to toe. "'Course, I can't say that I'd mind having him stuck over my berth, 'specially if he took off the acorn hat and the metal chest thing."

"Maud!" Glory's face flamed, but the stranger with the elegant-sounding name seemed unaware of the bawdy nature of Maud's comment.

"Thou must givest me that mirror." He strained against the daggers but stilled at the sound of rending cloth.

"Oh, I don't understand him," Glory muttered.

"*Thee* must*eth* givest me that mirror?" He seemed as perplexed by his mirror obsession as she was.

"I already said no."

"To heck with the mirror. Let's unpin him, Glory." Maud rubbed her hands together, and her eyes sparkled with anticipation. "I'm short, so I'll take the low parts."

*   *   *

Dante found his attention rudely distracted from his predicament when the aging crone called Maud wrenched the daggers from around his hips and gave him a lusty pat before stepping away. And then Gloriana moved to take her place, and Dr. Dee's cursed magic glass might have shattered for all the notice Dante paid it again.

The top of her head just reached his chin, and from her drifted the most intoxicating scent ever devised by God.

His arms ached from the effort of holding them so that the daggers would not tear his sleeves beyond repair. Gloriana removed the knives above one arm and then the other, and he lowered them gingerly to his sides. His limbs prickled from the shift in position; he suspected they would tingle even more if he followed his inclination to wrap them around Gloriana's narrow waist.

Two daggers atop each shoulder still pinned his cape to the wall. He gritted his teeth against the exquisite agony of her hand brushing so close to his neck as she worked those daggers free. A soft sound of frustration escaped her as she tugged at the last one, as if it had bitten deeper into the wooden wall than she'd meant it to.

Her eyes met his with rueful, silent apology, and he marveled at how rare that was, to forge unspoken understanding with someone he did not know at all. Then she stepped closer still, to lend leverage to her strength. She rested her hand briefly against the metal breastplate covering his heart, then suddenly snatched it away, as if his body heat had rendered the steel as scorching as the door of an oven. She summoned a deep breath and touched him again, but this time she used only her fingertips to brace herself. He wished his chest armor might dissolve; indeed, he couldn't understand why it did not, since her closeness had set his blood to boiling. Her breath caressed his cheek, reminding him that he had not taken any air himself for the past moment or so, ever since her first light, tentative touch.

She pulled the last dagger free and, tilting her face toward his, gifted him with the full splendor of her smile. He was looking down at her, his lips hovering mere inches from hers, when his damned ostrich feather bobbed between them.

She sneezed. Once, and then again. Then she turned away and stepped back so that she stood next to Maud once more.

Dante might have remained affixed to the wall for all the good his freedom did him. He wrenched the cabassat from his head and tucked it beneath his arm. It struck against his breastplate, giving off the dull clunk of metal striking metal, and both women started at the sound, as if neither had ever heard a man move about in partial armor before. He suddenly felt every inch the fool she'd claimed he looked. His abrupt motion had freed his hair to brush against his shoulders, and he knew it must be hanging in gnarled, sweat-soaked strands after its long stint stuffed into the cabassat.

Maud's eyes did indeed widen at the sight of his hair. She glanced quickly at Gloriana and then back at him again, only this time there was speculation in her eyes. She tugged at Gloriana's sleeve. "He wants your mirror, Glory."

"Well, he can't have it."

"You've told me a thousand times that you don't even like the stupid thing."

Gloriana shrugged. "I might not like it much, but it's

the one thing the women in my family could always depend on." She sent a wounded look in Dante's direction, telling him without words that she had found few things worthy of her trust. She meant to hold on to her mirror at any cost.

The tip of the ostrich feather drifted before his nose, and he pursed his lips without thinking, intending to blow it away. Gloriana blushed and touched two fingers to her lips. The gesture, so artlessly feminine, roused male triumph within Dante—it told him that she had been willing to accept his kiss before the cursed feather split them apart.

"You're not using your head, Glory. If he wants the mirror so much, maybe he'd be willing to take on the job to earn it. *And . . .* " Maud paused for a broad wink, which her quickly raised hand did nothing to hide. "Maybe you could convince him to accept another form of payment a little later. I'm getting awfully tired of shoveling horse sh—"

"So am I," Gloriana interrupted. She faced Dante with her hands clutched together before her breast, creating a most tempting display when the folds of her gown parted ever so slightly. Eagerness and reluctance warred for mastery of her features. "Would you? Work for the mirror, I mean?"

At that moment, with her soft, blushing tremulousness calling to his blood, Dante would have shouldered any task for the mere pleasure of looking at her. His throat seemed to be in accord, for he couldn't manage a coherent word, only a garbled sound betraying his desire.

"No. What was I thinking of? I can't give up the mirror. And even if I could, it isn't enough. The job's too hard."

So she regretted offering her mirror in exchange for

menial labor. This he could not allow, for he must possess the mirror. He scrambled for the right words to tell her that he was indeed strong enough for any kind of labor, however lowly.

"Thou lookest upon a very, very hard man."

His reasonable comment sent the women into an inexplicable flurry of embarrassed giggles.

Gloriana recovered quickly with a sudden shift into determination that he doubted forged steel could penetrate. "The job is available, but the mirror is out of the question."

"Show him some cash, Glory. Maybe he asked for the mirror because he doesn't think you have any money." Maud pulled an elaborately beaded pouch from the dressing table and pressed it into Gloriana's hands.

Hope flared in her features. "I never thought of that." She busied herself with the pouch, drawing forth and discarding an astonishing number of objects from its seemingly limitless depths. "Here's some." She abandoned the pouch and approached him with several small greenish-gray parchments clutched in one hand, opening the other to reveal a handful of coins, some copper and some contrived of a metal that aped but failed to equal silver's brilliance. Of gold there was nary a hint.

"Here's a week's pay."

"That's a lot of money, Glory." Maud sounded somewhat envious.

"I know. And I'll double it if the trip takes longer than a week. You won't find any job in Arizona that pays half so well."

"Pay?" He could not hide his scorn. "Thou seekest to foist this collection of moldy parchment and base metal upon me in place of the mirror?"

With a huff of annoyance, she shoved the money back into the pouch. "There, now you see why I knifed him," she said to Maud. "He's rude and insufferable and crazy as a loon. I don't want him within ten feet of me or my mirror."

"Can't blame you, honey."

"You may leave now." Gloriana spoke as if dismissing a servant.

"Not without the mirror."

She pursed her lips. "Let's get him out of here."

"That trick Manjou taught us?"

"Mmm-hmm."

With that, the women commenced a concerted effort of patting and pushing and prodding with their hips and knees, nudging him relentlessly toward the door. Although he knew their combined female strength was no match for his own, they seemed to possess some unearthly skill that enabled them to force his body to do their bidding. It called to mind the time a chance wave had upended his small fishing boat, and he, a strong swimmer, found himself unable to hold his course against the surging water.

His ability to resist was further sapped by the exquisite tremors that shivered along his limbs whenever Gloriana's weight pressed against his body.

They gave him no time to savor the sensation, for he was unceremoniously forced through the opened door like grape pulp squeezed from its skin. He found himself on a small platform, where ash stung his eyes and the *clackety-clackety* increased to deafening proportions, drowning out his shout of protest.

The wind tore the ostrich feather from his cabassat. The realization of the speed at which they traveled tore the objections from his throat. His fingers tightened around the inadequate rail that was all that stood between his quaking person and doom.

"Heck, he wasn't half as balky as Manjou's baby elephant," Maud remarked just before Gloriana slammed the rail car door in Dante's face.

He heard the distinct sound of a bolt being shot into place. Gloriana had barred her door against him. Her impertinent dismissal should have filled him with outrage. Instead, he found himself grateful that the windowless portal provided no means for her to witness the humiliating weakness that gripped him as he stared at the monstrous but wondrous conveyance that carried him, and which convinced him as nothing else could that he had indeed traveled forward in time.

The train wailed, a hauntingly forlorn sound, one that made him want to tip his head back and howl in accord. He caught a final glimpse of his ostrich feather, tumbling helplessly in the wind, and it reminded him of how helplessly he, Dante Trevani, was adrift in the currents of time. He, who had always held himself friendless by choice, felt all but paralyzed with a loneliness no other soul on this earth could hope to understand. All he had known, everything he had touched or smelled or tasted—everything was so long gone that even memories of them no longer existed.

He stared at his hands, white-knuckled from his grip on the rail. They were unchanged, even to the V-shaped scar along his thumb that marked a careless slip of a fruit knife. The rail, simple in design and no different in purpose than any other he'd seen, was fashioned from iron more finely wrought and smoother than any he had ever seen. The rail edged a platform that bounced and jolted him about, providing him with an excellent excuse for standing struck witless. Except his wits had not fled; if anything, they had sharpened, and took delight in piercing the illusion that he was in complete control of the situation.

He controlled nothing. Not the madman who'd sent him here; not the mirror that the madman had decreed capable of restoring all Dante had lost; not the passage of time that made a mockery of everything men thought important. With bitter clarity he realized that even if he did manage to return, time would erase all he had achieved. And of all the countless people who lived in 1888, not one of them would spare a thought for Dante Trevani, whether or not he succeeded in returning to his own time.

He remembered Dee's taunt: *You will forever be what you are right now, a man of no consequence.*

He began drawing huge, rasping breaths, not caring that the soot he breathed threatened to choke him. The very air taunted him with the odor of brimstone. Perhaps he ought to accustom himself to such unpleasantness, for to a man of no consequence, hell itself could not be worse.

But then again, it might.

The laughter bubbling in his throat had little to do with humor. How his subordinates would nod with resignation. They would not be surprised to hear that at the very moment Dante Trevani considered succumbing to despair, he still attempted to weigh the results of his decision, still believed that anticipating the variables would give him control.

Engaging in the familiar habit restored some of his hopes and dimmed a bit of the despair. Meekly accepting what had happened would ensure that Dee's contemptuous prediction came about. Struggling against it might consign him forever to obscurity . . . or bring him more than he'd ever dared dream.

All he needed to do was batter down Gloriana's door, wrest the mirror from her clinging hands, aim it toward the sun, and pray that such a witless exercise would send him hurtling backward more than three hundred years.

The battering and wresting were simple enough; 'twas the praying that seemed beyond his abilities just then. Which was just as well, since the sun crouched low in the horizon, offering nary a single ray that looked capable of carrying a man across centuries.

Morning would arrive soon enough, bringing with it a fresh, bright sun. Dee had cautioned that time might pass more swiftly in the past than in the future Dante was experiencing. But certainly he could spare one night. So brief a time, he hoped, would not alter matters beyond salvation.

Besides, during the night he might think of a way to coax the mirror from Gloriana without causing her to hate him. It might make it easier to pray, and believe, if he departed with her smile lighting his soul.

4

For the first time in her memory, and despite suffering through an all-but-sleepless night, Gloriana yanked her blanket to the side of the bed and sat up anticipating the sunrise.

Circus life suited late risers, but it was more than the need to recover from a late-night performance that kept Glory lolling in bed most mornings. There didn't seem much reason to get up early if fussing with her wardrobe and practicing her act were all a woman had to occupy her time.

But that day things were different. That day she had to . . . She blinked, wondering what on earth had prompted her to leap out of bed so quickly that it might have been Christmas morning and she only six years old, filled with the certainty that she would find something new and wonderful in her stocking.

Something new and wonderful. Her mind conjured up the image of Dante Trevani. Well, blast the man! She'd sent him packing. His face—even if it was a rather handsome face—had no business intruding on her pleasant morning. She'd gotten up early to watch the Arizona sunrise, not sigh over a man who'd turned down her job.

And so Gloriana watched the gap in the curtains, awaiting the arrival of dawn. No glorious burst of sunlight occurred to herald its arrival, only a subtle shift from inky darkness to murky light. She wouldn't complain about its turning out overcast on the one day she wanted to watch the sunrise if it meant some relief from the godawful heat.

Without the sunrise to occupy her mind, thoughts of Dante Trevani returned to plague her. She couldn't imagine how she'd managed to store up so many memories of him in such a short time. She would swear she'd been more concerned about protecting her mirror than watching him. And yet he was there in her mind: the tightly leashed power evident in every long, lean inch of him; the way sunlight struck the bronze highlights in his hair and his eyes; the brief, revealing flickers of emotions he'd tried so hard to hide from her. Confusion. Confidence. Panic. Determination. This Dante was an intriguing mixture of vulnerability combined with strength.

It occurred to her that maybe Dante affected her in the same way as the moving pictures she'd seen earlier that year, as the guest of Mr. Thomas Edison. She'd been so awestruck by the moving images that she'd been unable to think or talk of much else for days afterward. But little by little the images had faded and the wonder had receded, until now even her most determined efforts to recall what she'd seen in the Menlo Park laboratory resulted in little more than a gray blur flickering in her mind.

Dante Trevani, a big gray blur. She couldn't wait for

that to happen, and there was no earthly reason she should feel sad at thinking she might one day be unable to summon his image in her thoughts.

He didn't want her job, and she'd sent him packing. That was probably what weighed on her mind, because the arrival of dawn meant it was time to tend to those horses before they started neighing their silly heads off and banging their hooves against the walls of their stalls, demanding their breakfast. And since Dante had refused the job, she'd have to do it herself.

Maud's raspy breathing—she insisted she "breathed rhythmically" and that Glory was being unfair to call it snoring—told Glory that her friend still slept in her snug little bed on the opposite side of the car. She would wake in an instant if Glory touched her shoulder, and the two of them could make relatively short work of the feeding and mucking-out. But then Maud would demand an explanation for the dark smudges the mirror showed under Glory's eyes and for the indefinable drag she felt on her spirits. Better by far to care for the horses herself.

She eased open the door. It was so cloudy that she didn't have to worry about the brightness wakening Maud. She squeezed through and closed it silently behind her. And then someone swung down from the roof and nearly sent her falling back into the door.

"Dan . . . Dante?" she quavered. She pressed her hand against her breast. Her heartbeat had accelerated, but it was from a swift surge of delight rather than from fear.

A slight smile tugged at his lips, and she felt like an idiot for questioning his identity.

"Gloriana," he acknowledged. "I bid thee good morn."

"Look at those thick clouds. I'll bet it's going to rain. It sure is a good morning."

"Soothly, I wouldst prefer the sun."

She snorted in disbelief. "I, um, soothly wouldn't! I hope it rains straight through to Holbrook. When it's sunny, these rail cars heat up like bean cans in a camp-fire."

He leaned forward with his hands gripping the edge of the balcony's roof, which drew his sleeves taut against his biceps and revealed them to be much larger and more rounded than Glory had recalled during her late-night imaginings. She swallowed, her throat suddenly gone dry, and then noticed that he'd shed his metal vest. His shirt was undone almost to his waist, and she could see fine whorls of copper-brown hair curling over the planes of his chest and then arrowing down over the well-defined muscles of his abdomen. There was a casual grace about him, as if he'd spent much time honing his strength, and he seemed to be uncommonly easy within his powerful body. Gracious, not even Benny Neider, the circus strong man, boasted a physique like Dante's!

She'd never seen anyone who looked less like a sta-ble hand.

"What are you doing here?" she demanded when she found her voice again.

"Thou knowest what I want."

The roughness of his voice, the craving for posses-sion that it conveyed, struck an answering chord some-where low in her belly. She found herself swaying ever so slightly, and not because of the rolling motion of the train . . . and then she realized that his comment had nothing to do with seduction.

He was still after her mirror. Damn the man!

"Don't even think of trying to steal my mirror." He

dropped his hands from the upper ledge and straightened, sending her a look of affronted dignity that didn't fool her for a minute. "I'm warning you, Maud's in there watching over it, and she . . . she has a gun."

Her threat seemed to amuse him. "Fear not, Gloriana. I wouldst not wrest the mirror from thee by foul means."

"Then what were you doing on the roof of my coach?"

"Marveling at the surrounds. And feeling the wind in my face." He spoke with wonder tingeing his voice. "Not even the armada's finest ship attains such speeds as this conveyance."

It gave her an odd feeling to think of Dante sitting cross-legged on the roof of her rail car, studying the passing landscape with his face tipped toward the sky and his hair streaming in the wind, the way a wild stallion might stand atop a mountain peak to view his domain. Why, she could fancy that she heard the stallion neighing, that its drumming hoofbeats thundered over the earth . . .

"Oh, God, the horses!" Glory recalled with a moan.

The need to calm Blizzard before he kicked a hole in the side of the car outweighed her worry over whether Dante might try to sneak into her coach and steal the mirror. She surged over the coupling bridge and burst through the stable car door, calling the soothing nonsense words and the secret name that always gentled the stallion when he was in one of his fractious moods.

Blizzard greeted her with a sharp, trumpeting whinny. Crystal, the mare, sent her a welcoming nicker. Glory left the door propped open so she wouldn't have to light a lantern. Seeing how eagerly the horses strained toward her made her want to rush straight to them with consoling pats and gentle strokes. As much as she disliked the chores associated with caring for her horses, she loved the animals, and it pained her to sense their confusion and unhappiness at being confined aboard the train for so many days.

She stood close enough so each animal could push its muzzle against her shoulder. All the while she kept up the familiar patter of nonsense words while she scratched around their ears.

"Blizzard . . . Sweetzel . . . Darling?" Glory gave a small yelp of surprise when Dante came up behind her and echoed her silly words in her ear. "Missus Crystal Zee?"

Blizzard lifted his head and flared his nostrils at the intrusion, and then, to Glory's amazement, he simply huffed softly and rested his muzzle atop her shoulder.

"He's not usually so accepting of strangers," Glory said.

"This horse and I are not strangers. I madest his acquaintance last night."

So Dante hadn't spent the whole night perched on her roof while she tossed sleeplessly beneath him. Maybe he'd reconsidered taking the job and had thought to get on her good side by performing some of the chores . . . but no, a quick glance around revealed the stable car's usual chaos.

"These are pure-blooded Arabian steeds," Dante remarked quietly. "I would not have expected to see such outside of a royal stable."

"Mr. Fontanescue breeds Arabians because he believes they draw bigger crowds than mongrel horses. Not every horse is suited for the arena, so he provides every performer with a pair of the, um, rejected ones to draw our wagons during the parades. That Mr. Fontanescue sure knows his business. You should see the people line up when we hit a new town! I've had

Blizzard for three years. Mr. Fontanescue gave Crystal to me earlier this year."

"Why wouldst he gift thee with such valuable steeds when thou art so inept at caring for them?"

He asked the question before she could finish explaining that Mr. Fontanescue also thoughtfully provided a veritable horde of stable hands to tend to his performers' horses. She'd never given a thought to learning how to do it herself. The contemptuous way Dante raked his gaze over the stable car, taking in the mess she and Maud had made of things after tending the horses for only three days, just flat-out irritated her so much that she didn't bother enlightening him.

"I'm not inept."

To prove it, she grabbed the pitchfork from the wall. She turned the tines curved side down, knelt near the lower rails of Blizzard's stall, and began drawing small clumps of soiled bedding toward her. Dante chuckled. She swung about and glowered at him. "Feel free to help with Crystal's stall."

"That I cannot do, for we have reached an impasse in our negotiations."

Dante folded his arms across his chest and leaned back against the wall. Why, that smug, arrogant . . . man. Glory realized with a flush of anger that he intended to just stand there and watch her work.

She found herself angling her body into uncomfortable positions to avoid sticking her rump toward Dante's impassive face. She could feel his eyes following her every movement, and though she couldn't hear it, she felt sure he continued to laugh at her technique. Inept? She'd show him inept. She applied the pitchfork with more enthusiasm than usual, imagining that each scrape of the tines shaved an inch off those bulging biceps that he refused to employ on her behalf.

Despite working harder than ever, despite working up a most unladylike sweat, it seemed to take hours to scrape all the dirty straw under the stall rails. Especially after Blizzard stamped, catching the pitchfork beneath his hoof. The impact jolted along the handle and almost numbed her hand, but she persevered, murmuring softly to the stallion to soothe his impatience.

"Aye, shift thy dainty-wainty hoovesy-woovesy, Blizzard sweetzel darling," Dante echoed mockingly. "Gloriana, thou approachest this task all wrongly."

She'd suspected as much, but she wouldn't give him the satisfaction of admitting it. "This is the way I like to do it." She moved to Crystal's stall and began all over again. She worked in silence, or as much silence as could be expected on a moving train with two hungry horses shuffling and snuffling at her efforts. After an eternity, she had the soiled bedding cleared away, and she began hoisting forkfuls of fresh bedding over the rails and dumping them into the stalls.

"I am forced to admit that thou art not inept."

She felt a little glimmer of pride. His forced admission made all her hard work worth it. "I told you so."

"Nay. Thou art completely unfit for the task at hand."

She let the pitchfork clatter to the floor. Dirty straw caked her skirt. Sweat trickled into her eyes and ran in a squiggly path down her neck to the valley between her breasts. Dust and chaff clung to her hair. Horseflies buzzed all around, every once in a while diving toward the exposed skin on her hands and face. Her hands were sore and reddened, and she knew that a whole batch of new blisters would follow.

He still leaned against the wall, looking impossibly cool and elegant despite his ridiculous clothing. Not a speck of straw clung to any part of him. He didn't look tired or disheveled, but disgustingly, infuriatingly strong and competent.

"Thou shouldst feed the beasts ere mucking out their stalls, and wait a bit to let them purge their innards, so that their bedding stays fresh longer," he suggested helpfully. "Thou shouldst remove the steed from the stall ere—"

"If you know so much, do it yourself."

"I would, most willingly, if thou wouldst agree to pay me with the mirror."

The mirror, always back to the mirror. "A true blue-blooded gentleman wouldn't even ask for payment from a lady, let alone demand her most valuable possession."

As soon as she said it, Glory realized that her comment had hurt Dante in some way.

He probably had no idea that he'd betrayed his emotion, for he shuttered his expression with a swift, frightening skill that told her he was a master at hiding his feelings. Only someone like herself, whose livelihood had long depended upon gauging strangers' reactions, would have caught the subtle tensing of his jaw, the careful remoteness that settled over his features, when she'd told him he was no gentleman.

She wondered what forces had contributed to forging a man of such haughty, deliberate detachment. And she wondered what she was doing, getting herself tangled up with someone like him, and practically daring him to stick around to boot.

It didn't add up. A man who took such pains to develop an impervious exterior should never allow such a common barb to pierce his hide. A man with pretensions toward toughness shouldn't be traveling through rough-and-tumble Arizona Territory dressed like a court jester.

That morning he'd told her he'd been riding on the roof, which was surely the most dangerous place on a train. And yet only the day before, he'd appeared completely startled when he realized they were in motion. Her heart speeded up at the memory of the way he'd sworn to protect her, as if he feared they were trapped on a runaway stagecoach or something really dangerous. He'd acted as though he'd never ridden aboard—never even *seen* a train—in his life, as though someone had scooped him up from a backward, remote homestead in the hills and plopped him down in the middle of a modern-day nightmare.

She remembered some of his incomprehensible comments: *Dee's boasting was not idle—he hath shifted me into the future.* Why, Dante had behaved as if he really believed that outrageous statement!

The train whistle wailed. The squeal of wheels against iron rails intensified. The metallic shrieking set Glory's teeth on edge, but she could tell by the speculation kindling in Dante's eyes that he found the noises fascinating.

Just so might a half-tamed tiger listen and learn while its cage door clanged and rattled, studying the sounds that marked its captivity, probing for weaknesses, waiting for its chance to escape. She tried to suppress the shiver that arose at remembering the dangers inherent to tiger taming, and she told herself she was glad Dante didn't want the job she'd offered. She didn't need a stable hand who would bolt at the first opportunity, nor did she want one who entertained delusions of traveling through time.

Just then Maud stumbled through the door, yawning mightily and rubbing the sleep from her eyes. "There you are, Glory." She yawned again but clapped her mouth closed quickly when she caught sight of Dante. "Oh, good, he decided to take the job after all."

"No. He's just standing around annoying me, as usual. Come on over here and help me feed these horses." She stared glumly while Blizzard pawed at the fresh golden straw she'd so laboriously heaved into his stall. She'd never admit it, but Dante's advice to feed the horses first made perfect sense. She knew the mess Blizzard and Crystal would make all over that fresh straw after they digested their meal. If she'd thought about it a little, she would have done a better job. Instead she'd been treating her horses like people, getting them all cleaned up before serving their dinner.

"Well, durn, Glory, I was hoping you'd already finished with them so we could go to the dining car. I'm so hungry, my belly's about to explode."

"Your belly explodes when it's too full, not when it's empty. You can worry about blowing up *after* you stuff yourself full of strawberries and cream and oatmeal and bacon and eggs—"

An ominous rumbling sounded from Dante's direction; Glory cast a quick look at him and thought she saw him blush.

"Sounds like he's just as hungry as I am," Maud remarked.

"Long time between meals, hmm?" Glory took little satisfaction at commenting upon Dante's apparently impoverished state.

"I daresay none aboard this conveyance wouldst believe me if I numbered the days since last I ate."

Even though she was still powerfully irked that he'd stood by and made rude remarks while he'd watched her work, she felt a pang of concern. Maybe his odd behavior stemmed from hunger rather than pure male cussedness. A tender spot in the middle of her palm burned, hinting at the blisters to come, and she decided there might be a way to solve both their problems.

"Breakfast costs ten cents. If you can't afford to buy it, I'll stand you to it, providing you take care of the horses for today."

His lips thinned, and he looked ready to argue. She was too hungry to get into another argument, and so sore she felt as though she might burst into tears if he turned down her offer. If he said one more thing about wanting to be paid with her mirror, she would just whack him in the head with her pitchfork and let him lie there and starve.

"Hotcakes and sausage and honey and biscuits . . . mmm," Maud rhapsodized.

"Well?" Glory prodded.

Dante pressed a hand against his stomach and gave Gloriana a curt nod of acceptance, one that she could tell cost him a great deal of pride. Funny, but she felt rather embarrassed herself, as if using his hunger to get her way, even partially, had somehow diminished her own opinion of herself.

"We'll bring his plate back here," Maud said. When both Glory and Dante moved to object, she sent them an exasperated glare. "He sure can't go to the dining car dressed like *that*."

Dante sighed and crossed his arms over his chest, looking as if he feared they meant to overpower him and strip him naked.

"I'm afraid she's right," Glory said. Her fellow passengers bedecked themselves in their finest while savoring the superb fare served aboard the Atlantic and Pacific Railroad. The dining car steward would probably deny them admittance once he caught sight of Dante's tights and puffy pants. Glory felt absolutely certain that Dante would despise being laughed at and ordered out of the dining car while dozens of passengers pointed and snickered.

"Do you have a spare shirt and britches stashed somewhere on the train?" Maud asked.

"Dee hath stolen everything from me with his fiendish tricks, save for these garments I wearest. I thought playing with him a harmless entertainment, but his fumbling demeanor was but a ruse that led me to sorely misjudge his skill."

"That'll teach you not to gamble," Maud said before Glory had a chance to figure out what Dante was talking about.

"Aye," he agreed, with a somewhat embarrassed nod.

Glory's spirits lifted, though it didn't make a bit of sense that it should perk her up to think of Dante as a failed gambler rather than a lunatic. "Oh, that explains everything, then. You got yourself tangled up in one of those high-stakes games I've heard about."

"The stakes run higher than I first believed, 'tis true." Dante nodded again.

"Even took the clothes off your back and sent you off with just that metal vest and that upside-down acorn thing on your head." Maud managed to sound admiring. "You boys must've got liquored up pretty good."

Dante scowled briefly, and then his expression shifted into confusion. "My command of thy tongue be not so profound as I hadst thought. Verily, I comprehend not 'liquored up.'"

"You got drunk," explained Glory. Though she had better reasons than most for nursing a deep-rooted aversion to alcohol, the notion that Dante had imbibed a bit too much cheered her up even more, so she launched into an explanation with enthusiasm. "Men are always getting drunk. Especially while they're gambling." Yes, alcohol-inspired delusions would explain everything that was strange about Dante. "If you really did some serious drinking, it can take days for it to wear off. That's why you're confused. And I bet that's why you're talking a little funny and making some of those, um, outrageous comments."

"Would that I gripped a stout tankard of ale between my hands now," he muttered, confirming her diagnosis; she knew drunkards craved additional drink to stave off alcohol's unpleasant aftereffects.

Glory studied him frankly. The drunks she'd known usually squinted through bloodshot eyes; they often staggered, and they always reeked with a yeasty, stale scent reminiscent of the odor wafting through an open saloon door. But she had touched Dante the day before, when removing the daggers, and she had smelled nothing but his clean, masculine scent. And that morning his skin glowed with good health; his movements were strong and purposeful. Perhaps he simply held his liquor better than most, for a wild session of drinking and gambling provided the only logical explanation for his behavior. Sitting on the roof of the train and raving about shepherds overtaking England, indeed!

"Come on, honey, you have to clean yourself up or they won't let you in the dining car, either."

Maud tugged at Glory's sleeve, and Glory became aware once again of her bedraggled state. She had come to hate this stable car over the past few days, and even her love for her horses couldn't hold her in it for a minute longer than necessary.

Dante stooped to pick up her discarded pitchfork. The motion caused his shirt to fall open and gave her another good look at the fit, sculpted torso it covered. He turned toward the horses, and she noticed the swing of his hair against his back, the way his broad shoulders tapered to the strong column of his waist. Blizzard pushed his muzzle into Dante's chest, an affectionate nudge that would have sent her flying halfway across the car, but it didn't budge Dante one inch.

"Glory!" Maud tugged again. "I'm starving."

So am I, Gloriana thought, wondering why the sudden awareness of an empty, gnawing ache inside her made her want to linger in the hated stable car rather than dash from it with all speed.

INTERLUDE
The Tower of London, 1555

A furtive scuffling outside his cell woke the prisoner John Dee.

Or perhaps it was not the scuffling so much as the erratic pounding his heart commenced at the sound. A glance toward his tiny window proved that night still reigned; the moon, lurking behind clouds, did little to illuminate the edges of his spare, cold cell, and so he could not judge the threat posed by his unexpected visitor when his door creaked open and then swung shut without the lock engaging.

Henry VIII, dead and buried these past ten years, had set the precedent for midnight executions of Tower prisoners. It was a precedent his son Edward had followed before his untimely death, and one his daughter Mary seemed eager to continue now that she ruled as queen of England; indeed, her people had taken to calling her "Bloody Mary."

"No, not yet. Please! I have not yet seen my predictions fulfilled," Dee moaned, ashamed at giving voice to his fear, but utterly unable to prevent it.

"Dr. Dee?"

An executioner would not have bothered to whisper his name, and certainly would not have done so in such a soft, feminine manner.

"Aye," Dee managed to croak.

"'Tis me, Elizabeth." With the soft sound of cloth brushing the floor, his visitor scurried to his side.

"Royal . . . Royal Highness?" Dee clutched the threadbare blanket to his chest. "But why, my lady—"

"Shh. No one must hear you call my name. I cannot be discovered, lest Mary hear of this visit. She already suspects the worst of me. If she hears of my doings this night, I might find myself lodged permanently in the next cell, with my only view that of the man who helped me swinging from the gibbet."

She moved into the small area brightened by the moon, and Dee could see that it was indeed Elizabeth Tudor who knelt in the rushes next to his bed. Her thin face took on an added pallor, and her red-gold hair, her most remarkable feature, might have been as dull gray as a field mouse's fur for all the color it showed in the moonlight.

"You must know I do not hold you responsible for my imprisonment," Dee whispered, assuming she had come to apologize for his incarceration.

"Oh!" said Elizabeth, with such surprise that Dee realized she hadn't spent a single moment worrying over whether or not he blamed her. She plunged immediately into the subject he suspected might be the true reason for her clandestine visit. "Dr. Dee, this horoscope you cast that roused Mary to such a fury . . . "

"Aye?"

"Is it true?"

Dee glanced around at his comfortless cell and pressed a thin hand against a chest still pounding from the fear this dead-of-night visit had prompted. "Your sister had no trouble accepting my predictions as true. Which portion do you doubt, my lady?"

"I don't *want* to doubt any of it." Elizabeth leaned closer, and her changeable eyes glittered like steel-colored diamonds. "I want everything to be just as you said. I want to be the best beloved of all the Tudors. I yearn for *my* star to ascend and shine brighter than that of any who has gone before me. I believe your horoscope predicted that I shall be queen, and I very much want to be queen, Dr. Dee."

She paused, but Dee knew she had more to say. He waited. She gathered her breath and continued. "It frightens me to think of what I must do to make this come about."

Her level gaze met his. It was unflinching and unapologetic despite her virtual admission that she was quite willing to eliminate her sister or anyone else who stood between her and the throne of England. Small wonder that Mary, who knew this sister of hers better than anyone in the world, had grown hysterical at Dr. Dee's horoscope, which predicted a glittering, adulation-filled future for Elizabeth.

He chose his words carefully. "You worry your head needlessly, my lady. You need do nothing but wait."

"Wait." She gave a most unroyal snort. "I have been waiting all my life."

"Then you must be patient and tolerate it for a little longer. Surely that is not so frightening."

"I shall tell you what is frightening about waiting. Women who wait for the things they want grow old and bent-boned and silly. A crick-backed, querulous queen is naught but a joke to the men she must command."

"You will rule in splendor, my lady. Glorious, unmatched splendor, and far sooner than you think."

"Your horoscope made no mention of a king."
Elizabeth tilted her chin, and Dee fancied a shudder of
revulsion shook her slender frame. "Who do you predict will rule at my side?"

"I daresay there would be a veritable army of men
clamoring for your hand, my lady. You alone would be
the best predictor of their individual success. Save, of
course, there being a betrothal already in place that
grants you no choice . . ." He allowed his voice to trail
off suggestively, wondering how she might answer
him.

"I have been betrothed a half-dozen times or more."
She sniffed, showing her opinion of her would-be suitors. "None more significant than the ink it took to write
our names."

Dee clucked sympathetically to hide his relief that
his meddling with Dante Trevani had gone unnoticed.

"Save one," Elizabeth added after a brief pause,
destroying his cautious relief. She curled one hand
against her breast and with the other stroked an object
at her wrist. In the moonlight Dee saw the shape of a
turtle with fiery, flashing diamonds for eyes. Her voice
softened. "One of them tried to be kind to me. I . . . I've
often wondered what happened to him."

"Do you regret that he did not press his suit?" Dee
felt an awful certainty that she was referring to Dante.

"Not at all." She shrugged, and the softness fled her
like clouds scudding past the moon. "If this one man
had come as arranged, my own imprudent tongue
would have given me no choice but to wed him. I wonder if your horoscope would have predicted such grand
things for me if I found myself married under such
onerous circumstances, Dr. Dee."

Her words indicated some doubt, but no uncertainty
marked Elizabeth's face. She rose and looked down her

royal nose at him, and Dee knew this gesture would characterize all their future dealings.

With an imperious nod Elizabeth Tudor took her leave, and John Dee remained shivering in his dark prison cell.

5

"*Glory, the dining car's* at the other end of the train."

"I know." Gloriana ignored Maud's hungry protest and entered yet another passenger car. Her searching gaze skipped over the male occupants, who all looked discouragingly familiar. She'd already interviewed every one of them.

"Breakfast is going to be over before you're done fooling around."

"I'm not fooling around. I had to spend extra time making sure Dante couldn't wiggle the lock open to our sleeping coach and steal my mirror while we're away."

"If you're so worried about that, we ought to hurry and eat, so's we can go back and stand guard."

"Not until I find someone to take that job."

She'd hire anyone, pay any price. Anything, rather than use Dante's apparent poverty to get her way again. It had taken her years to learn how to zero in on another person's weaknesses and turn them to her advantage for the act—to provoke laughter, to convince the skeptical, to awe the incredulous. She'd often embarrassed her targets; she'd never before embarrassed herself.

They made their way through two more passenger cars before Glory spotted a man she hadn't seen before. "There, Maud. I don't remember talking to him about the job."

Maud shook her head. "I never asked him to apply. Look at that suit he's wearing. And the hat and umbrella. He's a dandy, Glory, not a stable hand."

"You shouldn't jump to conclusions. Maybe that's his Sunday suit."

He greeted them affably and listened with great politeness while Glory outlined her predicament, and then just as affably and politely asked them to leave so he could return to his business papers.

They fared no better with two similar types. Glory eventually admitted defeat and allowed Maud to tow her toward the dining car. And there, in the corner, sat the potential answer to her prayers.

The tables immediately surrounding him sat empty, and Glory understood why when she approached and caught his odor. He exhibited every sign of drunken debauchery that she'd failed to find in Dante. His hand shook as he lifted his coffee cup. He slurped at the steaming liquid, and some of it dribbled from the corners of his mouth into a matted beard that looked capable of soaking up an entire urn's worth of coffee. He swung bleary eyes toward her as she approached, and he did a poor job of stifling a belch when she paused at his table.

"Oh, God, I just lost my appetite." Maud moaned. "Not him, Glory."

"Sir?" Glory practically whispered, and then cleared

her throat very quietly. Maybe, if he didn't respond, she'd just keep on looking. "Are you by any chance in need of a job, sir?"

"Dunno. Lemme check." He commenced lurching from side to side until Glory feared he might topple from his chair, but it seemed he was merely trying to reach behind himself. He withdrew a flask from his rear pocket, held it toward the window and frowned, and unscrewed the lid. He peered into it and then turned it upside down, tipping it toward his tongue with a hopeful expression that died when nothing dripped out. "'Pears I do need a job, little lady," he said dolefully. "When kin I start?"

Maud moaned even louder.

"Aren't you even going to ask me what kind of job it is? Don't you want to know how much I'm willing to pay?"

"Don't matter, so long's I git enough fer drinkin' money. When do I start?"

Well, there he was, the solution to her dilemma. Glory studied her potential employee and couldn't dismiss the image of another man, one who'd never relinquished a shred of dignity despite hungering for longer than he cared to admit. Dante. She should be reveling in the notion that she could fling his demands for her mirror right in his face.

Maybe she'd better state her terms up front with this fellow before he started hankering after payment she had no intention of offering. She slid into the seat across from him.

"I'd like to settle the details with you here and now," she said.

"Suit yourself."

"The job involves complete care and feeding of two horses while we're on this train and during a little side trip I want to take. I want them given exceptional care. I'm very fond of those horses."

He shrugged and cast a longing look toward the empty flask that he'd set alongside his coffee cup. "Nags is nags. When do I get my first pay?"

"When the job is complete."

"Aw, hell." He scowled and lifted the flask again. He sighed. "How long?"

"A week. Maybe two."

"You stayin' on this train fer two weeks?"

She distinctly remembered telling him there would be a side trip involved. "No. We will be disengaging our cars from the train when we reach Holbrook. From there we're going to visit my ranch in Pleasant Valley, and then—"

"Pleasant Valley?" He jolted upright, as if all the coffee's invigorating effects had struck him at once.

"Yes."

"Pleasant Valley, *Arizona?* That place what's surrounded by them Mogo-lon Mountains?"

Glory had mispronounced the name of the mountain range herself until corrected by a railroad conductor. "The pronunciation is *moy-an,* even though it's spelled M-o-g-o-l-l-o-n."

"Don't keer whatcha call 'em. I ain't interested in no job what takes me closer than a hunnerd miles o' that place." He struggled to his feet and steadied his wavering stance by bracing one hand against the tabletop while he stabbed a grimy finger at Glory. "You'd best stay away from Pleasant Valley, little lady. Hell, there's so much ambushin' and bushwackin' goin' on there that the Apaches is linin' up to take lessons."

Gloriana stared wordlessly while her spirits plunged to her toes. This wasn't the first time that an eager applicant had suddenly developed an aversion to the job she offered after he learned her ultimate destination. Some had suddenly remembered pressing business elsewhere, and others had declared they couldn't spend so much time away from their own places. One even claimed he'd forgotten he was on his way to pay his final respects to his dying mother, who couldn't depart this earth without setting eyes on her boy again. They'd all made their feeble excuses in the manner of men who feared that telling the truth might brand them as cowards.

"I wish somebody would tell me what's so bad about Pleasant Valley."

"Don't you read the papers?"

"Why, no, I don't." He leaned back and sent her a look of such disbelief that she felt compelled to defend herself. "I travel a lot, and it always makes me sad . . . I mean, it seems like a waste of time to read about towns and people I'll never get the chance to know."

To her surprise, the disreputable wretch showed more honesty than any of the others. "Folks're dyin' in Pleasant Valley, miss."

"I know. My pa was killed there. But it was an accident."

"Yeah, and I'll bet it was one o' them Hash Knife cowboys what caused the accident."

"What are Hash Knife cowboys?"

"The lowest, schemin'est scum of the earth, is what they are. They ride fer the Aztec Land and Cattle Company, what uses a hash knife brand on its stock. The Hash Knife outfit wants to winter goddamn sheep down on the Tonto Basin. That range always belonged to cattle, and the cattlemen ain't takin' kindly to lettin' goddamn sheep ruin their grass. Pleasant Valley's the only spot where there's a rift that lets them

through the mountain. Them boys'll do anything fer
their bosses, even if it means killin' innocent home-
steaders what's aimin' to scrape a livin' from that soil.
Yer pa probably tried to stop them from drivin' sheep
across his land."

"I . . . I knew it had something to do with a disagree-
ment between cattlemen and sheepmen, but I had no
idea it was so bad."

The man tempered his words with an unexpected
kindliness. "You jest take them horses yer so fond of
and make a little side trip through to Californy. It'll be
better fer you. I swear it."

He rose, stifled a belch while he nodded, and staggered away, lurching more than the train's swaying
could account for.

Maud lowered herself into his vacated chair. Neither
she nor Glory made any effort to summon a waiter.

Maud leaned forward and gripped Glory's hands.
"Honey, I'm starting to get just the tiniest bit nervous
about this trip. Maybe you ought to reconsider your
plan. Do what that lawyer fella suggested and come
back here in a couple of years."

"I can't wait that long. For one thing, any claim
jumper can move onto the ranch if I don't show up and
let people know I intend to take it over."

"You said you're not going to take up ranching,
Glory."

"I know. I . . . I just have to see the ranch. And I
have to see it now. Those Hash Knife cowboys won't
bother me when they see I'm just there for a visit."

"You've been living on God's earth for twenty-four
years without so much as a glimpse of Arizona. Surely
you could manage to get by for a little while longer."

Glory decided to try to articulate her reasons
before Maud offered another objection. "My mother

always claimed that settling on a place like that would kill her. My father always said he'd die without land to sink his roots into. So he stayed on his precious ranch and married a woman he didn't love, and Mama kept traveling and drank herself dead of a broken heart, and now I'm stuck with the ranch that killed them both."

"All the more reason to wait, unless you're hankering to add your stone to the graveyard."

"I have to see it now. If I wait too long, someone else will move in and change things, and then I'll never know."

"Know what? That a bunch of murdering mutton-lovers wants to take over that land the easy way?"

Glory shook her head and pressed a hand over her heart. "There's something about that ranch that's eating away at me inside. I have to see it. Get it out of my system. Get myself back to the way I was before, or else *I'll* be the one looking for a job."

Maud pressed her lips together tightly. Glory knew there was no protest her truthful friend could make. Mr. Fontanescue's generosity with his horses was but one example of the way he pampered his performers. Jobs with his circus were even more highly coveted than star billing with Colonel Cody's Wild West Show. Entertainers and acts badgered the circus owner into conducting impromptu auditions at virtually every city the troupe visited. Mr. Fontanescue prized loyalty and offered it to his employees in large measure, but he never allowed sentimentality to cloud his business judgment. His performers understood that their jobs were secure only so long as their skills awed the crowds.

There had been a gradual deterioration in the quality of Glory's performances in the four years since her mother's death, and it had grown more pronounced since she'd learned about inheriting her father's ranch.

Since that day, a secret voice inside had taken to whispering, *You don't have to be here. You have somewhere else you can go.* Always at the most inappropriate times, such as when she was trying to overcome the stage fright that gripped her before each performance, or when hecklers—male hecklers—called out compliments about her physical attributes and shouted promises that prompted other men in the audience to roar their own comments. *Come on over here, Red, and I'll show you what's real and what's not!*

Glory's mother, Katherine, had possessed the knack for turning those taunts into good-natured cheers. Glory had never seen Katherine freeze with revulsion or tremble with panic or tilt her head to listen to the secret voice that always seemed to be urging Gloriana to flee from the circus ring.

"Losing that job might not be so bad," Maud said. "There's others to be found."

"Oh, sure. I'll bet there are at least a dozen positions for circus illusionists posted at the Holbrook general store."

"I ain't talking about taking another circus job. I'm talking about settling down on that ranch you inherited. Raise yourself a family. That's more than enough work for any five women, from what I've heard about homesteading."

"In case you haven't noticed, I don't have a husband."

"Then find one. Forget about hiring a stable hand and find yourself a husband instead."

"No." Carlisle women didn't settle down, raise families, bake bread.

"I told you men are plumb woman-starved out here.

You'd have every single fella for forty miles lined up to make you his missus. They'd be so busy fighting over you that they'd forget all about grazing them dumb sheep and cattle."

"No."

"Glory, honey, you know Katherine would've wanted you to—"

"Don't try telling me my mama would've wanted me to marry." Anger, and a sudden, aching longing for her laughing, spirited mother, flared through Glory.

"I didn't mean to insinuate that your mama would've urged you to take a husband." Maud spoke with quiet dignity, and Glory felt a stab of remorse for doubting her friend's motives. "Nobody knows better than me how much your ma relished her independence. If she hadn't treasured it so, you'd have grown up on the very ranch you're so determined to get killed over."

"Then what would she have wanted for me?" Glory's voice cracked. "Tell me, Maud. Tell me."

Maud slumped, suddenly looking every day of her fifty-nine years. "She would've wanted you to listen to that fella who just walked away. She would've wanted you to turn your back on this place and run as fast and as far away from it as you could. But not on account of the danger. On account of some kind of hungry thing inside her that never did get satisfied."

"Like your belly?" Glory tried joking, but Maud would have none of it.

"Circus life suited her." Maud's eyes appeared suspiciously moist. "I ain't so sure it ever suited you half so well. You take after your pa; you did from the first minute, when you smiled at the midwife instead of squalling. It comes hard for a woman to say this about another woman, but I don't think your ma did the right thing, keeping you from your pa for all these years."

"She didn't keep me from him," Glory said softly. "He just built himself a life that didn't include us."

But Harry Trask had known where they were, and he'd somehow managed to have a letter delivered to Katherine at least four times a year, no matter how obscure the stops the Fontanescue Circus made.

Glory had always been able to tell when Katherine received one. Her mother's usual effervescent manner would dim; she would darken their rail coach's windows, don her most sober clothing, and stay behind to "rest" after sending Glory to the meal tent with Maud or one of their other friends. Glory had learned to recognize the scent of bourbon from the way their car smelled on those dark days.

Katherine had never missed a performance. But on letter days it seemed to Glory that her mother's act took on a frantic tone, that her professional smile wavered just a little, that her beautiful eyes surveyed the crowd with dull despair. Until the applause began. Then Katherine's shoulders would straighten. She would throw her head back with a proud tilt to her jaw, sending her glorious red-gold hair cascading down her back. She would breathe extra deep on letter days, filling herself again and again with the stale tent air, as if it nourished her more than the food she declined on those days.

She would hold Glory close after letter-day performances. With the two of them still shaking from the after-show shivers, she would forget her own admonitions about maintaining a moderate tone of voice. "Oh, *this* is the very best life, Gloriana!" she would exult, half laughing and half crying, leaving Glory uncertain as to whether her mother was telling her a truth or asking her a question.

Glory always found a new dress or trinket laid out on her bed right after a letter day.

"Your father sends his love," Katherine would say while Glory lifted her new treasure and held it close, longing for her father's embrace instead of the impersonal caress of cloth or metal. Sometimes Katherine would tell her things about her father, describing the ranch where he lived, revealing the existence of a half-brother and half-sister whom Glory secretly envied with all her heart. She would never give in to Glory's pleadings, though, for an explanation of what had caused the rift between Katherine and Harry, nor explain why Harry Trask claimed Katherine Carlisle was the love of his life but had married another woman.

The ranch drew Gloriana, promising the answers she had always been denied.

"Let's order breakfast," Glory said, waving her hand to catch a waiter's attention. "You might want to sit there jabbering all day, but I'm starving."

Dante tongued the kernel of corn from one side of his mouth to the other. He'd popped it into his mouth after pouring generous measures into each steed's feed bucket, and he occasionally bit against it while tending to the familiar chores that accompanied the keeping of horses. He'd not managed to dent the rock-hard corn, though Blizzard Sweetzel Darling and Missus Crystal Zee contentedly munched away, grinding their own portions easily between their more powerful teeth. He wondered at the horses' obvious enjoyment, for he had not gained the tiniest hint of taste from his corn, and any man as hungry as he should be especially attuned to the pleasures of food. A hunger so overpowering that he'd tried nibbling on horse corn—that was why he'd taken on this demeaning chore, to earn some bread and eggs and bacon.

No. He might be able to present this excuse to others, but Dante would not lie to himself. As a soldier in his father's army, he had learned to tolerate fierce hunger. He had learned how to relieve it when the opportunity presented itself and to ignore it when food could not be found. If hunger alone had held him in thrall, it would have been a simple matter for him to overpower Gloriana, gain the mirror, and wait for the return of the sun so that he might transport himself back to the year 1544. He might be dining at the king of England's famously generous table instead of gnawing upon horse corn.

Instead he found himself mucking out stalls, hoping Gloriana would soon bring him his breakfast, and wondering whether it would please him more to feast upon the food or the sight of her.

But it was Maud's slight form that eventually barreled through the door, balancing a tray laden with two platters of food.

The sharp-eyed crone noted his disappointment. "Sorry it took so long. We got involved in a . . . conversation, and Glory worked herself up into one of her headaches. I hate seeing her suffer, but it suited me this time."

"I would not have suspected that thou takest pleasure in another's pain," Dante remarked.

"Naw. I wanted to talk to you alone, is all, and that headache couldn't have come at a better time. I made her crawl into bed to nurse it, and I convinced her it'd only get worse if she brought this food to you. It wasn't hard. You ain't exactly one of her favorite people right now."

"That surpriseth me not, given her determination to

make a menial servant of me." He allowed himself a moment of righteous indignation to fuel his desire to return to his own time and claim the woman who would wed him or no other. He told himself that Elizabeth surely would not consign *her* favorite to a position involving the care of horses.

Maud set the tray upon a bale of straw. "Come on over here and chow down." When he hesitated in his confusion over her words, she crooked a finger at him. "Come on, Dante. You've waited a long time for this food. I know what it's like to be hungry. I have something to ask you that might get a better reception if you listen with a full stomach."

Soldiers also learned the value of eating quickly, quietly, and so neatly that not even a smear of sauce remained on the plate. Maud took a seat upon another bale and watched with apparent relief while Dante made fast work of the first plate of food, as if it eased her spirits to realize he possessed some table manners. He turned his attention to the second platter as well, and only after it was forked clean did he wonder whether she'd meant it to provision him for the balance of the day.

She clapped her hands over her knees and sat forward in the manner of a man setting himself to bargain. "Okay. I have a proposition for you."

"Okay," he echoed, liking the sound of the word.

"I'll try to help you get the mirror."

He had not entertained this possibility, as Maud had seemed so staunch on Gloriana's behalf. The proposition held promise. "Okay."

"Don't be so blasé about it. I said I'll *try*—but there are a couple of conditions attached."

"Okay."

"For one thing, you'll have to convince Glory that

you changed your mind about the job and that you've reconsidered taking the mirror away from her. She probably won't believe you right off. This train's stopping in Winslow later today, and if I know Glory, she'll approach every man who gets on board before she asks you again. We have to come up with some kind of plan to make her give the job to you before she finds someone else."

"Okay."

For some reason, his repetition of the very word she'd taught him caused her to frown. "You're not crazy, are you?"

"Nay."

Even such a simple denial caused her lips to part and her breath to catch with doubt. After a pause, she merely shook her head. "I guess I'll have to believe you, on account of I don't have much choice. You can't let her know that me and you are in on this together. It'd hurt her feelings something awful if she knew I was plotting to get her mirror away from her. And she'd be madder than spit to hear I think she needs a man to protect her. She hates depending on anyone, always did."

He, who had spent a lifetime learning to depend only upon himself, understood. And yet an uncomfortable lurching in his chest stole a bit of his breath. "Danger doth threaten Gloriana? Tell me more."

"A couple of months ago a lawyer came to tell Glory that her pa had left her some property. He told her that her pa had been accidentally killed because of some local grazing dispute, and he strongly recommended that she stay away from the place for a little while, until matters settled down. He didn't offer any details, which made me suspicious as hell, considering the source."

"Lawyers." Dante made a contemptuous sound low

in his throat. "Ever the same, it seems. Not even the passage of centuries can alter their perfidious natures."

"Well, I guess you ain't crazy after all, if you hate lawyers." Maud brightened. "Anyway, Glory seemed completely disinterested in the ranch. I thought she had taken that lawyer's advice. But she started making mistakes in her act, and it seems she's doing a lot of daydreaming. Lately she's taken to turning all absent-minded and teary-eyed for no reason."

These symptoms, which so confounded Maud, sounded remarkably normal for the women of Dante's acquaintance. He continued to listen politely, keeping in mind that she had hinted at helping him gain possession of the mirror.

"The circus had just set up for a three-week run in Santa Fe, and then out of the blue Glory took it into her head to visit her inheritance. She said that on account of Santa Fe's being so close to Arizona, we'd only have to take a short leave from the circus."

"Good tacticians plan their travels to avoid unnecessary tedium. 'Twas a logical decision, wouldst thou not say?"

"Heavens, no! Except for winter breaks, Glory ain't never spent two days away from that circus in her whole life."

With that one sentence, Maud illuminated for him the intriguing inconsistencies he'd witnessed in Gloriana—all smooth and polished one moment, shy and uncertain the next. Not unlike a convent-raised female, who emerged from the nunnery fully prepared to shoulder the management of her husband's estates, yet understanding nothing whatever of life's passions.

"I confess I am growing confused, Maud, about the task thee . . . thou hast in store for me. Dost thou desirest that I urge Gloriana back to the circus?"

"Yes. No. I mean, she's determined to keep her job with the circus, so you don't exactly have to urge her. But she's just as determined to visit that durned Pleasant Valley. I suspect that things there are worse than she expects. From what I hear, we could be riding into an all-out range war, not some little grazing dispute. What she needs is a bodyguard."

"Bodyguard?"

"Someone to protect her. You'd be perfect, seeing as you have all that experience as an assassin. So here's the deal. You take on the stable hand job, so's you can secretly watch over her, and I'll do everything I can to convince her to give you the mirror."

"It soundeth as though there be slim chance for success. Thou hast said she is determined to keep the job that requireth her to use the mirror."

"I'm hoping that she'll change her mind about the circus when she gets to Pleasant Valley."

Pleasant Valley. The name evoked birdsong, burbling streams, a woman tending her kitchen garden beneath a gentle sun while springtime breezes stirred tendrils of her red-gold hair.

Maud's thoughts seemingly ran in accord. "Pleasant Valley. It sounds like it should be such a nice place, doesn't it?" She leaned forward in her eagerness to share a confidence with him. "Glory's no more suited to the circus than you are to this stable hand job. She ain't worldly like me. She doesn't know any other way of life. She ain't never been to school. Heck, she won't admit it, but she can't read so good, and so she never even studied history and all them magazines with the fashions and such. She grew up with her ma filling her head with all sorts of crazy notions about freedom and being a star."

Being a star. Dante rolled that phrase through his

mind, finding it wonderfully easy to imagine Gloriana glittering more brightly than all the other lights in the firmament.

"What Glory's never figured out for herself is that her ma's dreams were her ma's dreams and don't have anything to do with what Gloriana wants from life. I'm just plumb scared to death that she'll spend the rest of her days reaching for what her mama always yearned for, instead of looking for what will make her happy."

"Thou thinkest she will find happiness in this Pleasant Valley?"

"I don't know. I'd be happy if it just gets her to thinking in that direction. One thing's for sure—she won't find happiness if she gets herself killed over a couple hundred acres of grass."

While Maud had been rambling about stars and dreams, Dante had been trying to fashion a rejection of her plot. Her blunt statement suggesting that Gloriana might die obliterated his half-formed refusal and sent Dante's blood surging.

"I will protect her."

And so, as quickly as that, he eliminated all possibility of simply wresting the mirror from Gloriana. Even worse, he pledged to protect her on an elusive search for happiness when Dee had warned him that the passage of hours in this time might differ from that in the past. Dante's common sense hammered against his skull, urging him to call back his words. He knew he should heed his instincts, for they spoke with clarity, while these swirling urges to shelter Gloriana and hold her safe from harm confused him.

And then it came to him: Perhaps he had responded so impulsively because some deeply buried part of his mind realized that protecting Gloriana was the first challenge Dee meant to fling his way.

He considered his limited knowledge of Gloriana's circumstances. Much like Dee claimed Elizabeth would one day do, Gloriana apparently found herself in unlikely possession of her father's lands. Violence and upheaval swirled about her. Elizabeth and Gloriana. Gloriana and Elizabeth. Their situations mirrored each other, though on different scales. Resolving Gloriana's relatively minor dispute would prove he had the strength to overpower an enemy and the wisdom to make allies of those who had every reason to mistrust him. If Dee had devised this clever way of preparing Dante for the challenges he might face once married to Elizabeth, perhaps he was not quite the lunatic he had seemed.

Royal consort! Honor and respect. His sons the equal of his father's legitimate offspring. The very notion sent his heart racing.

And that quivering excitement, so at odds with his usual careful demeanor, roused an inner warning. Any warrior who charged into battle while under excitement's spell risked losing everything. Some accused Dante of being too calculating, too methodical, too eager to weigh every option before making a move. Most of those who derided his careful planning lay moldering in the ground, while he lived to fight again and again. He would do well to remember the secret to his longevity: anticipating every likely outcome and avoiding surprises.

He would try to remember it later.

"Well, what do you say?" Maud asked.

"I will lend my sword arm to that cause."

"You don't have a gun?" she asked, peering toward his hips, as if she suspected he might have somehow hidden such a cumbersome treasure upon his person.

"Nay."

"And I don't suppose you have the money to buy one when we stop in Winslow tonight." At Dante's shrug, she sighed. "Oh, well, I guess I could buy it for you. You do know how to shoot a gun, don't you?"

"Of course." He could not keep from straightening his shoulders with pride, knowing Maud could not fail to be impressed with his vast experience. "I long ago mastered the falcon and scoppietti. But such small arms pale in significance, considering that I have twice fired a fine Swiss harquebus."

"Only twice?" Maud asked with dismay.

"Twice be two times more than most men."

"What the hell is a harquebus?" Maud's puzzlement creased her brow. "Is it like a Sharps rifle or a Colt revolver?"

"Mayhap," he ventured cautiously, mindful that his knowledge of English weaponry was rather limited. Admitting ignorance of the nature of Sharps rifles and Colt revolvers might lead Maud to reconsider her offer.

"Well, which one is most like a harquebus?" Maud spoke quite testily. "I need to know so I can buy the right one for you to carry around and show off."

Her comment so astounded him that Dante could not speak for a moment. She spoke of purchasing a harquebus—a weapon coveted by kings—as if acquiring one posed no greater challenge than ordering a crock of butter from the village dairymaid. She spoke of carrying it about—as if one man could brandish its awkward six-foot length for more than a few paces without staggering beneath its weight.

Maud apparently misread his astonishment for uncertainty. "I thought that if you just wore the gun on your hip and looked sort of tough, nobody would bother us."

"Wear it on my hip?" Dante frowned, certain now that Maud was jesting with him. The transport and firing of a harquebus was an affair that required several men, beginning with those who bore it as carefully as a nursemaid carrying her lord's firstborn, to the armsman who balanced the gunrest upon which the long bore of the harquebus rested, to the shooter who aimed with the careful precision of one who counted the cost of every shot. "Who would helpest me shoot it?"

Now it was Maud's turn to look as shocked as if Dante had told her he required assistance to spoon his soup into his mouth.

"Assassin, my eye." She glowered and looked disappointed all at once. "I was right the first time I saw you. The only way you could hurt someone is by ramming them with your acorn hat."

"One hardly becometh a world-renowned assassin by resorting to a gun." Dante stifled the smile prompted by Maud's obvious ignorance of fighting. "I have shed far more blood with a simple foil. A sword," he amended when he noted the deepening of her confusion.

"Oh, so now you're world-renowned. I guess I'd better get you a sword, though lord knows where I'll find one in Arizona."

"I could make do with a soldier's sword," Dante offered, so relieved to realize that Maud did not intend to retract her promise to help him acquire the mirror that he resigned himself to bearing a clumsily fashioned weapon. "I would, though, that thou seekest out a foil, if it please thee, Maud. A graceful weapon with a flexible blade that will bend at my will and yet pierce Gloriana's enemies' hides with deadly ease."

"I like the sound of that." Maud nodded her approval. She ran an assessing glance along his form. "I guess I'll have to get you some clothes in Winslow, too."

"Why hast thou this obsession with my garments?"

"Because you don't look mean enough."

With that, Dante tipped his head back and sent her his fiercest glower, one that sapped the strength from grown men's knees.

She widened her eyes admiringly. "Say, that's pretty good. Now, all I have to do is figure out some excuse for buying you all this stuff without making Glory suspicious. Speaking of which, I'd better get out of here before she starts wondering why I've been here so long."

"Mayhap thou couldst tell her that thou and I have been gambling, and that these objects thou must provide me represent thy losses."

She slapped her knee and chuckled. "I'm starting to like you, Dante."

There was no reason why such an offhand statement should tease a smile from his lips, but it did.

She paused before leaving to grip his hand with a firm shake to seal their bargain. "You'll keep her safe, won't you?"

"Aye. I give thee my word."

He had not realized how stiffly she'd been holding herself until his promise sent her slumping with relief. But only briefly. "Well, that gambling story will explain why I'm buying you clothes and weapons. We still have to figure out a story that'll make her believe you don't want her mirror. It won't be easy. She has a suspicious nature when it comes to men."

"I could tell her I find myself enjoying caring for these horses."

"Nobody would believe that."

"They are magnificent beasts, Maud."

"They're pains in the a—neck, is what they are.

Naw. She'd suspect right off that you're hiding the truth. I do have an idea that might work, though." She edged closer to the door, giving the impression that she meant to bolt the moment her suggestion left her lips.

He sighed, certain from her demeanor that she meant to say something that would displease him, and motioned with his hand for her to continue.

"You might've noticed Glory has a real pretty way of speaking."

"Aye. I noticed." He had more than noticed; his brief exposure to her honeyed tones had created a longing in him to hear more.

"Her grandma came from England. Glory talks sort of like her. I thought maybe I could tell her you're kind of embarrassed about the real reason why you don't want money for the job."

"The real reason is because I wantest the mirror."

"I can't tell her that! I thought that maybe I could . . . I could tell Glory you'd like her to teach you how to talk."

She quivered like a doe who'd just scented a wolf.

So those *thees* and *thous, -eths* and *-ests,* continued to plague him and mark him as a foreigner. Dante thought about the suggestion. Indeed, it was fitting that accepting this challenge might prepare him to communicate better with Elizabeth. He nodded his acceptance of Maud's idea.

And with that, Maud fled.

He welcomed the chance to be alone, with only the horses and their soft sounds to accompany him, while he restored his mind to its usual order.

Everything that had happened to him since entering Dr. Dee's squalid parlor had conspired to steal his wits. No doubt it all had a perfectly logical explanation that for the moment eluded him. He would puzzle it out in his usual fashion, studying every aspect, envisioning an appropriate reaction to every possibility, so that nothing took him by surprise.

The mirror would belong to him eventually. That was the most important thing to impress upon his mind—the mirror, not Gloriana. Possession of the mirror, not the woman. Protection of fragile, centuries-old glass, not the tender blushing flesh of the woman.

Time would be his ally. Time would help him fashion a way to repay the meddlesome Dr. Dee by returning to his rightful place and time. This venture he meant to embark upon would, by Gloriana's own reckoning, last no more than two weeks, perhaps less. Two weeks. Fourteen days. It would pass in a twinkling, he was sure.

Even if Dee's warning that time in his era did move at a different rate proved true, what of it? Could one day in the nineteenth century be two days in his own time? Or five? Ten? Surely no more than ten days. At most, he might trade ten times fourteen days, a hundred and forty days, of ruling as royal consort while ensuring Gloriana's lifelong happiness.

It seemed a bargain, though the knowledge that he would not be present to witness her happiness dimmed its luster just a little.

Besides, he rather fancied the idea of helping Gloriana defend her inheritance against a handful of insolent shepherds. Engaging in blood sport always had the refreshing side benefit of clearing a man's head.

His contemplative solitude lasted but a moment. A frantic scratching at the door heralded Maud's return. She poked her head into the stable car.

"You know, on second thought, I'm not so sure I can

pull this off by myself. She knows me too well. We'd better develop a plan."

"Thou thinkest I might be a better liar?"

"No. I think *she* can't think when you're around. We'll have her agreeing to everything we say before she figures out we're up to something."

6

"*You lost* how *many* hands?" Glory asked. She'd been so concerned about Maud's prolonged absence that it must have affected her hearing.

"Seven." Maud ticked them off on her fingers. "Britches, shirt, hat, razor, gun, and a ... a whatchamacallit, Dante?"

"Foil."

"Foil." Maud ended her list with a quick dip of her head that managed to make her look embarrassed and smugly pleased with herself at the same time.

Maud was up to something. *They* were up to something.

"What on earth is a foil?"

"A nasty sword, right, Dante?"

"Aye."

"Why would you make her buy you a gun *and* a sword?"

"Because I quakest in fear of sheepmen."

Glory hadn't seen a single indication that he would

quake before the devil himself. Frightened men huddled in corners. They kept their arms close to their sides and sneaked worried little glances all around the room. Dante propped his elbow against her armoire, all elegant grace. A subtle softening around his lips made her think he was having fun.

"That's only six forfeits, not seven. Besides, Maud, you never lose at poker."

"Today wasn't my lucky day." Maud put a woebegone expression on her face. A suggestion of tears clung to her lashes. She met Glory's skeptical gaze directly, without the slightest hint of guilt.

Maud was lying through her teeth—Glory just knew it. Dante, too—imagine him winning seven hands from a con artist such as Maud, who'd learned from the best shell game operators in the business! He'd already admitted he was no great shakes as a gambler, though his stone-faced countenance would do any card sharp proud.

"What game were you playing?" Glory asked, looking straight at Dante.

"Seven card stud!" Maud shouted.

Dante's lips tilted, and his eyes narrowed with pleasure. "Stud. My favorite pastime."

She'd never heard so much rumbling richness in any man's voice. It roused an unfamiliar quivering from somewhere low in her belly. "I . . . I didn't know you had cards with you, Maud. Where are they?"

"Why, I . . . I threw them out the window, I got so frustrated at losing." Maud blinked and smiled, looking quite pleased with herself. "Yep, right out the window. They're probably scattered from here back to New Mexico by now."

The train whistle wailed, announcing that they were approaching the Winslow station. The train slowed a little, and then unexpectedly lurched, sending both Glory and Maud crashing into Dante.

Glory thought at first that he might still be wearing his metal vest, because plowing into Dante's chest wasn't much more comfortable than slamming into a solid wall. But then his arms came up and encircled both her and Maud, pulling them hard against his sides while he braced his back against the coach wall. His leg shifted against Glory's as he tensed his muscles. His upper arm clamped against her shoulder, and his forearm pressed firmly against her belly. Goodness, she didn't even know that people could flex their forearms. She could feel Dante's strength and warmth clear through her robe.

Eventually the train's motion steadied. She found her balance but felt curiously incapable of standing alone. She swayed just a little as Dante's hold upon her eased. He kept his hand at her waist until she straightened, and then he let it fall away, his fingers almost imperceptibly tracing the swell of her hip. The featherlight caress weakened her knees all over again, but she moved away from him before it became noticeable. And she was glad she did, because only a few moments later the train chugged and jolted to a halt, which would have thrown her against him once more.

Maud didn't appear to be the slightest bit discomfited by her proximity to Dante. "Say, Glory, there's one tiny little detail I think I forgot to mention."

"Oh?"

Maud's "tiny little" omissions always meant trouble. For once Glory welcomed it, because dreading what Maud might do gave her a good excuse for the fluttering sense of foreboding that filled her just then.

"Well, you sort of have to keep Dante company while I shop in Winslow."

"What?"

"He's going to hold my belongings hostage until I get back with his winnings. He doesn't trust me, isn't that right, Dante?"

"Thou art correct, Maud. I am a most untrustworthy man."

"No! That's not what . . ." Maud glared at Dante and then slid a furtive glance at Glory. "That's not what he means at all, which leads me to my next point—"

"There is no next point." Glory decided to put a halt to Maud's conniving, without waiting to learn what it would lead to. "What on earth do you expect me to do with him while you're shopping?"

Dante sucked in his breath, which made the cloth of his embroidered shirt stretch taut against his chest. The sight stirred in Glory vivid memories of spending a few all-too-brief seconds leaning there just minutes earlier. He didn't say a word, and his expression was as unrevealing as it had been when Maud began this whole charade. From the glint in his coppery brown eyes, though, Glory could see that he was imagining a thousand pleasant diversions they might share while Maud haggled with the Winslow shopkeepers. She felt a wave of heat begin at the base of her throat and make its way downward, peaking at each spot where Dante's flesh had pressed against hers.

"Do him a favor and teach him to talk," Maud said, and then she slipped through the door.

Silence reigned briefly, pierced only by the muffled sounds of activity coming from outside their car. Men called to one another, horses whinnied, and over the incessant clanging of the station bell she could hear the shrill laugh of a child excited at greeting the train.

A long, loud hiss made Dante's head snap up.

"It's just the engineer blowing off extra steam,"

Glory said, remembering that he seemed unfamiliar with train travel.

"Ah. To me, it soundeth likest a hundred blacksmiths had all at once plunged freshly forged horseshoes into cold water."

She'd heard that sound a thousand times but had never thought of anything quite so picturesque. Now that he'd mentioned it, his observation sounded rather sensible. But like so much of what he said, it made her wonder what caused him to view the world the way he did.

"Don't mind Maud," she said. "Don't get offended because she commented about the way you speak. She didn't mean to hurt your feelings. She just says whatever's on her mind without bothering to cushion her opinions in pretty words."

"A plain-spoken ally."

"Yes, exactly." Gloriana cast him a grateful smile for understanding. "She's the best friend I've ever had."

"Allies are not always friends."

"I would trust Maud with my life."

He nodded gravely, as if he had good reason to have faith in Maud, too. "And so I shouldst then trust her opinion that my manner of speaking requireth improvement." Gloriana gave him a tentative nod. "Very well. If thee . . . thou wouldst instructest me, Gloriana, I wouldst showest my appreciation by caring for thy horses for the next fortnight whilst forgoing wages."

"Oh, would you?" Relief rushed through her, and then almost at once it was overcome by raging suspicion. "Wait a minute—what about my mirror?"

He shrugged, as if he'd never expressed a bit of interest in it. "Maud will fetch a shaving glass along with my other winnings. Britches, shirt, hat, razor, gun, foil, and mirror."

Maud *had* mentioned losing seven hands of poker.

But he had seemed downright obsessed by her mirror. That particular mirror, the one he claimed belonged to a sorcerer. Now he was acting as if he just needed to add any old mirror to his shaving kit.

"I will have done once and for all with learning my *thees* and *thous,* my *-eths* and *-ests,*" Dante said, interrupting her suspicions.

"That's easy enough."

"Ha! 'Tis a welcome opportunity for me, to learn from thee. I have yet to master many aspects of your tongue."

"What did you study—Shakespeare's plays?"

"I did not." He looked so affronted by the possibility that she couldn't help wondering if he even knew who Shakespeare was. "I have ever known the wisdom of hiring one well versed in the skills I seek to acquire, and so I hired the services of one whose rates proclaimed him to be the best private tutor of English."

"You should ask him for a refund," said Gloriana. "Nobody except Quakers says *thee* and *thou* anymore. We just say *you* all the time."

"Why didst scholars not simplify the English tongue in this way centuries ago?" he marveled.

Glory didn't know how to answer that question. "And the only words that end in *-est* are those that mean the most of something, like the *greenest* grass or the *fastest* horse."

"The *beautifullest* woman?" he asked softly.

She didn't need that compliment to tell her that he'd warmed to the notion of her teaching him. His face was inclined toward hers; earnestness illuminated his bronze eyes, and his full lips were parted as if he meant them to utter more pretty words until she swooned at his feet.

"The *smoothest* flatterer," she shot back. She turned away, toward the window, and pulled the curtain to the side, peering through the glass and pretending a sudden, overwhelming interest in the outside activities.

Her effort to place some distance between them failed miserably. He came up behind her, and she could feel his heat cross the inches separating them until it warmed her back. When he spoke, his lips were so close to her ear that she could feel the words stir her hair.

"It would seem that many who ride this conveyance have departed to walk whilst stopped here in Winslow. Dost thou— Do you not partake of exercise, Gloriana?"

"I got all the exercise I need taking care of those horses this morning."

"If you are afraid of sheepmen, I shall offer you my arm to cling to."

He seemed determined to goad her into walking outside. To her amazement, she found herself blurting out the shameful truth, which she'd never admitted to a soul. "In small towns like this, people stare at strangers when they get off the train. I don't have to endure that when I'm not working."

"Ah." He didn't press for an explanation as to why a woman who earned her living by performing before huge crowds should so dislike being stared at by strangers. His restraint should have left her feeling grateful; instead, it showed a perception she found disconcerting. She wished Maud hadn't left her alone with him.

"Gloriana, I thank you for thy—"

"Don't say *thy.* Say *your.*"

"I thank you for your instructions. I have oft thought—"

"It's *often,* not *oft.*"

"I have often thought English wouldst—"

She heaved an enormous sigh that lifted both her shoulders.

"One doth not say *wouldst?*"

"Right. One doesn't say *wouldst* or *shouldst,* or even *dost* or *doth,* for that matter."

"Mayhap I should simply hold myself silent."

She slanted a wary glance at him over her shoulder, fearing another of his misplaced compliments.

"It's *maybe,* not *mayhap.* And maybe you're right. Maybe it's best if we both keep our mouths shut for a while."

She winced inwardly at the shrewish tone she'd used to badger him into silence. It wasn't his fault that she couldn't seem to keep her thoughts in line when he spoke to her.

"Very well. I will silently inspect this place so I need not fear being attacked by marauding shepherds while I await Maud's return."

He hadn't made a single mistake with his words. She should have complimented him, and it made her feel like a liar when she didn't.

He then proceeded to ignore her. He stalked through the train car, poking into every corner and eyeing everything suspiciously, as if he expected sheepmen to be lurking behind chairs or hiding inside trunks. In less than two seconds, Gloriana wished he'd start talking funny again so that she would have something else to think about rather than the unconscious grace and power that marked every move he made.

And then, in another two seconds, she wished she could simply disappear, because he'd worked his way into the trunk holding her haphazardly folded underwear.

"Name this for me," he ordered. From his fingers dangled her Madame Boadecia corset—the one that thrust her breasts outward like buckeyes splitting their husks.

"Dante!" She barely managed to croak the rebuke through her mortification.

He merely cocked a brow questioningly and allowed the corset to swing to and fro.

"Oh, for heaven's sake!" She retreated into prickliness. "It's my costume underwear."

"Underwear?"

"Yes, underwear." Her embarrassment didn't abate a single bit when she realized he didn't understand what she meant. "I don't know what they call it where you come from, wherever that is, but you must have seen something like it before."

"Underwear." He repeated the word while ignoring the opportunity she'd given him to reveal his native land.

"Underwear."

They couldn't stand there all day saying the word *underwear* to each other. Well, maybe they could, but she didn't think her modesty could stand it. She tried couching an explanation in words he might more easily understand. "Um, let's see. It's something one wears beneath one's garments."

"But 'tis filled with bones." He indicated the whale-bone stays.

"Of course it's filled with bones—it's a corset."

"I have seen corsets. They are worn like jackets outside one's garment, not under . . . wear. This one is far too fine. It must be a church-devised punishment. I wouldst . . . would repent all my sins most eagerly if forced to wear such."

"Men don't wear corsets like this."

This information sent relief flickering over his features.

She explained further. "Only women are foolish enough to punish themselves by squeezing into them. And since that particular kind of corset enhances a woman's figure in a . . . well, a sort of sinful way, I doubt very much that the church approves at all."

"Then the devil himself must be responsible." He gave a low, rumbling chuckle that spoke of familiarity with deviltry and something more, and his whiskey-colored eyes twinkled in a way that made her spirits lighten. "The devil in league with a fallen but still celibate priest, for no man would willingly permit his woman to garb herself in such. 'Twould deny him his rightful freedom of her soft flesh."

"Well, um, it, um . . ." Her mind had gotten caught on *it would deny him his rightful freedom of her soft flesh.* So much for guarding her modesty! With such an outrageous statement echoing in her mind, she couldn't summon an explanation for how important it was that her appearance distract her audience while she performed her simple circus illusions. Her inability to explain didn't seem to matter. Dante paid no attention to her stammering. He stared with frank curiosity from her robed, uncorseted figure to the underwear, probably trying to imagine how it confined her embarrassingly generous curves.

His regard left her acutely conscious of her state of undress. She'd shucked her dress earlier, so it wouldn't wrinkle while she rested in an attempt to cure her headache. Headache? Gracious, it hadn't troubled her at all since he and Maud had charged into the car. She'd simply pulled her robe over her chemise and thought nothing of the impropriety of greeting a man in such an outfit. Growing up within the circus and coping with the lack of privacy, changing costumes and helping one another primp in communal dressing areas, and then stripping away the garish outfits before succumbing to exhaustion in half-clothed camaraderie had long ago obliterated that sort of embarrassment.

Though the thick cotton robe covered her whisper-light silk chemise, she suddenly felt all but naked. She had never noticed before that each breath she took sent the silk she wore sliding against her skin in an infinitesimal caress. She had never realized that the fine hairs along her arms could lift and quiver with anticipation. Her figure had blossomed when she turned fourteen, but in the ten years since, she'd never noticed the weight of her breasts, or that little shivery tingles of delight seemed to radiate from their tips. The tingles grew even more delightful when she watched Dante's thumb probe the length of a corset stay. His touch lingered at the seam that would rest just beneath the tender underside of her breast the next time she donned that corset, and that realization made her draw a huge, rasping breath.

"Art thou—Are you in danger of taking a fit, Gloriana?"

Dante's question doused all her unfamiliar sensations. Good lord, what had she been doing, turning all fluttery and female just because he pawed at her empty corset?

"I'm fine," she wheezed. "Just fine."

"Certes? Such gaspings and swayings often mark the onset of a fit. I have seen several people struck down exactly so."

"I am not gasping and swaying, and I'm in no danger of taking a fit." He fixed her with a dubious stare that would serve any medicine-show hawker well, so she gathered the shreds of her dignity about her and devised an explanation for her lapse of control. "I'm just not in the habit of entertaining men in my private coach."

"You have been entertaining me?" He peered around, looking as disappointed as a small boy who'd learned he'd slept through an elephant parade.

She took advantage of his distraction and snatched her corset from him. She shook it beneath his chin.

"You've been plenty entertained for the past few minutes, buster."

He stared down his nose at the corset, and then his tawny glance swept her from head to toe, enmeshing them in a visual intimacy. A faint smile tugged at his lips.

"Aye," he said. "Now that I think upon it, I daresay you are proving most diverting, Gloriana."

"Okay, that's it." She spoke sternly but felt as inept as a beginning juggler as she tried to hold her robe closed while hanging on to the corset and reaching for the doorknob. She had to move Dante out of her coach before she succumbed entirely to these uncharacteristic squeakings and swayings and self-consciousness. "I don't care whether you trust Maud or not. You can just take yourself to the next car and wait for her to bring your winnings to you."

"I am afraid to go outside dressed as I am." He sent her such a cocky, confident smirk that she doubted he'd ever found himself afraid of anything.

"You've been wearing those clothes since I first met you."

"Exactly so. And where have they gotten me, but to mark me as easy prey for gamblers?"

"Easy prey my eye. You beat Maud at seven hands, remember?"

"I might not be so lucky if a sheepman comes along and forces poker upon me."

"Oh, for goodness sake!" She fumed, tapping her foot in exasperation. His protests were blatantly ridiculous, but she didn't see how she could dare him to tell her the truth without prolonging their conversation. "You just have to cross the coupling bridge and balconies into the stable car. You won't draw much attention if you cover yourself up and move fast." She jutted her chin toward an armoire tucked in the corner. "You'll find a long black cape in there. It's a lot plainer than yours. Once you pull it around yourself, you won't look too noticeable."

He looked as if he meant to object. She glared at him until he sighed and trudged to the armoire.

But when he pulled her black cape from the armoire and swirled it around his shoulders, her promise didn't hold up. That cape, when she wore it, swathed her from neck to toes with a thoroughness that made nuns' habits appear skimpy in comparison. On Dante, it didn't even close at the neck. His shoulders were so wide that the cape gapped open over his chest. And it fell only to his knees, leaving his calves exposed.

If *she* were a sheepman, she'd run screaming in fear at the sight of him.

"'Tis meant for a much smaller man," Dante observed. He stroked the silk lining and then drew the cape taut over one arm, where it hugged the sculpted curves of his biceps.

"It's not a man's cape. It's mine," Glory said in a squeaking voice. Why her strong voice squeaked, she didn't know. But for some reason she suddenly felt small and delicate and prone to exciteable outbursts. "It's part of my costume when I do my Madame Boadecia act. I wear it when I first enter the ring, and then I sort of fling it open to get everyone's attention."

"You delight in revealing that underwear?" Dante asked softly, with a meaningful look toward her corset.

"No! Yes! I mean . . ." She swallowed to stifle the turning sensation in her stomach. It had been some time since she'd acknowledged that combination of revulsion and stage fright that accompanied every one of her performances. How she despised posing and smiling before the crowd—and yet it was a necessary diversion, something that would redirect their attention. Few suspected she was really picking up clues from her cohorts, who mingled with the audience before the performance and used a wide variety of signals to feed her the information they learned to help her perform her feats of illusion. "What I mean is, the corset is covered by . . . another bit of frippery."

"Thus, 'tis worn under frippery. Underwear." Dante nodded sagely, stroking the cape's lining.

"Something like that." Glory's skin warmed, and she wondered if he realized that the silk he was fondling usually clung to her bare limbs.

She forced those thoughts away, only to have them replaced with the worrisome notion that sending him into the next car meant he could simply walk away. There wasn't much to hold him to his word. She'd helped him with his English and given him a cape to cover himself, though she didn't truly believe he feared meeting sheepmen, no matter how he was dressed. Anyway, he could simply waylay Maud in town and claim his winnings. Then she'd be back to searching for a stable hand, which was surely the only reason she was worrying so much about his sneaking away.

"Would you . . . would you like me to act as a lookout for you?"

She knew at once that she hadn't fooled him with her oh-so-casual offer of assistance.

"I daresay I can cross a pair of balconies without being accosted." He studied her unsmilingly while his fingers tugged at the cape without succeeding in stretching it over his full breadth. "I will not desert my post, Gloriana. I will care for . . . your beasts and hold all safe against harm. I swear it."

She noticed the slight catch in his voice. "Hold *all* safe?" she whispered.

"All."

She couldn't help the little rush of pleasure sparked by his pledge or prevent herself from thinking that he spoke of protecting more than her horses. Nor could she stop the tiny internal voice that scolded her for practically melting with delight at the realization that he'd spend virtually every moment of the next two weeks in her presence. And she couldn't shake the certainty that no other man's declaration would have struck her so profoundly as did this vow made by her half-tamed, caped champion. She didn't entertain one bit of doubt that he could protect her against an army of range warriors.

Well, he'd been honest about admitting that he meant to watch over her. She might as well admit that she saw through his ruse.

"You can stop pretending you're afraid of sheepmen."

"Maud will be distressed to learn I have somehow . . . spilleth the beans." He looked chagrined.

She'd skipped the -*eth* part of the English lesson. "Don't stick -*eth* onto anything," she said. "And Dante, I'm not a fool. I know I could be in big trouble, and I'm grateful that you're willing to help. But I'm still not willing to part with my mirror, no matter what Maud might have promised you."

"Maud promised nothing. Of you, Gloriana, I would demand only what you are willing to give."

His growling murmur all but seduced her with its reverberating intensity. He studied her through slitted eyes that didn't quite hide the feral gleam of anticipation glowing within.

"I just want to see that ranch," she whispered.

"I have been wondering, Gloriana—what is a ranch?"

His puzzlement set her aback. It sometimes seemed that half the population was either homesteading a ranch or wanted to homestead one. The country swarmed with immigrants eager to claim free government land and make their fortunes, and Dante's foreign accent had led her to believe he might be a potential homesteader.

Goodness, she'd even heard circus folk musing over the homesteading dream. Not a season ended without someone declaring they meant to disengage their rail cars permanently from the caravan and put down roots on a little patch of ground where a body could raise its own food and not worry about the success of the next performance. Glory had never been able to listen to those wistful dreams without growing weepy. Probably because her mother had taught her that a *real* circus performer would sooner die than settle down.

"Well, a ranch is a bunch of dirt and grass, to raise cows on."

"Ah." Dante swept her with an assessing glance. "Thus you are a cowherd."

"I most certainly am not a cowherd!"

"You are now." Dante had that look upon his face, that put-upon, long-suffering expression that men wore when they were certain their knowledge would prove superior over anything a woman might come up with. "You have a ranch. So you must be a cowherd."

"I never met anyone who likes to jump to conclusions the way you do," Gloriana ground out. "You've been doing it from the first minute."

"Jump to conclusions? Nay. When information is given to me, I merely consider all options and put forth the most logical choice." If anything, the look upon his face became even more self-congratulatory. "I dislike surprises, and sound, logical expectations always prevail over surprises."

"That's what you think. I sure never expected to inherit anything from my father."

She caught a fleeting glint of something in his eyes that whispered, *Nor do I.* And then it was gone, coupled with a smooth diversion that forced her to shift her attention away from him and onto defending her actions yet again.

"You race to claim this unexpected inheritance despite being warned to stay away.... 'Tis a bold course for a woman to pursue."

"Oh, I'm anything but bold." She gave a self-deprecating shrug. "I just want to see the place. I've always been curious about it."

"I daresay 'tis far more than womanish curiosity at stake here."

She hadn't expected such an astute observation from him. He made her delve deeper into her own reasons for the irrestistible pull this ranch land exerted upon her, to articulate them to someone other than Maud for the first time.

He studied her with an intent curiosity that reminded her of the way she'd examined the first electric lamp she'd ever seen, trying to figure out how glass and wire and invisible gases combined to create illumination. She usually abhorred being the object of such blatant scrutiny.

Instead, in the same way that electricity brightened a

lamp, Dante's vow to protect her rekindled her hopes. His interest warmed her soul. She felt herself leaning toward him like a newly sprouted seedling groping through mud to reach the constant, dependable sun.

"Why, you're just like a big old light bulb, Dante."

She hadn't realized she'd whispered her observation aloud until Dante scowled at her. "Light bulb? Do you cast yet another slur against my garments?"

She'd embarrassed him with her inane outburst; she'd embarrassed herself even more. If anyone was like a big old light bulb, it was she—why, the red must be glowing from her cheeks like twin beacons! What she should do was clamp her lips shut and get him out of that car, which was what she'd meant to do for what now seemed like a lifetime. So what if his vow touched her heart, if his old-world, courtly concern probed beyond the facile motives other people would readily accept? She didn't owe him a glimpse into her innermost thoughts. And yet she found herself chattering on, as eager as a squirrel sharing the discovery of a hidden cache of nuts.

"My father left that land to me. To *me.*" She gave a short, bitter laugh. "His will stated it plain as day: 'I leave all my lands and property, all my earthly possessions, to my beloved natural daughter, Gloriana Carlisle.' His beloved daughter. Ha! He never acknowledged me in public until his legitimate children died. You probably can't understand why this whole thing gets under my skin."

"Many things about this situation lend me pause, Gloriana." He spoke dispassionately, his face as expressionless as finely chiseled granite. Not one speck of understanding radiated from him, but neither did she sense any of the unspoken pity that she'd feared her confession might prompt.

And there was no reason on God's green earth why she should feel a soul-deep certainty that Dante did understand. She wished that he would gather her into his arms for a big, mutually reassuring hug, for something about the way he held himself told her that he needed one just as badly as she did.

"What about your father, Dante? Is he kind to you?"

"My father is not important just now."

His rebuff stung, and, like acid, it dissolved the tentative trust that had sprouted in her heart. She remembered that he'd used those exact words to dismiss her question about the Elizabeth he'd seemed so concerned over when they had first met. Here she'd gone and spilled her deepest, innermost thoughts, and he hadn't told her a single important thing about himself.

She knew almost nothing about this man who had pledged to watch over her. Almost nothing? Hell, she knew absolutely nothing about him.

Never give your heart to a man who keeps secrets, Gloriana, her mother had always slurred in her bourbon-inflected voice. *He'll only leave you and go back to what he's hiding.*

She couldn't imagine why her mother's warning had popped into her head at that moment. She certainly had no intentions of giving her heart to Dante Trevani, mystery man.

"Maybe you ought to go check on the horses now," she said.

He nodded. "Do not fear if you hear noises outside your door ere nightfall. 'Twill only be me checking upon the latches."

"You will?" She'd meant to sound authoritative, as if she expected him to perform this chore to ensure her safety. Instead it betrayed her doubt that he'd stay with her.

"Gloriana, I am, for the most part, a man of my word."

"For the most part? I wonder what part of you I shouldn't trust."

She said it lightly, jokingly, to reduce the tension between them the way she would handle an annoyed member of an audience. But he didn't respond in kind. He inclined his head toward her and paused just before the door. He looked back at her with a mixture of warning and regret marking his strong features. His next words confirmed every lesson her mother had ever taught her.

"Perhaps you should not trust me at all. That way you will not be disappointed."

7

"You let him get away."

Though the bottom half of Maud's face was hidden behind the pile of men's clothes she held, Glory knew from Maud's tone of voice that her friend's lips would be tight with disappointment.

"Dante didn't get away. I sent him to the stable car."

"Why on earth would you do that, after I worked so hard to figure out how to leave you two . . ." Maud grimaced and let her voice trail away.

"Don't bother trying to keep up that phony poker story. I know all about you two working in cahoots."

"You're not mad?"

"Furious." Glory softened her comment with a smile. "You were right to worry about our safety. I guess I was just so set on visiting that ranch that I blinded myself to the danger. Speaking of which, I don't see you carrying any gun or sword."

Before Maud could answer, the train whistle sounded, announcing their imminent departure from

Winslow. From somewhere outside, the conductor bellowed, "All aboard! Next stop Holbrook!"

Holbrook. A day and a half away. And then only two more days of wagon travel to Pleasant Valley.

"Couldn't find no harquebus or sword in Winslow," Maud said, picking up the conversation as if it had never been interrupted. The train began its first, jerky movements, and she went to the window, which framed the receding town. "Nobody knew what I was talking about when I asked for a harquebus. No swords here, either, but a fella here said he'd wire on ahead, on account of there's some Hopi Indian fella in Holbrook owns a sword. He might be willing to sell it. Won't matter if he's not. If Dante's run off, we won't have any other world-renowned assassins waiting to use it."

"He'll be in the stable car."

Maud gave a skeptical snort.

"He will," Glory insisted. "He gave his word."

"You say that like you believe him."

"I . . . I do." Glory found those two words hard to form.

"Hmpf." Maud turned about, craning her neck toward the ceiling. "Yoo-hoo! Anybody around here see a tall redheaded gal by the name of Gloriana Carlisle? There's an impostor here in her rail car."

"Maud!"

"Well, the Gloriana Carlisle I know spent half her life swearing she'd never fall for some man's fancy promises."

"He didn't make any fancy promises. He needs the job."

Maud hooted her scorn. "What's he going to do with that big pay he earns—cook up a pot of mirror stew? Maybe he's been real anxious to chew on some antique glass to toughen him up for his next assassination.

Maybe he . . . uh-oh." Maud put an abrupt halt to her wild speculations when Glory let out a soft sob of disbelief. "I just messed up, didn't I?"

"Oh, Maud." Glory's agony came out in a choked whisper. She didn't know which hurt worse, Maud's conniving against her or Dante's lying about it. "You know how important that mirror is to me. To *us*. How could you?"

Maud let the clothing tumble to the floor. She wrung her hands. She looked as if she wanted to step closer to Glory, but something in Glory's expression must have stopped her. "I just told him I'd *try* to convince you to give him the mirror. I didn't promise him anything, honey. I swear it."

Maud promised nothing. Dante hadn't exactly lied, which cheered her up just a tiny bit. But he hadn't been exactly truthful, either, which sent her spirits plummeting back down.

"I won't try at all to convince you to give him the mirror." Maud's eyes brimmed with tears. "Please, honey, don't be angry about this. You know I'd never do anything to hurt you. I wouldn't have a home if it weren't for you and your ma taking me in when I got scared of walking the ropes. Mr. Fontanescue would've tossed me out on the street like some useless sack of garbage—"

Glory raised a shaking hand to stop Maud's pleading. She knew the extent of Maud's gratitude and never felt comfortable hearing about it. She treasured Maud's companionship so highly that she considered their arrangement a more than even trade. Except at times like this, when Maud's good intentions outweighed her common sense.

"I know you didn't mean anything by it, but you did it. Now I have to figure out how to handle this."

She wanted to wail in frustration, but she'd caught herself squeaking earlier with Dante, and she'd be damned if she'd do it again. Strong women maintained a moderate tone of voice, her mother had always said, and won their arguments by the force of their logic. Plus they always maintained self-control and never based their decisions on emotion.

The trouble was, Glory had never been too strong on logic, and her self-control seemed to have flown out her rail car's window when Dante Trevani stuck his handsome head through it and promised he'd die rather than let her come to harm.

"If I tell him right now that he can't have the mirror, he's bound to leave us unprotected. But if I pretend I don't know what you two cooked up, he'll stick around thinking he's going to get the mirror. Oh, God, listen to me—I'm starting to sound just like him, trying to anticipate what the logical move would be."

"Aw, Glory, honey, you know you don't have a logical bone in your body." Maud took one tentative step, and when Glory didn't move to stop her, she rushed to Glory's side. She gave Glory a comforting squeeze around the waist as she led her to her stool. "You stop worrying right this minute, or else your headache'll come back. I'll take care of everything."

Glory groaned.

"I will." Maud stooped and gathered the spilled clothing. "I'm going to take these to him. I won't breathe a word about our plan."

"What plan?"

"Why, I don't have it exactly made up yet, but it'll come to me. Now you get dressed for dinner. Wear something pretty, so Dante will be so bedazzled he won't have any space in his stubborn head for thinking about that mirror."

"You mean he's going to have dinner with us? You took him enough food earlier today to feed ten assassins."

"I know. And he ate every scrap so fast you'd have thought he hadn't tasted food for a hundred years. I guess it takes a lot of fuel to keep all them muscles primed for action."

"Um . . . ," Glory choked out, remembering the way the muscles in question had stretched her silk cape.

"If he was my man, I'd sure enough keep him stoked."

"Oh, God," Glory moaned.

Ten tables sat empty of diners. Ten. Dante counted them again to ensure accuracy. Another half-dozen presented empty places for any who cared to sit, unlike their own small table, which barely accommodated the three of them crowded round its inadequate surface. There was no logical reason for the elderly Miss Hampson to stop and inquire whether she might dine with them. Even less reason existed for Gloriana to immediately leap to her feet with a delighted assent and then filch a chair from a nearby table and wedge it between herself and Dante so Miss Hampson might sit.

Dante chewed another portion of meat. His pleasure in the delicacy called beefsteak dwindled with each word that Miss Hampson spoke. And the garrulous old woman managed to string together hundreds, maybe thousands, of words before pausing just short of expiring from lack of air. After drawing a breath she prattled on, meandering with no logical progression from one inane topic to another.

Gloriana hung upon every witless utterance. She trained those wondrous emerald eyes upon Miss

Hampson, sparing him and his new finery nary a glance. Her soft, rose-tinted lips were parted, but her face was turned away from Dante, and so he could not feast upon the sight of their moist, lush fullness. She limited her comments to "Oh, my!" and "Tell me more, please!" which encouraged Miss Hampson to drone on and on in her quavering, old-woman's voice when Dante's ears all but burned for the balm that came only from Gloriana's honey-smooth tones.

Dante did not feel it wise to pick up his knife just then, so he speared the remaining slab of beefsteak with his fork and tore a chunk from it with his teeth. Would that it were Miss Hampson's throat! His brief enjoyment of that thought fled when Maud sent him a sharp kick to the shins. In his surprise he swallowed his beefsteak unchewed, and it nearly choked him. Would that it were Miss Hampson the meat was choking . . .

"Listen to this," Maud hissed.

"So," said Miss Hampson. She fortified herself with a breath of such volume that Dante knew she meant to launch into a particularly long string of words. "I'm going to lock myself up in my berth and force my chair under the doorknob for good measure, and pull the shade and cover my head with my pillow until we leave Holbrook. I declare, there ought to be a law against trains stopping at the town that holds the reputation as the wildest place in all Arizona. Endangering fragile unmarried ladies like ourselves! And nobody but that dandified Sheriff Owens to keep order. He's too fine by half, even his name. Commodore Perry Owens. What kind of name is that for a sheriff? I guess it doesn't matter what his name is, on account of he's made himself a reputation as a dead shot. Holds a rifle in one hand and a pistol in the other! Why, they say his hair hangs halfway down his back and that he keeps it just as shiny as a girl's, and you know that means he must brush it at least a hundred strokes every night. What kind of sheriff tends to his hair like that? And you know the rumors about how the cowboys love to torment men who have long hair—"

"What," Dante interrupted, "do I need fear from cow-boys?"

He suspected cow-boys might be a particularly loathsome breed of creatures that were half men and half cattle, conjured by Dee himself to test Dante's mettle. It would prove prudent to prepare himself against the torments devised by such abominations.

"Oh!" Miss Hampson's eyes blinked with the same rapidity with which her tongue uttered words. "Oh, oh, oh. Why, I didn't notice you had such long hair, Mr. Trevani! I'm sure you're not a sissy like those cowboys think. Sheriff Owens surely proved he's not a sissy! I do believe it's on account of those half-breeds, who don't cut their hair on account of their spiritual beliefs or some such, and the meaner cowboys like to make fun."

Half-breeds. His assumption had been correct. Protecting Gloriana against such devil-spawned atrocities seemed a worthy challenge, bound to impress Dee. "What is a sissy?"

"Someone who likes boys better than girls," Maud blurted.

"Maud!"

"She's entirely right, my dear." Miss Hampson nodded with remarkable tolerance for a lady of her years. "Anyway, as I was saying, you'd best do the same, Miss Carlisle. Hole yourself up in your car like a hibernating bear until we're well away from Holbrook."

"I can't do that, Miss Hampson. We have to leave the train at Holbrook."

This, at last, stilled Miss Hampson's tongue. She sat there opening and closing her mouth in indecision.

"We're not going to stay in Holbrook," Maud offered. "We're heading out to Pleasant Valley as soon as we get provisions."

"Pleasant Valley!" Miss Hampson shrieked the name. "Oh, oh, oh. This is even worse. You cannot, under any circumstances, go to Pleasant Valley."

"I have to go. I own property there."

"Those Hash Knife boys will never let you keep it. Don't you read the papers? There's a terrible, horrible feud going on there. Why, Sheriff Owens has taken to meeting every train for fear that hired guns are getting off in Holbrook just so's they can take up sides in the war! If he doesn't know a man, he makes him state a good reason for being there, or else he claps him straight in jail. He wouldn't do that if he was a sissy, now would he? Even though the cowboys thought he might be one because he carries his gun on his left hip with the butt facing outward. What kind of way is that for a sheriff to carry his gun? He has to reach clear across his belly to draw his gun. Don't seem to slow him down none, though, especially since he holds a rifle crooked in his other arm at the very same time. Walks around like he's cradling a babe in his arms. They say he can shoot with that rifle without even taking aim. What kind of way is that for a sheriff to shoot a rifle? They say the outlaws laughed at him when he first came to town, on account of his hair and the way he holds his guns, but he killed most of them, and now the rest are too scared to show their faces, and Holbrook might not be such a bad place after all if they could just clear up that ruckus down in Pleasant Valley and stop all those hired guns from coming into town."

"You know what, Glory?" said Maud. "I think I

caught your headache. If you all will excuse me, I think I'll go back to our car and lie down with a cool wash-cloth on my forehead."

Dante pushed his plate away, his appetite having fled upon digesting the information gleaned from Miss Hampson's gush of words. Each turn of the train's wheels brought added confirmation that they aimed for a situation sane people would not dare approach. A quick glance toward Gloriana revealed that her face had paled; she had drawn back from the table, as if she meant to distance herself from even the sound of the words *Pleasant Valley.*

I'm no fool, Dante, she had said, but this latest information from Miss Hampson made him less inclined to believe her words. All his instincts cried out for him to argue against going to the ranch. The subtle tension in her posture and the pallor of her skin told him that she would listen and agree with but the slightest coaxing on his part.

And yet . . . and yet.

No kingdom passed easily to its queen—not England to Elizabeth, not even a bunch of dirt and grass, fit only for raising cows, to Gloriana. If Dante failed to help Gloriana secure what her father had left her, he could never hope to convince Dee that he would serve Elizabeth better.

He suddenly wished he had not dined so well upon the beefsteak. The meat was a delicacy he doubted even kings regularly enjoyed in his own day, and it served as a pointed reminder that he'd eaten this dinner in the year of our Lord 1888, not 1544. A sourness developed in his gullet. What manner of man was he to encourage Gloriana in this dangerous escapade for the sake of proving himself worthy of a woman who had already lived her life?

The hairs at the back of his neck prickled, a warning no soldier ever ignored. He looked up and saw Gloriana's eyes fixed upon him. He read hope and faith in her eyes, coupled with a reluctance that told him she fought those soft virtues. She had looked at him just so when she'd called him her big old light bulb, whatever that was—an 1888 endearment bestowed upon a 1544 man who planned treachery.

The man who dares love a queen cannot pretend to have her interests at heart while secretly working toward his own goals. Dee's taunt came upon him unbidden.

"Something wrong with your dinner?" Glory whispered.

He shook his head.

Miss Hampson droned on, oblivious to both Maud's desertion and their shift in attention.

"If half of what she says is true, we'd be fools to continue through to Pleasant Valley." Gloriana's words eerily echoed his own thoughts.

"Aye."

He felt a calmness descend upon him. If she talked herself out of the journey, he would say naught to change her mind. He had allotted two weeks to this task. Other challenges were bound to present themselves during that time.

"Um, Dante, are you having second thoughts?"

She did not meet his eyes. She concentrated instead upon the teacup she clenched in her hands. Given her firm grasp upon it, it should not have clattered as much as it did when she lowered it onto her saucer. Dante's first impulse was to soothe away the doubt and fear she fought so hard to hide.

But while he weighed the potential outcomes of following that course, a second, less noble, notion presented itself for consideration. Gloriana's options grew slimmer with each passing moment. No other man aboard the train was willing to go with her to Pleasant Valley, and she could not search for someone in Holbrook, for admitting that she traveled without a bodyguard risked calling down the wrath of the Hash Knife cow-boys upon her.

Thus if Dante withdrew his services, pretending that Miss Hampson's account had led him to regret taking the job, Gloriana would be forced to make a decision: call off the journey or continue without a protector. At that point Dante could offer her one more option—he could agree to continue serving as her bodyguard if she gave him the mirror.

She betrayed the extent of her trepidation by whispering, "Well? Have you changed your mind?"

Dante had learned much about the art of negotiation by watching his father. The negotiator who pressed hardest, who betrayed anxiousness, ultimately paid whatever the other demanded. By begging for an answer, Gloriana had lost the battle. Victory was within his grasp; he need only negotiate the terms of surrender. But for once, bargaining gave Dante no pleasure.

He feigned contemplation while Miss Hampson began holding forth on the merits of compulsory education for females.

"Dante?"

He wished it were passion rather than dread that caused his name to tremble upon her lips. He could not bring himself to lie outright to her, so he chose a circuitous route to his destination.

"You could come back later, when your circus season ends."

She smiled then, with such radiance that he knew he would spend all the days given him in his own time regretting that he would depart from life long ere she was born and graced the earth with this smile again. "If I'm afraid to do it now, when I have you here to protect me, I'll probably never come back. I'll always wonder about it—always. Can you imagine, Dante, spending the rest of your life angry with yourself because you took the easy way out?"

"I am trying to avoid such regrets myself," he said. "Perhaps that is why I am considering these second thoughts you have asked me about."

She swayed a little in her chair, but not from the motion of the train. "Everybody keeps saying the range war will calm down and it'd be safer to wait. I think I'd find myself in even more danger if I came back later."

"What could be worse than flinging yourself into the midst of a war, Gloriana?"

"Trying to claim my inheritance after someone stronger takes it over."

She could have chosen no better words to remind him of how closely her situation mirrored that of Elizabeth Tudor.

"But 'tis your birthright."

"I guess you don't know too much about the unwritten laws of the range. Arizona Territory isn't quite as law-abiding as the United States. That ranch is fair game right now for anyone who cares to move in and claim it. I won't be able to hold on to it. The neighbors probably think I have no right to it anyway, so nobody will take my part if a claim jumper moves in."

"Perhaps the sheriff Miss Hampson reveres so highly might defend your rights to the ranch." He detested implying that another man might do a better job of protecting her, but he had no choice if he meant to force her to hand over the mirror.

"I doubt Sheriff Owens has jurisdiction clear down

to Pleasant Valley. And even if he did, why should he stand up for me? I travel almost constantly with the circus. I don't vote anywhere, and I don't pay taxes in Arizona. The law in these parts has to please the folks who live here, the ones who have influence."

"Gloriana." He said her name and then paused, for every ounce of his being protested what he must do. "I cannot stand up for you, either."

"You promised. You gave me your word."

Her reminder shamed him. He could offer no defense of his honor without jeopardizing his plan. Rage—at himself, at Dee for putting him in this unenviable position—swept through him. "I will do as I promised only if you give me the mirror."

He braced himself for an onslaught of tearful pleading, for a barrage of angry insults. She did something far worse. She accepted her defeat with the familiarity of one who had often been forced to follow a path not of her choosing. Disappointment radiated from her, directed toward him and with an intensity that told Dante he'd killed far more than Gloriana's career with his selfishness. He'd destroyed her illusion that he might be a man worth trusting.

He wanted, fiercely, to call back his demand, to convince her it had been nothing but a ploy. Anything, if it would only restore the gentle softness that had until now marked her regard for him.

"You bastard," she whispered.

"So I have been called all my life."

He had endured the taunt times beyond counting without suffering so much pain as he did upon hearing it from Gloriana's lips. The loss of her respect, her good opinion, seemed to matter more at that moment than the attentions of Europe's most glittering royalty.

"What are you two bickering about?" Miss Hampson

must have paused long enough in her narration to realize that they had been ignoring her. "Lands' sake, Miss
Carlisle! I haven't seen a body so teary-eyed since my
mama back in 1865, when she heard the news that Mr.
Lincoln had been shot. Gracious, more than a quarter
of a century ago, and I can still see those tears as plain
as day . . ."

"I'm so sorry," Gloriana whispered to Dante while
Miss Hampson droned on.

Her apology so stunned him that Dante found himself speechless.

"That's probably the meanest thing one person can
say to another." Her eyes shimmered with a depth of
understanding that could come only from enduring her
share of similar slurs throughout her life. "I haven't been
fair about this. I want *you* to risk your life for something
important to *me*. It's only fair that I pay you with something that's equally important to you. You hold up your
end of the bargain, and I'll give you my mirror. I'll worry
about how to replace it in my act later."

"Are you certain?"

"I have to see that ranch."

He remembered Maud's wistful hope that Gloriana
would find happiness on the ranch, away from the circus. He remembered the light in Gloriana's eyes when
she had declared that her father had acknowledged her
with this land.

Gloriana's determination to go on at all costs proved
he must help her. He must keep her safe. To impress
Dee, yes, and succeed at his challenge, yes. But for
other reasons as well, such as restoring luminous smiles
and soft glances—reasons that were not worth wasting
time thinking about just then.

"I will keep you safe, Gloriana. I will give you good
value for the mirror."

She bit her lip and stared down at her teacup.

Having decided upon his course, he realized that his 1544 battle skills might need improving to match those of men who were trained upon the weapons of this day. There was one way to ensure success, he knew: He would hire himself a tutor.

He directed his questions to Miss Hampson, who pursed her lips in disapproval when he interrupted her discourse on the hygienic liabilities of the inside sweatbands of ten-gallon hats. "This Sheriff Owens is not a sissy or a half-breed?"

"Oh, my, I should say not!"

"And he wears his gun upon his hip?" He had doubted Maud when she'd stated that men did this.

"His left hip," Miss Hampson specified. "I hear tell he's considered the fastest draw in Arizona."

"Ah. The fastest means the best."

"So they say."

He had found his tutor.

Gloriana relished the luxury and privacy afforded by her private rail coach, but keeping to it so much had the negative effect of making her a curiosity when she moved among the train's conventional passengers. Each foray to the dining car and back had turned into something like a miniature circus parade, with Glory and Maud the only attractions. Edging through the narrow aisles while the train clattered and tested their balance seemed little different than making her way down a rutted street while the town residents lined up to gape at the passing parade.

But this time Dante led the way from the dining car, and the passage held no terror.

Well, perhaps *terror* wasn't the right word, Gloriana

amended. She couldn't possibly be terrified by parades, considering that she'd participated in circus parades at least once a week throughout her entire life. They were part of the job—to create interest in the performers, to entice the townsfolk into parting with their hard-earned coin for a few hours of entertainment.

She'd been in more parades than she could remember, but she'd never stood on the sidelines during a single one. Only now, watching Dante sidestep a carelessly outflung leg here, a slumbering child's rump there, did she understand the lure of a parade.

Maud had outfitted him entirely in black. To make him look mean, she'd said, and so much like a desperado that nobody in Pleasant Valley would dare attempt to hurt Glory while Dante stood by her side. But to Gloriana, his black garb and his bronze flecked hair once more called to mind the exact colors of a half-tamed tiger and created an aura of danger that was not entirely related to his bodyguard duties. He moved with a tiger's quick, lithe precision. His coppery brown eyes swung with apparent disinterest over each and every occupant of each and every car they passed through, the way a jungle cat sometimes feigns boredom when assessing its prey—a boredom that shifts into lethal intent just prior to the tiger's dealing its victim a deadly swipe with its paw.

Those damned black clothes! She wished he still wore his puffy pants, because they'd minimized the taut fitness of his flat belly and narrow hips. She couldn't move her gaze away from him, no matter how she scolded herself over the impropriety of staring at a man's backside.

She paid the price for her distraction when a crate of hens tucked beneath a bench suddenly burst into cackling discord. Startled by the sound, she backtracked a step and tangled herself in the handles of someone's sewing basket.

She would have regained her equilibrium instantly. Circus folk relieved the endless tedium of traveling by teaching each other their skills, and Glory had learned many balancing techniques from Maud and from any number of acrobats. Dante couldn't know that, though. He'd had to support her once before when the train had lurched and practically knocked her off her feet. So she couldn't blame him for catching hold of her elbow, for drawing her close against him, for bending low to murmur, "I have you, Gloriana."

I have you, Gloriana. She nodded mutely while he shifted his hold upon her. In the space of two seconds he went from supporting her left elbow in a perfectly acceptable gentleman's gesture to something completely improper. He crossed his arm behind her back to grip her right elbow, and then curled his other hand over the flesh of her upper left arm. This drew them so close together that she could hear her calico skirt swish against those damned black britches. When her shoulder blade pressed into his chest she could feel the beat of his heart.

Not even married couples would dare walk around in public clinched together like this, but he didn't loosen his hold one bit as they walked the entire length of the car. Well, what did she expect from a half-tamed tiger of a man? A proper young lady wouldn't tolerate such liberties for a single minute, let alone revel in the heady sensation of being totally enveloped by him. His chin skimmed the top of her head. His shoulder towered above hers. His body shielded hers so completely that the whole trainload of passengers could line up and stare and they wouldn't be able to see her at all.

Stifling, oppressive—those were words Glory's

mother had used to describe the turn a woman's life took if she let a man gain any control over her. Dante's physical presence did indeed overwhelm her, but there was nothing oppressive in his light touch. She knew without trying that he would drop his hold if she made the slightest motion to free herself. She didn't want to. With Dante deflecting the sounds and the stares, she felt freer than she ever had.

"Will you open the door?" There was a husky edge of uncertainty in his voice. It matched the indecision in her heart.

If she did as he asked, she gave tacit approval of the way he held her. If she refused and demanded he tend to the task as any true gentleman would, he would have to let go of some part of her and might even step away from her entirely. She remembered the pain crossing his features when she'd said he was no gentleman, the hurt he'd betrayed earlier when she'd called him a bastard.

Gloriana opened the door.

She had to stifle a little sound of frustration when the open door revealed her stable car directly ahead of them. She usually anticipated reaching it because it meant the end of her passage through the train; on this evening she wouldn't have minded being escorted through another car or two. Dante pulled her infinitesimally closer as they stepped onto the balcony, and they stood there motionless until the train's vibrations slammed the door closed behind them. The clacking wheels and the whistling wind were enough to deafen her, which could explain why all Gloriana could hear was the sound of her own heart, hammering faster than their deliberate stroll could account for. They began walking again in unison, taking short, careful steps across the narrow walkway that bridged the treacherous coupling. Dante's arms provided surer support than any metal railing. She opened the door to the stable car without waiting for him to ask.

He'd left a lantern burning low but had taken the precaution of wedging it so tightly into a nook that Gloriana knew there was no danger of its falling and starting a fire. He maintained his hold upon her until they reached the center of the car, each step progressively slower than the one preceding it, and then he let his hands fall away.

Blizzard and Crystal swung their fine heads toward them. Blizzard's nostrils flared wide, and he whooshed in anticipation. Crystal sent them her usual welcoming nicker.

"Ah, they have been awaiting the return of their stable boy."

A hint of humor laced Dante's words, so Gloriana knew there was no reason she should feel ashamed for having relegated him to that status.

"I'm sure they're happy to see you, but I'll bet they're more excited about this." She withdrew a handful of sugar cubes from her pocket, which sent Blizzard's head nodding. "They know I always steal a few from the sugar bowl at dinnertime."

"Sugar?" He plucked a pair of cubes from her palm and held them between his fingers, examining them as closely as a fairway vendor checking for loaded dice. "I have never seen it take such form. Are you certain 'tis sugar?"

She'd never met anyone who'd seemed the least bit puzzled by sugar cubes. Then again, she'd never met anyone who found train travel so mystifying, or who traveled through the American West without knowing anything about homesteads or ranches. She'd pegged him as a backwoods hick the first time she'd met him, an ill-clad, confused foreigner who spoke like a Quaker.

He'd certainly altered over the past couple of days, losing some of his charming naiveté but gaining an aura of command that, she suspected, came far more naturally to him. He now looked and sounded every inch the Western gunslinger—except for the boyish longing in his eyes as he stared at the sugar cube.

"Try one for yourself," Glory dared him.

"You try it."

"Uh-uh. I already had two lumps with my tea."

"The horses, then."

Blizzard and Crystal eagerly obliged. After they had lipped the sugar from her palm, Glory rinsed her hands with a dipperful of water from the bucket hanging near the door. She'd never thought of keeping a bucket filled with clean water in the stable car, and a quick glance around told her that it was only one of the many improvements Dante had made.

She had thought it such a good idea to bring her own wagon along, but she'd caught her toe a dozen painful times against the wheelbase, which took up the far corner of the rail car. The rest of the wagon disassembled easily, but the darned base had to remain intact, and she'd never managed to walk by it without kicking it or scraping an elbow on it. Dante had arranged straw in front of it and heaped sacks of oats and corn on top of the wheelbase. Not only did it eliminate the likelihood of getting hurt, it also meant he could scoop grain without bending in half. Glory wished she had thought of it.

Over in another corner, a blanket stretched over a mound of hay. His sleeping pallet, no doubt, judging by the length of it and the belongings—his metal hat and vestlike thing and his poker winnings—stacked in a neat pile alongside it. She sternly quelled the soft little flutter she felt when she realized she was staring at Dante's bed.

Blizzard stretched his neck until his questing muzzle brushed her hand, looking for more sugar. Glory nodded toward the two lumps Dante held.

"You see, they haven't keeled over and died. Now you try it, or else hand them over so I can give them another treat."

He sent her a brooding stare, and then lifted one cube to his lips with all the enthusiasm of a child being forced to swallow a dose of castor oil. His tongue darted out and pressed against the cube, and at once his expression transformed into one of sheer delight.

"Sugar," he stated, as confidently as if he had been trying to convince her of the cube's identity all along. He slanted a cocky grin at her. "Watch this."

He tossed the cube into the air, an effortless gesture that nonetheless caused a considerable amount of bunching and bulging of his biceps. He tipped his head back. His loosely bound hair fell away from his face, revealing the strong planes of his cheek, the corded column of his neck. He caught the sugar cube with a casual grace any sword swallower might envy. He faced her with a triumphant smirk, his lips compressed and moving in such a way that she knew he was sucking that blasted sugar cube straight into oblivion. He came closer and held the second cube out toward her.

"No. You have it."

He shook his head, and then swallowed before speaking. "Nay. 'Twould be piggish and a shocking breach of manners."

"I—"

"'Tis sweet, Gloriana. So very, very sweet."

His teasing smile faded away, to be replaced by a look of naked longing that, she knew, had nothing to do with the sugar. "Sweet," he whispered. He reached toward her with the cube between his fingers; his hand trembled just a little. He stroked her lower lip with the sugar cube. She edged the tip of her tongue out and tasted the hint of sweetness that he'd left.

Each took a shuddering breath at the same time.

"'Tis like you, Gloriana."

"M-Me?"

He stroked her lip with the cube again, and it seemed that the shaking passed from his hand straight to her limbs.

"Aye. A smooth surface with sharp edges, carefully molded to protect its inner sweetness and innocence. You, Gloriana."

She didn't feel the least bit innocent as she closed her eyes and tilted her face toward his, waiting for him to press the cube to her lips again. Instead he groaned, and she heard the dull crunch as his fingers compressed the cube into powder. Fine grains clung to his fingers; she knew this because he traced her lips with his sugar-coated fingertip, and she could not resist the urge to taste him.

"More?" he murmured in a husky rasp while his lips brushed against her forehead.

She had never realized that her forehead could feel anything except sweat or the sting of sunburn. But then she had never before found it being kissed while held in a half-tamed tiger of a man's embrace, with his uncompromising lips somehow softer than velvet against her skin. All at once it seemed that every inch of her body had a direct connection to the place where Dante's lips pressed against her forehead, and that secret pathways developed from that spot to link with a nameless ache somewhere low in her belly.

"More," she whispered. "More."

With another low groan, he captured her lips with his, and she realized that her forehead possessed little ability to feel in comparison with her mouth.

It shouldn't have surprised her that a man who could flex the muscles in his forearms would possess lips capable of equally astounding movements, but it did. The few kisses she'd permitted over the years had been quick, furtive things, either hard and dry or mushy and moist—nothing so hot, so demanding, as Dante's lips claiming hers.

He twined his fingers in her hair, drinking of her lips like a man who'd thirsted for a lifetime. Gloriana did the same, luxuriating in the feel of his hair slipping between her fingers, thrilling to the thunder of his heartbeat, which drowned out the noise from the train. He tasted of sweetness and salt, the essences of pleasure and survival, and Gloriana knew a woman could live forever upon the sustenance she found there.

He swung her easily from her feet into his arms, and before she could decide whether to protest or urge him to hurry, he'd crossed to the car's far corner. He settled her atop his pallet with a kiss that trailed over her neck and then left her flesh to skim over her shirtwaist. She wanted to whimper with frustration when he lingered over the mound of her breasts, his warm breath penetrating her tightly buttoned shirtwaist.

And then he moved away from her. His chest rose and fell with the same rapid, inadequate breaths that shivered through her. He knelt ramrod straight, his head turned slightly to the side, with his jaw jutted skyward. The wary, self-protective stance of a proud man accustomed to many forms of rejection.

"Dante." A more accomplished woman would know endearments, pretty words, to soothe away that rigidity.

Gloriana Carlisle knew little about men, and virtually nothing about this particular male. "Dante Trevani."

The simple calling of his name roused a smoldering satisfaction in his eyes. With a wordless murmur he surrounded her, pressing her into the pallet, so much taller than she, so much wider. She knew that every inch of her belonged to him, for this moment, for always.

His hand moved down her shirtwaist with such dexterity that her buttons proved no hindrance. "This manner of dress well suits a man's temperament," he murmured when her lapels fell aside to bare her camisole. He rubbed the thin cambric between his fingers and then tugged at a silk ribbon until the neckline loosened. He gave a low, triumphant laugh as his hand delved past the neckline. "No underwear."

"I most certainly am wearing—" She always felt secretly guilty for not wearing a corset under her day dresses, but her camisole qualified as underwear. Gloriana's staunch defense of her undergarments dissolved into a gasp of pure pleasure when Dante's hand cupped her breast. She remembered his disdainful rejection of the corset: *'Twould deny a man his rightful freedom of his woman's soft flesh.*

If Dante were her man, if she were his woman, she would never regret abandoning her corset again.

She wrapped her arms around his broad shoulders and pulled him closer. They kissed, the sweetness of sugar still upon his lips and his tongue. Her body abandoned all connection to her brain, and she marveled, as if from a distance, that she knew how to arch her back and thrust her hips in perfect accord with Dante's beguiling movements.

He'd unbuttoned her skirt, and his hand weighed heavy against the double drawstrings of her petticoats. She felt him tracing the knots, slipping his finger through the placket to touch the soft flesh of her belly. His restraint asked her silent permission to continue.

All of a sudden she was mortified that he would be in such cool possession of himself while she craved his touch so much that all sense of decorum had fled. How could she have so easily forgotten all her mother's warnings, all Maud's lectures, about the way men relished pursuing a woman? "I'm . . . I'm not proving to be much of a challenge for you," she whispered.

"Challenge?" His hand stilled.

"I shouldn't make it so easy for you." Misery laced through her, for to her mind, her admission signaled a capitulation that no decent woman should take such pleasure in anticipating.

He touched his forehead against hers, and a huge shudder coursed through his body. "Challenge. I never . . . I never considered one coming from this quarter."

He pulled away from her, all the while staring down at her with such avid hunger, such raw need, that she shivered from the force of it. "Dante?"

"Forgive me, Gloriana." He pressed his hand over his eyes, as if he found looking at her too painful to endure. "I pray John Dee's soul is blistering in hell at this very moment."

In one swift, smooth motion he was on his feet and then through the door, silently rejecting her before she could embarrass herself by begging him to stay.

She could do nothing more than simply lay on his pallet for a moment, pinned there by equal measures of humiliation and guilt. She'd behaved like a wanton, flinging a lifetime of caution to the winds. She deserved every bit of the pain that threatened to crush her heart the way Dante had crumbled that sugar cube between his fingers. Thank God her horses were the only witnesses to her shame.

She rose eventually and buttoned her garments with shaking fingers. Her hair had come loose during some part of their lovemaking, and the ends had managed to pick up some bits of straw. She did her best to rake it clean, then brushed her skirts and angrily rubbed the tears out of her eyes. She immediately wished she hadn't done that. Millie Voskamp, an actress, had taught her how to cry beautifully for the stage, with crystalline tears brimming and dripping without turning her all sniffly and red and puffy. The minute she tried wiping the tears away, though, the skin beneath her eyes swelled up and colored like ripe tomatoes. Maud would be sure to notice and ask why she'd been crying. She prayed Maud might be asleep so that she wouldn't have to answer any questions at all.

She didn't have any answers to give, anyway. Dante had proven all the advice right. He'd charged off the minute she'd admitted she was no challenge. He'd seemed to be enjoying himself up till then. Not as much as she'd been, though, for he'd mentioned somebody else's name— though she could not recall whose, for her whole being had been so consumed with Dante that she probably would not have been able to recall her own name either. She'd been reveling in sensation, willingly abandoning her soul to hell, and Dante had been roundly cursing someone, hoping he was in hell. . . .

John Dee. That was the name he had said. The so-called sorcerer who, Dante had claimed, had once owned her mirror.

The damned mirror. It all came back to the damned mirror. Dante's seduction had been nothing more than an attempt to woo her into handing over her mirror before he finished his job.

She steeled herself against the anguish that shafted through her at the realization, and then she stiffened her backbone and her pride. Whatever it was that she'd said about a challenge must have convinced him that she'd caught on to his little ruse. And she *was* on to him now. He wouldn't find her defenses so easily breached next time. Indeed, there would be no next time. She wouldn't let him within five feet of her—at least not in a romantic way—ever again.

Still, when she crossed the narrow bridge over the coupling between her stable car and her traveling car, she couldn't help remembering the solid, reassuring way he'd guided her across the vibrating expanse.

Maud, to her relief, was indeed in bed. She greeted Glory with only a muffled "'Night, honey" before rolling over again.

Glory stepped out of her clothes and left them lying in a heap. She would stuff them into the bottom of her deepest trunk, and maybe by the time she got around to finding them again, she'd be able to wear them without imagining Dante's callused fingers toying with each button, with every ribbon.

And then she lay in her own bed, sleepless, staring at nothing, while hot tears trickled down her cheeks. They continued falling until much, much later, when the sound of booted feet crossing her roof told her Dante had settled himself into his watchful position atop her coach.

INTERLUDE
January 15, 1559, Westminster Abbey

At precisely the hour the stars had decreed, the cathedral doors clanged open and Elizabeth Tudor began her solitary march down the aisle.

Some had protested the unseemly haste of holding a

coronation only two months after the death of her sister Mary. Many had voiced outrage over the enormous sums of money Elizabeth had borrowed to spend upon the celebration.

The stars had demanded that Elizabeth take the crown on this day. The charts had decreed it should be an occasion of unrivaled splendor. Elizabeth had heeded John Dee's advice, as he had predicted so long ago.

But amidst the glory of Westminster Abbey, Elizabeth paid Dee not the slightest consideration, did not spare him, her royal astrologer, so much as a single glance. Just as well. The heavily embroidered tunic she'd given him itched like the devil. It would not do for his lady Elizabeth's Grace to witness him standing there scratching throughout her coronation.

The royal choir chanted in soaring harmonies. The Bishop of Carlisle presided in robes of uncommon fineness, surrounded by hordes of fawning acolytes. A host of prominent bishops and cardinals had refused to conduct this holy ceremony for fear of offending those who disputed Elizabeth's right to the throne. How they must be regretting their cowardice, Dee thought. They would learn soon enough that Elizabeth Tudor never forgot an insult.

She took the chair of state before the high altar. Four times Carlisle proclaimed her queen. Four times the close-packed crowd roared its approval, in an undulating wave that commenced at the altar and swelled to the masses of Elizabeth's subjects who waited outside.

A curtained pew revealed its purpose when Elizabeth disappeared into it and emerged soon after garbed in a robe of royal purple velvet, embellished with a mantle of silk and gold. Trumpets blared a joyous fanfare when she slid a ring symbolizing what she would call her marriage to the people of England upon her right hand.

Glorious spectacle, my lady, Dee had urged, and it gave him great pride to see how Elizabeth had obliged.

Not one crown, but three. First, the holy crown of St. Edward rested briefly upon her red-gold tresses. Next, the imperial crown of England, rumored to weigh more than seven pounds. She lifted her head and balanced all that weight upon her slim, supple neck. The gold and the jewels showered her Tudor hair with a priceless rainbow of color, a glorious, splendid display to mark the start of her reign. But even one so determined as she could not bear such a heavy burden for any length of time. The third crown, lighter, less ostentatious, took the imperial crown's place.

"'Tis the crown Henry had made for the whore, her mother," whispered someone standing behind Dee.

Elizabeth meant to walk from the abbey to Westminster Hall once Mass had been said to solemnize her coronation. The route had been carpeted, and hordes of adoring subjects lined the pathway, cheering and staring.

"Walk with me, Dr. Dee," Elizabeth commanded when she passed him in the aisle.

Elizabeth had always seemed to relish moving through crowds. That day she manifested a white-lipped tension, a flickering trepidation, that was completely at odds with the usual pleasure she projected. Dee had thought she would find the exercise even more enjoyable while carrying the scepter and orb that marked her as queen.

"You make a beautiful queen, Highness."

"Fishing for compliments, Dee, merely because you lent your precious looking glass to me for my toilet?"

Dee bowed his head, making no comment. No doubt

nervous humors were the cause of both her unusual demeanor and her cutting wit. He knew her mercurial temper would shift, causing her to regret her imperious remark. She did not disappoint him.

"Forgive my agitation, Dr. Dee. The mirror was much appreciated."

He waved off her remorse. "'Tis understandable, Highness. You have more important concerns on your mind this glorious day."

"That is true, isn't it?" She cast him a mischievous look that was replete with satisfaction and self-congratulation. "But I fear my worries at this moment are of a less profound nature. It seems I have lost my favorite bracelet." She lifted her arm and bared her slender wrist for him.

"Your turtle bracelet is well known, Majesty. Whoever finds it will be certain to recognize it as yours and return it to you promptly."

"No doubt expecting a royal favor in return. I will order a search for it ere it gets trod into shards by a careless boot."

She tilted her head, and at once a manservant appeared at her side. "My turtle bracelet has gone missing. Begin searching for it in my dressing room. I remember admiring its reflection in the mirror and touching it there for luck. I noticed it missing whilst donning my robe in the curtained pew."

"I will crawl each inch of the way between those places, Majesty, even to sifting the rushes if need be."

"Aye, you will," said Elizabeth. "I will have that bracelet back." The lackey sprinted away. "Will you dine at my side, Dr. Dee? I feel the need to hold at least one friend close today."

Dee accepted the boon with a modest inclination of his head, while his heart commenced a furious pounding. It was all coming about as he'd predicted, all of it! Lest Elizabeth sense his gloating, he gestured toward the milling throngs. "These are all your friends, Majesty."

"I do not worry over them. I worry over the others, those with influence, who might seek to wrest away from me that which is mine by my father's decree."

"None will succeed, my lady, if only you remain true to yourself."

She stared at him for a moment with both naked hope and utter loneliness warring for mastery of her features. Neither won; after that brief moment of vulnerability, her expression shifted into its normal unreadable lines. "There is none other to be true to, Dr. Dee."

She turned merry then, quickening her pace, stopping occasionally to ruffle a comely child's hair or accept a posy from a blushing lass. Her good spirits continued through the minstrels, the jesters, and the opening courses of her coronation banquet. Her laughter rang forth again and again, as if to offer her an excuse for not hearing the grumblings and whisperings of discord weaving their way round the hall.

The whispering ceased when, with a great clanking and clattering of hooves, Elizabeth's champion, fully armored and mounted upon his war horse, charged into the hall. Sir Edward Dymoke. He cast his gauntlet upon the floor and wrenched his helmet from his head. Cupping one ear, he turned his aristocratic head as if listening for gossip.

"I challenge any man who questions my lady's right to this throne!"

Resounding silence answered his challenge.

Elizabeth accepted Dymoke's homage and then sent him away.

"It seems you have at least one who will defend you with his life," Dee remarked, hoping to provoke her into complimenting *him* for his own unwavering support.

"One man is all a woman needs, providing he is the right one," Elizabeth answered.

8

Glory closed the hasp of her largest trunk. She snapped the lock shut and tugged to make sure it had caught. And then she tugged it again.

They'd arrived in Holbrook nearly an hour earlier. Soon, she knew, the station master would be knocking at the door to tell her they were ready to disconnect her two rail cars from the rest of the train and put them on a siding, where they would await her return from Pleasant Valley.

"You're still mad at me," Maud said.

"No, I'm not. I'm just going over all the details in my mind." Weighing all the options, hoping she'd planned for every contingency—just like Dante. She shook her head and tugged again at the lock. She certainly hoped he wouldn't pop into her mind every time she tried making a rational decision, though she would have been far better off if she'd considered the outcome before kissing him the night before. Then again, she couldn't have predicted his abrupt departure.

"Well, you're awful quiet, and you're looking peaked to boot."

"Anyone would look peaked after such a long time cooped up in a train. I'm just tired. I didn't sleep so well last night."

"You're still worried about that mirror. I don't see it on your dressing table."

"I hid it."

"Where?"

Glory bit her lip and pretended she hadn't heard the question.

Maud's face crumpled. "I knew it. You don't trust me anymore."

Remorse stabbed Glory. "I do so. It's Dante I don't trust."

"You'd tell me where you hid it if you trusted me. Since you're not telling me, you must be afraid that I'll spill the beans to him."

"Oh, Maud, you won't mean to, but you might. He can be . . . awfully persuasive."

Speculation glimmered in Maud's eyes. She leaned forward, her lips parted in avid curiosity.

A commotion outside interrupted before Maud could demand an explanation. Glory had never heard such a welcome ruckus. She rushed to the door and flung it open. She pressed her hand to her throat when she saw that the disturbance centered around Dante, who stood near the stable car ramp.

Dante was scowling, his mighty arms crossed. Her cape flapped from his shoulders, revealing his outlandish metal vest and puffy pants. The throng of townspeople milling about couldn't fail to see his unusual attire.

Dante had that scowl fixed upon an aged Indian who weaved around in front of him, practically staggering beneath the weight of a huge old sword he held high in the air.

"*Bahana!* Conquistador!" the Indian shouted. The sword blade waved dangerously with every syllable, but Dante never flinched. "Conquistador! *Bahana!*"

"Oh, lord," cried Maud from behind Glory's shoulder. "Looks like we're going to have to go and save Dante from that Indian so there'll be something left for the murdering sheepmen to hack up later."

A drunken knight had once disparaged Dante's parentage within Dante's hearing. Dante had promptly challenged the oaf, and the two men, in full dress armor, had pounded each other black and blue beneath the merciless sun.

The knight had ultimately conceded, but not before dealing Dante a telling blow to the head. Dante could still remember the clanging thud that had echoed through his skull and the brief but disconcerting separation of mind from senses. The taunts shouted by his tormentor had sounded garbled and distant. Light had struck his eyes painfully while illuminating nothing. Though he'd stood with feet firmly planted, heaving his sword about and blindly finding his mark, he'd had the uncomfortable sensation of somehow having drifted apart from his earthly body. It had lasted mere seconds, and yet that experience had affected him more profoundly than events that had dragged on for far longer periods of time.

Dante felt that same dislocation now. He stood next to the frightening but fantastical conveyance called a railroad train, his feet firmly planted in 1888 dust. And yet standing so close that Dante could smell him, an elderly Indian brandished a sword exactly like those his father's armies had carried in their conquest and plunder of New Spain in the 1540s.

"Conquistador!" the Indian bellowed. Obviously tiring, he wedged the sword tip into the dirt and used the weapon for balance while he thumped at Dante's breastplate with all the deliberation of a kitchen wench testing a melon for ripeness. He gave a satisfied nod. "Conquistador!" The Indian had somehow recognized Dante's attire as being very like that worn by the troops of Hernán Cortés, Charles V's Spanish general, who had conquered the New World.

It was enough to make Dante momentarily doubt that he'd traveled through time, but though his doubt lasted only a moment, it left him feeling a wistfulness that he dared not examine just now. Evidence abounded that he had indeed been shifted away from all that was familiar to him. He had but to reach one arm's length to touch the train, feel its power shudder through his arm, and know that guildsmen of his own time could not have built such an awesome wonder. The rough but substantial buildings lining the streets of Holbrook and the sheer number of saddled horses standing idle hinted at a widespread prosperity that commoners of his day had ever yearned for but had no hope of obtaining from the firmly entrenched noblemen.

The crowd rushed toward him, their faces lit with interest and excitement. None among them seemed to hold precedence over the others. This aura of equality alone would have been enough to convince him that he'd journeyed to some strange place, even if Gloriana had not confirmed that Dante Trevani had left the year 1544 behind.

And yet there stood that Indian, the very twin of one of the New World people called the Moqui by the

Spanish. Several of these Moqui had been taken as
slaves and displayed at Charles V's court by soldiers
returned from New Spain. Dante, a callow youth
scarcely into his teens, had reveled in the tales of the
untold riches begging to be plundered. Dante had
befriended one of the captives, and had thus learned
secrets that astonished his young soul. His Indian friend
had told him that the Spaniards were wrong to call
them Moqui—his people were truly called the Hopi.
The Indian had told him of the *bahana,* the white
brother of Hopi legend who would someday return and
lead the Hopi to glory. For this reason, and to their own
detriment, the Hopi welcomed all white visitors in
hopes that the true *bahana* had returned. He had
taught Dante a secret handshake that would lead the
Hopi to trust him, if ever Dante acted upon his boldly
declared intention of claiming some of New Spain's
riches for himself some day.

Dante used that secret handshake now.

The Indian matched him motion for motion.

"Conquistador," the Hopi said again, but with the
awed reverence of one who was witnessing a religious
effigy come to life. He pressed the sword hilt into
Dante's hand. The weapon had the familiar grip and
heft of the Toledo blades Dante had practiced with endlessly while honing his skills. It fit snugly into the empty
scabbard at his waist—it might have been the twin to
the blade he'd left in the care of John Dee's servant
more than three hundred years earlier.

Dante quickly assessed the crowd after he sheathed
the sword. None seemed amazed to find an Indian in
their midst. None of the men carried swords, sheathed
or unsheathed. None wore a breastplate. None wore
capes or ostrich feathers or cabassats. Most wore
tough-fibered breeches and shirts similar to what Maud

had given him, but of faded blues and duns rather than black. Wide, square-brimmed hats shielded the men's eyes from the sun.

The women wore nunlike headgear; their gowns hugged their upper reaches and flowed in wide gathers from their hips to the ground. An astonishing number of the women had been afflicted with pitiable deformities—not even extra yards of cloth and elaborate ribbons could hide the hideous growths that projected from their buttocks. The cloth of some sported flowered designs that only the most skilled weavers would dare attempt, but not one of the wearers had the look of a highborn lady able to afford such luxury.

They were all so strange. But they pressed close to one another, exchanging glances and whispers, at ease with one another. They stared at him with a kindred watchfulness that told him he'd gotten it all wrong—he was the strange one there. Not of their time, but no longer of his time, either.

A realization of his isolation pierced his soul, and in that stark moment the sound of his pulse was the only thing he could hear. It was as if each thump of his heart pulled him that much further from his own time and place, mocking him with the knowledge that those he knew and cared about were so much dust and bones, no longer capable of feeling any pulse at all. Charles V, Elizabeth Tudor, Dr. John Dee—all were naught but long-dead personages, their stories fodder for scribes.

And what of Dante Alberto Trevani? For all his life he had fought the taint of his bastard birth, had clawed his way up and held his tenuous perch by sheer force of will. It was not hard to imagine that his disappearance had caused scarcely a ripple of concern. It might have, truth be told, prompted a great deal of relief, if not outright rejoicing. Elizabeth, John Dee, and his father would rearrange their affairs as if he'd never existed. What sort of welcome would they offer once the mirror was his and he returned to his own time? He did not require the prophetic powers of John Dee to know the answer.

He would be in the way once again.

Unless he returned so quickly that no one had time to mark his absence.

"All is in readiness for you, *bahana,*" the Indian said. "Come. I will show you the sacred cave of my people."

"He ain't no banana and he don't care about no sacred cave! Stand away from him!" Maud's strident challenge rang over the platform.

With a great deal of murmuring and swiveling of heads, the crowd parted to reveal Maud plowing her way toward him, glaring fiercely over the garments piled in her arms.

Gloriana followed. His blood stirred at the sight of her. Of all those who had lived in either 1544 or 1888, she alone might regret his disappearance. Or would she? An inner voice taunted him with the knowledge of what might have been had he stayed with her the night before. Another part of him whispered he might have found this daytime meeting even more uncomfortable had he slaked his lust knowing there could be no future for them.

But something within him rebelled at such a notion. Loving Gloriana, claiming her as his own, could never be likened to a mere slaking of lust.

How many men, he wondered, found themselves struggling with cravings that led them to desire one woman above all others, all the while knowing such passions were forbidden?

Gloriana had changed garments. She wore a gown that fit in the manner of the other women's dresses, even to the grotesque projection from her rear, though he knew from recent experience no such projection existed. Upon Gloriana, the simple green cloth clung and flowed in sinuous ripples that had nothing to do with the quality of material and everything to do with the elegant body moving beneath it. It was the smooth, sharp-edged Gloriana, with her circus smile firmly in place. As she moved into Maud's path the murmuring increased in volume, with the spectators' heads pivoting in tiny increments that kept pace with each of her graceful, fluid steps.

She hated being the object of staring; she had told him so. And yet this smooth, sharp-edged Gloriana seemed untroubled by their blatant gawking. He yearned for a glimpse of her sweet innocence, but he feared that his behavior of the night before might have dissolved it forever.

"Who is *she?*" Dante heard a bearded man marvel.

The woman standing next to the man caught him in the midsection with her elbow. "Who is *he?*" she countered, indicating Dante with a movement of her chin. "Why was Mr. Blue hollerin' at him? Mr. Blue never hollers."

"He never lets anyone touch that old sword of his, neither, but it plumb looks like he's gone and handed it over to that stranger."

"Anybody in town expecting visitors?" called yet another. The query seemed to hover over the crowd, prompting a few of the men to lift their heads in challenge to Dante's presence and some of the women to huddle closer together. Their murmuring turned as low and ugly as winter thunder, and intensified until it spewed toward Dante like dark, invisible venom.

Gloriana's gaze flickered over the crowd. A tiny, almost imperceptible line creased the center of her forehead. And then a dazzling smile transformed her features. She pivoted toward Dante and flung her arms wide with welcome.

"Sweetheart!" she cried.

She plucked at her skirts, lifting them a scant inch or two from the platform. She ran toward him. The motion plastered her skirt against her legs and sent her hair streaming behind her in glorious disarray. She all but bowled over Maud and the Indian, and she crashed into Dante with more joyous abandon than his favorite hunting dog had ever shown in welcoming him home.

"Ouch." She maintained her wide smile and looked upon him with rapturous delight while softly uttering the small whimper of pain. "That chest thing you wear is made out of real hard metal."

He opened his mouth to agree, but all that came out was a stifled gasp when she twined her fingers together at the back of his neck and pulled him close. "To my everlasting regret," he whispered, thinking how delightful Gloriana's soft form would feel against his body without a quarter-inch of forged steel separating them.

She tugged at his neck and brought his head down. She tilted her face up, and he could feel her warm breath against his skin as she lifted her lips. God's blood, he had feared she might never speak to him again, and here she meant to kiss him before all these people!

"Why on earth are you wearing that stuff when Maud gave you decent clothes?" she whispered against his lips.

"Again this obsession with my clothes. I covered my person with the plain cape, as you told me to do before. And I might ask the same of your appearance—what has happened to your nether reaches, Gloriana?"

"My nether reaches?"

He ran a quick hand over the bulge at the back of her skirt.

She gasped. "How dare you! Stop that at once! That's my bustle."

He gladly ceased fondling it; there was no pleasure in stroking what felt like a cloth-covered basket. "Do you not remember that Miss Hampson warned us to expect trouble? My defenses are few enough. I must needs employ them all, even unto my chest armor." He tried not to notice how his breath stirred her hair, how the sunlight picked out its red-gold strands and gilded them even more until it seemed she glowed with an angel's fire.

"Well, it's too late to regret it now." She leaned back while maintaining her grip around his neck. Her broad smile belied the worry in her eyes. "Don't just stand there. Hug me."

"Hug you?"

"You know, a little squeeze."

"Squeeze?"

"Oh, bother, I keep forgetting you're a foreigner. Just hurry up and wrap your arms around me." When he hesitated, she hissed in frustration. "Dante, I know how to read a crowd. You look strange and sort of threatening dressed like that. These folks seem all riled up. We'd better not let any of them know you're a world-renowned assassin."

"And bestowing a hug-squeeze upon you will confuse them?"

"It might. They might think you're just my sweetheart." She bit her lip, as if she wished she could swallow those words. "Don't worry, I'm not trying to force you into a role you're obviously not interested in. I just could use a little help to pull this off. Pretend we're in love for a few minutes, that's all."

So it was pretense, all of it—her feigned delight in seeing him, her bold public show of affection. Still, he deserved no more; indeed, a man of principle would discourage anything more. It was time to remember that he had a job to perform, a challenge to meet.

He ignored the part of him that rejoiced over this particular aspect of the assignment, and he tried to feel workmanlike and dutiful as he did his job, embracing her as she'd requested. His right arm curved round her waist. The bustle provided a handy ledge for resting his hand above the gentle swell of her hip. His left arm bent at the elbow, with his hand riding higher, just below her shoulder blade, where the rise and fall of her breathing seemed to shoot straight up his arm and into his heart. Or maybe he just noticed her breathing more now that his own lungs seemed to have stopped working—he had forgotten to draw breath the instant his arms encircled her.

There was nothing workmanlike and dutiful about the way his clasp upon her tightened, drawing her close until the folds of his cape settled around her. Two bodies covered as one, an intimacy usually relegated to the bedchamber. A man, he thought, might find contentment holding Gloriana within a hug-squeeze forever, shielding her from all harm.

But he learned at once that, enfold her as he might, he could not protect her from verbal assault. A large woman, florid-faced and quivering with self-importance, shouldered herself to the forefront of the crowd. The gown she wore closely matched Gloriana's in cut and color, but it required such an abundance of cloth to cover her ample form that all sense of style was lost. Her rear sported the grossest protuberance Dante had yet seen. A man might pull up a chair and work his account books upon the flat ledge jutting from her backside.

Her pudgy finger stabbed toward Gloriana. "I know who she is," she blared. "She's Harry Trask's circus brat." Clearly, Dante thought, despite the passage of three centuries, society continued to sneer at those who did not fit into its approved mold.

Gloriana stiffened within his arms, and it seemed that she too suddenly forgot to breathe. Someone's high-pitched nervous giggle was shushed into silence. The crowd's murmurs changed in tone, taking on a derisive edge that he recognized all too well.

"How dare she show her face around here!"

"Circus people! My land, as if things in Holbrook ain't low enough already!"

The large green-garbed woman glanced about with smug satisfaction. "I been keepin' an eye open fer her ever since she sent that there telegraph through my husband's office."

"Reading other people's personal messages." Maud quivered with fury. "Bend over, Dante, and ram her with your acorn hat!"

Though he had never in his life assaulted a woman, it sounded like an excellent idea to Dante. He reluctantly let loose of Gloriana but stilled when she placed a hand on his upper arm.

"What do you think you're doing?"

"My job." He could not bring himself to move away while her hand anchored him at her side, so he contented himself with turning his fiercest glare upon the crowd. Some, he could tell, were merely curious. Others shrank away from his deadly regard. Still others met his gaze with belligerence, while more than a few dared to look upon Gloriana with a smirking disrespect that caused him to tighten his grip around the sword hilt. "Stand aside, Gloriana. I am well accustomed to teaching manners to churls."

"Set him loose, Glory," Maud urged.

"No. I can handle this. Just . . . just go along with whatever I say."

She swung about and stepped forward until she was nose to nose with the stout harridan. With a toss of her head, Gloriana sent her hair flowing over her shoulders. The sun struck sparks from it, sparks akin to those raised by two clanging swords. Her voice held a lethal edge, like that of the most finely wrought weapon, as she brought it to bear upon her tormentor.

"Yes, I'm Harry Trask's daughter." Dante recognized the false civility in Gloriana's voice. "And who might you be?" She took yet another step toward the woman, forcing her to yield a few inches and angle her head to look up at Gloriana like a supplicant making obeisance to her queen.

"Mrs. Loudon," the woman gasped. "Mrs. Henrietta Loudon. I'm . . . I'm the telegraph clerk's wife."

"Oh, a clerk's wife. I was hoping to be welcomed by someone important."

Mrs. Loudon's face mottled with outrage, but she kept her plump lips clamped shut. Someone tittered their amusement, and at the sound Mrs. Loudon's skin paled to a deathly white.

"Gloriana," Dante murmured warningly, thinking Gloriana's inner boldness was leading her into heedlessly and needlessly forging herself an implacable enemy.

She swiveled to face him, and in that moment he realized she was neither brave nor commanding. Her eyes betrayed the bitter knowledge that she was all too familiar with these sorts of confrontations. That she knew only a show of strength and determination could suppress the slights, the blows to her pride. He understood, for he had faced many such situations himself and handled them in much the same manner. He'd sometimes feared that someone with a more acceptable position would call him out and reveal him for the uncertain, secretly ashamed bastard that he was—that he *had* been, until his physical strength developed to match his inner strength and men had ceased taunting and tormenting him over what he could not change.

But Gloriana would never acquire a man's strength. She sought to hire his—and he meant to withdraw it from her all too soon. He would do well to remember that he would be leaving her as soon as Maud obtained the mirror for him. It was wrong of him to interfere with the way Gloriana handled her enemies, to encourage her to depend upon him, when he would be deserting her and leaving her to her own devices soon enough.

No, not deserting her. Meeting a challenge and claiming his reward.

He welcomed the new flurry of motion that drew Gloriana's attention back toward the crowd.

A golden-haired man strode into the group. He stood a few inches shorter than Dante, wore his hair just as long, and sported an equally fine mustache. He cradled a rifle in his arms and wore a pistol, butt side out, riding on his left hip. Unlike the dun- and blue-clad townsmen, the newcomer wore a white shirt and dark breeches over which he'd stretched sections of fine leather whose sole purpose seemed to be to prevent the insides of his legs from rubbing together.

Long-haired and too fine by half, Miss Hampson had

said in describing the renowned Sheriff Commodore Perry Owens. This man could be no other.

"Okay, folks, let's get a move on!" he cried with authority. "Roustabouts can't get through to unload the train—you're throwing it off schedule."

"Aw, Sheriff Owens," one of the townsmen complained, confirming the man's identity. "Things was just gettin' good 'tween Henny Loudon and this redheaded gal. I'll bet you don't know who she is!"

"That's just what I mean to find out. The only thing that's gettin' is you all, and what you're gettin' is out of here," Owens stated. He shifted the rifle until it rested against his hip. "Go on now, get."

With surprisingly little objection, the crowd dispersed until only Dante, Gloriana, Maud, and Mr. Blue stood with the sheriff. He tucked his gun beneath his left arm.

"Since all that trouble started down in Pleasant Valley, I make it a habit to greet all strangers gettin' off the train," Owens said, with no trace of welcome marking his words. "Holbrook don't need any more trouble, so if you're here to sign on with the feud, just keep movin'."

"We're not here to cause trouble," said Gloriana, virtuous intent all but dripping from every word. "I'm here to claim an inheritance."

"So Henny Loudon pegged you right after all. You're Harry Trask's by-blow."

There was a silent, uncomfortable pause before Gloriana spoke again. "I'd prefer the term *natural daughter,* Sheriff."

"You know, ma'am, your pa asked me to watch out for you if you ever showed up. It might be easier if I just called you by your name, but I'm damned if I can remember that fancy moniker Harry told me," Sheriff

Owens said. "And I apologize if I come across so hard, but I'm sheriff of this here town, and I'm paid to be suspicious of strangers."

"Gloriana. Gloriana Carlisle." Gloriana's frosty demeanor thawed slightly as she introduced herself. The sheriff then tipped his head Dante's way. "And that's my, um, this is Dante Trevani, and he's, um . . ."

"He ain't no bodyguard, that's for sure," Maud interjected. "He's her . . . he's her fee-ann-say. I'm what they call a chaperone, and I'm keeping an eagle eye on them until they're married."

Gloriana's gaze, wide with dismay, met Dante's.

"Well, hell, we got a churchman or two, if you're thinking of hitching up here in Holbrook." The sheriff nodded at Dante and offered his hand. "Commodore Perry Owens, at your service."

Spurning the hand of the man who Dante hoped might serve as his tutor could not help Gloriana's cause. But hearing himself unwillingly betrothed yet again made Dante's fingers curl around the hilt of his sword.

Gloriana stood with her hands gripped together. The wind whipped at her skirts and tousled her hair, but those flutterings did not disguise from him her barely perceptible trembling.

His betrothed. Never to be his wife, no matter what Maud had said.

He would be gone long before Owens questioned why he had failed to give Gloriana his name. It seemed he was destined to come close to marriage and be forgotten instead, whether in this time or in his own. With him forever gone, Gloriana's memory of him would grow dim in years to come, until even the look of his face, the color of his eyes and hair, would be forgotten.

He wished such thoughts had not occurred to him, and so he cast them aside.

Go along with whatever I say, she had begged. He would have preferred a few moments of quiet thought to weigh the possible consequences of doing so, but there was no time. If it eased their passage through Holbrook and made Gloriana feel safe, he could submit to one more betrothal.

He shoved his hand into Owens's and pumped vigorously. Sheer radiance flowed from Gloriana, accompanied by a blindingly beautiful smile that held no hint of artifice. Perhaps she would smile at him like that every once in a while, until he left her. But even if he saw Gloriana's smile only this once, he knew it would never fade in his mind.

"The woman who is to be my wife . . . ," he began the lie, and then found himself shockingly thick-throated when she slipped to his side and tucked her hand between his side and his elbow. He supposed a truly betrothed man might cover his lady's hand with his own, and so he did, all in the interest of doing his job well. Her fingers felt impossibly delicate, her skin smoother and cooler than the lushest silk. "My betrothed . . . "

"No need to apologize for her raisin' Henny's hackles, Mr. Trevani. Redheads is always feisty, and Trask, her father, was one stubborn son of a bitch. She comes by it natural." Owens spoke with good humor but did not smile. "Besides, Henny Loudon's always walkin' around here like a pot of sour milk anxious to curdle."

"I'm sorry if I upset her," Gloriana said, not sounding the least bit contrite. "It won't happen again, because we won't be here very long."

"That's right." Maud punctuated her statement with

an emphatic nod. "We're heading out as soon as Glory completes some business dealings she arranged through the telegraph."

"You, Miss Carlisle?" Owens appeared puzzled, and he cocked his head questioningly toward Dante. "You allow your fiancée to handle business?"

"My betrothed . . ." Again the simple act of imagining Gloriana taking on the status of wife clogged Dante's throat.

"He's a foreigner." Gloriana rushed into an explanation, one that Dante could tell had not been well thought out in advance. "He can speak a little English, but he can only read and write in, um . . . well, darn, I plain forgot what language that was, sweetheart."

"Bohemian," said Maud.

"No, Ital—" Dante began.

"That's right, I tell you, he's Bohemian." Gloriana smiled prettily and fluttered her eyelashes. "Thanks, sweetheart. You know that's such a hard word for me to remember."

Dante opened his mouth, determined to defend both his mother country and his hard-earned skill with English, but Gloriana shot him a warning glance that stilled his protest. He remembered her asking that they go along with whatever she said; he gave a curt nod to show her he would, albeit grudgingly, play along.

"Ain't met any Bohemians up to now." Owens rubbed his chin, scowling with thought. "Is that the way they all dress?"

"Um, that's his circus outfit," said Gloriana.

"Why's he wearing his circus outfit for traveling?"

"He was practicing his act," said Maud. "And, er, Bohemians have a rule—at least circus Bohemians—that they won't ever practice without wearing their outfits." She hurriedly stuffed the clothes she held into Dante's hands. "Here, Dante. You can change into your regular clothes now that you're finished."

"Hmm." Owens tucked his weapon under his arm and took a few slow, measured steps around Dante, studying him from various angles. "What d'you do in the circus, Mr. Trevani?"

"He's a trapeze artiste," Gloriana burst out.

"Aye," Dante confirmed, wondering what on God's earth a Bohemian trapeze artiste might be.

"Didn't know that Atlantic and Pacific railroad cars came equipped with practice trapezes." Owens seemed to have accepted the women, but reserved deep suspicions about Dante. Dante assumed a soldier's pose, recalling how Miss Hampson had warned that Owens often clapped suspicious-looking strangers into his jail.

"Oh, heck, Dante don't need any trapezes to practice on." Maud dismissed the very idea with a flick of her hand. "Those rail cars have little balconies on them, and he just swings himself from car to car like a big old ape."

Dante knew men who spent as much time honing their wits as their weapons. He'd always found their dependence upon their barbed tongues amusing, and somewhat pitiable, since he was certain that it stemmed from inner cowardice or lack of manly strength. He wished now that he'd practiced the art himself, for all his swordsman's skill could not eradicate the image Maud had painted of Dante Alberto Trevani disporting himself in the fashion of wild African apes.

"Sounds dangerous," said Owens.

"It sure is. That's why I make him wear this." Gloriana rapped her knuckles against Dante's breastplate, raising a metallic thud. "It protects him in case he falls."

"It won't stop a bullet," said Owens. "You could all cover yourselves with metal from head to toe, and it ain't gonna help you stay alive in Pleasant Valley. Bill Mulvenon's the sheriff down there in Yavapi County. He'll be hauling your carcasses out of there inside of a week."

Dante had taken lightly none of the many warnings they'd received, but hearing this steely-eyed, commanding man so confidently predict their demise quickened his pulse. "No harm will come to her unless I die first."

"You probably will," said Owens. "Though I'd recommend you see to it that she goes before you do. You got any fire power to compare with these?"

Without giving Dante time to puzzle out his statement, the sheriff reached across his waist and pulled his pistol from the contrivance strapped to his left hip. Owens hitched his other hip, and the rifle that rested there seemed to leap into his free hand. Lifting each weapon in turn, he said, "Most men can't handle a rifle and a pistol together, on account of the difference in size. I say a gun is a gun, and in these parts a man damn well better know how to handle one, no matter the size. Watch that old piece of rope tied to that hitchin' post over there."

With minute twists of his wrist, the sheriff sent the pistol twirling round his finger. "Watch this, ladies." He spun the rifle butt forward until a loud metallic click sounded, and then let the butt fall back. Then, holding both weapons at hip level, Owens swiveled toward the frayed rope he'd indicated. With a loud double roar, the guns at his hip exploded . . . and the rope, severed neatly, dropped into the dust.

Gloriana slanted a sideways look toward Maud, who shrugged almost imperceptibly before ostentatiously stifling a yawn. The two women applauded politely, but Dante detected no real admiration in their gesture.

He, on the other hand, was all but overcome with wonder at Owens's feat. To think that mankind had so refined guns as to make the aiming of them unnecessary and to enable one man to wield a brace of them without help!

The sword he gripped suddenly seemed more a child's toy than a weapon capable of great destruction, and he knew that what Owens had said was true—his armor could not stand against men brandishing guns by the pair.

Ever since arriving in this time and place, he had held himself watchful and wary. He knew that blundering about or talking of how he had been transported could easily mark him a fool or a lunatic, and his own blustering might deafen his ears to knowledge he would need in order to return to his own time and place.

But what had holding his tongue, watching, and waiting brought him? Nothing but yet another betrothal, the loss of his true nationality, and a blow to his dignity. Bohemian trapeze artiste! Big old ape! Surely this could not be the challenge Dee had predicted for him. He had been in the future for only a few days and already he had swallowed more humiliation than he cared to stomach.

It was long past time to cease watching and waiting. He had to begin acting like a man.

"Sheriff Owens," Dante asked, "do you ever hire yourself out as a tutor to one who profoundly respects your fire power skills? We trapeze artistes are not well versed in the handling of guns."

"Dante, no!" Gloriana protested.

But Dante could tell that Owens was both flattered

and intrigued at the notion. "I have a couple of spare hours right now," the sheriff said.

"Excellent," said Dante. "Maud, you shall oversee the unloading of the horses. Gloriana, you will go attend to your business. The sheriff and I have men's work to do."

9

Gloriana watched Dante stride away at Sheriff Owens's side. He'd slung the new clothes over his shoulder, and he examined the sheriff's pistol as he walked.

"This is just awful," she whispered. "This is the worst thing that could have happened."

"I'll say," Maud agreed. "I never expected he'd turn out so bossy. 'Maud, you shall oversee the unloading of the horses,'" she mimicked in a dead-on imitation of Dante's accented command. "Goddamn Bohemian."

"Um, I think that's part of the problem." Glory swallowed. "I don't think he's a Bohemian. He might be a Quaker."

"A Quaker?"

"Mmm-hmm. Remember all those *thees* and *thous?* And Quakers are sort of religious, aren't they? They probably don't approve of circuses. That could be why he didn't seem too happy when we called him a trapeze artiste."

"Well, then, he should've told you something about himself so we didn't have to make it up on the spur of the moment."

Their need to dissemble brought home to Gloriana how secretive Dante had been about himself. He was a regular mystery man, and now she'd gone and announced to the world that they were going to get married. Not that it mattered. They were just passing through Holbrook. They wouldn't be around long enough for anyone to care whether they ever got married or not.

"All he told us was that he was an assassin. I didn't think it was a good idea to admit that to the sheriff, considering how suspicious he seemed."

"Of course, it was a *much* better idea to stand there and stammer as if you didn't even know the man. Lucky for the both of you that I'm such a fast thinker. I thought you had this bodyguard thing schemed out, Glory."

"Hiring a bodyguard was your idea, Maud." Glory spoke absently. "Everything happened so fast I didn't have time to think! And maybe that's for the best. Sometimes you jinx things by planning too far ahead."

"I guess you're pretty safe on that account."

Maud's sarcastic rebuke stung. "I know Dante believes that a person can plan for every contingency, but I can't. How in the world could I have expected that he'd go walking off with the sheriff? You know how men love to brag to each other. He's bound to let it slip that I hired him because he's an assassin. What good would it have done to prepare a story ahead of time? Come to think of it, how did I know I'd end up with a closemouthed foreigner who wears metal shirts?"

"Conquistador," offered Mr. Blue, who emerged from the shadows near the stable car. "My people have been waiting for centuries in the hopes that one such as he would return. Now that he is here, we can take all of you to the sacred cave that hides in the mountains rimming your land."

"Oh, him and that durned cave!"

"Don't insult him, Maud." Glory turned to Mr. Blue. She wasn't sure why he kept calling Dante a conquistador or why Dante's arrival pleased the Indian so much, but she could figure that out later, when she'd settled a matter she found more pressing at the moment. "Are you saying you can guide us to my ranch?"

The Indian nodded with a broad smile. "I have crossed the lands from Holbrook to the Mogollan Rim once each week for more years than I can count."

"Well, at least he stopped calling Dante a banana." Maud sent an apologetic smile Mr. Blue's way, turned toward Gloriana, and squeezed her hands. "I'm sorry for being so mouthy, honey. I know you don't have a scheming bone in your body. I should've helped you make up a story. Let's work on a new one right now."

"No, you go on. Unload the horses, like Dante said. Do you think you can put the wagon together yourself?"

"I guess so, seeing as I've done it a hundred times or more."

"Good. Then I'll take care of my business and we can leave for Pleasant Valley as soon as I take care of all those pesky details."

"Me and my wife will help you with your horses, old woman," offered Mr. Blue. "We're good with horses."

"You're on," Maud said.

When her friend disappeared into the stable car, Gloriana forced her lips into a smile and turned to face the street.

All through her conversation with Maud she'd felt tiny prickles at the back of her neck and little shivers along her arms. Showman's instinct, her mother had called it, telling Glory that it warned a performer when someone in the audience was paying attention to the wrong thing at the wrong time. Gloriana knew she was being watched.

Sure enough, when she turned, she saw the townspeople. They'd dispersed, as Sheriff Owens had ordered, but not very far. Some of the men leaned against hitching posts. Others fiddled with harnesses and saddles while staring at her over their horses' backs. A few women strolled slowly along a board sidewalk; a few more hovered in doorways, peeping around the jambs.

She let her gaze skip over the storefronts. Armbruster's Blacksmith Shop and Brown and Kinder's Livery Stable hunched alongside Main Street on the north; more bars than any decent town had a right to offer lay in an appropriately haphazard line along the south.

At the very end of the street stood the dusty edifice proclaiming itself to be the Coconino Bank. She patted her pocket and took heart at the familiar sound of rustling paper, her copy of the telegram that snoopy Henny Loudon had admitted to reading. Gloriana hoped its mundane contents had bored the busybody to tears—all she'd done was arrange to have funds transferred to the Coconino Bank from her Florida account. But to claim her money and purchase the supplies they'd need for the trip to Pleasant Valley, she'd have to walk past each and every gawking resident of Holbrook.

Her audience was curious, true, but also wary and more than a little hostile. They stared at her with the you'd-better-give-me-my-money's-worth attitude that marked the worst opening night crowds.

Something within her, something warm and hopeful that she'd scarcely been aware of before, subsided at the realization that she wasn't welcome there. But what had she expected? That Holbrook would fling its arms open wide and make her an honorary citizen?

It would've been nice, Glory thought, but so what if they didn't? She wouldn't want to call such a backward, dusty place home anyway. Why, she'd just shrivel up in this town and turn all pucker-lipped, like Henny Loudon.

You tend to the business, Dante had said, as if he had no doubt whatsoever of her ability to deal with all these hostile people.

Taking a deep breath and tipping her chin up the practiced one-half inch that made her look confident—at least in front of her mirror—Gloriana started walking.

The sun struck hot in this strange Arizona land. Dante had long ago shed his cape, cabassat, and chest armor. He doubted that any but desert-bred infidels would fare well in this place, where heat shimmered from the sere, sandy earth and where any plant daring to poke above the ground found its leaves burned brown.

A pox on John Dee for shifting him to such a wretched clime! Dante deliberately drove all memory of Italy's gentle sun and cool mountain breezes to the back of his mind as he squinted at the heat-distorted landscape and aimed his pistol at his target. The glass bottle shattered, sending a shower of glass fragments toward the substantial pile his previous efforts had accumulated.

"You're a natural," Sheriff Owens said, clapping him on the shoulder. "If you and your little lady buy yourselves a couple of Colts like this one, you won't have a bit of trouble."

From behind him came a gentle correction. "We won't be buying any guns."

Dante turned at Gloriana's comment. He felt a swift surge of pride when he realized that she must have witnessed his quick mastery of Colt marksmanship, and he had to resist the urge to whirl about and prove his skill again by destroying the lone bottle still perched atop the fence rail.

"How fared the business, Gloriana?"

"I'm afraid I have some bad news for you, Dante," she said.

"Excuse me," Owens broke in, "but I'll be darned if I didn't forget an important appointment. You drop off that pistol at my office when you're finished practicing." Sheriff Owens sent Dante an apologetic shrug, nodded at Gloriana, and took off in a ground-eating lope toward town, leaving Dante and Gloriana alone.

Dante studied her, noting now the subtle difference in her demeanor. Though he had no good reason for thinking it, he doubted the debilitating heat accounted for the change. He felt certain her fine skin seldom betrayed such an unnatural pallor. He possessed little familiarity with her moods, and yet the thin line of her lips and the suspiciously bright glitter of her eyes told him she stood in dire need of the hug-squeeze she'd asked of him earlier. He did not understand what had forged Gloriana Carlisle, but he somehow knew that bestowing the hug would shatter her tenuous calm.

So he merely remarked, "We must purchase guns. Sheriff Owens confirms the worst of what we have already heard. We are riding into danger."

"We're not going to Pleasant Valley." Gloriana stared at the pile of glass and spoke with words as chipped and lifeless as those glittering shards. "I've changed my mind. You can go on about your business. Find yourself another job. I won't be needing a body-guard."

He knew that the mirror would not be his if he did not stay with her, but he bit back his protest. He was utterly certain that any attempt to dissuade her would force her into hardening her position.

At the same time he wished she would turn those wondrous sea-storm eyes upon him and speak to him as if he were more than an annoying hireling whose services were no longer required. She stared only at that pile of splintered glass, but without the slightest hint of fascination or a bit of regret over the ruination of so much painstaking craftsmanship.

It came to him then that he had at other times witnessed individuals turn such attention upon some innocuous object. Truth be told, he'd done it himself, when he was younger and lacked confidence in his own abilities. He remembered developing an inordinate interest in the number of blades of grass sprouting in front of his nose the first time he'd been unhorsed at a tourney. He'd counted them again and again, praying that the jeering, taunting crowd would tire of its sport and drift away before he had to stand and face their mockery. It was embarrassment and failure that led to that sort of evasiveness. What had Gloriana endured over this past hour that had affected her so?

His fingers curved over Owens's pistol, and he realized with breath-stealing suddenness that he would gladly shoot whoever was responsible for stealing the light from Gloriana's eyes.

"Why?" he asked, limiting himself to one word lest he mark himself a hotheaded fool.

"I just changed my mind, that's all."

But he could tell there was much more to it than that. The woman who'd approached this place so eagerly was now wilted like a rare flower that had been transplanted into a new garden without sufficient moisture to sustain its roots. Flowers possessed remarkable powers of recovery, but the wise gardener studied his charge before rushing to attend to it. The smallest sip of water could enable a flower to lift its perfumed head and stand tall, while an overabundance might drown it.

Gloriana's spirits certainly seemed to need lifting. And somehow Dante didn't think overcoddling would do the trick.

"So Owens was right. I should not have entrusted business to a female."

Her head snapped up. Her eyes snapped, too, but with outrage. She drove her hand into a pouch at her waist and pulled forth a folded document, which she crumpled and threw to the ground, stomping it into the dirt. "I handled the business just fine, I'll have you know. It's these birdbrains here in Holbrook who got everything all mixed up."

Dante bent and rescued the document. Not quite parchment, though a curious sort of printing tracked over its smooth surface, and it was obviously designed to be read like a parchment. He rubbed it between thumb and forefinger, testing its slipperiness, hearing its soft rustle. He'd heard that a new substance was finding favor with scribes and scholars—*paper,* they'd called it, claiming that a material made of wood and cloth rather than animal hide would make the written word available to more people. This document he held looked nothing like wood or cloth, but as it was not parchment, it had to be paper.

Guns. Glass. Paper. Treasures so common that men felt free to shoot bullets without aiming, to shatter glass without regard to rarity, to grind written words into the earth without sharing them with others. The paper in Dante's hand was palpable evidence of a time and place that did not belong to him. His hand should never have known the feel of this paper, the grip of a Colt revolver. Dee had flung him far, far into a future that possessed more wonders than his mind could absorb.

Awesome wonders, but none so magical as one slim, defiant woman, bravely blinking back tears. He moved to shield his desert rose from the merciless sun; while he dared not touch her in her present prickly state, at least his shadow cloaked her with his presence.

With difficulty he tore his attention from her so he could read the document. Its spare manner of printing was wondrously simple to decipher, but its message only reminded him anew of how little he comprehended about this place and time. "I am sorry, Gloriana. I do not understand this."

"Neither do I." Her gaze targeted the glass pile once more. "Something funny's going on around here. That's my copy of the telegram. That snoopy old busybody Mrs. Loudon admitted she'd read the telegram. But the bank manager tells me that he never received the wire."

"This is paper." Dante waved the document for confirmation, and after a slight hesitation Gloriana nodded. "This paper is your copy of the telegram." Dante flapped the paper before Gloriana, and she nodded again, although somewhat quizzically. "What does a telegram have to do with wire?"

"Well, they're the same thing."

Dante snorted his disbelief. "The nature of wire

could not have changed so much that it could be confused with paper."

"They call them wires," Gloriana insisted. "I guess because of the way the messages go out over the, well—" She pointed back toward town and shifted her finger skyward, where a number of dark ropelike strands hung between poles, all far too high to be of any use to anyone save giant wild apes. Or perhaps Bohemian trapeze artistes. "Wires—you know, tap. Tap tap tap. Tap tap." She curved her fingers and with each *tap* struck at the air the way a tutor might rap an inattentive student upon the head.

"All of this tapping somehow conveys a message," Dante guessed, giving up for the moment his intention to convince her that paper could not be called wire.

"Exactly!" Gloriana seemed to brighten at his acceptance of her outrageous explanation. "Anyone with an ounce of sense in their heads could read that message and know I transferred money from my Florida account to the Coconino Bank here in Holbrook."

Dante bent his head toward her missive once more and read it again more carefully. After reading only a few words, his lips curved, and though he tried to stifle it, he could not prevent a soft chuckle.

"Gloriana, if you ordered the wording of this document, you alone are to blame for any confusion caused by it."

"Don't be absurd. I've been transferring funds from one bank to another for years now. It's not safe for a woman to carry lots of money with her."

He remembered Maud telling him about Gloriana's difficulty in reading and wished he had not placed the blame upon her. "Listen while I read. 'I, Gloriana Carlisle, hereby authorize you to transfer one hundred fifty dollars from my account to the Coconino Bank in

Holbrook, Arizona, stop.'" His chuckle grew into a genuine laugh. "How like a woman, to order a man to do something and then call him to a halt with the next breath."

"Why . . . why . . . that's not what that means at all! That's just the way they write telegrams." When Dante sniffed his disbelief, she insisted, "It is! Everybody knows that 'stop' in a telegram doesn't mean anything."

"Ah, then perhaps you meant nothing by putting a stop to our trip to Pleasant Valley."

"No! I mean, yes, I meant it. I'm not going."

She drooped once more, his rare and precious blossom. The heat-stirred dust seemed to settle over her, dimming the luster of her hair, dulling the sheen of her skin. He suddenly felt as though he would do anything in order to see her eyes alight once more.

"Very well," he said, watching her carefully. "You may hand me the mirror now as forfeit."

"What? You didn't do anything to earn it."

"But I stand ready to do so. 'Tis your own breach of contract that deprives me of the opportunity."

"We don't have a contract. We never signed any papers."

"Where I hail from, a man's word binds him more tightly than any signature on fragile paper that might be crumpled into a ball and ground into the dust."

"Well, that didn't seem to stop you from practically blackmailing me into handing over my mirror." Dante flushed at the reminder of how he'd reneged on his word. "If you don't like the way we run things here, maybe you should just go back to wherever you came from. I, for one, would be glad to see you go."

She turned from him and strode determinedly away. Dante's vision wavered, and his breath came in quick, hard gasps. He searched his mind for the reason he was breathing like a winded stag and felt pain arrowing into his heart. The sun, he thought. Yes, it must be the sun, exacting its toll on his heat-weakened body. Or perhaps it was her reminder that he was far from home and he knew he was unlikely to return to his own place and time without the mirror she seemed so bent upon withholding from him. Those were the only two possibilities; he refused to consider any others, absolutely refused. He would not admit the possibility that her repudiation of him had anything to do with this unfamiliar ache clenching his heart.

"Do you forget," he bellowed after her, "that your own lips have branded me as your betrothed before this entire village?"

Her stride faltered and she came to a halt. With an angry swish she jerked her skirts to the side and glared down at the ground, but even from where he stood, Dante could see that no irregularity in the earth had caused her to stumble. And nothing impeded her from continuing her march, save for the challenge he'd flung at her.

He crossed the ground separating them in less time than it took him to think of doing it, and when he reached her, he found he could not think at all. Her chest heaved, like his own, with the effort of drawing sufficient breath from such overheated air. Her parted lips glistened with a light, dewy sheen. The tip of her tongue flicked over them, lending additional moisture that promised to slake a man's every thirst, if only he dared partake of her bounty. A sweltering breeze, mocking them with its lack of freshness, gave her skin the shimmer of fine porcelain and lifted a tendril of her red-gold hair, sending it whipping against Dante's face. The sun teased a delicate perfume from Gloriana, triggering an appetite within Dante that he could not possibly indulge.

"I only called you my fiancé to protect you," Gloriana said. "It didn't mean anything."

"Do you ever mean anything you say?"

"Are you calling me a liar?"

"I will list the facts, and then you can tell me the possibilities. You promised me the mirror in payment for serving as your bodyguard, and now you deny me the chance to earn it. You besmirched my nationality and accorded me a profession you know I do not have. You called me your betrothed and now say it meant nothing. You ordered the banker to transfer money and then told him to stop."

"I *told* you that all telegrams are written that way!"

"So *you* say," Dante answered in a tone that conveyed every ounce of his doubt. "But most damning of all, you delivered a touching speech that convinced me to risk my life by guiding you to your inheritance, and now you say you've changed your mind, that 'twas not important at all."

"It's not important." She tightened her lips as if determined not to let a single word escape. "I just changed my mind. It was a stupid idea."

"I do not believe you." At his words she gasped, but her outrage sounded unconvincing to Dante's ear. "I know something of what it means to receive acknowledgment from a negligent parent. Even one who thinks himself . . . herself well inured to the parent's disinterest finds himself . . . herself incapable of scorning the offer. So you tell me, Gloriana. If you are not a liar, what is the explanation for the contradiction between your words and actions?"

"I'm not a liar."

"A storyteller, then."

"Why do I have to be anything? Why can't I just be . . ." She whirled away from him, into the stifling heat, but not before he heard her despairing whisper. "Why can't I just be . . . afraid?"

Once more agony speared him, this time to the depths of his soul. Without pausing to think how she might react, he lifted his arms to encircle her shoulders. She did not shudder away from him; rather, she leaned back against him, almost imperceptibly. She fitted against him with a perfection that no other woman's body had ever achieved. He tightened his arms, pressing her shoulder blades into his chest and resting his chin atop her head, and closed his eyes with the wonder of it when she did not pull away.

Her scent, her softness against him, and the living heat of her created a yearning ache within his loins, a trembling within his limbs. His manhood surged, aching for the warmth of her flesh, but pressed impotently into her cursed bustle. Perhaps he should be grateful for its presence, for he felt so heavy and hard that she might be excused for believing he'd melted down his cabassat and chest armor and shoved the resulting ingot into his breeches.

"What frightens you, Gloriana?" All of him had turned thick, even his whisper.

"You."

Stricken, he let go of her and stepped away. She slanted a glance at him over her shoulder, revealing the crest of one pink-tinged cheek. He wondered where else her blush might evidence itself, and then mentally restructured his thoughts lest he give in to his thoroughly masculine urge to crush her to his chest again, but this time face to face, so he might feel her breasts against his skin and partake of those luscious, promising lips.

"You must know I would never hurt you."

"I . . . I do know that." She stared at him with complete bewilderment, as if her own words had astonished her. "But you do just *awful* things to me."

His pride demanded defense. "Other women have not thought my embrace, my kisses, so . . . awful."

"Oh, you mean last night in the stable car?" She gave a false, shrill laugh. "Not that. That was kind of, um, nice, but I didn't mean anything by it. And we probably shouldn't stand so close together like this, out here in the open for everyone in Holbrook to see. Even if they do think you're my fiancé."

As she spoke he had the answer about where she blushed—she blushed everywhere. The most delectable shade of pale rose colored her skin from forehead on down, disappearing into the neck of her bodice. A man required no imagination at all to envision her firm, thrusting breasts glowing pearly pink against his sun-bronzed hands.

She intruded upon his lustful thoughts. "The trouble with you, Dante, is that you make me think too much."

Well, there was a blow to his male vanity. While he'd been overwhelmed with the need to protect her, consumed with desire for her, reveling in the fit of their bodies and struggling to control his passion, she'd been *thinking.*

"Dante Trevani, one of many applicants, court jester, the big old light bulb, Bohemian trapeze artiste." He muttered the insults aloud to remind himself of the low regard she held in him.

She pressed her fingers to her lips, but not in time to prevent a nervous giggle. "My mother always said that a worried-natured girl like me could think herself into a convent. The bank manager probably made an honest mistake. There's no good reason why I'm imagining that somebody's trying to keep me away from Pleasant Valley."

"You believe there is a conspiracy against you?"

She shrugged, looking rather shamefaced as she did. "It does sound kind of crazy when you put it that way. I wish my mother were here—she'd know what to do. She had a real knack for following her instincts. She did her best to teach me everything she knew."

"Such as?" Dante asked softly.

"Such as the idea that a woman's life doesn't have to be drudgery. A woman can be a star and never have to worry about darning a man's socks or eking out a meal for a hungry family with nothing more than a skinny rabbit and a handful of wild onions."

"I had not realized that women despised their wifely duties." Dante had spent little time in female company and knew virtually nothing about the way women structured their days. When visiting his own mother, she had seemed to take inordinate pleasure in dismissing her servants so she might herself prepare his favorite dish or ply her needle to construct a special garment for him. He had not realized she begrudged every mouthful, every stitch; nor had the wives of his friends shown disgust for their lot in life.

He shook his head in bewilderment. "The women I know always seemed happy to me, with their children clustered about their skirts. Their husbands teased them and sampled their fare, holding them playfully about the waist whilst the women laughed and pretended to scold the men for keeping them from their cooking."

"Well," Gloriana said. "Well." She blinked, as if clearing her vision, and he wondered if his words had somehow betrayed the longing that sprang up within him at his mention of the family life he'd often yearned to experience for himself. "Maybe *some* women like that sort of thing," she said, "but not me. No, not me. I wouldn't like that at all. I'm a Carlisle woman, and show business is in my blood, you see. I'm like an actress, born and bred to the stage."

Perhaps her profession explained the tiny wobble in her voice, the quickly banished wistfulness in her expression. Those who sought to entertain others needed to master the art of creating false emotions, Dante knew, though he could not imagine why Gloriana would seek to convince him with her demeanor that she desired wifehood and motherhood above all else while disparaging those states with her words.

"I have never before met an actress," he said, stopping short of admitting that females who aspired to the stage were reviled in his day. An attitude that might prevail even in Gloriana's day, he realized, considering the cruel remarks flung at her earlier by the Holbrook townsfolk.

"Actresses are special women." She spoke with the flat intonation of a student parroting memorized verses. "A man can't expect us to shackle ourselves to some godforsaken homestead, to give up the excitement of the circus, to abandon our dreams, just so he can indulge his."

"And what of love, Gloriana? Did your mother teach you nothing of the love that flares between a man and a woman, until all differences are melted in its flames?"

She smiled then, a dreamy softening of her features that made him ache with the need to touch her. "Love. Oh, yes, my mama taught me plenty about love. If a man really loves a woman, *he'd* give up everything for *her,* not the other way around. That's what I'm waiting for, Dante. I'm waiting for the good guy to come hitch his white horse to my rail car and follow me wherever I want to go. The heck with land, the heck with his job, the heck with everything. When a man can look me in the eye and tell me he's turning his back on all that junk, then I'll know he's a man worth loving."

Abruptly Dante's passions cooled. He could never be the man Gloriana awaited. He stood there consumed with an inappropriate craving for her—and a constant, gnawing desire for all the possibilities he had left behind: a queen, an entire kingdom, a throne, the respect of all those who had ever sneered at his status . . . and revenge so sweet and pure that it would sing through his veins when he claimed it.

The mirror. He must have the mirror. He could not have—he did not *want*—a woman who would look upon love and marital responsibilities as a form of slavery. He had never expected to find love in marriage, but neither did he relish the thought of claiming a wife who regretted every moment she spent in his presence.

Gloriana as wife—ha! Where had such a notion sprung from?

From their contrived betrothal, of course, and from his dilemma. He had marriage on his mind. If he wanted to enforce his betrothal to Elizabeth Tudor, he had to travel back to his own time. Gloriana's last-minute balking could be one of Dee's infernal challenges.

If by some chance the throne of England were cleared for Elizabeth, her claiming of it would not be an easy thing. There would be counterclaims, and political factions, and all sorts of intrigue conspiring to keep it away from her. Gloriana likewise suspected a conspiracy to keep her away from her inheritance. Dante could not allow her admittedly faulty intuition to stop her from glimpsing a sight she desperately longed to see.

Surely he could help her wrest from her banker a sum of money so small it could be sent through a wire. If he could not manage these things, then he could not hope to protect a queen from truly formidable enemies.

"Let us visit this bank manager, Gloriana. You are a newcomer to this place, and he might have thought to take advantage. He may have a change of heart when he sees you will not be denied."

She shook her head. "It still doesn't feel right to me. The whole thing is turning out to be more dangerous than I expected. If someone wants my land that badly, they can have it."

"I have never heard such a ridiculous statement in my life."

Her chin tipped up. "What's so ridiculous about it?"

Oh, Gloriana, you are not such a wonderful actress. She tried to act so brave, and yet even one so blinded by ambition as he could see the genuine fear that clouded her eyes, the almost imperceptible trembling that came upon her when he suggested returning to the banker.

Dante was convinced that Gloriana would regret it forever if she allowed her fears to triumph. Perhaps he would not despise himself quite so much if only he could help her conquer those fears.

But, if he were honest with himself, he would have to admit that he would ever deserve her derision. She waited for a man who would cast all ambition aside for the sake of her love, and he was a man who would suffocate love's tiniest spark for the sake of his ambitions. Gloriana or Elizabeth. Love or ambition. He could not have both; he must turn his back on one.

"Coward," he said, not entirely certain whether he intended the insult for her or himself.

Her eyes widened. "Did you . . . did you say *cowherd?*"

He did not think she had misheard him. She was giving him a chance to retract the word. It gave Dante a moment's pause. He could smile, go along with her, pretend he'd made another mistake in her tongue. Or he could continue forcing her to adhere to a course she hesitated to follow.

The decision would be the same whether he did it for love or ambition, he realized. No matter his motive, Gloriana would see her ranch and Dante Trevani would see his challenge through. It should have cheered him to be able to rationalize that Gloriana would not be hurt by his decision. Instead, it made him feel like a fraud.

"I called you a coward," he said, allowing some of his own self-loathing to sharpen his tongue. "You turn your back on your legacy because a lowly *clerk* withholds your own money from you."

Her eyes widened even more.

"You scorn your father's dying wish. You call yourself a special woman, above the drudgeries and toils of common life, and yet you scurry away like a serving girl caught wearing her mistress's gown and aping her betters."

She attempted to slap him with a movement so quick that Dante's fencing master would have applauded. He caught her wrist. His heart wrenched at the fragility of her bones, at the anger he felt vibrating from within her.

"Let us visit the banker," he repeated.

She jerked her wrist from his grip. "I've already been to see him. I'm not some yellow-bellied female who needs to depend on a man to take care of her business."

"I know that." Her lips parted, as if she wanted to swallow the essence of his confidence in her. "Nonetheless, a touch of my new sword might help him remember your telegram."

She turned away from him, but even though he could not see her face, he could tell by the set of her slim shoulders that her pride warred with her fears. When she whirled about to face him, it was again the smooth, sharp-edged Gloriana he saw, every inch the consummate actress, smiling, betraying nary a trace of rage or humiliation.

He would not have managed it half so well.

"I don't think it would be a good idea to stick him with your sword, but that sure would be something to see."

He made a noncommittal sound, for it did not seem at all appropriate to give voice to the image he nurtured in his mind's eye—brave, beautiful Gloriana Carlisle tending his fires, with a clutch of his children clinging to her skirts.

10

She was going to kill him, that's what she would do.

She could see the Holbrook newspaper headlines now: "Gloriana Carlisle, Circus Star, Murders Alleged Trapeze Artiste Dante Trevani." On second thought, maybe it would be better for her career if there weren't any headlines. She would wait until they were out in the middle of nowhere and *then* she would shoot him dead, right between those mesmerizing, beautiful eyes of his.

She probably couldn't do it. She would never shoot a rabbit, let alone a man. Let alone Dante.

So maybe it was a good thing, after all, that he'd angered her so much that she'd agreed to go to Pleasant Valley against her better judgment. Maybe things would be every bit as wild and dangerous as she feared, and some mean, nasty outlaw sheepman would plug him right in the forehead and save her the trouble.

Gloriana stomped ahead of him straight through town, taking grim satisfaction in raising dust clouds that drifted through the air and then settled over the gawkers still hanging around. For some reason their staring didn't bother her at all this time around. She huffed with the effort; Dante sauntered alongside with an easy feline grace that went right along with those coppery-brown eyes of his.

She slammed open the door of the Coconino Bank and stomped over to the manager's desk. Slamming and stomping felt damned good; she resolved to do both more often. She planted her hands on the polished desktop and cleared her throat loudly to get his attention.

"Give me my money."

The manager sat up like a twitchy little gray ferret, his poor excuse for a mustache quivering while he nervously licked his lips. *Good lord, Dante pegged him right.* How could she have allowed such an insignificant little clerk to scare her? Shooting the both of them sounded like an even better idea than shooting Dante alone.

"I-I told you, Miss Carlisle, we didn't receive the telegram. . . ."

Dante slid the crumpled, dusty copy of her telegram onto her hand. And he winked at her! A sly, sideways wink that she knew the bank manager couldn't see. Well, that wink, and that rather nice look of admiration, were not going to make her forgive him for his high-handed behavior. No, she wouldn't forgive him, even though without his nagging she would never have summoned the nerve to march back past all those watching eyes to accost the manager. She slammed the telegram onto the ferret's desk.

"You've already shown me that, Miss Carlisle," the manager whined, blinking furiously. Those blinks turned into a wide-eyed stare when Dante sat on the edge of the desk and ran his finger along the sword hanging from his belt.

"Miss Carlisle, my betrothed, was thinking about why you had refused to give her her money," Dante said. He ignored Gloriana's fierce glower and repeated, "Thinking. She is a most thoughtful woman." He stroked the sword blade, then winced—rather dramatically, Gloriana thought—and showed them a few drops of blood welling from his thumb.

The bank manager shivered back into his chair.

Dante pressed his thumb to his mouth, looking very thoughtful himself. "Miss Carlisle always seeks to grant the benefit of the doubt. 'Tis one of the many qualities that have made me sick with love for her. Is that not right, sweeting?"

Gloriana smiled in response, thinking, *You're sick, all right.* She had to admire—grudgingly—how he had that bank manager pinned to his chair like a gopher cowering before a coiled rattlesnake, all the while making it look as if returning there had been her idea. He was playing with the manager with all the skill of a performer who'd spent the past ten years of his life hustling scams. Yes, she thought, it must be admiration for his performance that had caused the odd little flutter in her belly to start up, not the fact that he'd lied about being in love with her or that he'd called her something stupid like "sweeting." Curse the man!

"Perhaps you did receive my lady's telegram, and then something quite important occurred which completely drove all thoughts of this telegram straight from your mind. Is that possible? 'Twould be an understandable mistake."

"Er . . . er . . . ," the manager stammered. Dante leaned forward, as if he meant to help the manager pull the words from his throat, and the scared man went on.

"That's it exactly! I remember now! I had just been handed a telegram when the bank's most important customer came in, and of course I had to direct all my attention toward him."

"Of course," Dante rumbled. His eyes narrowed with the satisfaction of a cat watching a mouse skitter in its direction. "And who might this important customer be?"

Damn, he was good! Gloriana thawed toward him, but ever so slightly, and only because this was turning out to be fun. Not because he'd earned his way back into her good graces. Not at all.

"Why, everyone knows—" Abruptly the manager snapped his flapping jaws shut. "I couldn't possibly reveal that information to a couple of strangers."

"A pity," Dante said. He sent her another all-but-imperceptible wink, urging her to play along with him, just as she'd asked of him earlier. "Now I must needs track him down, a task that always sours my good nature."

"Oh, no, don't turn sour, Dante!" Gloriana feigned horror.

"Forgive me, sweeting, for I know 'tis not a pleasant thing for you to witness." He turned a glum expression upon the bank manager. "And I ask your forgiveness in advance as well, considering you will be blamed for the havoc I wreak."

"Blamed? Havoc? What . . . what . . . ?" The manager gulped.

"I must confront your best customer in his home and search through his papers, of course."

"You wouldn't dare," the manager whispered.

"I would not?" Dante asked with deceptive softness.

"You shouldn't dare him," Gloriana cautioned. "He is a Bohemian, you know."

Dante sent her a dark glower, which she answered with a smile—and she didn't need a mirror to tell her it looked rather smug.

He gave a little motion of his head and perked up as if he'd just had a thought that pleased him immensely. "Ah, but perhaps this personage will not mind when I burst through his door and begin flailing my sword about. He will understand—I daresay even Sheriff Owens will understand—when I explain to him that such violence is necessary because you have lost my lady's telegram."

The manager whimpered.

Gloriana leaned toward the manager and gave his shoulder a reassuring pat. "Don't worry. Dante won't hurt him too badly, providing he doesn't try to put up much of a fight."

"You don't understand." The manager's face had drained of all color. "You can't . . . I'm not supposed to . . . Owens can't be called in on this. . . ."

Dante hoisted his sword into the air, tip skyward, and squinted along its length, as if examining it for nicks.

"Put that damned thing away!" the manager burst out. "That telegram didn't get mixed in with anybody's papers."

"Ah. You have suddenly remembered where it is."

"Yes, damn you. Believe it or not, I was being difficult for your own good." The manager stood, somewhat shakily, and braced his hands on his desk. He called toward a clerk who sat still as stone behind an iron-barred window. "Hawkins, bring me one hundred and fifty dollars. Now."

A tense silence held them all in its grip. The manager seemed both frightened and furious, refusing to so much as look at the money while Hawkins counted it out. Hawkins peeled each greenback from a thin roll of bills, moistening his finger between bills, announcing the running total in a quavering voice. Dante watched closely, his head swiveling from Hawkins's shaky grip toward Gloriana's outstretched palm, as if he'd never seen anyone count out a stack of greenbacks before.

"One hundred and fifty!" Hawkins shouted the final total, then scurried back to his station before Gloriana had the chance to recount.

"Your wire money?" Dante asked. Gloriana nodded as he caught the edge of a bill between his fingers and rubbed it. "I would have preferred gold," he said.

Gloriana shot a look at the manager, who stood so pale and quivering that she didn't know whether he would faint or punch them if they made another demand.

"This'll spend just fine, Dante," she said. "Let's get out of here."

She wanted to whoop with delight when the Coconino Bank's door banged shut behind them, wanted to thump Dante's shoulder in congratulations and salute their triumph.

Instead of sharing her glee, Dante looked every bit as sour-natured as he'd threatened.

"What next?" he barked. "Is Maud ready with the horses and wagon?"

Gloriana glanced toward the train. "Not yet. We still have time to stop for supplies." She interpreted the disinterested grunt he made as a request for directions, and she pointed toward Thurgood's General Store. "The store. Over there."

He stalked through the open door and then came to a dead halt, so unexpectedly that she plowed into him from behind. It was like walking into a mountain. His arm shot out and caught her before she stumbled. It seemed to be a completely instinctive gesture, for he paid her no attention whatsoever while his viselike grip helped her gain her balance, and then he set her loose without sparing her a glance. He was far too busy gaping at the store's loaded shelves.

"God's blood, but even my father's largest holding does not boast such a wealth of goods in its stores."

"Finest in Holbrook." A smiling storekeeper came to greet them with his hand extended for shaking. "Alfred Thurgood. I can outfit you for any—" His sales spiel broke off when he caught sight of Gloriana. "You're the one who came in on the train today. Harry Trask's girl."

She nodded. "We're heading out to Pleasant Valley. We'll need enough food for four or five days, and some matches, and—"

"Sorry. Can't help you." Thurgood shoved his hand into his apron pocket. His expression shuttered. "Everything in the store's already spoken for."

"But you just said—"

"I can't help you!" For a moment it seemed as though regret and self-loathing were visible in the storekeeper's eyes. His glance darted around, and then he lowered his voice to a whisper. "I'm warning you, miss, nobody in town is going to sell you a thing. You might as well get back on that train and head out of Holbrook. It's for your own good. Please. Get back on the train."

The storekeeper's genuine concern affected Gloriana far more than the bank manager's self-centered terror. Icy tendrils of fear curled around her heart. Her mouth turned so dry that she had to lick her lips before she could tell Dante that she'd changed her mind again, that they weren't going anywhere near Pleasant Valley.

"No customer will find this flour acceptable," Dante said before she had a chance to speak. And in front of her startled eyes, his sword flicked out and sliced a gash in the top of a sack holding enough flour to feed an entire circus for a month, even after a small mountain of it cascaded through the gash. "Gloriana, if you will point out the goods you require, I shall search for ones with similar defects."

The storekeeper's lips twitched. He appeared amused, and strangely satisfied, by Dante's outrageous behavior. "Hold on there, pardner. You want to stick any more sacks, just do it to me—I'm a sack of shit for kowtowing to them Tewkesburys on this one."

"Tewkesburys—these are Hash Knife cow-boys?" Dante asked.

Thurgood grunted an assent. "Old man Tewkesbury and his half-breed sons use the Hash Knife boys like their personal army. Us folks here in Holbrook would be better off locked up in a stockade—we'd be safe from them that way."

Dante studied him with somber intensity. "Would a minor stab to the arm serve?"

"It'll do, providing I cringe enough when I show it to them. We'll take care of that business after I help you with your order."

Gloriana stared from one to the other in bewilderment. "What on earth are you two talking about?"

"Flouting your enemy, Gloriana."

Dante moved about the store with Thurgood, who suggested item after item until they had amassed an enormous pile of goods.

Gloriana watched in amazement, and finally she ventured a comment. "Excuse me. You're selling us too much."

"You're not likely to find any supplies out at your place, miss." Thurgood hefted another sack into Dante's waiting arms. "You'd best stock up here while I'm inclined to oblige you."

"You don't understand." Gloriana didn't want to come right out and admit that she intended to make such a whirlwind round trip to Pleasant Valley and back that the train Mr. Thurgood had urged her to reboard might still be sitting there when she raced back to Holbrook. "I can't spare more than a few days on this, um, visit."

"You might wish to stay longer," Dante grunted, hoisting a bundle. He deposited it on the board sidewalk outside, where it would be easy to collect once the wagon was ready for loading.

"No. Absolutely not. I must rejoin the circus before it leaves Santa Fe." Thurgood tossed a sack of sugar to Dante, who caught it like an experienced stevedore and balanced it atop the stack of goods. "Stop that, both of you! We couldn't possibly use twenty-five pounds of sugar. Goodness, we won't even have time to boil all the beans in that sack!"

"I daresay Maud will spill a goodly portion of these beans." A twitch of his lips told her he was joking—joking!—heedless of the threat posed by Tewkesbury's mob.

She found herself trotting back and forth between the two men, who continued weighing down the front porch with goods. She waved for their attention. "Look here! All we need is a few pounds of flour, a couple of cans of beans . . ." Dante and the storekeeper ignored her, adding sacks of cornmeal and salt, tins of crackers, and a basket of fresh eggs to the heap.

Dante sniffed skeptically at the pickle barrel. Thurgood challenged him to taste one, and Dante all but swooned with rapture, crunching away with his eyes closed.

"Dozens of these," he ordered. "Dozens."

Thurgood asked for an embarrassingly small amount

of money when he added up their purchases. "Wish I could just give it to you," he said, "but it might be some time before I'm able to regain the trade this'll cost me."

"We shall not forget your kindness," Dante said solemnly. "Or your courage."

"Don't you worry none about my courage," said Thurgood. "You just keep up your own." The storekeeper bent his elbow and began unfastening his cuff. "No sense in ruining a good shirt. The missus would wring my neck."

Before Gloriana could protest, Dante pulled Thurgood's arm straight out. He felt along the storekeeper's sinewy forearm and then skewered Thurgood with his sword. Blood welled from the wound, which Thurgood stanched with the edge of his apron.

"You will not suffer unduly from that thrust," Dante said. "'Tis well placed." Thurgood flexed his arm while Dante sheathed his sword, and the two nodded congratulations at each other like candidates who had just successfully completed some bizarre ritual for joining a secret society.

A tiny droplet of blood glistened at the tip of Dante's boot.

He had wanted the money from the banker, and he had gotten it by promising violence and havoc. He had wanted supplies from the storekeeper, and he had gotten them, at the cost of the blood soaking Thurgood's floor. He wanted Gloriana's mirror. Would he pursue it with equal ruthlessness if she put up any resistance?

"Let us leave this place," Dante said. He gripped her just above the elbow with the same hand that had so callously plunged his sword into Thurgood's arm. "Maud must have the horses and wagon ready by now."

"It takes a while to get it all together," Gloriana said absently.

She let him propel her along toward the train, looking for all the world as if they were a happily betrothed couple spending a carefree afternoon shopping in Holbrook. Nobody would ever guess that with each step she waged a battle with herself. Dante's determination to travel on to Pleasant Valley ran contrary to what all her instincts told her to do. And yet in her heart she ached to see the ranch, yearned to sit in her father's favorite chair and watch the sun rise and set over the land he had treasured so much that he had abandoned the woman and child of his heart.

Dante would take her there. And he would protect her. He had promised. She didn't have to like him. In a way, it was a good thing that she'd witnessed his ruthlessness, for now she would be sure to maintain a healthy wariness around him. No more hugs or teary confessions. No more kisses. Most of all, no more kisses. He had proven himself far too skilled at manipulating people. She would do well to remember how easily he adapted himself to whatever circumstances he found himself in.

For instance, he was staring at her now with doubt. He'd slowed his step as if he was no longer interested in reaching Maud and the wagon right away, as if he'd sensed her inner uncertainties and pretended to share them. She didn't trust this new mood of his for one minute.

"Gloriana, I have been thinking."

"I thought that was my job, *sweeting*," she shot back.

His sun-bronzed skin flushed, just a little. "This resistance throughout the village strikes me as worrisome. It hints at a true conspiracy against you."

She sniffed; he already knew that she'd suspected as much. "Don't tell me that *you* want to back out now."

"Never!" Both his brows lifted at least an inch. "I but

meant to say that we must approach your new holdings with the utmost stealth. We must apper as innocent and inconspicuous as a band of pilgrims bent upon visiting whatever religious shrines might be nearby."

"I don't think Arizona is known for its shrines," Gloriana said. Just then they rounded the corner of the train depot. "Oh, look! Maud and that Indian fellow got the wagon together!"

Blizzard caught sight of her and greeted her with his customary trumpeting whinny. Crystal nickered a shy welcome of her own. It often amazed folks to see two such fine-boned horses pulling Gloriana's circus wagon, but they didn't realize that the wagon's framework was a marvel of special springs and engineering, or that the high painted sides were constructed of a special wood so light that a single woman could dismantle the wagon and put it together again at her convenience. One of her grandmother's gypsy lovers had built the wagon, and it had been handed down from Carlisle woman to Carlisle woman, just like the private coach and stable car, and just like the mirror Dante coveted.

Gloriana's wagon wasn't suited to be lived in over the long term, unlike some of the other circus folks' wagons, but it served well enough to carry Glory and Maud through parades and on the short jaunts between towns that weren't served by the railroad. The bold paintings on all sides made the conveyance look far more imposing than it actually was. Gloriana had never cared much for those giant-sized likenesses of her done in shocking reds, yellows, greens, and blues, but they too represented the continuation of a Carlisle tradition. It comforted her sometimes to know that if she ever scraped off the top layers of paint, she'd find pictures of her mother and then her grandmother, their images and memories underlying and supporting her now that she was in charge of the Carlisle act.

Dante staggered to a halt at the sight of the wagon, and she remembered that he'd mentioned something about traveling inconspicuously. For once she was glad that her wagon was considered rather sedate by circus standards. "If you think my wagon's something, you ought to see Mr. Crenshaw's. He's a real magician. His wagon draws way more attention than mine."

He whispered something in a language she couldn't understand, and then he shook his head.

Blizzard tossed his head and curved his neck, pointing his elegant muzzle toward the sky for another whinny. The stallion always had been rather talkative in a horsy way, sort of like her friend Etta's Siamese cat, which yowled and gave its feline opinion on everything.

Dante's gaze seemed riveted upon one particular painting of her, which showed her leaning forward in her Madame Boadecia corset, her red-tipped index finger beckoning while her green eyes glittered with a provocative look that Gloriana was convinced existed only as a wishful thought in the artist's head.

"Perhaps . . . perhaps we might hire another conveyance."

All at once she'd had enough—enough of Dante's insulting her courage, enough of tradesmen refusing to give her service for her own good, and definitely enough of Dante's trying to boss her around.

"I'd never hitch Blizzard and Crystal to anything heavier than my wagon. And I refuse to board my horses in some rat-infested stable in this town. We take my horses and wagon or we don't go at all. Those are your options, Mr. Trevani. One or the other."

"We go." Then—in order to save face, she supposed—he rattled off a list of demands. "We shall leave here as soon as I load the provisions, in full light, so all in town are witnesses to our safe departure. We shall travel only during dusk, darkness, or the predawn hours. And when we arrive at your inheritance, we shall first ascertain whether there are any caretakers or servants to mark our approach, and then we will take possession in full daylight."

"I don't like traveling at night. It's too easy for the horses to turn a leg."

"The timing is important, Gloriana. You must trust me in this."

"No traveling in the dark." He moved as if he meant to argue over it some more, but she lifted her hand. "Maybe you do know what you're talking about, but I'll never trust you, Dante Trevani, ever again."

She would have sworn that her insult, her overall demanding behavior, brought a gleam of satisfaction to his eyes.

11

"*So where did you hide* the durned mirror?" Within the confines of the wagon, Maud's stage whisper sounded louder than normal conversation.

"Shh!" Gloriana glanced toward the roof. Its solidity reassured her that Dante, sitting outside and driving the team with Mr. Blue, couldn't possibly have heard Maud's question—a question she would have to answer, or else Maud would badger her to death. "It's in the false bottom of my trunk."

Maud rolled her eyes. "I'll bet he'll never think of hunting for it there. Lordy, Glory, everyone knows trunks have false bottoms. That's probably the first place he'll search."

"*You* didn't look in the trunk, or you wouldn't have had to ask me where I hid it." Maud flushed, and Glory smiled indulgently. "Besides, I'm not so sure Dante knows much about . . . well, trunk compartments and other things." Gloriana didn't quite know how to articulate her certainty. "He seems flabbergasted by the most ordinary things, like dollar bills. And then, on the other hand, he seems to be able to read people's minds and know just what to do."

Quickly she recounted the bloodletting incident at Thurgood's General Store and how Dante and Thurgood had come to an almost instant understanding after the exchange of a few seemingly innocuous words.

"I think you ought to check on that mirror, just in case," Maud argued.

"He couldn't have found it. He didn't have a chance to search my trunks when he hauled them out of the rail car. And he sure as heck wouldn't be driving this wagon now if he had the mirror. No, Dante couldn't possibly have stolen that mirror from me. It'd be a waste of time to check."

Two minutes later, Glory's best gowns lay scattered in jewel-toned heaps on the floor while she and Maud eased the false bottom from her trunk.

She breathed a sigh of relief when the mirror's smooth surface reflected the weak sunlight that penetrated the wagon's small window. "There. Safe as houses."

"You'd better find something sturdier, like an army fort."

"Oh, don't be such a worrier, Maudie. The trunk was only a place to put it temporarily, until I could put it into its real hiding place, which I couldn't get to until the wagon was put together. Remember that secret panel built into the wall near the door?"

Maud cast a dubious glance toward the panel in question. "It's a good idea, but we'd better check and see if it'll fit. That mirror has more edges and curlicues sticking out than a gingerbread house."

Taking a deep breath to stifle the mild revulsion that always gripped her when she handled the mirror, Glory plunged her hands into the trunk and lifted the looking glass from its hiding place. It came free smoothly, easily, and yet she heard something fall back into the trunk with a rattling noise.

"Oh, darn, I think I broke one of those curlicues."

"Good," Maud said. "If it's broken, maybe Dante won't want it anymore, and you won't have to worry about tricking him into letting you keep it."

But when Glory pulled the mirror entirely free and propped it against a cushion, it appeared undamaged.

"Hmm." She studied it carefully. That mirror was so old, its frame so darkened by time, that nobody could recognize what kind of metal it had been to start out with. She didn't see any shiny edges that might indicate a break in the old metal. And the blasted thing *did* have more fancy carving than it needed—the whole zodiac, and strange symbols that someone had once told her were mathematical signs. If a little chunk of all that folderol had broken off, she'd probably never notice— and neither would Dante, she thought gloomily.

She'd definitely heard something fall, though. To satisfy her curiosity, she bent back into the trunk and at once saw a small black lump wedged into a corner. "Something did break off," she called to Maud as she reached for it. And then she let loose with an ear-shattering squeal when the black lump slithered through her fingers.

"Glory! What on earth?" Maud hunkered down next to her and peered into the trunk. "You act like you latched on to a snake or something."

Glory shivered. "I think it was a worm, or a big old spider with long legs."

"Well, you must've scared it off with all that shrieking. All's I see in here is this dirty old bracelet." Maud stretched out her palm to show Glory. Dangling from each end of the lump was a slender chain that Glory hadn't noticed.

Like her mirror, the chain sections were blackened with age. The lump part of the bracelet, though dulled by time, hinted at marvelous craftsmanship buried beneath a layer of sooty grime.

"Where did that come from?" Glory marveled. "I've never seen it before."

Maud held out the bracelet as far as her arm would permit and squinted at it. "What is it? Looks kinda like a bug, but who would make a bracelet shaped like a bug?"

Glory tugged the bracelet away from Maud and rubbed some of the soot and scorch marks away with her handkerchief. "Oh, my! It's not a bug, it's a turtle." She knew Maud's eyesight wasn't good enough for her to see all the exquisite detail carved into the turtle, so she did her best to paint a word picture for her. "This fat part's carved like a shell, and it's real fancy, with gold lines and green enamel. There's a cute little gold tail sticking out its backside. Bugs don't have cute tails. And this little sparkly thing in the eye—I can't be sure, but I think this might be a diamond. *Two* diamonds, one in each eye!"

"Well, a turtle bracelet sounds just as dumb as a bug bracelet, especially if it has diamond eyes. It'd call so much attention to your hands that you'd never get away with a single trick if you tried to wear it while you were doing your act. Whatever possessed you to buy such a useless hunk of jewelry, Glory?"

"I didn't buy it. I told you, I've never seen it before. It was just . . . there. With the mirror. Like . . . like all those other things."

"Oh." Maud's flat tone conveyed her instant understanding. "You'll be wanting to put it out of your sight, then. With all those other things."

There really weren't all that many "other things." A small handful, and, like the turtle bracelet, all had carried traces of age and scorching. A gold button, intricately carved, embellished with a circlet of tiny pearls. A thumbnail-sized red stone that glittered the way Glory had always imagined a ruby might, but it surely couldn't be a real ruby. A cloth circle embroidered with gold and silver in a fanciful pattern, stitched to a shred of torn silk, hinting that the circle might have once been fastened to a luxurious garment. A collection of pure white, beautifully furled feathers, sort of like the one Dante had worn on his hat, but bound at the bottom into a wedge that had a ragged, singed edge, almost as if the feathers had once formed a lady's fan. And now this diamond-eyed turtle bracelet.

Strange, elaborate fakes, of course. The gold, pearls, and ruby couldn't possibly be real; if they were, they'd be worth a queen's ransom. And if someone had set those feathers or that embroidered silk on fire, they would've burned so fast they couldn't be saved. Glory had often taken them from the place where she kept them locked away, turning them over in her hands, trying to imagine what sort of person might own such useless trinkets—and why they would torment her by leaving them near her mirror for her to discover.

"Yes, I'll put this with the other things. In a minute or two." She draped the bracelet over her wrist. The turtle gleamed against her skin. With the application of a little elbow grease, the chains might shine again, too. She flexed her fingers, noticing that they seemed more graceful, more slender, with the turtle bracelet calling attention to her hand.

Out of the corner of her eye she caught her reflected image in the mirror, and she found herself unable to look away; it was almost like secretly watching someone else model the exquisite bracelet. The bracelet's true owner, whoever she might be.

And then, as if Glory's idle thought had commanded the mirror, the image shimmered and shifted until it reflected a woman much like herself, tall and slim and red-haired, but bedecked in a gown fashioned of yards and yards of shining silk. Elaborately embroidered circles of gold and silver were appliquéd to the gown. A row of gold and pearl buttons dipped from her shockingly low-cut bodice to her waist. Some sort of metal contraption—a crown, it looked like—anchored her hair in place, with a hundred glittering rubies peeping between her curls. The turtle bracelet graced her wrist, and its tiny diamond eyes caught the light as she snapped her fan and slanted provocative glances over the feathers toward the tall, broad, bronze-eyed man who seemed enchanted by her feminine wiles. . . .

"God, I hate this thing!" Gloriana swiped at the pillow cushioning the mirror, heedless of the mirror's fragility. The looking glass fell facedown with a quiet thud.

"No, you don't." Maud spoke with the patience of one who had made the same remark a thousand times. "Let's hide it in the wagon's secret panel, and then we'll put that bug bracelet with the other things. You won't ever have to look at it again."

"That's right. I won't ever look at it again." Glory tore the bracelet from her wrist and let it dangle from her fingers the way a squeamish girl might handle a bait worm. She glanced down at herself, reassured by the familiar lines of her green cotton day dress, by the sensible cloth-covered buttons fastened clear up to her properly high neckline. Not a speck of embroidery. Not a glimmer of a jewel. No ridiculous feathered fan, and certainly no provocative glances cast over the top of it at any men, bronze-eyed or otherwise.

She wondered what Dante might think of her hands if she wore the bracelet for him. She refastened the bauble around her wrist.

"I hate that mirror," Glory repeated.

His native Italy was a land of mountains and sunshine, but Dante had never felt so close to the sky as he did driving Gloriana's wagon across the land called Arizona. He understood now why some of the conquistadors had chosen permanent exile from their homeland in order to settle in this new world.

Always before, the earth had filled his vision and taken precedence, with the sky capping it with a narrow layer of bright beauty. Here it was the opposite, although he could not fathom why. The earth seemed little more than a base for the huge bowl of the sky, even though mountains to equal Italy's loomed in the distance. The sun even seemed to burn hotter; he could feel it searing the tops of his hands, the tip of his nose, the skin stretched over his cheekbones.

Sunburn! His father's fair-skinned Hapsburg soldiers often complained of it. As a child, he'd asked his mother to explain sunburn to him, and she'd told him that one benefit of melding Charles's Germanic Hapsburg blood with her Italian heritage was a Mediterranean complexion that never noticed the sun's sting.

Thinking on it now, he couldn't remember his mother ever mentioning any other benefit of her illicit liaison with Charles. She, obviously, had never paused to consider the consequences of her actions.

He shook the memory away. He had developed a distressing propensity for latching on to any stray thought rather than pondering his predicament. This endless wagon ride had afforded him hours of uninterrupted thinking time, and he'd frittered them all away, gaping at the passing landscape like a prisoner newly sprung from a windowless dungeon.

Then again, what sensible man would waste a minute's thought upon Dante's dilemma? Only a lunatic would lend credence to the notion that Dante had traveled through time, that it had taken a blistering blast of heat reflected from a mirror to send him here and give him his first taste of sunburn.

Above all, he did not want to think about Gloriana or the callous manner in which he had ignored her fears and tormented her into making this trip. She possessed something he wanted, and he meant to take it from her, even if it meant risking her life—or, at the very least, her livelihood.

He found it disconcerting that the object in question was a mirror—a mirror that he might have glanced into hundreds of years ago, to see his own familiar visage. All firm-chinned and self-righteous he'd been in those days, so certain that he'd been wronged, so certain that Charles V had had no good reason other than selfishness for seducing and then abandoning Dante's mother. Dante was grateful, in a way, that Gloriana had hidden the mirror away from him. If he looked into it now, his face would be the same. But the self-righteousness would be replaced by the knowledge that his behavior was far more despicable than his father's. His father had been driven by loneliness and the passions of youth, whereas Dante refused to acknowledge lone-lieness and could not claim youthful impulsiveness. Pure, mercenary intent made him covet Gloriana's mirror, and he would abandon her the moment he had it.

He put a stop to those thoughts, too.

Mr. Blue, who with his wife had been scouting ahead on spotted horses the likes of which Dante had never seen, circled back to the wagon. "The sun goes soon, *bahana*. There is good water here, so we should make camp now. Me and the wife, we will do for you. Soon we will show you the sacred cave."

Dante nodded, grateful beyond expression that the Blues would tend to the making of camp. He had hours ago passed beyond weariness. A bone-deep exhaustion such as he'd never felt held him in its grip. But even exhaustion was a grand feeling, considering that he'd lived through several centuries since last sleeping well and that by rights he should be staring down from heaven's eternal rest onto the pile of moldy bones that had once been his body. He climbed down from his perch and saw to the unharnessing of Gloriana's splendid horses.

He was not so tired that his keen eyesight should fail to mark the location of the good water Mr. Blue had promised, but though he raked his gaze over every inch of the surroundings, he could not find the trees or luxuriant greenery that would indicate a stream.

"My wife will show you," the Indian advised when he asked, and Dante obediently led the Arabians in Mrs. Blue's wake.

She might have been much younger than her husband—and might just as easily have been much older. Her hair gleamed with the blue-black radiance of a raven's wing. She carried an enormous pottery jar and rode with an easy grace that belied the deep wrinkles in her face and the prominent veins in her hands. Dante didn't know whether she could speak, although she was not silent, for she hummed continuously, stopping her strange, rhythmic sounds only to catch an occasional breath.

The horses began pulling at their reins just as Mrs. Blue waved her hand toward a clump of grasses. Delicate green shoots poked through the brown and brittle matted grasses hugging the ground. The pitch of her humming changed, and then Dante realized that she was somehow harmonizing with the sound of clear, cool water splashing over stone. She dismounted and parted the grasses to show how they had grown over the narrow stream, protecting the precious water from the thirsty sun.

"You take your water first, Mrs. Blue," he said. It was absurd to think that horses could understand his spoken words, but Blizzard let out an annoyed-sounding huff and jerked at his reins. Crystal merely uttered a horsy sigh of resignation.

Mrs. Blue watered her mount and filled her jar and then left after bestowing a shy smile upon him. Dante let the Arabians suck at the water for a moment and then pulled them away. They had not been overused and were in no danger of belly cramps, but he walked them as carefully as any groomsman coddling his master's best racing steeds. He let them drink again briefly and walked them some more. Absurd, to be forcing horses to walk after they'd pulled a wagon for dozens of miles, especially when he was himself so tired that his legs staggered beneath him. Darkness would indeed come soon, as Mr. Blue had promised. There was no reason for him to spend so much time upon this minor chore, no reason at all to prolong his absence from the camp—except that he didn't want to face Gloriana.

But he would have to face her, if only to wrench the mirror from her hands. And he should do it quickly, before the pleasure of watching Gloriana bloom amidst so much raw beauty blinded him to his other ambitions.

"Drink your fill," he murmured, letting the horses' reins slide through his fingers. "But take your time about it."

The scent of cooking drew Dante into camp an hour later. Eggs and butter, a hint of onion, bacon, and coffee—a veritable feast prepared by Mrs. Blue in the middle of the Arizona wilderness. She was humming as he walked toward the circle illuminated by the campfire, and he watched her deft hand reach into a pouch at her waist and withdraw a pinch of powder, which she stirred into the pot. The aroma changed in a subtle, enticing way. Herbs, in a camp. Some things about this century showed a marked improvement over his own time.

Maud hunkered close to the cooking pot like a street urchin determined to filch a taste. Gloriana sat on a blanket next to Maud, her back propped against a pile of cushions and her legs curled gracefully to the side. She stared into the campfire with disturbing intensity. She seemed oblivious to the smell of the food and Dante's arrival in camp. There was a tautness about her, a tension in her posture that was at odds with her casual pose.

"Has Mr. Blue gone to seek out his sacred cave?" Dante asked, noting the Indian's absence.

"Naw. He just went to fetch more firewood." Maud inclined her head toward Gloriana and rolled her eyes. "She wants a big fire. A really big fire."

"This climate, 'tis like Africa's." Dante felt the inexplicable need to defend Gloriana's desire. "The heat of the day disappears quickly once the sun deserts us."

"I don't get cold," Gloriana murmured.

"Naw, she just gets scared," said Maud.

"Maud!"

"It's true. You've been jumpy as a jackrabbit ever since you stepped out of that wagon."

"Perhaps she is hungry," Dante suggested, just as Mrs. Blue pushed plates into Maud's and Gloriana's hands.

"Well, this ain't gonna help her any." Maud held her plate out at arm's length. "Naw, looks just as bad from far away, like a big old pile of blue horse shi—"

"Maud!" Gloriana interjected again, more forcefully. "Don't insult Mrs. Blue's scrambled eggs. She's doing her best out here in the middle of nowhere."

"Then you eat it. I'm not gonna risk it."

The Indian woman offered Dante a plate, which he accepted gingerly. He found his lips quirking with amusement; the contents of his plate did somewhat resemble blue horse droppings.

And yet a tantalizing scent wafted toward him from the plate. He'd eaten worse-looking food, certainly worse-smelling food, and survived. His stomach urged him to fill it, so he dipped his fork into the blue mass and stoically filled his mouth.

"Looks like you're gonna need to hire yourself a new bodyguard, Glory," Maud murmured.

Dante meant to tell her that she was wrong and that Gloriana would not need a new bodyguard—not unless he ate his way into oblivion. He meant to tell her how wonderful Mrs. Blue's scrambled eggs tasted, but couldn't spare the time for words when his stomach was demanding another portion.

Mr. Blue returned to the camp and let an armload of wood rattle to the ground. He took one look at Maud and Glory clutching their untasted plates of food and began to chuckle. He reached into Mrs. Blue's pouch and withdrew a pinch of the dried herb she'd used.

"Chamiso," he said, letting the herb drift into the fire. "Cooking ashes from the four-wing saltbush plant. These ashes nourish our bellies and lend the holy blue color to our foods. We mean to use much chamiso to color all your foods blue, for this journey you undertake requires all possible help from the gods, *bahana*." Mr. Blue's solemn gaze held no hint of teasing.

"The holy color is your namesake?"

"No. Some white men mocked our religious beliefs and began calling us Mr. and Mrs. Blue for sport. Soon all of Holbrook followed suit. It does not trouble us."

"I would rather call you by your given name," Dante said quietly.

Looking both pleased and amused, Mr. Blue held up a forestalling hand. "Hopi names do not flow easily from white men's tongues. I am comfortable with the name given me by my white brothers, *bahana*."

"He doesn't care for nicknames," Gloriana told Mr. Blue, even as Dante sought the right words to voice his objection.

Something warm blossomed within him at the realization that she had divined this useless bit of knowledge about him from their brief conversation when first they'd met. A man like himself could claim precious little as his own, and so he guarded his bastard name assiduously. No woman had ever understood anything about his innermost thoughts, although to be fair, he had to admit that he'd never encouraged any woman to try.

"'Tis true that it puzzles me to find you so willing to abandon the name that is yours by right of birth," Dante said.

Mr. Blue merely smiled. "It does not matter what name others use to draw my attention. A man finds his identity within, in his soul and in his heart, and not by what other men call him to his face."

Such a thought had never occurred to Dante before.

Maud sampled the fare with wrinkle-nosed trepidation, which blossomed into a delighted smile once she swallowed. "C'mon, Glory, try your supper. You'll feel more like yourself after you get some food in your belly, even if it is blue. The food, I mean, not your belly."

"There's nothing wrong with the way I feel." Gloriana swallowed some of her meal. "Just leave me alone."

"She always turns prickly when she's scared," Maud remarked to no one in particular.

The shame of knowing his goading had contributed to Gloriana's fear weighed heavy on Dante's soul. He endured it for long moments while they ate, until the guilt stole his pleasure in his food. "Perhaps it is my fault," he admitted. "I have forced her to make this journey against her will."

Gloriana stood abruptly, dropping her now-empty plate into the dirt. "Will you two stop it? I'm not prickly, Maud, and I'll have you know, Mr. Trevani, that I'm not so easily manipulated. You didn't force me into doing anything I didn't want to do."

She edged closer to Dante as she spoke, until they stood nose to nose. With his vision so filled with Gloriana, it was as though the others of the party had drifted out of existence. Her eyes flashed with a glorious emerald blaze that reduced the role of their campfire to that of sparking the red-gold highlights from her hair.

"You wanted to turn your back on your inheritance and leave Holbrook without making this trip," Dante reminded her.

"Maybe that's what I said, but that's not what I meant." Dante must have betrayed his confusion, for she gave a rather exasperated sigh. "A person can change her mind, you know. Maybe someone like you, who weighs the pros and cons of everything he does, never says anything that he regrets later."

"I have made mistakes," he said quietly. "That is why I try so hard to balance my words and actions."

"Well, I don't care if everything balances. I regretted calling off the trip almost as soon as the words were out of my mouth. When you badgered me into coming anyway, all it did was help me save face."

"Then why does your pulse race? I see it beating in your throat, Gloriana, with the desperation of a trapped bird fluttering to escape a net."

She stared at him for the space of one of her racing heartbeats; her eyes betrayed dismay at having been caught out. Then she straightened her shoulders, and the green fire returned to put an end to her momentary lapse. "My blood's boiling because I'm standing here arguing with a bully."

"I am your bully?"

"Wipe that sappy smile off your face! I just insulted you."

"But you called me your sweetheart." Dante did not know what a sappy smile might be, but the one prompted by her endearment felt quite delightful.

"I did not. I called you a bully."

"Where I hail from, *bully* means 'sweetheart.'"

"Well, that doesn't surprise me at all. From what I know of men, sweethearts can turn into bullies right quick."

"Simply by remarking upon the way your body reveals your inner fears?"

"Oh, good grief, we're back to that again. You're worse than one of those terrier dogs Mr. Fontanescue keeps around to kill the rats." She turned on her heel and stalked to the fire, where she wrapped her arms around her slender waist as if she'd suddenly caught a chill. "All right. If you must know, I am a little nervous. But not because we're going to see my inheritance. Maud, you probably understand how I feel."

"I'm not so sure I do, honey."

The Blues had, at some point during their argument, drifted away from the campfire, leaving only the three of them.

"I've . . . I've never spent the night with . . ." She paused to gulp and cast a nervous glance Dante's way, and something primal and male leaped to life within him at the thought that she might be trying to say she wanted to spend the night with *him*.

Her lips parted, and the firelight played over their lush fullness. Her tongue darted out to moisten them. Dante could not breathe, lest the rasping sound drown out the sweet invitation he felt sure those lips would soon utter.

"I've . . . I've never spent the night out in the open with so few people around me."

"That's true." Maud nodded. "This is a hell of a lot quieter than circus camp."

"I always thought it would be nicer if camp weren't so hectic. I thought I'd sleep better without all the noise and all the smells. Instead, I feel all puny and helpless, like one of those stars could just fall down out of the sky and squash me. It . . . it makes me want to throw up."

So much for Dante's amorous hopes. He pulled a few small logs from the pile Mr. Blue had left and nudged them into the fire, hoping the motion would cover his disappointment. "You pine for your circus friends?"

"No, I wouldn't say that. I know I'll be seeing them all in a week or so." Slowly, with halting steps, she walked back to him. "I guess I just miss the closeness, the camaraderie." She settled on the blanket next to Maud.

"Camaraderie?"

"You know—stuff like sitting around the campfire and telling stories."

"Ah! As we soldiers do."

"Tell us some soldier stories, Dante." Maud leaned forward.

"Such are not fit for ladies' ears."

"Durn." Maud pouted for a moment, and then she brightened. "Well, maybe we ought to tell regular stories, if it'll make Glory feel better."

Dante crouched down across from her, and Gloriana's agitation vanished. It just wafted away, as if it had to make room for the scent and warmth emanating from him. Maybe all she'd needed was to keep another living, breathing human body within touching distance; maybe she wouldn't have gotten so out of sorts. But she'd been sitting smack up against Maud earlier when the frightful fluttering had started within her.

Back then Dante had been nowhere in sight, and a tiny little voice inside had whispered that he might not be coming back.

Of course, that was all nonsense. He'd made it clear he wouldn't leave until she turned over her mirror. But that knowledge didn't lessen the impact of her realization that her inner turmoil had started to diminish when he'd stalked back into camp. Or that it had quieted to nearly nothing when he expressed concern for her well-being, only to be replaced by a different sort of fluttering altogether when he'd smiled at the absurd notion that *bully* meant "sweetheart."

"Ghost stories," Maud suggested.

"Nay!" Dante seemed shocked at the very idea. "'Tis worse than telling soldiers' tales, to deliberately provoke spirits." This struck Maud as funny, for she launched into a snorting, hiccuping laugh. Glory could swear Dante blushed, although it was hard to tell with the light of the campfire dancing over the planes and hollows of his finely chiseled face.

An idea popped into Glory's head. Maybe she could use the opportunity to learn a little bit more about her mysterious bodyguard. "Let's talk about what we're going to do after we finish this trip."

"That's an easy one," Maud said. "I'll be tagging along with you, like I've been doing for the past five years."

"Maud has lived with me since she retired from the circus," Glory explained to Dante.

"I did not retire. I'm on a whatchamacallit . . . a leave of absence."

"Maud used to be a tightrope artiste."

"Don't say 'used to be.' I'm the best in the world."

When Dante cocked his head quizzically, Glory launched into a fuller explanation. "You know, where they string a high wire way above the ground."

"In the manner of those wires you showed me in Holbrook."

She had to think for a minute before she remembered the telegraph wires she'd pointed out to him. "Heavens, no. I'm talking about big, thick, ropy wires, stretched between two platforms. Until her eyes went bad, Maud used to scamper across those high wires like a little squirrel."

"A rope dancer," Dante mused.

"I like the sound of that better than being called a squirrel," Maud grumbled. "Squirrels come by their ability natural. I had to work real hard to dance on the high wire."

"And your advanced age and failing body forced you to retire," Dante said with a teasing twinkle in his eyes.

"Failing body! Ain't nothing wrong with this body." Maud stood and strutted about, shocking Gloriana with the way she thrust out her breasts and waggled her butt. "It's my damn eyes. They didn't go bad—they got better, in a way. All my life I couldn't see more than two feet in front of me. Then when I hit fif— I mean, when I got a little older, the durned things switched on me. Now I can't see anything up close, and the minute I step on the wire I can see that hard old ground down there just waiting for me to smash down onto it." She shivered and dropped back onto the blanket.

"That man we saw in Nashville said spectacles could help you," Glory reminded her.

"I'd look like somebody's old granny, wearing spectacles on the high wire."

"Plenty of young people wear spectacles."

"You show me a photograph of Marietta Ravel wearing spectacles, and I'll order a pair."

"Marietta Ravel and Maud were sort of like rivals," Glory explained.

Maud snorted. "There wasn't nothing to be rivals about. I was better than she ever was. I'm still better, and that's all there is to it. I'll prove it as soon as I get around to working my act again."

Glory and Maud had rehashed this argument a hundred times, to no avail. Glory knew that no matter how vociferously Maud might deny it, her fright had escalated into an unconquerable fear. Maud would never again be able to walk ropes without risking the sudden loss of nerve that could send her plunging to her death. Glory abandoned the argument and turned to Dante, hoping her casual attitude hid her intense curiosity. "What about you, Dante? What do you plan to do after you finish your bodyguard chores?"

"Once I have the mirror, you mean."

Glory felt her false smile falter. "Oh, sure. That's what I mean."

"Ah. But I have been taught that a man must wait his turn until the ladies have finished. You first, Gloriana."

Curse the man! He had a very smooth way of turning the tables on her. Still, she thought she detected the pulse leaping in his throat—a sure sign of nervousness, according to him. She wanted to press him, take advantage of that tiny crack in his composure. But even though she'd known him for only a short while, she knew in her heart that he and Maud were alike in that he'd never give up questioning her until she told him her plans, so she might as well just get it over with. Besides, there was nothing much to tell, and it would put him on the spot that much faster.

"We're going to rejoin the circus in Santa Fe."

He waited, obviously expecting more.

"That's it. We'll hook up my rail cars to the circus train and be back in business the next day."

The sound of snapping logs and the yipping of a coyote punctuated the ensuing silence.

"There is no joy lighting your spirit when you tell of your plans, Gloriana."

Joy? What was joyful about resuming her Madame Boadecia job? The awful truth of it was that Glory had so thoroughly enjoyed these past few days away from the circus, even with the strain of learning the true nature of her father's death and all the bad news about Pleasant Valley, that she'd deliberately avoided thinking about returning to the circus. Nor did she want to think about how Madame Boadecia would be welcomed back into the Fontanescue Circus if she ended up turning her mirror over to Dante. She wasn't half as good a Madame Boadecia as her mother had been; without the mirror, she wouldn't be any good at all.

She shrugged and lowered her head to cover the blasted pulse that recommenced pounding at the base of her throat. "This year's season doesn't have much longer to run. When winter strikes, we'll head for Florida. I love Florida."

"Florida! I know many things about Florida."

Dante accompanied his declaration with a huge ear-to-ear smile that flashed strong white teeth against his sun-bronzed skin and added a heart-stopping twinkle to his eyes. She hadn't ever seen him smile like that—and now Gloriana couldn't stop staring at him.

Men usually appeared friendlier and less threatening when they smiled. Not Dante. His delight at hearing the name *Florida* seemed to wipe away the endearing trace of confusion that he occasionally let surface. It made him seem taller, stronger, and completely self-assured, without a trace of weakness. It reminded her that he wasn't an ordinary man, but a highly skilled, mirror-stealing assassin.

She should run. She should grab Maud's hand and drag her along, the two of them hiking their skirts and getting as far away from Dante Trevani as they could. And yet all Glory wanted to do was stare at him and say *Florida* again and again so that he'd keep smiling at her.

Thank God he seemed oblivious to her inner turmoil.

His beautiful eyes took on a dreamy cast. "Florida. My God, the tales Ponce de León told at court of discovering that place and its wondrous Fountain of Youth . . . "

"Didn't know they hauled folks off to court just for

lying." Maud, an inveterate stretcher of the truth, sounded a bit apprehensive. Glory grinned, and Maud bristled. "Well, do you think I'd look like this if there was a fountain of youth in Florida?" She poked one elbow skyward and tapped the soft flesh hanging under her upper arm. "This'll start sagging any day now. Anyway, you'd think Dante'd make up a better fib. Everyone knows Christopher Columbus discovered this country, not that Ponce person."

"Perhaps you speak of the noted Italian explorer, Christoforo Colombo," said Dante. Glory, still mesmerized by the subtle change in him, didn't have the heart to correct his pronunciation. Especially when he added, with a tinge of regret, "I never had the chance to meet him."

"I should hope not." Maud leaned back, the way someone might jump clear of a raving lunatic's path. "He's been dead for a million years."

"Columbus hasn't been dead nearly that long," Glory amended quickly. She remembered how persnickety Dante had been regarding the exact number of years that had passed since her grandmother had acquired the magic mirror. She hoped he wouldn't ask for a clarification of the number of years that had passed since Columbus died, because she sure as heck didn't know. Besides, how on earth had she gotten sidetracked into swooning over Dante's smile and discussing dead explorers when she'd truly meant to pry a few secrets out of him?

"Your turn," she said. "Tell us what the future holds for you, Dante."

Just like that, Dante abandoned his smile and easy pose. Glory sensed that he seldom revealed that gentle, smiling side of himself, and it made her sad to think he'd probably never allow her to see it again.

"You would not believe me if I tell you."

"Sure we would," said Maud. "We'll go along with anything you say. We won't laugh, no matter what."

Glory had never witnessed a man struggle so to get a few words out of his mouth. He caught his breath, started to speak, and then snapped his mouth shut. He scratched his head. He shifted until he sat in the dirt with his arms draped loosely over his bent knees. He did the whole breath-catching, starting-to-speak routine over again. "You would not believe me," he repeated finally, glancing away.

"Oh, for goodness sake, just tell us, or I'll break the stupid mirror right over your head." Maud shifted onto the balls of her feet, ready to make good on her threat.

"No, you must not do that." Dante raised a hand like a Chicago policeman directing carriage traffic. "If you break it, I shall be trapped here forever."

He sounded as appalled at the prospect as an innocent man would upon learning he'd been sentenced to life in prison. Glory felt an odd little quiver inside at the realization that he didn't enjoy spending time with her. Well, so what if he didn't? Considering how stubborn he could be, Glory certainly didn't want him hanging around. He'd only pester her endlessly about why she hadn't adequately weighed the consequences of allowing Maud to break the mirror.

"I'll keep her away from the mirror if you tell me why it's so important to you."

He shook his head.

"You don't have to feel ashamed if you're running away from . . . from trouble or something. Sometimes it seems like half the people in the circus joined it to make a fresh start. You can't tell us anything we haven't heard at least a dozen times before."

"If only that could be true." He cast her a dark

frown. "I am the only accursed soul to be saddled with such extraordinary circumstances."

She decided to take a page from his own book of stubborn insistence, though she sweetened it with an encouraging smile. "Go ahead, tell us. You're among friends here."

Her comment appeared to startle him. He stared at her as if nobody had ever suggested they might be his friend.

"Very well. I . . ." He paused for a deep breath, long enough for Glory to fear that he was going to launch into his delaying tactics all over again. "I fell victim to a sorcerer's tricks," he finished quietly. "Dr. John Dee used that very mirror to shift me to this place from the year of our Lord 1544. I must possess the mirror in order to return to my own time."

Well, she had to hand it to him. She truly had not heard this story from anyone before.

"1544? That's more than three hundred years ago! You're saying you used my mirror to travel through time?"

"It has been three hundred forty-four years, to be exact, since I foolishly visited the accursed Dr. Dee at his home in Mortlake, England."

A muffled snort came from Maud. Glory practically gored her with her elbow to shut her up. She felt certain Dante would quit spinning his elaborate tale if Maud laughed out loud. As for herself, she felt like bursting into tears. She couldn't sense one ounce of trickery emanating from him. He believed his far-fetched tale with every fiber of his being, which meant he was either a lunatic or . . . or nothing. She could think of no other option.

"You don't want to go back to 1544, Dante." Maud gained control of her laughter, apparently remembering that she'd promised not to laugh at anything Dante told her. She started rattling off objections as if she believed he might actually use Glory's mirror to travel back in time. "Hell, that's the whatchamacallit, the Dark Ages, back then. No toilets. No running water. They had plagues, and people didn't have any teeth."

"I must go back."

"I'll bet they didn't have railroads back then, did they? Or sewing machines. Or—"

"Maud, I cannot stay here. I have vowed to return."

"You probably want to get revenge on that Dee fellow."

"That is true. And there is also one other matter." He sent Gloriana a look fraught with apology. "I must claim what Dee seeks to deny me."

"Oh, that's right. He stole your clothes and money."

"No." He grew pensive, and Gloriana feared once more that he had changed his mind about telling his story. He leaned over, pulled a stick from the stack of firewood Mr. Blue had left, and began poking at the campfire.

The flames leaped higher. Tiny bits of burning ash glittered like miniature fireflies. The brightness illuminated Dante's face. He looked at her, and she read a bittersweet regret in his expression.

"Dee sent me here to prevent me from marrying Elizabeth."

"You're ... you're engaged to be married?" Gloriana whispered.

He tightened his lips, the very lips that had so thoroughly plundered her own the night before. Lips that apparently had no business being pressed anywhere but against his precious Elizabeth's. His glance flickered toward her, and he flushed, as if his thoughts mirrored her own.

"Her pa took against you and ran you off, huh?" Maud asked eagerly.

"I had no chance to discuss matters with her father, though I meant to confront Henry Tudor about the betrothal. Dee has taken it into his head that Elizabeth will inherit the throne but that she must rule as a virgin queen. She has vowed to marry me or no other. So you see why I must return. I shall become her royal consort upon our marriage."

He sat there trying to look humble but not succeeding at keeping the light of ambition from his face, while the meaning of his statement slammed into Glory's heart. He was involved with another woman. A woman who would make him into something important, something sort of like a king.

Maud tugged at Glory's sleeve. "Elizabeth Tudor? Ain't that the queen your mama named you after?"

"Yes. Oh, my God, yes, it is." Mortified to realize that thinking of Dante's marrying another woman had completely blinded her to the absurdity of his statement, Glory jumped to her feet. "He's making all this up. I told him when I first met him that my mother had named me after a dead queen in a poem. *The Faerie Queen,* by Edmund Spenser. But you probably know all about that, don't you, Mr. Trevani?"

"Nay. I have never heard of Edmund Spenser. Nor have I ever heard Elizabeth called Gloriana."

"No wonder Mr. Blue called you a banana," Maud shouted, as angry as Glory now. "The insides of your head are just as mushy as a banana!"

Gloriana curled her arms around her waist in a reflexive action prompted by a sudden aching sensation within her. The movement pulled her sleeve up away from her wrist, revealing the turtle bracelet she still wore.

Now Dante too rose to his full height. He caught her hand in his and drew it up to inspect the bracelet. "Where did you get that?" His voice had turned so hoarse and low that it might have been a tiger's warning growl. "That is Elizabeth's bracelet!"

She jerked her hand free. "What is wrong with you? According to you, my mirror belongs to somebody named Dr. Dee. According to you, my bracelet belongs to somebody named Elizabeth." A terrible notion came to her; she remembered how he had called her Elizabeth when he'd first come upon her in the rail car, how stunned and disbelieving he'd been when she told him she wasn't his Elizabeth.

The night before, he'd held her and kissed her and made her ache for more. Now she had an explanation for his sudden withdrawal. "When you . . . when we . . . Those nice things you said, when you . . . kissed me, all those words and kisses belonged to Elizabeth, too."

His head snapped back as if she'd slapped him. "Nay! Gloriana, the feelings I hold for you cannot be compared to the regard I hold for Elizabeth."

"Of course not. She's your betrothed. I'm just some circus strumpet you thought it might be fun to dally with until you meet up with your precious Elizabeth again."

Oh, God, she'd learned nothing! All those years of watching her mother pine for a man who couldn't turn his back on his prior commitments, and here she was doing the very same thing. How could she have been so stupid? The turtle bracelet slid over her arm, cold and hard. She should have kept her heart the same way. She clasped a hand over the bracelet; it would serve as her talisman forevermore. "You're not taking this away from me."

"You may keep the bracelet. But I am warning you,

Gloriana, the mirror will be mine." She met his gaze with defiance, but it withered before the ruthless determination in his. "It will be mine, no matter how you might try to hide it or otherwise keep it from me. I will not be denied."

There were probably a hundred rude retorts she could have made, a thousand witty comments, but something seemed to be clogging up her thought processes. All she managed to do was haul back her foot and kick him square on the shin.

And then she couldn't run away from him because her toes shrieked with the agony of striking what seemed to be solid oak. Maybe there was something to be said for thinking out the consequences before taking action. She winced, expecting Dante to treat her to an ear-blistering scolding at the very least.

Instead, Dante simply turned away and disappeared into the overwhelming darkness that rimmed their tiny camp.

12

Dante stalked through the darkness, cursing his stupidity. What had he expected? That they might believe him?

You are among friends. His heart tugged at the very memory of those words, at the sweet curve of Gloriana's lips as she'd urged him to tell her the truth. And like a jabbering monkey—nay, the big old ape Maud had called him—he'd done it. He'd given Gloriana far more of the truth than she had to know. Far more than he wanted her to know. He'd never meant to tell her about Elizabeth, about his betrothal.

Why?

Every bit of his energy should be directed toward returning to his rightful place and time, upon claiming the woman and kingdom that should be his. Why did he regret telling Gloriana about Elizabeth? There was no logical reason to withhold the truth from her. There could be no honorable motive in deceiving her, only the prolonging of the sweet dalliance he'd reveled in over the past few days.

He knew that once she realized he had pledged his troth to another, she would never again look at him with that wondrous light in her eyes.

As if his thoughts had conjured her, he heard a soft footfall behind him.

"Dante?"

The moon had risen, bathing this awesome land in a soft silver glow that outshone a thousand of his father's finest candles. He turned to her and, with a lurching of his spirit, saw the regrettable change in her that he had expected. She picked her way around tufts of rough grass and over the moonstruck earth with a brisk, businesslike air. She reached his side and looked up at him, and it was as though a cloud had covered the moon, for there was no light in her eyes.

All his life Dante Trevani had ached to be noticed, to have the admiring attention of crowds and important personages fixed upon him. At that moment he would have traded a lifetime of unremitting adulation for one of Gloriana's real smiles, there in the dark, where nobody but he would ever see it.

"I did not expect you to follow me."

"Then I guess you didn't weigh all the options when you stormed out of camp."

He hadn't. He'd let remorse and self-loathing propel him away.

"I am sorry, Gloriana. I know that the words I spoke wounded you." *As they did me,* he added silently.

"What words?" She frowned, conveying great puzzlement, and then understanding dawned upon her. "Oh, all that stuff about your betrothal to what's her name, Elizabeth Tudor. I don't care about that."

"You . . . you do not care?"

"Of course not. What you do after you finish this job is your own business. All I care about is my mirror. That's why I followed you. Now that I know what you want to do with it, I have an idea."

She certainly seemed self-possessed and filled with purposeful intent, not at all a weeping, reproachful female who'd just learned that her paramour had hidden a secret betrothal from her. The realization should have pleased him. Instead, it filled him with a nameless ache that threatened to buckle his knees.

"When this Dr. Dee person sent you through time with the mirror—"

"You believed me," he interrupted, unable to hide his astonishment. He'd been so entirely certain that she thought him a fool. And then he regretted his outburst, for her composure wavered.

"Oh, Dante, no woman in her right mind would believe that story."

"But you do. You would not have followed me if you did not believe me."

"I . . . I guess that makes me a crazy woman."

He cursed the moonlight that stole all color, for when she lifted her eyes to his he saw only grays and charcoals, the cold colors of Elizabeth's eyes, and not the emerald fire of Gloriana's. But Gloriana's eyes swam with a silent acknowledgment that warmed him even better: *I believe in you, Dante Trevani.*

She absently stroked the bracelet gracing her wrist. "This bracelet, which you said belonged to Elizabeth . . . Well, I have a whole collection of unusual things that just appeared out of nowhere. They always turn up somewhere near the mirror."

"Like me."

Her weak smile held no trace of happiness. "Yes,

like you. And I've lost a number of things that simply disappeared after being placed close to that mirror."

As he intended to do. "Like me," he repeated.

"You're not mine to lose, Dante." She glanced away, but not before a slight tremor coursed through her. "Anyway, I've never been able to figure out why those things come and go. The mirror frightened me once with some rather . . . otherworldly aspects. I'm willing to consider the possibility that all that stuff traveled through the mirror. And if that's true, you could have come here that way as well. Thinking about so much stuff traveling back and forth gave me an idea."

Dante nodded warily, listening.

"You didn't own the mirror when you came here, did you?"

"No, I did not. 'Twas Dee's own."

"You more or less showed up by chance, wherever the mirror happened to be."

Dante doubted chance had anything to do with finding himself in what had once been called New Spain; he had always hankered to make his mark there. Dee had vowed that Dante would find everything he had ever desired: a queen, a kingdom, a place where he was not in the way. Here he'd found Gloriana, who needed him, even if it was only to help her claim the small kingdom that belonged to her. "I believe Dee knew where I would find myself once he sent me through the mirror. And the bracelet you wear proves there is a connection between that time and this."

She nodded. "All we have to do is figure out how to send you through the mirror."

"I know how 'tis done. Dee angled the mirror so that a sunbeam struck off it onto my forehead, and then *pfft*—I came here."

"That's the only part that troubles me. That's exactly the way I use the mirror—except it sets things on fire; it doesn't make them disappear."

Dante recalled that it had felt as if all the heat of the sun burned into his skin after Dee directed the mirror toward him. "Human flesh might prove more resistant to flame. And perhaps in the interest of protecting the mirror, you diverted the light ere it completed its work."

She made a small sound of discovery. "That would explain why everything I found was all black and sooty around the edges. I thought maybe it was just useless, dirty stuff nobody wanted."

Like me, Dante thought.

She resumed her brisk air. "Well, anyway, all that goes to prove you don't have to take the mirror with you. I'll aim that mirror toward you until you leave for, um, whatever year you have to go to, and I won't have to worry about losing my job."

Until that very moment, Dante had not permitted his thoughts to dwell upon his actual leave-taking. It struck him now that when he left he would never again have the slightest hope of seeing Gloriana's smile . . . unless she were to bestow it upon him as she sent him on his way.

"You would help me, Gloriana? You would be the one who sends me away from this place?"

"Dante, you know how important this mirror is to me. I wouldn't dare trust just anyone to expose it to the sun. My grandmother always warned us that the mirror is so old and fragile that too much sunlight could shatter it."

"Dee told me that very thing."

It struck Dante as odd that they were standing there side by side in the moonlight discussing the proper handling of a time-shifting mirror as if it were the most logical thing in the world. What was oddest about it was the sudden urge he felt to race back to camp and kneel before Maud so she might act upon her threat to smash the cursed looking glass over his head.

Now that Gloriana believed him and would help him, it would be only a handful of days before he could return to his own time. The achievement of his heart's desire was within reach.

But only a few days away as well was the moment when Gloriana would so eagerly direct a sunbeam at his head, knowing it would part them forever. It appeared that all she cared about was making sure her mirror survived the exercise.

"Which hand will you use, Gloriana?"

She stared at him quizzically. He caught one of her slender hands within his own and held it to his lips. "This one? Is this the hand you will use to tilt the mirror and send me away from you?"

He felt a tremor course along her limbs and knew her bright, businesslike demeanor was crumbling.

"Why not? You'll stand there and let me do it."

"Aye." The acknowledgment escaped like the final breath of a dying man.

"How . . . how could you?" she whispered. A heartbreakingly poignant catch garbled her words. "How could you?"

He almost wished she would kick him again—anything but reveal this inner pain, which was far greater than any he'd ever meant to cause. Just a moment earlier he'd been nursing a hurt of his own because she reflected none of his own inner turmoil; now he regretted every word he'd uttered over the past hour, for he alone was responsible for the agony she suffered.

He drew her toward him. She resisted, but just a little, and only for a heartbeat. And then, with a muffled sob, she settled against his chest. He held her lightly, hesitant to tighten his arms around her, as he so desperately wanted to do, because he was afraid he might never let her go if he did.

"I never meant to hurt you, Gloriana."

"That's what men always say."

A pang of raw jealousy speared through him at the thought that some other man had found his way beneath her protective smoothness. "You are so familiar with men who . . . deceive?"

"No. I've never let a man . . ." He did not know whether it caused him pleasure or pain to hear her admit that she had permitted no man but he to get close enough to wound her so. "My mother warned me about men like you. Men who keep secrets, who hide commitments that will tear them away from you. You . . . you're just like my father."

The moon darted behind a cloud. It reappeared almost at once, and all its light seemed directed upon them. Beneath such unforgiving illumination, a man could not hide his shameful secrets.

"How strange. I was just thinking I find myself acting just like mine."

"What do you mean?"

"My father seduced my mother, knowing full well that he could never marry her."

He would swear no thought of marrying Gloriana had ever flitted through his mind. So why, then, did his heart threaten to falter, as if it had just witnessed the shattering of his most cherished dream and could find no reason to continue beating?

"That's exactly what my father did to my mother. I swore I would never let it happen to me."

He could not help remembering that long-ago day when he'd held a sobbing Elizabeth Tudor in his arms and known he could never act as a loving husband toward her. He'd known then that Elizabeth would mature into the sort of woman who cared for no one but herself, whose own grasping nature would make it impossible for her to trust a man, whose utter selfishness would never let her love one.

He held a sobbing Gloriana now—a woman who cared so much about other people that a simple conversation about the father she had never met sent her into shivering despair. Despite all her brave words about being a star, about not needing a helpmate in her life, Dante knew she turned away from men in order to guard her heart against pain. He regretted he could not spend the balance of his days teaching Gloriana to trust him, teaching her to love *him*.

But his course was already set. He must return to his time and fight for the status, the wealth, the respect that had been denied him all his life.

And he would forevermore be haunted by the memory of an emerald-eyed beauty whose wondrous eyes lit up for him, Dante Trevani, regardless of whether he had those things or not. He ached to possess her once, just once, to feel her silken-smooth limbs wrap about his, to feel her breasts swell and her womanhood flow for him, for him.

He made a sound of self-disgust when he realized that the clamor in his loins could so overwhelm his good intentions. He strove for control. "I swore I would never behave as my father had done. I am sorry that the one thing we have in common is all this pain, Gloriana."

"Pain has nothing to do with it, at least from the man's point of view."

"You are wrong." When she sent him a questioning look, he tried to explain the understanding that had only just then begun to occur to him. "My father once tried to explain to me what had happened between him and my mother. I was barely sixteen at the time, filled with self-righteous wrath over having been brought bastard into this world. I accused him of making excuses to cast himself in a better light. Such a callow, stupid youth I was! And yet my father was but the same age when he found himself heir of a kingdom that would one day encompass most of Europe. Too young to actually rule, stymied at every turn by the phalanx of advisors and ambitious men who sought to rule through him. He met my mother, who fell in love with Charles the man and not Charles the king. They enjoyed one summer of love in Italy. Just one."

"Did your mother deliberately keep you away from him?"

"On the contrary. My mother ever tried to advance my cause. She endured much humiliation to keep me at court, within my father's sight. As I grew, my father came to appreciate my abilities. He paid me well, better than others who boasted some skill with the sword. To assuage his conscience, I thought. My mother thought 'twas his way of showing affection, for he could not openly favor me over his legitimate son."

"My father always sent money," Gloriana whispered. "I always secretly dreamed that he'd show up one day, stand in the audience, and watch our act, and that I would just look at him and *know* that he was my pa. My mother told me he couldn't do that because it would hurt his wife and children too much."

"My mother always urged me to try to be more forgiving. She often said that sometimes circumstances force decisions upon us that all but tear out our hearts. Although I once had the temerity to offer those words to Elizabeth, I . . . I never understood their meaning until this night."

Gloriana swayed in his arms. "Why did our parents do this? Why did they proceed with such doomed affairs?"

"Because of this, Gloriana."

He caught her lips with his and kissed her with all the passion he knew he would never feel again. She clung to him, answering with a sweet ardor that shredded the remnants of his honor.

The garments Maud had provided him he shed with welcome ease. Gloriana's proved more difficult and more delightful. He celebrated each liberated button with a kiss against the flesh it had covered. He peeled away the clinging cloth of her bodice and the delicate fabric of her underwear, traveling every newly exposed inch of flesh with lips and tongue and fingers.

Their clothes made a soft bed upon the sandy soil. He loomed over her, drinking in the sight of Gloriana drenched in moonlight. Every perfect curve, every exquisite indentation was silvered like the rare and precious treasure that she was.

She reached toward him and trailed her fingers over his chest, curled her fingers in his hair, rested her hand against his skin, the moon revealing the contrast of her pale perfection against his swarthy soldier's skin.

"I've . . . I've dreamed of seeing you like this, Dante."

Her admission sent the blood pounding through his loins.

"I have not dreamed of you," he uttered hoarsely.

A shadow came over her expression.

"Nay, 'tis not what you think." He shuddered from the effort of explaining when he ached to be loving her. "I grow awkward with words just now, Gloriana. I mean that one must sleep in order to dream. I imagined you like this in every waking moment. My lips have traveled your flesh and my tongue has tasted your sweetness a hundred times, a thousand times, and yet none of those imaginings can equal the splendor of you now."

She quivered and whispered his name, and he was lost.

He had possessed more women than some men, fewer than others, but always some part of his mind had remained detatched, observant, perhaps even a little disinterested in the mechanical aspects of slaking his physical needs.

Gloriana was soft murmurs and sighs; she was hot silk and heated honey. And Dante Trevani was naught but her lover, completely and totally immersed in the gift of her femininity.

He knew he ought to be protecting her from his full weight, but he could not deny any part of himself the delicious sensation of her silken skin caressing his rough hide. He knew he ought not hold her so tightly, but he could not assuage the need he felt to press her close, to absorb her into his very essence.

Her body, so slight and delicate in comparison to his own, amazed and humbled him with its resilient strength. She bore his weight; she encouraged his embrace; she arched against him, maddening him even more with the gentle thrust of breasts and hips against his surging flesh.

"Dante." His name was like a caress from her lips, and it ended with a soft gasp when he could wait no more and probed the soft folds of her womanhood. Then 'twas his turn to gasp, for she came virgin to him. She sheathed him more tightly than he had believed possible, all hot and wet and melting, until he clenched his teeth against the need to thrust and thrust until he burst inside of her.

Some detached part of his mind stirred ever so slightly, enough to chide him for taking advantage of her innocence.

"Gloriana . . . are you certain—"

She hushed his question with a kiss that quieted his conscience and gave his tongue more pleasurable pursuits than the forming of words. She wrapped her legs around his hips, clutched his shoulders, matched each shift and thrust of his body, as if she too felt the compelling need to become one with him in every way.

"Love me, Gloriana," he whispered. "Love *me*."

"Yes."

He claimed her then, as gently as a man could when he had lost all discretion and when a primal masculine desire drove his every breath. His triumphant cry echoed through the darkness, striking their ears once, and then again, and then once more, growing fainter with each echo.

They lay belly to belly for a long time, listening to the sounds of each other's heart.

She made a slight movement, and his senses returned. There might be stones pressing into her back. And now that passion had been spent, she might find his weight less endurable. He shifted until he lay with her stretched against his length.

Her hair spilled over his chest, filling him with the scent of lavender and falling against his skin with the softness of rose petals. Few women of his time took such care with their hair. Those who followed the soldiers always wore caps to cover hair that smelled of wood smoke and grease. The finer ladies doused their tresses with perfumes that never quite masked the vague unpleasantness that came with infrequent washing. Seldom did women of any status unbind it for lovemaking, for few cared to endure the troublesome business of brushing out the resulting tangles.

Gloriana's hair slipped like silk through his fingers, supple and softly scented as though she washed and brushed it every day.

"Your hair," he murmured.

"Oh, is it tickling you? It's so wild that it's always been a trial to me." She caught it back with a practiced hand. The movement bared her breast. With one quick motion, Dante gripped her about the waist and slid her higher so that he could catch the tip of her breast in his mouth. She sighed with pleasure and clung to him, letting her hair fall free to drift over them, providing a curtain of privacy for the shocking things he did to the front of her while she moaned and shuddered in his hands.

She gave herself completely. He took everything she offered, and he knew with utter certainty that doing so meant he would roast forever in the fires of hell. Maybe, just maybe, he could endure those eternal flames by recalling the memories of this one night spent in heaven.

It was a very long time later that she stirred from where she lay curled upon him.

"Maud will come looking for me if she wakes up and finds me gone."

"Let her look. She cannot see very well, and she will not know that at this moment you appear very soundly ravished."

"Dante." She giggled, a girlishly happy sound that made him smile. "Come on, let's go back."

He didn't think he could bear it just then, to walk into camp and fill his sight with the horses, the wagon, Maud, all the evidence of the temporary nature of his stay.

"You go, Gloriana. I shall stay here to savor the sights and sounds of this place. I know I shall never see its like again."

She flinched at his deliberate reminder that he would be leaving soon. He wanted to reach out and hold her close, apologize for hurting her, but forced himself to remain still. Soon their leave-taking would be of a more permanent nature. They would both do well to remember it, and prepare for it, for it would require a courage and purpose of mind that even war had not forged within him. *The wounds you will suffer will not bleed, but will cause greater pain than the loss of life or limb.* Dee's warning haunted him, and now he understood.

A wolf howled. The faraway keening struck an answering chord in Dante. Some claimed there was a magical breed of wolves that mated for life; should one of the pair chance to die, the other spent its lifetime yelping from a loneliness that could never be erased. What would Elizabeth Tudor think, Dante wondered, if he one day succumbed to his regrets and she caught him baying at the moon?

Glory listened to the wolf and wondered what she had ever found so frightening about such a sad, aching cry. That cry called to her now, echoing straight into her bones, where it found a kindred anguish.

Once Dante left, she might as well just track down

that old wolf and sit beside it, howling at the moon in harmony.

Her throat had gone tight, the way it always did before she cried, but no tears sprang to her eyes. There probably wasn't a drop of moisture left inside her after all those things Dante had done to her. Or maybe this was the first stage of spinsterhood—people did call spinsters "dried-up old maids," after all, and now she understood why. The right man made a woman feel all the sweet torrents of spring rushing inside her. Without him, it might as well be the hot drought-stricken weeks of August all the time.

"Would you move your, um, hip, please?"

He obliged, shifting his weight so she could tug her skirt from underneath him.

The moon bathed them both in a revealing light that even Mr. Edison's Pearl Street power plant couldn't duplicate. She couldn't imagine why she didn't feel embarrassed to death, sitting there buck naked with Dante, all lit up by the moon. Maybe it was because he seemed so utterly unconcerned about his own lack of dress. Maybe there *was* a bit of the wild Bohemian in him after all, because Glory felt pretty sure that none of the men she knew would sprawl so nonchalantly without so much as a napkin to cover their groin.

But Dante didn't seem . . . naked. No more naked than a sleek and supple tiger sunning himself upon a rock next to his well-satisfied mate. He seemed perfect and beautiful, and her traitorous fingers itched to stroke every well-defined inch of him. To prevent herself from acting upon that impulse, she tried to shake some of the dust from her skirt.

That was a mistake.

Dante coughed. The dust made her sneeze. She'd never realized that her breasts bobbed when she sneezed, but they did. Dante must have noticed it, too, for his cough ended with a sort of garbled, hungry sound that made her want to feel like springtime again.

She clutched the skirt against her chest. Now, surely, modesty would return. Instead she felt a heady sense of power at the way Dante's body tensed and hardened, brought to attention by the merest glimpse of her breast. All her life she'd tried to captivate crowds, but no success had ever felt so grand as the knowledge that at that moment Dante Trevani's whole being was riveted upon her.

Her mother's obsessive pursuit of the crowds' roars suddenly took on new meaning for Glory. So too might she search her whole life to recapture this sensation. Thinking of her mother slammed home the bitter reality of what she'd done.

She'd followed Dante out there because she'd had a damned good idea about sharing the mirror, but honesty demanded that she admit, at least to herself, that she'd wanted to salvage some semblance of pride as well. She'd wanted him to know it didn't mean a thing to her that he loved someone else. Not a thing.

And then she'd gone and given herself, body and soul and heart, to him, a man who would not stay. Who could not stay. A man who belonged to another woman. A man who had kept secrets, but who had honestly divulged his intentions well before she'd given in to the quivering yearning that had seemed to grip her from the moment she'd met him.

Are you certain? he had asked. *Are you certain?*

The ache in her throat intensified. Surely now the remorse would begin, the tears come in a flood. Instead she found herself thinking, *I am certain that I would have always regretted sending him away without loving him first.*

Yes, *she* would be sending him away, with her own hand. Somehow a brittle laugh escaped her tight throat.

He sat up at the sound. His hand wavered toward her, and then he pulled it back to rest upon his knee in the manner of one who is uncertain whether his handshake will be accepted.

"Gloriana?"

She waved off his concern and concentrated on finding her shirtwaist. She turned her back toward him and shook the shirtwaist free of dust very carefully.

"I would not have you regret what we have done tonight, Gloriana."

"Regret? Oh, my, no." The blasted tears that could have fallen unnoticed moments earlier now rained from her eyes like miniature cloudbursts. She did her best to hide the way they thickened her voice. "What's to regret? I'm merely carrying on the tradition of the Carlisle women."

She didn't bother looking for her chemise or petticoats—as thoroughly as Dante had loved her upon them, they'd be so ground into the dirt that no wind could lift them away. She'd find them in the morning. She pulled on her shirtwaist, fumbling a bit with the buttons, and then yanked on her skirt. "First my grandmother, then my mother, and now me. All of us hopping into bed with men who . . . well, it doesn't matter."

Her unwed grandmother had borne her mother, and then her unwed mother had borne her. And now Gloriana's belly might shelter the seed of a tiny baby girl who would grow up to carry on this heartbreaking tradition. A copper-eyed, graceful little girl who would never know the half-tamed tiger of a man who'd fathered her on the moonlit Arizona desert, because her mama had sent him traveling through time.

Well, at least she was going to *try* sending him through time—providing his crazy story proved to be true. He'd certainly leave her regardless. One way or the other, she would lose him, and she didn't suppose it mattered in what century he ended up deserting her.

She fastened the final button. This wasn't so different, she thought, from the way she felt when she finished fussing with her costume before taking the center ring. She found her performance smile and her performance voice, and she whirled with them in place to face Dante.

"You know, I've been thinking."

"Again." His expression shifted from concern to dejection, and he glanced down at himself as if he'd just that moment realized that he was sitting there stark naked.

"Maybe we ought to practice."

"Ah. Such thoughts I encourage." He cast a possessive glance up and down her body that made her shiver, and sent her a hot smile that made her insides tremble.

"Not that." Whether she meant to discourage his lustful thoughts or her own, she couldn't say. "We ought to try sending something through the mirror. I'd hate for you to get caught halfway or something."

He inclined his head toward her wrist. "The bracelet, the other things you mentioned—they came to you unharmed. And the items you lost did not get caught halfway, else you would have found them. There is, too, the comfort of calling upon your vast experience with the mirror's otherworldly aspect."

Her vast otherworldly experience encompassed the accidental shifting of a glass paperweight by about four inches. Neither her mother nor her grandmother had ever warned her that the mirror was capable of such a trick. She'd told herself that she'd imagined the paperweight's movement, and to prove it, she'd manipulated the mirror until a sunbeam was focused on a hatpin. The hatpin had shot off the table as if it had been loaded into an invisible slingshot. Before she could lower the mirror, the sun had caught the plaster model of her hand that an admirer had given Gloriana and rolled it from palm side down to palm side up. Afterward she'd hidden the mirror from her sight, consumed with a superstitious dread of flirting with the unknown. She hadn't tried moving any more objects since then.

None of those objects, she realized now, were the sort of thing that easily caught fire. They'd just . . . moved. But none of them had disappeared. She shuddered to think how it would affect her if she directed the mirror toward Dante and he disappeared right before her eyes.

A tiny voice inside her whispered, *He might change his mind and stay if he sees it doesn't work.* She quelled that voice at once.

"I never sent or received any of those things on purpose."

He nodded at her approvingly. "Thus, 'tis logical to attempt the feat purposely to see what the results might be."

"We can try it at first light. That way, if we don't get it right the first time, we can keep practicing."

His gaze flickered down toward her turtle bracelet.

"No. Not this." She clapped her hand over it. She'd be damned if she'd let Elizabeth Tudor have *everything.*

"What, then? I possess little save for my garments. My chest armor, perhaps?"

"No. Not anything that belongs . . . back there. Something from this place, so you'll . . . so you'll . . ."

So you'll look at it and think of me, her soul cried.

"So you'll be able to show it to Elizabeth and prove that you had this little adventure." She searched the nearby ground. When she spied the edge of her chemise crushed into the dirt near Dante's hip, she indulged for a moment the notion of sending that—let him explain another woman's underwear to his precious Elizabeth! But then moonlight glinted off the pad of a low-growing cactus. She plucked the pad, careful of the spines. "I'll bet you don't have cactuses like these in—Where is it you're going, anyway?"

"London," he said absently. He accepted the cactus pad from her. "Some of the conquistadors tried bringing strange spiked plants back to Spain, but none lived through the journey. I saw what survived—naught but dried brown clumps studded with needles. I daresay none there will have seen such as this. It might provoke a furor."

"Send a note along with it explaining you'll be coming along as soon as you finish your bodyguard duties."

"A note. 'Tis an excellent idea, Gloriana. Dee warned me that the passage of time might be different in that place than it is here, and she might be wondering. . . ."

His thoughts were obviously centered upon his Elizabeth and not upon her, upon traveling through time and not upon savoring these final few moments spent with Gloriana Carlisle. She longed suddenly for the dark shelter of her wagon, for Maud's deafening snoring—anything to numb her against what she felt at this moment.

Her mother had found her numbness in a bottle.

Glory remembered the scent of bourbon souring

their wagon in the days following a letter from her father. Men and their damn letters . . . She knew, though, that while she craved the deadening of her senses, she would never destroy herself over that, the way her mother had done. She wondered what Elizabeth would sip after reading Dante's note. Champagne, maybe, to celebrate his constant devotion. Glory certainly hoped Dante wouldn't try writing to *her* through the mirror once she'd sent him on his way. The last thing she needed was a correspondent from the sixteenth century.

Her glib thoughts threatened to crush her with the realization of how truly, utterly apart he would be from her. She took a step away from him, and then another and another, and felt ashamed to realize she'd been hoping he'd say something to keep her by his side.

"I don't suppose you have writing supplies." She asked the question over her shoulder.

"Nay."

"I'll leave my stationery box on the wagon steps for you."

Dante had never found a missive so hard to fashion, and not merely because of his unfamiliarity with Gloriana's writing instrument or the astonishing smoothness of the paper. His difficulties began with the salutation.

Dearest Elizabeth struck him wrong, for there was nothing dear to him about her, and the face that swam in his memory at the word *dearest* was not Elizabeth Tudor's.

My betrothed would not do, either, for it served only to remind him of the day in Holbrook when Gloriana had called him her sweetheart, pretending she meant to marry him. She had set aside her aversion of crowds in order to perform without a circus tent, to embrace him and turn the crowd's ugly mood into indulgent smiles.

Even the vague *my lady* roused a denial within him, for the one a man called his lady ought to be the woman ruling his heart, not the one capable of fulfilling his ambitions.

Perhaps, Dante thought, he would use *my lady* tempered with the awkward phrasing Dr. Dee had seemed so fond of using.

For my lady Elizabeth's Grace, Dante wrote. Perfect. Formal, distant, all smoothness and sharp edges, the ideal manner of addressing a woman whom Dante suspected lacked the inner melting sweetness of a sugar cube.

It took him the entire night to craft a few carefully worded sentences. Because time might be passing differently in Elizabeth's day than in Gloriana's, he would have to avoid stating a specific date for his arrival. He did not want to incur Dee's wrath by revealing the full extent of the sorcerer's treachery—he might find himself dealing regularly with the cursed conjurer if Dee's predictions about Elizabeth's reliance upon him proved to be true. He did not want to express effusive regret at his separation from Elizabeth, for he truly did not feel any regret; he meant to return, and so there was no need for regret. And he did not want to express his eagerness to return, because . . . because . . .

Because I do not want to return.

"I do not want to return." He repeated the astonishing truth aloud.

But it could not be true. Returning meant claiming a queen and a kingdom as well as the respect and power appropriate to one who carried the blood of kings in his veins. This weak-willed wavering, this yearning to stay by Gloriana's side, could likely be traced to the ache she roused in his loins.

He forced himself to push aside the utter certainty that Gloriana, his sweet Gloriana, meant far more to him than just a particularly enjoyable bedtime romp.

He bent his head to his letter.

Forces beyond belief have sent me far away. I do not know when I will be able to return. I mean to try, but success is not assured.

He imagined Gloriana standing before him, smiling as she deflected a ray of sunshine toward his head. He imagined himself lifting his hand to deflect the ray, saw his mouth forming a denial, felt the air reverberate with the force of his shouted "No!"

The images seemed so real, so alive, that sweat sprang to his brow. His hand shook, and an ink stain blotched his paper. He ought to begin the letter over, but he feared he might never again get beyond the salutation.

I have been told you will enjoy great happiness, Elizabeth. I pray you will realize all your ambitions.

Dante Alberto Trevani

It took him the night long to craft it, and it said none of the things he'd meant for it to say. There was no bold demand that his rights be enforced. No firm promise to soon stand at Elizabeth's side. No claiming of the position of royal consort, no admission of his intention to involve himself thoroughly in the ruling of her country. Rather, the note smacked of a leave-taking, of a gentle disengagement from vows and ambitions of his own that should have bound him to an uncompromising course.

It was practice, nothing more, he told himself. He would do better with the next letter—but nay, no more letters would be necessary. He would follow soon enough and present his demands in person.

Gloriana came to him at dawn. She held the mirror clasped to her breasts. The pale light revealed dark smudges beneath her eyes and a pallor to her skin, the same marks of sleeplessness that no doubt ravaged his own countenance.

Neither of them spoke. It was as though there were no words left in this world to be said between them.

She led him toward a small copse beyond the edge of their camp. He understood that the leafy canopy would shield the mirror from the worst of the sun.

He withdrew from his shirt the awkward packet he'd made of the cactus pad and his note, and he balanced it atop a rock. Sunlight worked its way through the trees, and she angled the mirror against her hip, catching a ray and sending it dancing over the ground until it settled upon the paper packet.

A wisp of smoke spiraled from the packet.

"It's going to burn," she said.

"Hold steady, Gloriana."

She kept the mirror in place. The edges of the paper glowed orange. "It's going to burst into flame any second now," she said.

"Hold steady."

"I don't want to expose the mirror to the sun too much longer."

A corner of the paper unfurled, and a tiny flame danced at its tip. And then the packet quivered and rolled to one side, smothering the flame.

"Hold steady, Gloriana," Dante urged again when

she began shaking so hard that she lost the sunbeam.

She tried again and this time stood as firm as the rock supporting his packet. The packet smoldered. It quivered. It rolled. With a sharp sizzling sound, it disappeared.

Gloriana's gaze sought his. Her eyes were as bleak as a puddle of seawater trapped behind the tide, as if all of her light had been spent in sending his packet to Elizabeth.

Gloriana turned the looking glass toward her chest and ran back to her wagon.

INTERLUDE
Mortlake, England, 1566

Lady Isobel Crompton backed away from the magic glass, shrieking and gasping until she collapsed into a dead faint.

Although such swoons were commonplace when consulting John Dee's mirror, Elizabeth's other ladies clutched at each other, all aquiver, so silent that nothing but the chattering of their teeth could be heard. Dee suspected a yearning for that silence had much to do with Elizabeth's frequent visits with her ladies. 'Twas said that the secrets they learned struck them so breathless that they could never discuss them in sensible terms.

His queen let loose with an exasperated sigh.

"For God's sake, Dee, let some light into this accursed chamber so the wench can be tended."

"Nay, Highness—the mirror—"

"The devil take your mirror! It has failed me this day!"

Elizabeth never told him what she expected to see

when she peered into his magic glass. He did not know, just then, how to soothe her ire.

"The sunlight is dangerous to it."

"Your queen orders you to open the shutters."

Dee's servant hurried to obey the queen without glancing toward his master for guidance. Dee swallowed his alarm. Elizabeth stood far too close to the magic glass.

"Then at least stand aside, Majesty, lest you find yourself sent—" He bit his tongue before spilling the entire truth.

"Before I find myself sent where?" she asked in the manner of royalty accustomed to choosing her own destinations.

"Sent . . . sent to the physicians, Majesty, with countless cuts upon your fair skin, should the glass shatter."

Elizabeth's thin lips compressed even more with frustration. "'Tis just as well I remove my person from the sight of that wretched glass. I would see you in your private study, Dr. Dee. Alone."

They left her ladies clustered round the supine Lady Isobel, waving burnt feathers beneath her nose and plying her with the sundry reviving potions women always carried about with them.

"Forgive my temper, John." Dee took heart; she never used his given name save when she was in an expansive mood. "I looked into your glass hoping to see the face of a man whose name I might offer to placate those fools demanding that I marry. I saw nothing."

Elizabeth flopped in a most unqueenly manner into Dee's favorite chair. Dee inclined his head, according her the automatic forgiveness that she always expected of him.

She seemed unconcerned whether he forgave her or

not. "I am out of sorts over this business with
Parliament. Those idiots have the temerity to suggest
they might halt my subsidies unless I settle the marriage
question once and for all."

"'Tis already settled in *your* mind, Highness."

This earned a mildly appreciative glance from her.
Her lips curled in a slight smile. "So it is. So it ever has
been. Thank you for reminding me, John."

She gathered her skirts and bounded out of the
chair. She charged through his hall, calling to her ladies
to attend her whether or not the spineless Lady Isobel
had revived. The queen had nearly gained her coach
when Dee's manservant came puffing through the door,
waving a small, soot-encrusted packet.

"Majesty! My queen!"

The servant's boldness so astonished Dee that he
made no move to stop him. Elizabeth turned, and the
manservant pressed the packet into her hands. From
where he stood, Dee saw that her given name, nothing
more, had been scrawled upon it.

"You have forgotten this, Majesty. I found it lying
next to Dr. Dee's mirror."

With a sense of impending doom, Dee watched helplessly while Elizabeth opened the packet.

"What manner of nonsense is this? Ouch!"

A bright spot of blood welled upon his queen's
thumb, and within the packet's wrapping lay a broad,
flat green plant of some sort, embedded with needle-
thin spines. She let the offending plant tumble to the
ground while her quick eyes darted over the packet
wrapping.

"What . . . what is this?" The color had drained from
her face as if it had all settled in the tiny drop of blood
oozing from her thumb.

Dee disengaged the wrapping from Elizabeth's hand.

It was paper, finer than any Dee had ever seen, and upon it stretched a signature he had hoped never to see again.

"Dante Trevani," Elizabeth whispered. "I remember him from when I was a little girl."

"Aye, Majesty." Dee heard the guilt in his own voice, and it caught Elizabeth's attention at once.

"You know something about this."

"You promised to marry him or no other." His misery stole all his pretense.

"How could you know . . . Have you been hiding this letter from me?"

"Nay, Majesty. I suspect . . . I suspect it came through the mirror."

She did not seem at all surprised by his explanation. "Just tell me this, Dee—is it true? Is he alive somewhere and intent upon returning to me?"

"Yes, Majesty."

An utterly feminine, beguiling smile, the likes of which he had never seen upon Elizabeth Tudor's countenance, lent a particular beauty to a woman who was not ordinarily accounted beautiful. "Thirty years, almost, since last he saw me and still he pines, eh, Dee? A handsome devil he was, too."

Dee prayed for the skill of one of her fawning courtiers. "I found him humorless and calculating, Majesty. Not at all the sort to appreciate the grace and wit of one so incomparable as you."

Her eyes narrowed with the pleasure of a cat having its back stroked.

"You do recall, my lady, that he is the bastard son of Charles V, and thus natural brother to Phillip, who was wed to your sister."

Elizabeth's shuddering aversion blossomed into disdain. "I refused Phillip. Everyone thought 'twas because he had been my sister's husband first. Truly, I could not accept a man whose father abandoned the responsibilities of his crown."

Charles V, prone to ill health and fits of melancholy, had abdicated his Spanish, Netherlands, and Italian thrones in favor of Phillip in 1555 and then secluded himself in a monastery. Some said his pious nature yearned for a monk's solitary devotion to God. Others, privy to the great man's thoughts, secretly whispered that Charles had never recovered from the unexplained desertion of Dante Trevani, the son of his heart. Dee's spies had sent him word that Charles's own diplomat had reported that the emperor was "constantly sunk in thought, and often he will weep so hard and with such copious shedding of tears, he resembles a child."

Charles never deigned to explain his melancholy, and none dared confront the world's most powerful man over the matter of his illegitimate son.

However, considering that Charles retained the elected office of Holy Roman Emperor and continued to involve himself in affairs of state through numerous letters to Phillip, it would appear that it was not a disinterest in ruling that had led to his abdication.

Dee kept this information to himself. Elizabeth's perception of Charles's actions suited him far better. Now, he judged, it was time to goad her into eradicating once and for all the threat posed by Dante Trevani—a man who appeared at this moment to be unusually determined and resourceful.

"This Trevani, I think, might be different. Ambition rules him. He would demand a strong role in your government. If the notion of marrying him pleases you, Majesty, I might find the skill to summon him from—"

Elizabeth's feminine delight had evaporated upon hearing that Dante might dare interfere with the absolute control she exercised as queen of England.

"Do not plague me with his whereabouts. See to it that he stays well away from me."

Elizabeth harbored a ruthless streak and was given to making vague statements that fell short of indicating her true intentions. Dee suspected he understood what Elizabeth meant by strongly urging Trevani to stay away, but he would have such confirmation from her own lips ere acting upon it.

"Suppose, my lady, that I am unable to prevent his return."

"Oh." She paused, and one could see her facile mind at work. "There would be no pleasant alternative then."

Once more Dee inclined his head, certain now that she meant for him to arrange for Trevani's demise.

"I should have to marry the bastard."

The letter dropped from Dee's nerveless fingers. He swayed, and might have aped Lady Isobel Crompton's flop to the floor if Elizabeth had not tapped him smartly upon the shoulder with her fan.

"I did give my word. And he has performed a singular service with this note. This letter, Dee, could not have arrived at a more propitious time. I can use his stated intent of honoring our betrothal to placate Parliament. Mayhap your infernal looking glass has not failed me after all."

No fury emanated from her. His position at court was safe. She meant to use Trevani, exactly as Dee had predicted all those years ago.

"Summon Cecil. You will accompany us to Parliament. I will make a pretty speech, and then you shall remain behind to explain to all those assembled idiots that my hands are tied regarding marriage so long as this Trevani lives. But do not name him, Dee. Say I am overcome with embarrassment over his continued absence but will reveal everything to them as soon as I bring my sensibilities under control."

She paused at the step to her carriage. With a movement of her head she indicated first the spiked plant and then Trevani's letter. "Oh, and Dee—fetch that trash and turn it over to my tiring woman. I would have it examined later."

And indeed it was a pretty speech she delivered to Parliament. Elizabeth sat with bowed head, every inch the subordinate woman anxious to please this houseful of most powerful men. They, in turn, did their utmost to assure her that their censure was meant for own good, for the good of the realm. She listened to their arguments in favor of marriage, and she endured the explanations of how peaceful succession was threatened by her failure to bear heirs for England. At the end of it all, she stood and spoke so quietly that they were forced into silence so that they might hear.

"I say again, I will marry as soon as I can conveniently . . . if God take not away him whom I mind to marry . . ." She paused, with the air of one hiding a great secret. "Or myself." There was the flicker of a smile on her face, as if she'd acknowledged her own mortality as a matter of course. And then she drew a great breath and turned toward Dee. Her countenance grew so unreadable that no man present could doubt that she withheld more than she told, and that John Dee might, if pressed, provide an explanation. "Or else some other great hindrance happen . . ."

There was more, all delivered in the choked tones of a woman struggling to master her weak female emotions. It was a trick she had long ago mastered. None save Dee sat close enough to witness that no tears clouded those cold gray eyes, or that when she lifted a lacy handkerchief to her lips it was not to mop away perspiration but to hide the smirk that rose when it became clear that Elizabeth Tudor had triumphed yet again.

13

Gloriana never bothered to fetch her underwear.

She thought about it as the wagon lurched over the plains toward her ranch. She'd abandoned her pride, her determination—good heavens, she'd given up her maidenhead—at the edge of the Arizona desert. She might as well leave her chemise and petticoats out there. She'd turned so dead inside, she ought to be considering erecting a granite monument to mark the spot where she last felt truly alive.

She felt a sniffle coming on. She tried to muffle it with her handkerchief, but Maud's sharp ears caught the sound.

"What's ailing you, honey?"

"Nothing."

"Nothing. I guess you're trying on those red, puffy eyes and that waterfall you call a nose for your new circus costume."

"I'm not crying."

"Of course you're not. Right now you remind me of Callie Ferguson and the way she waters up and snorts like a brood sow when she gets anywhere near the lion cages."

Maud's convenient explanation sent relief washing through Glory, even as the unflattering description raised her unwilling smile. "Maud! You shouldn't mock Callie. She can't help it. The poor thing doesn't even dare handle a barn cat without fearing she'll get so clogged up she can't breathe."

Maud lifted knowing eyes toward the front of the wagon. Dante sat just beyond that wall, driving Blizzard and Crystal over the treacherous terrain. "Well, I suspect you won't be suffering those symptoms much longer."

"No. H-He's going t-to . . . and I-I'm the one wh-who'll . . . ," Glory stammered, but any satisfaction she took in holding her tears at bay vanished when Maud burst into tears instead.

"This is all my fault!" Huge, gulping sobs sent Maud's shoulders heaving. "For years I've been telling you that you were too hard on men, that you expected too much of them. Of all the times for you to start paying attention. You should've never listened to me!"

Maud's profound anguish made Glory's seem trifling in comparison. Her concern for her friend outweighed her own misery. She guided Maud onto the bench and pressed a handkerchief into her hands, which Maud twisted and tugged while her tears ran unchecked.

"I should've . . . I should've suspected the worst when you told me about those Quakers. You're not worldly like me, honey. You couldn't be expected to know about Quakers."

"Know what about Quakers? They preach brotherly

love," Glory said, completely baffled by Maud's obsession with the religious sect.

"Well, that's true." Maud sniffed and sent Glory a prideful smile, as if she were immensely pleased by Glory's scanty knowledge. "But what they're really famous for is their insane asylums. I should've suspected the truth right off, when Dante came around spouting all those *thees* and *thous.*"

"Suspected what?" Glory whispered.

"Suspected that Dante's a runaway lunatic. Everything fits, honey. He was probably locked up in one of those Quaker asylums and stole those clothes he was wearing from a playacting troupe that stopped to entertain the madmen."

"Just because he dressed and talked funny doesn't mean he's a madman," Glory said, feeling compelled to defend Dante.

"Oh, I know that. But what about him thinking he can travel through time using your mirror?"

Glory clamped her lips shut. She couldn't think of a single way to admit she believed that part of Dante's story without sounding as though she belonged in an insane asylum herself.

Maud didn't seem to notice her silence. "You add in all the rest of it—claiming to be the son of some kind of emperor, claiming to be engaged to the queen of England . . . Crazy people always think they ought to rule the world. Hell, Glory, we got ourselves a certified lunatic driving our wagon. And last night you and him . . ." For the first time in Glory's memory, Maud blushed.

"You know?" Glory didn't bother trying to conceal her dismay. Before dawn she'd washed away all signs of lovemaking. And since then she'd been so careful to hide the minor discomfort she felt, *there,* reminding her with every movement of the gift she had given Dante the night before. "You didn't . . . you didn't watch us, did you?" She would just die if Maud had witnessed her wanton behavior.

"Oh, goodness no. I didn't have to see it to know what happened." She tilted her head and gave a bittersweet smile. "Bet you couldn't face yourself in the mirror today, could you?"

"No."

"Go look now."

Glory shifted over to her dressing table. Her mirror lay facedown upon it; she propped it upright and did her best to wipe out the memory of the way it had vaporized Dante's love letter to Elizabeth. Only then did she risk peering into it.

She hadn't applied any color to her face that day, but her lips appeared swollen and reddened beyond anything she'd ever achieved with her circus paints. She'd rubbed her eyes, so they were puffy, as Maud had noted, but the skin along her jawline and on her tender neck practically glowed, it was so pink. She touched her neck and shivered as she remembered the way Dante's mustache and pleasantly rough cheek had scratched against her.

"Men leave their mark upon their women," Maud said.

He had branded her. She touched her lips. It seemed as though they still throbbed, and she knew that if she licked them, she would taste Dante. Oh, yes, he had branded her, because that shameless notion sent such a spiral of delight coursing through her that she had to close her eyes to stay upright. When she opened them she was staring straight into the mirror, and she wasn't entirely sure that she'd regained complete control of her senses.

Her eyes looked all cold and gray instead of their usual plain green, and she could have sworn that for a fleeting second an elaborately furled lace ruff encircled her neck. A lace ruff? Good lord—clowns wore ruffs, not women. She blinked, and when she dared look at her reflection again, everything was as it should be. Except the pink at her neck seemed to have faded a bit—that was probably what had created the nonsensical image of a ruff, the blotchy pink contrasting against her normal paleness.

So. Already Dante's brand had begun to fade. Soon it would be completely gone, just like him. Gloriana returned the mirror to its facedown position.

"It doesn't matter if Dante's a lunatic," she said.

"You mean it doesn't change the way you feel about him?" By the way her friend's voice rose, Glory could tell that the possibility frightened Maud. But admitting that she would hunger for him whether he was sane or insane frightened Glory even more.

"It doesn't matter, because he'll soon be gone. I'm just a mediocre circus performer who can't even give him a mirror without counting the cost. Dante's looking for a woman who will make him a king."

The wagon lurched to a halt. While the harness was still jingling and the wagon still creaking, Blizzard issued a trumpeting challenge. An answering whinny came from far off, and by the time Glory had cracked open the wagon door, the drumming of approaching hoofbeats filled the air.

Maud squeezed in next to her and peered over her shoulder. Riders—a half-dozen or more—aimed straight for them.

"What is it? Oh, lord, do you suppose they're sheepmen come to cut off our heads?"

Dante swung down from the driver's bench. The

sight of him barely affected her at all, Glory told herself. Why, she scarcely noticed the way the sun struck bronze highlights from his hair, or that her flesh seemed to tingle at the sight of him. His gaze caught Glory's for a moment and then moved away. His lips thinned with disapproval—and something more.

"Mrs. Blue has already ridden for cover. I would have you two remain inside the wagon. Mr. Blue and I will tend to this."

"While we hole up like a couple of scared little bunny rabbits? Not on your life." Maud squirmed past Glory and landed feet first in the dust with all the skill she'd once used to come to earth after walking the ropes.

"Gloriana." Dante spoke her name with the sort of confident control she'd heard men use to send their wives scurrying to do their bidding. Well, she wasn't his wife, and he'd made it clear she'd never be his wife, which was probably a lucky thing for him, because she'd never taken kindly to scurrying at anyone's bidding.

She stepped down next to Maud and immediately wished she'd stayed in the wagon rather than face down the horde of gunmen riding toward them.

And then she saw it—a short section of split-rail fence, built for no reason but to hold the collection of whittling tools that hung from pegs pounded into its top rail. One end of the fence had shifted to rest against the twisted trunk of a tough little mesquite tree. A weathered three-legged stool stood propped against the tree as well. She'd bet anything that if she ran over to that tree, she'd see a stream cutting the earth next to it. The ground between her wagon and the tree was littered with sticks bearing the marks of whittling.

Dante cursed and left them to tend to Blizzard, who

plunged and snorted in an agitated attempt to free himself from the traces. Blizzard's trumpeting screams and the ground-shaking drumming of the approaching hoofbeats made normal conversation impossible, but Gloriana imagined she could hear her mother's bourbon-slurred voice on the night before she died. The bourbon must have turned Katherine maudlin, for she'd divulged a tiny snippet about Glory's father, something she must have read in one of the letters she would never let Glory read.

He sits on his stool in the evenings, whittling, listening to the wind in the trees and the water splashing in the stream. He says he thinks about us then, all the time.

"Maud," Glory said. "Dante. We're here." She stared down at the sticks that her father had whittled while thinking of her. Her lips started quivering, and even when she pressed them together they wouldn't stop. "This is my ranch."

Mr. Blue appeared from scouting the surrounding countryside. He added his strength to Dante's, and the two of them brought Blizzard under control.

"How many?" Dante asked.

"Eight."

The tally matched Dante's own. His eyesight had not been keen enough, though, to determine the detail he considered most important. "All armed?"

"Yes, *bahana.*"

"Bring your wife to the wagon."

"She is safe where she is, *bahana.*"

Buried inside Dante lay a secret place, an inner cave so dark and deep that nothing could penetrate. 'Twas there that he locked away the things that could truly hurt a man. When those who accompanied him into battle muttered over his iron nerve, his icy calm, none understood that he had consigned his hopes and dreams to that blackness within. Brave, they called him, and courageous, never realizing that the stalwart facing of his enemies was all that was left to a man who had little to gain and nothing to lose.

But until now he had assumed that lands, title, and respect were the only things precious enough to fight over. Until now it had been a simple matter to stuff the essence of Dante Trevani into his secret cave. It mattered not that there was pitifully little to protect. He forged willingly into battle knowing he might die, determined only to exact the toll of his enemies' death and to succumb with dignity if he should fail.

Now he had Gloriana to protect.

And so when he tried to bury his hopes and dreams this time, they screamed and kicked him into an awareness that he had more to lose than his long-held ambitions. He grew acutely aware of the overwhelming odds he faced. When he tried to place his faith in his strengths, he was tormented with the knowledge that he'd gained only the sketchiest sort of competence with his Colt pistol, certainly not enough skill to overcome eight gunmen. If he died in this battle, of all battles, he abandoned Gloriana to the horrors of cow-boys and failed miserably at the only thing she had ever asked of him: that he help her take possession of her father's lands.

And when Dante's soul confronted John Dee's in the afterworld, Dee would be bound to taunt him with this proof that he had been right to prevent Dante from marrying Elizabeth.

"Piss on Dee." Mr. Blue gaped at him, but Dante could spare no time just then to enlighten him. "Piss on the crown of England as well."

Those trifles fit easily into the blackness, and he gave a moment's thought to why he'd never before tried to bury them so.

"Strip Blizzard of his harness save for his headgear, Mr. Blue," he ordered. "I will have need of him shortly."

He turned Blizzard's reins over to Mr. Blue and stalked to the side of the wagon. Gloriana and Maud stood huddled together watching the riders approach, motionless in the manner of deer held spellbound by an onrushing wolf. Before they could protest his intentions, Dante tucked one small woman beneath each arm and hoisted them both through the yawning wagon door. He slammed it shut and secured the latch with a stout stick that God himself must have had a hand in providing, for the stick bore precisely placed knife marks and gouges to prove it had been shaped and shaved for exactly this purpose.

The women drummed on the wagon walls with a furor that threatened to drown out the noise of the approaching horses. He doubted that a thousand cats stuffed into the wagon's confines could produce such shrieking and hollering. Dante sighed. So much for keeping Gloriana's presence a secret.

"Gloriana!" he shouted, praying she could hear. "I have left you my sword. Use it on each other if you must."

His reminder of Sheriff Owens's warning bought a blessed silence lasting three heartbeats, no more.

Dante's hand lingered against the wagon door. The tremors caused by the women's pounding coursed straight to his heart. He repressed the urge to fling the door open and gather Gloriana into his arms, so that he might shield her with the width and breadth of his own flesh rather than the flimsy construction of these wagon walls.

He stepped back and strode off to snatch Blizzard's reins from Mr. Blue. He vaulted himself onto the furious stallion's back. The animal had been superbly trained; even its agitation over the approaching horses and its annoyance at being mounted at such a time did not interfere with Blizzard's instant obedience to the pressure of Dante's knees. Dante plotted an angled course to carry them well off to the side, so that the wagon would not be in the line of fire should all eight gunmen begin shooting at him at once.

Excitement surged through him. All at once it seemed a wondrously fine thing to be riding out to challenge his lady's enemies with a remarkable steed between his legs and a powerful weapon at his side. Blizzard's ears flicked, as if the horse relished the challenge as well, and he lengthened his ground-eating stride until Dante drew him up just short of plowing into the oncoming herd of lesser horses.

These cow-boys, he was relieved to notice, were not some monstrous offspring of humans and cattle but, rather, ordinary men mounted upon ordinary horses. Not sissies, for they all wore their hair short. Blizzard attempted to rear, but Dante reluctantly checked him, mindful of the slippery nature of his unsaddled perch. It would have been beyond magnificent to face these men with Blizzard screaming and pawing the air, his full mane and tail whipping in the wind while Dante controlled the stallion's lunges with his customary skill.

Such a display would have been echoing history, he realized, remembering Cortés's recounting of the landing of his conquistadors upon the shores of New Spain. Sixteen mounted men and a handful of harquebuses had been sufficient to defeat thousands. With this as

Dante's heritage, perhaps one man, one horse, one gun *could* stand against eight.

But it seemed no courageous stand would be required at all, for the newcomers reined in their horses and stared at him with simple curiosity only slightly tinged with hostility. Not one of them aimed a weapon at Dante, as if they were so confident of their superior numbers that his presence was but an insignificant annoyance.

"You're riding onto private property, stranger," said the man Dante assumed to be their leader.

"'Tis my lady's land, and I will fight to the death any who dare deny it to her."

Dante decided that there might well have been some taint of cow within these men's brains, for it seemed to take them an eternity to ponder the meaning of his words. Too, several chewed upon and then wiped from their chins some malodorous substance that called to mind the dribbling manner of cows enjoying their cud. It was difficult for Dante to maintain his wary edge in the face of their disinterest in the threat he posed. When one of them finally spoke, it had naught to do with his bold challenge.

"Say, boss, ain't that a circus wagon?"

All eight of their heads, plus Dante's own, swiveled as one to Gloriana's wagon. Dante cursed the artist who had so skillfully portrayed Gloriana's splendor upon the wagon walls. Her smiling countenance beckoned from one corner. Her delicious lips pouted from the portrait at another corner. A triple-sized Gloriana curved sinuously across the wagon's midsection, and from the midst of that image, seeming to burst through the far too enthusiastic rendering of her breasts, wriggled Gloriana herself.

She'd opened the small window and managed to

squeeze her upper reaches through the opening. Her efforts had cost her her hairpins and threatened to rupture the seams of her garment, which was pulled so taut against her breasts that her fleshly display rivaled the painted one. Her red-gold hair whipped in the wind, and even from this distance Dante could feel the warm heat of her emerald regard.

"By God, that *is* a circus wagon," marveled the leader. He tilted his head toward Dante. "Do you mean to tell me you got Glory Carlisle stashed in that wagon?"

"Her name is Gloriana."

"Well, hell, I'm Peter Henley. I'm her neighbor."

With whoops of delight, Peter and his men whirled their horses and charged toward the wagon. Dante had no choice but to follow, a humiliating position for one who'd entertained visions of impressing his lady with his willingness to defend her to the death.

"Glory! Glory Carlisle! Is that you?"

Gloriana ceased her struggles. She glared at Dante, and then turned her actress smile upon Peter Henley. "You sound like you've been expecting me, cowboy."

Peter bounded from his horse with an effortless skill that rivaled Dante's own. He doffed his hat and smiled up at her.

"Ma'am, now that I've seen you, I'd have to say I've been waiting for you all my life."

14

"So this is it."

Glory tried to muster some enthusiasm as she stepped through the door into her ranch house.

Maud gaped about, staring with wide-eyed dismay at the weather-beaten plank walls, at the newspaper stuffed in some but not all of the cracks, at the hard-packed dirt floor. She bit her lower lip firmly, and Glory suspected it was to keep from blurting out disparaging remarks about the inheritance they'd risked their lives to claim. She couldn't even bring herself to look at Dante to see what he thought.

Sunlight made a weak attempt to penetrate whatever it was that stretched over the single opening in the far wall—it looked as though somebody had nailed a well-scraped animal skin over the window instead of installing glass windowpanes. But even the dimness couldn't hide the cobwebs hanging from the corners or the scarred surfaces of the crude furniture scattered about the room.

"I guess I should've sent a woman over now and again to keep the place swept up."

Glory felt obliged to return Peter's apologetic smile. "I'm sure you have enough work on your own place without worrying about this one."

"I promised your pa I'd look after it for you. I feel right bad that I didn't get here in time to keep them Hash Knife boys from rustling off your pa's cattle."

The loss of a few cows meant nothing to Gloriana compared against Peter's friendship with her father. "Did you . . . did you know my father very well?"

"We were neighbors, Miss Glory. Ain't much time for socializing out here on the Arizona frontier, but we had our times. There's lots of stories I could tell you."

"I'd like that. I really would."

Peter beamed his delight. Dante scowled his disgust.

She toured each of the three rooms in turn. They afforded no more space than her rail car and wagon, and far less comfort. Peter and Dante dogged her throughout every step of her inspection. She couldn't turn around without knocking into one or the other of them. Peter responded to each inadvertent bump by stepping back with a polite apology. Dante just let her crash into him, absorbing the blow, touching her arm or her shoulder—for support, she supposed, except his gentle touch had the unfortunate effect of further endangering her equilibrium.

What would it be like, she wondered, to live in this house with Dante and several of his large sons filling it to bursting? A woman might have the time of her life, crashing like a billiard ball into all those big Trevani boys before ricocheting into the safety of Dante's arms. She could imagine the sound of her own joyous laughter well enough, but she'd never heard full-bellied mirth from Dante.

"Wait'll you see the barn," Peter said. "It's even better than the house. Your pa put up the feed before . . . well, for this season. I was going to move it onto my place if you didn't show up in time to use it yourself."

He showed them the barn, and she tried to appear suitably impressed by the stalls and by a room filled with harnesses and a variety of implements that looked heavy and apt to cause splinters.

"What's this?" she asked, stroking a low-lying object that had its front end imbedded in a bale of straw.

"It's a plow." Peter seemed amused by her lack of knowledge.

"And this?" She touched a box bearing a trio of *X*'s.

"Whoa! That's dynamite. Be careful around that, Miss Glory."

"Why on earth would my father store dynamite in his barn?"

"Pleasant Valley's a mountain basin, Miss Glory. There's solid rock not too far below the surface. I suspect your pa named his ranch Canyon Rock for a reason. He probably had to blast holes for fence posts and suchlike."

"Well," she said to Peter when they went back outside, "I can understand why nobody's tried to jump this claim yet."

"I drove off four so far."

Maud's derisive snort indicated that she shared Glory's disbelief.

"I did. And I would've kept driving them off until you showed up, on account of I promised your pa I'd try to keep the place open for you as long as I could."

"I . . . I appreciate it, Peter."

Peter smiled modestly over her halfheartedly expressed gratitude. "More jumpers'll be along. The Canyon Rock's a fine place, Miss Glory. The range war's the only thing keeping them away. Once matters cool down, someone'll move in."

A row of sawed-off stumps had been placed alongside the house. Glory imagined that her pa, his wife, and their two children must have sat there on pleasant evenings. The view they afforded was rather spectacular, with the lush Pleasant Valley grass rippling in the breeze, stretching over countless acres clear up to the forbidding face of the Mogollon Rim.

Glory had crossed the Rocky Mountains. She'd been up and down the comparatively gentle swells of the Appalachians and Ozarks more times than she could remember. Every crossing offered some element of danger and provoked plenty of cursing from the roustabouts charged with moving wagons and horses and elephants over land more suited to mountain goats. The Mogollon Mountains couldn't rival the Rockies for size or sheer grandeur, nor did they stretch seemingly without end, as did the Appalachians. But no mountain had ever presented such an impenetrable face as the rim encircling the Canyon Rock Ranch.

Even from this distance, she could understand why her land had proven to be a magnet for sheepmen seeking to gain access to Pleasant Valley. In direct line with the ranch house, a V-shaped crevice split the rim's face. She searched the rim as far as she could see without spotting another passage.

Peter must have noticed where her attention was focused. "It kind of fools you—from here it almost looks like the mountain rim's split in two."

"That's what it looks like to me," said Maud.

"Naw. Actually, the rift starts so far back on the plateau that you can't see the other end from here. It's miles long, and it's sort of a gentle grade from the top of the plateau down to the valley. Tailor-made for goddamned sheep. There're probably two, three out-laws lurking at each end of that passage right now. They keep men posted all the time so's nobody can close it up."

Glory knew then that the rumors were true. Her father's death had been no accident.

She lowered herself onto a stump. Maud followed suit, and then Dante and Peter took up stances in front of her like a pair of twin sentinels, facing the mountain rim with their arms crossed over their chests, as if they feared sheepmen might begin swarming through the crevice at any moment.

Two men, so alike and yet so different. Both tall. Dante's shoulders and upper arms loomed larger, appropriate for a man who claimed to be a world-renowned swordsman. Peter's thighs bulged more, with the strength of a man accustomed to spending the better part of his day on horseback.

Brown hair, both of them. The sun caught bronze highlights from Dante's. Peter's hair turned lighter in the sun, too, with little streaks reminding Glory of the color of sand. Dante's brown eyes burned with the cop-per glints of a half-tamed tiger's. Peter's brown eyes sparkled with lighter flecks that looked sort of like . . . sand. Dante's skin had been baked golden by the sun. Peter's too was tanned from long hours in the saddle, not pale like Glory's but brown like . . . sand.

And now the two of them, so alike, and yet so differ-ent, postured in front of her. Dante, firm and unmove-able, like the Mogollan Mountain rockface. Peter was equally imposing, but he projected the shifting, easily moved nature of a . . . sand dune.

Sand, they said, could erode rock.

It wouldn't surprise her one bit, Glory thought, if Dante and Peter decided to put that theory to the test.

They spoke to each other cordially enough, but so much hostility simmered between them that Mrs. Blue could probably use the sizzling heat to fry one of her sky-colored omelets.

"You're welcome to spend the night at my spread, Miss Glory," Peter offered. "This place ain't fit for cowhands, let alone women."

"Cow *hands.*" Dante cast a snide glance toward Peter's hand.

"No need to go to all that trouble, Peter. The wagon's outfitted for sleeping. We'll do fine there for tonight, and Maud and I can get this place cleaned up so we can sleep in the house tomorrow."

"Tomorrow!" Maud bolted from her stump. "You mean we're going to stay here for more than one night?"

"Of course." Glory blinked her surprise. "Goodness, Maud, we spent almost a week getting here, and you sound as if you'd like to hop back into the wagon and head back to Santa Fe right now."

"That's exactly what I'd like to do. This place gives me the shivers."

"One should always heed the instincts honed by a personage of advanced years," Dante commented, looking immensely pleased by Maud's trepidation.

"Goddamn Bohemian," Maud grumbled.

And then Peter came to Glory's side. Hunkering down next to her, he essentially repeated Dante's sentiment, except he couched it in terms Maud surely found more agreeable. "Miss Maud might have a point there. Pleasant Valley's no place for women."

"What about all the ranchers' wives?"

"They're all gone."

"Dead?" Glory whispered.

"Naw, don't fret about that, Miss Glory. The

ranchers set them up in Holbrook for the time being. Tom Blevans—he's another neighbor down the road apiece—set the example. First him and his missus took in Mrs. Gladden and her young'uns when her man got killed, and then he decided the womenfolk and young'uns'd be better off plumb away from the trouble. He'd be mighty put out with me if I didn't see to it that you followed suit. This whole valley's full of bachelors just now, Miss Glory, and I suspect that missing their womenfolk has something to do with the way things have gotten hotter around here lately."

Birds trilled from nearby trees. The wind sighed through the grass, sending dandelion puffs dancing over the meadows. The sun beat down upon them, hot, but tempered by the breeze. The warmth seeped into Glory's bones, and she shivered, for she knew this was not the sort of heat Peter referred to.

He misread her shiver. "Your ma didn't like it here very much, either."

"My . . . my *mother?*" She had thought he understood that Harry Trask's wife had not been Gloriana's mother. She braced herself to explain the embarrassing truth. "I'm afraid you're mistaken, Peter."

"Naw. Couldn't be two women in the whole world who look more alike than you and your ma. It's how I recognized you right off. 'Course, the circus wagon gave me the first hint." He ducked his head sheepishly.

"You're mistaken," she repeated. "My mother never—"

"I sure hate to disagree with you so soon after making your acquaintance, but she sat right where you're sitting right now, Miss Glory, and she had the shivers just like Miss Maud. Your pa kept saying something like, 'Look around you. Can't you feel it, Katy?' and she'd shake her head and say she'd just shrivel up from boredom and blow away in all this wind."

"When?" The harshness of her whisper caused Dante to bristle, as if he understood that Peter's revelation hurt worse than if he'd plunged a knife into her heart.

"Four years ago or thereabouts. 'Bout six, seven months after Harry lost his wife and young'uns to the cholera. She didn't stay but a few days. The womenfolk around here didn't exactly take to her—I guess on account of they knew how your pa had hankered for her all those years while he was married to his missus. And then your ma showed up, with Mrs. Trask hardly cold in her grave."

Four years earlier Katherine had dispassionately told Gloriana about the epidemic that had wiped out her father's small family. Glory had thought that Katherine would surely race to Harry's side, but she'd never spoken of him again.

They'd been performing in Fort Worth a few weeks later, when Katherine had confided that a minor medical matter required her to spend a week in a Dallas hospital. When Glory announced her intention to come along and tend her, Katherine had refused to allow it, reminding her of their responsibility to the circus.

Katherine had ordered new dresses made and bought new shoes. She'd had her hair restyled to suit a new, flattering hat. She'd made her preparations to leave in such a dither of excitement that Glory had questioned why she approached a hospital stay with such enthusiasm.

"It's a very personal matter that's been plaguing me for years, Gloriana," her mother had said. "You can't imagine what a relief it will be to have the pain . . . resolved . . . one way or another."

Glory had suspected cancer. She'd thought that explained her mother's failure to reconcile with Harry; Katherine wouldn't have wanted him to marry her out of pity. And when Katherine returned from her hospital stay in a state of drooping collapse, when she'd fished her bourbon bottle from her trunk and ordered a dozen more, Glory knew Katherine hadn't found her miracle cure. But she'd never had the chance to discuss it, for despite all Gloriana's pleading and cajoling, Katherine refused to explain. And she'd never again allowed herself to become sober for one single minute.

At dawn, three days after Katherine's return, they had found her crumpled form lying at the edge of Fort Worth's main street. There wasn't much to investigate. The sheriff surmised that during the dark of night she'd wandered drunk into the path of a wagon heading for the Chisholm Trail and that whoever had run Katherine over never even felt the small thump that would have accompanied the striking down of such a slender body.

"It broke your pa up real bad when he heard your ma died so soon after leaving here," Peter remarked quietly. "He'd started building a new house for her, on account of he'd thought this one might've been a little too rough, and that was what had made her run off. I can show you what he got done, if you'd like."

Glory gave him a curt nod. Her throat had clenched too tight for her to speak. Peter spoke so sincerely that she couldn't possibly doubt a word of the tale he'd told, especially since her mother's behavior fit so neatly with the story. She remembered her mother's telling her about her father's whittling beneath the tree—now Glory realized Katherine had been recalling not some little snippet she'd read in a letter but something she'd seen in person.

It was all true. Her mother hadn't gone to a hospital;

she'd come to Pleasant Valley. Katherine had lied to her, and she hadn't loved or trusted Glory enough to let her daughter help heal her broken heart. And to learn of it now, when strangers practically surrounded her! Giving in to the tears that ached to fall would betray that she'd first heard this shattering news from a stranger's lips rather than her own mother's.

Maud's hand closed around hers. Glory looked at her friend, asking her silently: *Did you know?* And Maud, with the familiarity of long friendship, somehow understood, for she denied any knowledge with a quick shake of her head. "Your ma would've wanted you to remember the good times," she said.

Remember the good times? Glory wondered. Remember that loving a man who pursued dreams at odds with his woman's desires had led to ruination and a yawning emptiness that not even a daughter's love could fill?

Such a man stood before her now. An immovable mountain of a man. Solid and impenetrable, with no crevices where a woman might take shelter.

Glory realized then that somewhere deep inside her she had nurtured a faint spark of hope, so deep and so faint that she hadn't dared acknowledge it. She could admit it to herself now, though. She had hoped Dante might change his mind about leaving, that he might have sort of liked the things they'd done at the edge of the Arizona desert enough to stay around and do them again and again—maybe even right there on that ranch, which didn't look so good just then, but which might sparkle and shine if a happy woman was given the chance to apply her dust rags and turn her garish costumes into bright window curtains.

Remember. Perhaps learning her mother's secret at this particular moment had been Katherine Carlisle's final gift to her. Dante sought revenge upon a sorcerer, the hand of a queen, the crown to a kingdom. All Glory had to offer was a weather-beaten three-room ranch house and a piece of land so dangerous that nobody in their right mind would try living on it.

"I guess my pa had his reasons for letting my mother go away," she said.

"And I guess he made a big mistake," said Peter. When Glory turned to him in surprise, he stood and scraped a booted toe against the ground. "If Harry Trask had had a lick of sense, he'd have followed your ma wherever she wanted to go. I know that's what I would do if ever a woman like you was to give me the chance."

There it was—the declaration Glory had always longed to hear. Funny how she'd always thought the vow of commitment would be the important thing, not the man who made it. She stole a peek at Dante. He stared through the open door as if he found the sight of Blizzard and Crystal grazing far more interesting than the tender moment unfolding before him.

Peter's skin flushed, but he tilted his jaw and curled his hands into fists at his sides, as if he meant to punch in the nose anyone who doubted his words.

"That's . . . that's very flattering, Peter," Glory said to bridge the awkward silence that greeted Peter's declaration.

His flush deepened, and her acknowledgment sent his head ducking shyly. He abandoned his belligerent stance. "Aw, hell." He cleared his throat. "I'm just gonna ride out and tell my boys to fan out through the valley, make sure no trouble's on the way. I'll keep them posted at your property lines while you're visiting."

"That's very generous of you, Peter. But I don't think

we'll need them. We're going to spend all day tomorrow cleaning and cooking, and then the next day Mr. Blue's taking us to visit his sacred cave."

"All the more reason to post a guard. You don't want someone riding in and taking you by surprise while you're working in the house. And you sure as hell don't want to leave the place empty—lord only knows what kind of unexpected company might be waiting to greet you. Gosh, it sounds like you're all going on a picnic. I haven't been on a picnic for years."

His wistful comment was so at odds with the warnings he'd been giving that it took Glory a moment to realize he was staring at her expectantly.

"Well," she said with a little laugh to cover her displeasure at being forced to invite him along, "I've imposed upon you so much already. I assume you're probably much too busy with your ranch work to join us when we visit the cave."

"Hell, Miss Glory, wouldn't matter if the President of the United States was planning to call on me. I'd tell him he'd just have to wait on account of I'm going on a picnic with the prettiest lady in the Territory. I'll bring a buckboard so's we can all ride together." He burst into a merry whistle and bounded away toward his horse.

"I too shall leave to assume my duties with the horses," Dante said when Peter left.

Gloriana lifted her hand, meaning to touch his arm and keep him where he was. But something about Dante had altered. An invisible shield seemed to have descended over him, erected to repel anything that came close. She pretended to scratch a nonexistent mosquito bite to cover the movement of her hand.

"Don't go now," she said. "Mr. Blue said his wife

would make us some kind of cornmeal drink. He promised it would be very refreshing."

"I think 'twould be best if I took my refreshment apart from now on."

"Dante—"

"I am . . . in the way here, Gloriana." A darkness settled over him, solidifying his invisible shield.

"I never said that."

"I learned when I was a child that the words need not always be spoken aloud."

She didn't know how he could make such a painful admission in that flat, emotionless tone. It tore at her heart.

"I need you." Her aching throat turned her whisper so faint she couldn't be sure he heard.

He did hear. But instead of keeping him with her, it drove him away. "Your need of me has diminished. Do you not remember what you told me about the manner of man you hoped to find someday?"

If a man really loves a woman, he'd give up everything for her, not the other way around. That's what I'm waiting for, Dante. She could hear herself saying it plain as day.

Dante nodded, as if he heard it, too.

"'Twould appear, Gloriana, that your wait has ended."

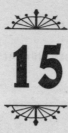

15

Gloriana threw open the wagon door and drew in great gulps of predawn air.

"This place could use a rooster," she declared.

"Mmnph" Maud's inarticulate grumble broke the rhythmic sleeping breathing. "Glory—what on earth? The sun ain't even up yet."

"I know. It's lucky I woke up when I did, or we would've gotten a late start. Mrs. Blue's already making breakfast at the campfire."

Glory left Maud rubbing the sleep from her eyes. She didn't mean to waste a minute of this day. She'd deliberately sought out her Annie Oakley suit with the short split skirt, because she didn't want her movements restricted at all. There was water to fetch and kindling to stack. Why, she could light the kindling she fetched and heat her water all by herself, and use it to scrub the kitchen table. Maybe she'd even tear that stupid animal skin off the window and let sunlight flood the room, so she could see the cobwebs and make sure she knocked down every one.

There were probably countless other chores that went into cleaning a real room. A room where people cooked and ate and conversed and watched the sunrise day after day. A room, one that stayed put and didn't go rattling off on a railroad track. A room that belonged to her and not some fussy Florida boarding-house widow whose face would screw into a prune-faced pucker if Glory dared set a jar of wildflowers on the table.

She'd have to learn what to do, because she'd never cleaned a real room before.

Mrs. Blue helped her once she'd finished with the breakfast, and Maud pitched in, showing a surprising aptitude with a broom. They caused such a ruckus, what with Mrs. Blue's joyful humming and Glory's and Maud's constant laughter, that the borrowed cowboys kept riding past the house long after all the coffee and breakfast had been devoured, like flies buzzing round a well-wrapped dessert cake. Even Mr. Blue ducked in from time to time, shaking his head at their antics, grinning at the grime that rimmed their eyes like raccoon masks. Every man on the place seemed drawn to the feminine gaiety.

Every man except one. Dante apparently intended to hold to his decision to take his meals apart from them. To live apart from them, too, for she had no idea where he'd bedded down for the night.

She vowed not to think about him, but when Mrs. Blue sat her in a chair and gave her what seemed like a full ton of dark sapphire-colored corn to grind between two stone implements, the repetitious task made it hard to keep him from her thoughts. His presence guided her high spirits the way a balloon skin trapped the heated air that made it rise. Containing her out-and-out exuberance, and somehow enabling her to soar. From the beginning, he had emboldened her, shielded her, encouraged her, believed in her. When he carried out his promise to leave, she knew her spirits would sink like a stone. If only he would stay with her, they could fly together, forever.

Maud pulverized a kernel of corn and gave a little grunt of satisfaction. "Are you wondering what it looks like?"

"What what looks like?"

"The house your pa was building for your mother." Maud shook the ground corn onto the discouragingly small heap they'd managed to accumulate. "I'll bet your pa never did a lick of housework after his wife died, so it's no wonder your ma didn't like it when she came to visit. This place ain't so bad now that we've cleaned it up some." She scowled down at the corn, as if it were responsible for her admission that she was growing to like the ranch.

Glory glanced around at the rough walls, the dirt floor, the crude stove. She'd never spent any time in a less welcoming place, nor had she ever felt so much at home. "No, it's not so bad," she agreed. "You gave me an idea, Maudie. I'm going to go out and find that house."

"Durn, I shouldn't have brought it up. Peter promised to show it to you. You shouldn't be going out on your own, what with them murdering sheepmen lurking all over the place."

"I think I'd like to visit by myself, at least for the first time."

"For the last time, if you go and get yourself killed. Make sure you scream good and loud before they cut your throat, so's we know which direction to send the search party to find your body."

"I promise I'll stay in sight of the ranch house."

"Oh, that's a relief. I'll just pull this chair out onto

the front porch so's I have a good seat to watch you get killed."

"Maud!"

"It's plumb stupid for you to go out there, Glory, and you know it." True concern creased Maud's brow. "Honey, take someone with you. Take Dante. He'll keep you safe."

If Maud thought Glory would be safe running off with Dante to some secluded hideaway, then Maud wasn't as worldly as she always claimed to be. Still, there was no stopping the little curl of excitement that wound around her heart at the thought.

"I'll ask him if I see him." She promised herself she'd run straight to Crystal and look neither right nor left. "Don't worry. I won't go past the line the cowboys are patrolling. And I'll turn back if I don't find the house in fifteen minutes."

She spotted Crystal dozing beneath the questionable shade thrown by a spindly-needled pine. Since she couldn't see Blizzard, it meant Dante was out riding guard with the cowboys. At least she wouldn't have to break her promise to Maud.

"Come on, you fat little sweetheart." She stroked Crystal's flank and scratched along the mare's back, surprised by how much the mare's girth had expanded over the past few days. "Dante's been feeding you too much corn. You look like you could use some exercise."

Dante rode into the yard and realized at once that the mare was missing.

He had no chance to inquire about her whereabouts, for Maud came storming from the ranch house, so angry that he would not have been surprised to see a column of steam rising from the top of her head.

"Some bodyguard you are."

Her insult hinted at danger surrounding Gloriana. "I left her with you."

"And what was I supposed to do—hog-tie her like a calf and keep her roped to the kitchen table?"

"If need be. Where is she, Maud?"

"Went off on her own to find that house her pa was building for her mother."

Dante sagged with relief. He'd found the abandoned shell while patrolling and had staked out one corner of it as his sleeping spot until his challenge here had ended. "'Tis not far, and no harm can come to her there. I shall fetch her home."

But he heard the unexpected drum of hooves as he approached the house, and it roused him to a fevered alarm. He nudged Blizzard toward a small grove, intending to approach with stealth, but the stallion's ears pricked and he nickered with comfortable satisfaction, easing some of Dante's worry.

"'Tis your lady approaching, eh, Blizzard Sweetzel Darling?" Dante whispered. He patted the stallion's silky neck and smiled when Blizzard tossed his head as though he'd understood. "Mine as well." It felt good to admit it aloud, even if only to a horse.

The hoofbeats continued to thud, but Gloriana and Crystal did not ride into view. Dante pressed his knees into Blizzard's sides, urging him forward. And what he saw almost made him wish that Hash Knife cowboys had captured Gloriana, for she surely would be safer with them than she was at that moment.

Crystal, with no apparent guidance, cantered along the rim of a huge newly trampled circle in the front yard of the unfinished house. Perched on the mare's smooth rump was Gloriana. Standing. Shoeless, and with her hair unbound, she posed with her arms open at her sides, her face lifted toward the sun, her eyes closed against its glare.

Her hair streamed behind her, richer and more luxuriant than a cloth-of-gold pennant heralding a royal presence. The wind, and the motion created by Crystal's endless cantering, plastered Gloriana's short garment against her skin, outlining the proud thrust of her breasts, the narrow curve of her waist, the soft swell of her hips. Her body seemed in perfect accord with Crystal's rhythm; though she appeared not to move, he could see the occasional slight tensing of a calf muscle, a compensating shift of a hip.

She looked like a goddess, graceful and splendid and blessed with unearthly beauty. Like a star coursing through the universe, burning brightly beyond any mortal man's reach.

She must have felt his regard, for when Crystal's circle carried them toward Dante, Gloriana opened her eyes. And she smiled at him.

Blizzard quivered beneath him, and then, sensing Dante's momentary lapse of control, the stallion leaped toward his mare.

Crystal never broke stride. Blizzard matched her pace, and the two horses circled as one. So smoothly did the Arabians stride that Dante found himself tempted to clamber to his feet atop Blizzard's rump. 'Twould be beyond magnificent to clasp Gloriana's hand in his and raise their joint fist high in victory while the Arabians circled until the end of time.

He felt Gloriana's hand against his shoulder and then a brief tensing as she paused, judging the horses' movements. A moment later she leaped onto Blizzard's back. She caught hold of Dante's waist, surrounding him with her slender limbs and silken hair and the scent of sun-warmed lavender.

She pressed her face against his back and tightened her arms around his belly. Laughing. Laughing with delight, her breath warm through the cloth of his shirt, burrowing her way ever deeper into his heart.

The horses slowed and then stopped. Dante clasped his hand over Gloriana's, claiming her and all her flaring brightness, if only for this moment.

"It's been too long since I've done this," she murmured. "I'll have to do it more often, or we'll get out of practice."

He tightened his grip upon her hand.

To his dismay she worked herself free and unwrapped her wondrously delicate limbs from around his hips and waist. She slid from Blizzard's back and gazed up at Dante, her eyes still alight with exhilaration.

"I could teach you, if you'd like."

"Teach me?"

"It's easier than it looks. Crystal deserves all the credit. Blizzard too, if you want to try. Mr. Fontanescue had them both very well trained before deciding they weren't suited to the arena."

He could not shift position at all, lest he shame himself and embarrass her with the evidence of how her ride had affected him. "I did not realize you performed riding stunts with the circus."

"Oh, I'm not nearly good enough for that—I just picked up the basics. There's lots of hours to fill between performances, so we're always teaching each other tricks. It passes the time, and it lets us help each other rehearse."

He remembered her apprehension at spending the night away from her circus companions. Here was more evidence of her dependence upon them. The realization did much to relieve his desire, but he still did not trust his body not to betray him. Circus folk were not the only ones in need of ways to pass time. He sought to prolong their conversation. "What is the most important requirement in mastering this trick?"

"A partner you can trust with your life."

"As you have entrusted me with yours, Gloriana?"

Gloriana had been talking about horses. About the wordless bond that connected a well-trained mount to its rider, enabling the rider to anticipate the horse's moves; about the loyal devotion that kept the horse on course when loud noises and distractions could cause it to shy and send its rider tumbling to her death.

Dante stared down at her. She shivered. His coppery brown gaze so easily pierced the practiced facade that satisfied other men . . . the facade she despised because it was all a lie. Dante bored right through it as if that facade didn't exist, going straight to her heart, and she reveled in the thought of baring her heart for him, only him.

Exhilaration gripped her. Here, on this ranch, she could take pleasure in her accomplishments without other people demanding the right to watch. Crystal could enjoy whatever horsy pleasure she seemed to take in working with Glory without being terrified by a liquored-up cowboy who thought his two-bit admission fee entitled him to shoot pistols to show his approval. Dante had watched her standing on the back of the circling mare, but not with the lecherous, slack-jawed stare that always sent revulsion coursing through her. He'd been afraid—for Gloriana. And when her skill became apparent, that fear had shifted into pride—for Gloriana.

His hand rested on his thigh. She slipped hers

beneath it and caught her breath at the way his muscles bunched in response and the immediate tightening of his hand around hers.

"I trust you more than I trust myself," she said.

"You should not."

He slid from the horse and enfolded her within his embrace. It wasn't enough. She wanted to be closer. She worked her toes into the earth and added its force to her own as she nestled against his heart, until she could feel his pulse pounding in time with her own. It still wasn't enough.

"You would not trust me," he murmured against her hair, "if you knew the thoughts consuming me just now."

She levered her hips against his, and there was no need for him to explain what he was thinking, nor for her to tell him that her own thoughts were in accord with his.

He led her across the weathered floorboards and through the skeletal frame of her father's unfinished house. To the back of the house, to a room she knew in her heart was meant to be a bedroom. She saw the neat pile of bedding, the metal breastplate, the acorn hat, all arranged with a soldier's orderly precision.

She wanted to mess it all up, destroy any hint that this was but a temporary resting place for him. She wanted to kick the breastplate and helmet into the weed-choked grass, where they would rust into nothing, and shred the puffy pants and embroidered shirt into such tiny strips that birds would carry them away to weave into their nests. She longed to tear the thong from Dante's hair, pull him down with her onto his pallet, and do unmentionable, exciting things to him, with him, in broad daylight, until the sweet sun-dried grass pallet burst at the seams and all trace of the time-traveling soldier dissolved, leaving only the half-tamed tiger of a man in her arms.

And so she did.

His head snapped back in surprise when she booted the chest armor out of the house. His lips quirked with barely contained amusement when the cabassat followed. By the time she got to shredding his old clothes, he quivered with a delighted anticipation that made her fingers ache to touch him, which completely destroyed her clothes-tearing abilities. Or maybe it was just that the cloth woven by those long-ago tailors simply proved more resistant, because she couldn't tear off a single strip. He caught his old garments away from her and crushed her hand against his shirt-front.

"Try this one," he whispered into her ear.

She splayed her hands across his abdomen, testing the strength of the stout homespun, craving the feel of the strong muscles surging beneath it. Simple unbuttoning won over the uncertainties of ripping, and she made quick work of the buttons, shuddering with delight when her fingers delved through the opening and traced heated tracks across his belly, around his sides, along his belt, and lower.

"God's blood, Gloriana," he whispered. He threw his head back and drew long, quaking breaths while she pressed her tongue against the line bisecting his chest and buried her face against the silken curls, breathing in his scent and knowing that it alone could set her aflame.

"Dante," she whispered. "Dante Trevani."

Her half-tamed tiger lost all restraint.

They did destroy the straw pallet.

But not before Gloriana whispered his name a dozen times more. Not until he surged within her and brought her again and again to such sweet, melting pleasure that she cried out from the exquisite agony of it.

He caught her head between his hands and demanded, "Do not close your eyes, Gloriana. Look at me. Look at *me*."

She looked, scarcely breathing while his belly slid against hers and his thrusts claimed her as his. She trembled again from an inner bursting warmth that struck higher, at her heart, and from seeing Dante's potent pleasure blur into an expression of utter belonging, as if he had found in her the one place in all eternity where he was meant to be. She understood his emotions so completely because they precisely matched the feelings sweeping through her. In Dante's arms she felt like a queen.

The very sky seemed to celebrate their joining, shifting from purest azure to a majestic purple shot with the sun's golden rays. The colors hung about Dante's shoulders like a royal mantle. Purple and gold . . . the colors of kings.

A woman who loved such a man, truly loved him, would not demand that he spend his days garbed in black homespun.

And she loved him. Oh, God, how she loved him, with an intensity that made her lifelong dreams seem pitiful and childish.

He slept afterward, and at first she feared she might not be able to break free of his embrace without waking him. But long hours of sentry duty had taken their toll on him. Or perhaps he didn't want to hold on to her—after all, it was she who had instigated their passion, knowing all the while that nothing had changed between them. He had made no promises, given no indication that he'd changed his mind about traveling back through time. He'd even removed himself from their small circle, taking his meals alone, claiming this remote sleeping place, as if he'd already begun to disappear from her life. And because she loved him, she must help him go.

He slept so deeply that Crystal's muffled hoofbeats did not make him stir. As she rode away Gloriana dashed the tears from her eyes and swore that she would send him back to his own time as soon as she could, because she never wanted to cry over Dante Trevani, ever again.

This time when Dante rode into the yard, Maud greeted him with scorn rather than worry.

"I wish I'd have paid you a wage, just so's I'd have the pleasure of asking you for my money back. I declare, this is the last time I hire a Bohemian bodyguard."

"I swear to you, Maud, that no man could have guarded her more closely." Curse his body's weakness! Sleep, the enemy of every soldier, had cost him the most important battle of his life.

"Well, I guess I ain't all that mad at you, considering she's probably safe."

"Where is she?"

"Went off with that Peter Henley fella."

Dante had never counted himself a jealous man. And truly, jealousy was but a weak echo of the pure, raw, violent need to reclaim what belonged to him that shot through him at Maud's words. "Went off?"

"Yeah, he brought some fancy two-seater and high-stepping horse. Saved me a headache, too, when they finally drove away. The two of them were yakking so much, you'd think they were direct descendants of that blabby old Miss Hampson we met on the train."

Dante knew Gloriana loved surrounding herself with companions. She had been the one to welcome Miss Hampson. She had missed her circus friends while they traveled from Holbrook. She pined for the friendly lessons taught by her fellow performers. And it seemed Gloriana craved cordial companionship so much that she had left his arms to go driving with another man, to go yakking with Peter Henley.

Dante realized that he barely spoke in her presence, but he could not see that he would ever change much. Talking was always the furthest thing from his mind when he was with Gloriana. No matter how much he might wish it, a man who had spent all his life guarding every word could not suddenly begin spilling his beans. Had he been able to express himself more freely, Gloriana would already know the feelings in his heart.

"Well, durn, they're back already. Hold on to your ears."

They were chatting, Gloriana and the man who had already vowed he would give up everything for her. Gloriana leaned toward Peter, appearing to hunger for every word that fell from his lips. Peter caught sight of Dante and paused in midsentence, and Gloriana swiveled her head to see what had taken his attention away from her.

She lowered her eyes to her lap and blushed. But she made no other acknowledgment of what had gone between them. The lowering of her eyes could well hide regret or satisfaction, her blush be nothing more than the mark of shame or delight.

That warm glow might have burned within him, for Dante's blood boiled through his veins like liquid glass bubbling through a glassblower's tube. Whether from shame or delight, she blushed for *him*. The wind lifted a tendril of her hair; he saw a bit of straw entangled in it and knew the straw had come from his own pallet. A true gentleman would master his raging pride and greet them with a pleasant smile. But Dante Trevani was no true gentleman, and Gloriana had known that from the very beginning. He told himself that he need not feel guilty, then, for the way his body betrayed him, surging and swelling at the sight of her, no matter that she sat alongside another man. He clenched his hands into fists and dug his feet into the ground lest he leap across the few feet separating them and claim her right in front of everyone, or kill Peter Henley without provocation.

Since he could do neither, he spun on his heel and sought the shelter of the barn.

Henley followed him a short time later. He approached Dante, slapping his driving gloves against the palm of his hand the way a courtier from Dante's own time might approach an opponent to declare a duel.

"I just want to ask you, man to man, whether you got any claim staked here."

They both knew Henley did not speak of lands.

I have laid claim to some part of her heart, as she has to all of mine. Dante's male pride demanded recognition; he ached to flaunt his possession of Gloriana. Doing so could destroy Henley's interest.

But Gloriana had left Dante's bed to turn to Henley.

"Gloriana must have explained our relationship to you."

"She said you're leaving any time now for London, England. Says you got yourself a fiancée waiting for you there. Says you're just working for her to earn your transportation."

Not a hint from Gloriana that they might have become more than employer and employee. It was odd how hearing his presence explained in a few brief sentences diminished the riches he thought he had found. "That is all true."

Henley let a small sigh of relief escape. "Well, good. Then I guess you and I won't be getting in each other's way."

"You intend to pursue her."

"Pursue her? Hell, I intend to slide a wedding ring on that gal's finger."

"You barely know her."

"Have you taken a look at her, Trevani? A *good* look at her?"

Dante had done little but fill his vision with Gloriana from the moment he had found her. He had studied her in lantern glow, savored her in moonlight, loved her in sunshine. "Aye." It came out with a quiver of longing, which he hurried to cover. "She is a beautiful woman. But there is more to her than beauty."

"I'll say. She's rich and talented, and the man who latches on to her won't have to brand another calf for as long as he lives."

"You mean to use her." Rage suffused him again. To think that Gloriana had longed all her life to find a man who would give up everything for her, only to find him clinging to her like a barnacle to the hull of a ship!

"No, I can pull my own weight. I'm thinking of becoming her manager, sort of like the way Butler manages Oakley." When Dante cocked his head in confusion, Henley added, "Frank Butler and Annie Oakley."

"I do not know those people."

Henley gaped. "I didn't think there was a person in this world who hadn't heard about Annie Oakley's stage act."

But I am not of this world, Dante thought. "You are a rancher, not a stage act manager."

"Ranching's damn hard work. I wouldn't mind taking off for a spell and lazing around the circus with Miss Glory."

"Gloriana's work is very difficult."

Henley snorted. "What, strutting her bosoms in front of a crowd?"

Dante forcibly held himself in check. How could Henley have spent any amount of time with Gloriana and not noted the tiny ways in which she betrayed her hatred of her work or the toll it exacted upon her spirit? "I do not believe you appreciate her."

"Hell, I'll appreciate her every day. Twice a day if she'll let me." And this time it was pure jealousy that surged through Dante at the anticipation lighting Henley's face. "I'll be one grateful sumbitch, I'll tell you. By hitching up with her, I'll go from Peter Henley, common-as-mud rancher, to Mr. Gloriana Carlisle, husband of a star. You'd damn well better believe I'll appreciate her for that."

"'Twould break her heart if she ever learned you married her for purely mercenary reasons."

Henley compressed his lips with exasperation. "I don't think I'm getting through to you. So what if I'm not in love with her at this very minute? She's beautiful. I can't wait to get her into my bed. I'll be forever grateful for what she can do for me. Hell, those are damned good reasons for getting married—folks did it all the time in the olden days."

As Dante himself meant to do.

"Who's to say love won't come along?" Henley continued. "I'll be doing my best to see that it does. I'll treasure her, Trevani, and follow her around so long as she has this urge to perform in the circus. And if she ever tires of it, we can come right back here. She'll have the best of both worlds with me. You have my word on it."

Dante could summon no further objections, not when his own situation so closely mirrored Henley's intent. Dante had seen Elizabeth only once, when she was six years old, and had spent no time at all in her presence compared to Henley's acquaintance with Gloriana. Dante could not even claim to be drawn to Elizabeth by her beauty or by a desire to bed her, as Henley could. Dante meant to marry Elizabeth Tudor for the most mercenary of reasons: because marriage to her would bring about riches and respect. That was exactly what Henley sought through a marriage with Gloriana.

Henley would treasure Gloriana. Dante would endure Elizabeth.

And still he wanted to drive away Gloriana's suitor.

Gloriana deserved better, much better. She should have a man who would love her without reservation . . . the way he, Dante Alberto Trevani, loved her.

The realization shuddered through him. He, of all men, would make the worst possible husband for Gloriana Carlisle the star. Never would he permit her as his wife to strut about the circus ring and show off her bosoms. He would chip every inch of the portraits from her wagon, for he could not bear to think of another man gazing at them with lustful intent. He would keep Gloriana close by his side, filling her slender belly with his babies again and again, and any man who dared call him Mr. Gloriana Carlisle would find his throat skewered at the end of Dante's conquistador sword.

Henley had retreated to the barn door while Dante had been lost in his thoughts. "So, tomorrow we're going on a picnic to see that cave your Mr. Blue seems so keen on showing us. My men'll stay on to keep watch over the place, if you care to join us."

The arrogance of the man, to insinuate himself into Gloriana's life and make Dante's presence superfluous.

"I am her bodyguard. I shall watch over her until she bids me stop."

"Maybe you won't want to watch too close tomorrow, if you know what I mean."

If Henley had leered or expressed any disrespectful intent, Dante would have gladly charged across the barn and smashed him into the wall. But Peter Henley merely blinked with the bewildered expression of a man who unexpectedly found himself falling in love. He left with a sappy smile curling his lips.

And Dante stayed where he was, wondering how he had ever come to crave the position of royal consort. Wondering how he could have willingly—nay eagerly—condemned himself to stand by impotently, watching his wife accept the accolades of her subjects, while men called him Mr. Elizabeth Tudor behind his back.

16

The wind blew without pause in Pleasant Valley, almost as though it had been trapped since the beginning of time within the bowl-shaped depression and had been searching ever since for a means of escape. It whistled against the mountain rim, rustled from the trees, and filled the air with a haunting Arizona melody unlike anything Dante had ever heard, especially with Mrs. Blue humming in celestial harmony with the sound.

"My people lived and died across all of this land." Dante followed Mr. Blue's sweeping gesture, which seemed to encompass the entire Arizona Territory. "Not just the mesas where we live now, but all of it. The Hopi still hold sacred the places of our ancestors. My charge is this cave." He gestured toward a particularly lush growth of mesquite. Without Mr. Blue's direction, Dante would have taken the dark background for heavy shade and not the opening of a cave.

"Never knew the sumbitch was there." Despite gaining this new knowledge, Peter yawned, as though bored by Mr. Blue's tale.

Peter and Gloriana sat upon the driver's bench of the exceptionally uncomfortable conveyance Peter had called a buckboard. The rest of them had crammed into the wagon bed, which had jolted their spines and jarred their teeth over every inch between Gloriana's house and this place near the base of the mountain rim. Mesquite trees and yucca flourished, proving that at this point the mountain had not yet hardened into the impenetrable face that loomed above them.

"The path to the cave poses no danger," Mr. Blue said. "The women can use the low-growing branches as handholds."

"Hell, let's just us men go," said Peter. "There ain't no need for the women to haul themselves clear up there just so's they can drag their skirts through some dirty old cave."

Mr. Blue's usually impassive face crumpled with disappointment. Mrs. Blue's humming took on a high, keening edge, the impossible sound of wind suffering pain.

Dante struggled, as he had since the ride began, with the urge to leap onto the driver's bench and bury his fist in Peter Henley's stomach, but this time so he might remove that superior smirk from the rancher's face. He was saved the trouble by Gloriana, who cast the swine a reproachful look that sent the edges of his lips drooping. She turned and placed a gentle hand upon Mr. Blue's shoulder.

"I'm looking forward to seeing that cave, Mr. Blue."

"So'm I," said Maud. She hopped from the buckboard, rubbing her posterior.

The path proved as easily navigable as Mr. Blue had promised, and it proclaimed the sacredness of the place they were to visit: Only God could have crafted the narrow stone ledge that provided easy footing and yet would never betray tracks, and only He could have grown greenery that held to its place without overgrowing the passage, that bowed round the sides and met over the top, so that anyone passing along the path would be completely shielded from a watcher's eyes.

At the mouth of the cave the wind blew sweet and cool, as if the cave itself might be the source of Pleasant Valley's constant breeze.

"Come," said Mr. Blue. "I will show you."

Evidence abounded of careful tending that had gone on for centuries. The stone floor, the stone walls, had been faithfully, lovingly swept free of debris until their surfaces shone almost like polished glass. Candles had been wedged into small crevices, but they were not needed on this day, for sunlight poured through a slim shaft piercing the roof.

The light flooding the small space illuminated for Dante the face of a ghost. For lying in stately repose upon a tilted rock shelf rested the mummified corpse of a conquistador.

The others in their group caught sight of the corpse at the same time. To the women's credit, none uttered more than a stifled gasp. Peter muttered a curse beneath his breath.

"I can think of better ways to work up my appetite for our picnic. I'll wait outside."

Dante found himself moving forward upon legs that felt as rigid as those of the mummy before him.

The wind moaned through the cave, cool and dry, dispelling rust and rot. Mr. Blue's Hopi ancestors had kept animals at bay. In any other place, Dante knew, dampness and burrowing vermin would have long ago destroyed all trace of the man resting before him.

The conquistador's metal breastplate, so like his own, marked him as a soldier who had marched for Francisco Vásquez de Coronado. Only his garments showed the ravages of time. Shreds of the ruined cloth fluttered in the breeze, their colors dimmed by the centuries but still vivid enough to remind Dante of the splendid display Coronado's forces had made when they departed for New Spain.

"I might have known him," Dante whispered, sinking to his knees. "I might have waved when his ship sailed from port."

"Look, Dante, there's an acorn hat like yours." Maud pointed to a ledge above the conquistador's head.

An empty scabbard rested there as well, and Dante knew that the sword he now carried had come from this sacred cave. He lifted the scabbard and studied its intricate carving but could find no hint of the conquistador's identity.

It could well be me, Dante realized with a sudden lurching of his heart. If his betrothal with Elizabeth had not demanded his presence in England, he would have sailed with his hero, Coronado, to explore New Spain.

"Why did you give me the sword?" he asked Mr. Blue, his voice gruff from the effort of hiding his inner turmoil.

"The Hopi have many legends. One is that when my people crawled from the underworld to live upon Mother Earth, a white brother came along with us. We called him *bahana,* for he was a being of supernatural wisdom. The *bahana* left us but promised to return and become our great leader. That is why we welcomed you when first your people came. We were wrong. The *bahana* was not among the conquistadors, but we have never stopped hoping our white brother will return. I wonder if you could be the man we seek."

Dante's dry, humorless laugh was caught by the breeze. "I possess no wisdom whatsoever, Mr. Blue. And I can barely lead myself through a difficult pass, let alone guide an entire people."

So what, then, was he doing hankering after a kingdom to rule?

Mr. Blue seemed unperturbed by Dante's listing of his shortcomings. Mrs. Blue's humming shifted into a sprightly lilt, and Dante recognized a soldier's march from his own day.

"I know that song," he said.

"My wife will teach it to another, as it was taught to her and to others before her."

Gloriana knelt next to him. With heartbreaking gentleness she smoothed the shreds of a cuff over the husk that had been the conquistador's hand. Her flesh, so smooth and warm and lovely, pulsed with life against the leathery remains. Dante reeled, so stunned by the contrast that he almost lost his balance.

In a few days, a week at most, Gloriana's beautiful hand would send him back to the past, where he would live out his days ere she was ever born. After that, Peter Henley might take hold of that beautiful hand with his own, and Dante would have no hand to stop him, for his life would have been long spent, and his remains would not be nearly as substantial as those lying before him.

But . . . he would have married Elizabeth Tudor and earned his place in history as her royal consort.

Gloriana did not read history, he knew. And so what did it matter if hundreds, even thousands, knew of the honor and respect he had attained, if Gloriana remembered him only as a man who'd chosen another woman above her?

Her lush lips moved with a silent prayer. Her wondrous eyes gazed upon the fallen conquistador with reverence, sorrow, and pity for a man who had ended his days apart from those he had loved. Dante always thought Gloriana's lips beautiful but preferred them swollen from his kisses, as well as her eyes dreamy with passion and her hair wild and free, forming a silken curtain of molten gold and red. A dead man could not ignite Gloriana's flames.

"Mr. Blue," she asked, "would it be all right if Maud and I picked flowers for him?"

"You honor my people's traditions." Mr. Blue inclined his head in a perfect if unconscious imitation of the courtiers crowding Charles V's court.

Would Gloriana someday gather flowers for Dante's grave? Nay, she would not—for he would rest far across the sea, where she would never go to seek out a marker that would be so ravaged by time that his name might not even be legible.

Despite the constant cool breeze, Dante found himself suddenly unable to breathe. "I shall wait outside."

He found a sun-drenched rock out of sight of both cave and buckboard and sat. He braced his wrists atop his knees and let his gaze sweep the basin formed by valley and mountain rim. He had never considered himself a man given to fancy, but with no effort at all he could imagine those flat acres dotted with cavorting white foals, all Blizzard's get. Those born of Crystal would be pure-blooded Arabians, the horses of kings. Mares of the quality shown by Henley's mounts would produce magnificent offspring as well.

During the seemingly endless buckboard ride, Henley had remarked that he'd captured wild horses to start his herd, horses he claimed were descended from those left behind by the Spaniards who had visited these lands centuries ago. They might have been the horses of the conquistador who slept in Mr. Blue's sacred cave. The stallion Dante had left behind at Mortlake might have sired the ancestors of the wild horses running through this land. Dante might be reclaiming a bit of his own property by rounding up a score of mares for Blizzard. A man could take pride in building such a herd.

He tore his thoughts away from that fruitless direction and wondered at the force that had caused the cleft in the mountain rim. In his own land, Mt. Vesuvius had wreaked similar havoc. Here he saw no smoldering volcano capable of cleaving mountains in two. Nay, that cleft had been caused by the Creator's capricious whim, exactly as Dante found himself caught here, all but split asunder by the desires that tugged him in opposite directions.

He did not know how long he sat in the meadow, phantom foals frolicking across it in his mind, until Gloriana came to him with her hair streaming in the breeze and her arms filled with flowers.

"Mr. Blue will guide you back to the cave," Dante said.

She sent him a mischievous smile. "I've already been there. These are for you." And she dumped her armload over his head, showering him with white and yellow blossoms. "That's better. You were looking far too glum."

Glum—ha! If she but knew the murky pit of melancholy threatening to drown him . . . It was difficult to maintain a woeful countenance, though, with a daisy tickling his nose, with Gloriana sitting next to him and the light once more dancing in her eyes.

He tossed his head, his hair whipping about him like Blizzard's mane when the stallion gave himself a hearty shake. The motion dislodged petals and blossoms and leaves and sent them pelting Gloriana. She laughed, making halfhearted protests, while flowers clung to her hair and to the soft cotton of her dress. A creamy white petal balanced precariously atop the curve of her breast. Dante blindly reached about him, gathering flowers into a posy, to keep his hands from taking that daring petal's place.

"Peter was right," she said. "This place isn't so bad."

"You like it here?" Dante kept his voice carefully neutral.

"Why, I believe I do." She seemed startled by her own pronouncement. "But that's probably because it's so different."

"Aye. Probably."

"And because I'll only be here for a short while."

As would he. "So you have told me time and again."

For something to occupy his hands, he began working a daisy chain. He wondered if she would be surprised to know that his fencing master had forced that female task upon his outraged male charges, claiming the deft touch it required kept one's hands limber. Curse his thoughts! Even such an innocent memory taunted him with a reminder of the way Gloriana's hands had felt upon him, so gentle and limber that she might have spent every moment of her life weaving daisy chains.

"Anyway, what I wanted to say is that I can tell you're anxious to be on your way."

A fragile stem snapped. Dante chose another.

"So if you'd like, we can try that mirror trick this afternoon."

"We will try the mirror trick when you are safely away from this place."

"Well, I might be sticking around here a little longer than I'd originally planned." A delicate shade of rose blossomed above her cheeks.

"You have found pleasant company here."

"Yes . . . yes, I have." The blush deepened, confirming Dante's suspicions that her thoughts dwelled upon Peter Henley. "It turned out to be a good thing after all that you made me buy so much food in Holbrook. Mrs. Blue promised she'd teach me how to cook."

"She spoke to you?"

"Not exactly. I sort of asked her, and she sort of hummed something that sounded like yes."

So she would have him postpone his destiny—and her own—while she learned the art of blue cookery. He did not believe it was sufficient to explain her dallying. "I thought your presence was required at the circus. I did not realize we had time to squander upon acquiring such a dubious skill."

"Oh, I don't intend for you to squander *your* time. Peter said he'd be happy to take over your bodyguard duties. He said he'd keep his men patrolling my boundary lines, too."

Dante mangled a blossom until its juices trickled over his fingers. Of course Peter would stand guard while she flipped blue pancakes and stirred blue oatmeal. Peter would cheerfully follow wherever Gloriana's whims led, and she would no doubt smile at him with every flip and stir. It was what she'd been waiting for, after all.

"You would feel safer with him than with me?"

"In some ways," she whispered.

He ached to take her slender waist between his hands and draw her against him, longed to kiss away the flower petals and undo her buttons and run his lips over her sun-warmed flesh. The agony in his loins demanded that he act upon his desires. The agony in his heart told him he dared not. With her own lips she had freed him of his promise, had confirmed that she had entrusted herself to the care of another man. He had no reason to stay.

He wove the daisy chain into a circlet and settled it on the wind-teased riot of Gloriana's hair. With little time left, with no money, there was no other gift he could give her. She touched it and traced its shape. Tears shimmered in her eyes.

"A crown?"

"Aye. *Per la regina il mio cuore,*" he murmured.

"What . . . what did you say?"

For the queen of my heart, he had said to the woman who could never be his.

"I am sorry. My excitement over your proposal caused me to lapse into my native Italian."

She did not notice that he had not translated his lapse.

"You're an Italian?"

"An Italian. Not a Bohemian trapeze artiste, nor a big old light bulb," he agreed with a bittersweet smile.

She touched her flower crown again, and it was as if the daisy's soft petal roused her to a fury.

"And I'm a circus illusionist, not the goddamn queen of England, so don't try pretending I'm someone else." She tore the daisy circlet from her head and stared at it with utter loathing before flinging it away. She stumbled away from him, threatening to break his heart with the despair her movement conveyed.

"Gloriana!" He bolted to his feet but had not taken one step in her direction before the mountain rim began echoing with the sharp cracks of gunfire. Blizzard's furious scream rang distantly from across the valley.

Henley thundered past, mounted upon one of the horses that had drawn the buckboard and leading the other. The harnesses jingled, the wagon leads trailed in the grass; he had not paused even to strip the gear away. Dante could not fault the man's instant response to the threat of danger. "Follow me! Sounds like the ranch house is under attack!" Peter shouted as he pounded past tossing the spare horse's reins at Dante's feet.

With two quick bounds, Dante gained Gloriana's side and gripped her shoulders hard. "Take Maud and the Blues. Go to the cave. Stay there until I come for you."

"But you haven't practiced much with that gun "

"I have my sword. Wait for me."

"But riding across the valley's dangerous. You'll be an open target for anyone."

"Gloriana, do as I say!"

She stiffened at his command, which he'd roared in the same tone that served to frighten reluctant soldiers into battle.

"Gloriana, I . . ." He shook his head and traced her determined chin with a finger that trembled both from the delight of touching her and with the battle lust raging through his blood. "Please go. You must know I would not take my leave of you in this way. But you show a distressing tendency for wandering, and I cannot fight at my best if I am consumed with worry that you might blunder into the fray."

"Dante?"

His warrior's instincts clamored, demanding that he leave so he might defend her. But when he looked and saw that she'd pressed her fingers against the spot he'd just touched, he found himself momentarily rooted in place. "Aye, Gloriana?"

"It's just a ranch. It's not a kingdom."

"I am finding," he said slowly, "that kingdoms are not the only things worth fighting for."

Glory hadn't known that a person could cry the way she found herself crying. Just sitting there with her back propped against the cave's smooth stone wall, and with nary a sniff or a whimper, her eyes dripped so many tears that she could probably have filled an elephant's water bucket.

The gun battle had raged for hours, it had seemed, until she would have traded her soul for a moment's silence. But silence had descended at least fifteen minutes before. Not one of the four of them had said anything stupid, such as "Well, I guess it's over" or "We should know anytime now." Each minute that crawled by made it less likely that the victors were the ones who knew that two circus women and two Indians hid in this cave, waiting.

Waiting for Dante.

Glory supposed that it went to prove she was a terrible person, but she couldn't summon more than a tiny bit of worry over Peter. He'd watched over the Canyon Rock Ranch for her before he even knew her, and he'd charged into a battle raging over *her* land without a second thought. He'd spent hours talking to her about her father, and, like a true gentleman, he had never questioned her distraction while she used that buggy ride to come to terms with giving up Dante. She owed Peter a debt of gratitude, but she couldn't even remember at that minute what he looked like. Sand, she supposed, which might explain why she found it so hard to fret about him. Nothing bad ever happened to sand. You could kick it, explode it from cannon shells, even shovel it into lion cages for the large cats to use and claw through, and each little grain survived intact.

Her mind was completely filled with the image of

Dante, her dark lover, bent low over the black buck-board horse's back as they raced across the valley. The sun struck bronze highlights from his hair and flashed silver against the ancient sword belted at his side. Bronze and black—the colors of a tiger charging any interloper that dared breach its den. Dante, her tiger, her mountain of a man. She had only to peek through the cave entrance, toward the rift in the Mogollon Rim, to know what happened when mountains stood against a superior force.

The cave, and its sleeping secret, confirmed beyond a doubt that everything Dante had claimed was true. She now knew also that he had somehow been sent journeying through time in order to bring her to this place, to make her fall in love. There was a purpose in it, a divine plan of some sort, but she couldn't figure it out while worry consumed her.

Maybe she'd never figure it out. Some things were beyond anyone's understanding.

"Ahoy!" someone called from outside. "Ahoy in the cave!"

"Oh, God, now we're under attack by sailors." Maud huddled close to Glory.

A piercing whistle, rather like the one Captain Spaniel used to send his dogs dancing through the ring, came next. It didn't sound threatening. Maud rolled her eyes.

Moments later Peter Henley burst through the entrance to the cave. "I hope you heard my warnings. I didn't want to just bust in and scare you." He lunged toward Gloriana and hauled her against his chest. He mashed her so tightly that she could barely squeak a protest or ask the question closest to her heart: *Where's Dante?*

"How bad was it?" asked Mr. Blue.

"Bad." While Glory gasped for breath and struggled in a vain attempt to break his hold, Peter pressed his forehead against the top of her head, where Dante's crown had rested. "Lost two men," he mumbled into her hair.

Dante. Grief struck her so suddenly that it sapped every drop of strength from her bones. Her collapse caught Peter by surprise, and so she escaped his cloying hold.

"He promised me he wouldn't . . . wouldn't take his leave this way. He *promised.*"

"Who promised, Miss Glory?"

"Dante."

"Oh." She glimpsed a brief flicker of pain dart through Peter's expression, and she knew she'd been wrong about nothing hurting sand. "Trevani's okay. Though I think he might've hurt his hand some when he bashed that sword against . . . Well, anyway, he said you'd hired him on at first to tend to your horses, so he stayed behind to take care of the mare."

"Did Crystal get hurt?" Oh, she ached for her mare, but it was amazing how hearing that Dante had chosen to stay with the horses rather than come back for her had strengthened her bones and steadied her voice. He had chosen to stay with the horses. She had no business worrying about him, aching for him. His absence made that clear.

"The mare spooked when those damned Hash Knife boys started shooting."

"She's afraid of gunfire."

"Well, damn them to hell and back. Your mare's been bred, Miss Glory, and they spooked her so bad she might abort."

Glory could only stare at him wordlessly, consumed by equal measures of shame for so easily doubting Dante's motives and of worry for her beloved mare.

"Best I can figure, the Hash Knife crowd heard you'd moved in and decided to scare you off. They set fire to the granary. The gear we found lying near the barn tells me they meant to burn that next, but they must've caught sight of your horses inside and their minds turned to rustling instead of burning. Those're damn fine horses, Miss Glory. Anyway, by the time the stallion started defending himself, the boys I left to guard your place must've woke up from their naps and helped him put up a little bit of a fight." Peter appeared embarrassed and disgusted by the failure of his men.

"Take me to him. I have to be with him." The hurt surfaced again in Peter's eyes, and though Glory could not call back her words, she did her best to temper his pain. "Crystal barely knows Dante. She might fare better if I'm there to help him take care of her."

17

Dante felt the subtle shift in the air when Gloriana entered the barn. With effort he maintained his casual sprawl against a pile of feed sacks. "Missus Crystal zee," Dante said, murmuring the nonsense name, "your mistress's touch will soothe you beyond measure. I know this to be true."

He also knew that Gloriana's touch could delight beyond pleasure, but he pushed that thought from his mind so he might direct all his attention toward the miserable mare.

Crystal stood spraddle-legged, her sides heaving, her elegant neck stretched low to the ground. Her normally expressive ears lay flat. Blizzard snorted, emitting a wheezing sound of concern now and again, and pawed continually at his bedding.

Dante felt Gloriana studying him, comparing each inch of his person against the image she held in her mind. He'd watched other women welcome their men home from battle with such intent perusals, which often ended with the women flinging themselves joyfully into their husbands' arms. Given her recent annoyance with him, he supposed he would have to content himself with knowing that her first concern had been for him rather than for her ailing mare. It was a small consolation when every inch of his flesh longed to feel hers pressed against it.

"You . . . you're not injured."

He shook his head. The wounds he suffered in the aftermath of battle did not bleed, and he had learned long ago to hide them from those who valued his cool head and steady sword arm.

Gloriana settled herself quietly in the hay next to him. She touched his upper arm. He felt her featherlight stroke from shoulder to elbow, felt her heat when her finger brushed his skin through a rent in his black shirt. He shuddered, wondering if his face betrayed how desperately he longed to gather her into his arms and feel the reassurance of her heart beating against his.

"Sorry," she said when he flinched. She made a rubbing motion with her fingers. "I was just . . . just brushing some straw from your sleeve. . . . Will Crystal keep the foal?"

"'Tis too soon to tell."

"I didn't know she was . . . well, you know. I mean, I thought she'd been eating too much corn."

"I assure you Blizzard would have been more attentive had he not already performed his job."

Gloriana studied her mare. "What about Crystal? What will happen to her?"

"You could lose her, too. 'Tis in God's hands."

Her eyes glistened, and he would not have blamed her if she burst into tears, for he felt a racking sense of desolation himself to think of so much waste for such little cause.

"You must leave in the morning, Gloriana. Take shelter in Holbrook. I will stay and look after Crystal until it is decided one way or another."

"The hell I will. I'm not leaving Crystal."

"I know fear has robbed you of your senses just now, but if you would just consider the options—"

"Options? How's this for an option—I'd like to kill each and every man responsible for doing this."

"I have taken care of that matter for you."

Some men reveled in killing. Some exulted in retelling each detail. And there were women who clung to every word, breathless with avid excitement—others who covered their ears and pretended their men were not capable of taking lives. Gloriana sucked in her breath and with trembling fingers traced his still-throbbing fist. Her healing touch accorded him a measure of forgiveness and absorbed some of the regret that always filled him when the battle lust drained away.

"I'm so sorry," she whispered. Something in his heart quivered and then crumbled, as if her understanding had breached an invisible wall. "I never meant for you to pay so high a price, even if it means it's safe to stay here now. Dante, I can stay here for as long as I like."

He whirled on her, taking Gloriana by such surprise that she cringed back against the feed sacks. He didn't touch her, but pinned her in place nonetheless, with his arms braced against the wall on both sides of her shoulders.

His eyes, smoldering with dark fires, revealed nothing of his thoughts. His lips hovered inches from her own. He smelled of gunsmoke and hard riding and the heady essence of himself, the scent she had savored on her own skin after he'd made love to her. A strand of his hair had escaped its thong. She wanted desperately to tuck it back in place but feared that she would not be content unless she cupped his head and bridged the gap that separated them, felt those magical lips and the brush of his mustache against her skin.

"You want to stay here?" he rasped, conveying so much disbelief that she might have announced her intention to enter a nunnery.

Glory wished she could call back her words. As usual, she'd spoken without weighing the consequences. No woman in her right mind would admit that despite all the danger, she'd found something compelling about this place. Hearing that Dante had eradicated the outlaws had filled her with such an unspeakable joy that she'd blurted out a truth she hadn't even admitted to herself up until then.

She admitted it all now. She wanted to stay. She wanted to save Crystal and her unborn foal and turn this land over to the raising of beautiful, spirited horses, and to hell with sheep and cattle.

The only problem was, she'd spent practically every moment since she'd met Dante convincing him that she loved circus life. She'd proven her total ineptitude around horses and hadn't even realized that her mare was pregnant. Telling him what was really in her heart would only brand her a scatterbrain in his mind, especially if she told him that none of her newly nurtured dreams would mean a thing without him at her side to share them.

Dante hovered over her, poised like a tiger waiting to pounce the instant its prey moved and betrayed its vulnerability.

What were the options if she told him? He probably wouldn't believe her—that was the first option. Or maybe he would, which would turn out even worse, because then his twisted sense of duty would compel him to stay on until he was sure she was safe. She could hold him that way, at least for a while.

She could hold him even longer if she preyed upon the passion that sizzled between them. She hadn't been able to resist touching him, to reassure herself of his living, breathing solidity, and she knew by the way his breathing had altered, by the simmering hunger in his eyes, that he mastered his desire with only the greatest of effort. She need only slide her hand through the gap in his shirt, curve it around his hot, muscled torso, and draw his weight down upon her. One kiss, one more touch given in the way she truly wanted to touch him, and so much passion would flare between them that they'd probably finish the job the Hash Knife boys had meant to do upon her barn.

Yes, she could kiss him and touch him and thus keep Dante by her side until he forgot all about Elizabeth and crowns and kingdoms. But maybe he never would forget. Maybe he'd pine away just like her mother; maybe he'd live in sullen misery like her father, yearning for something that would never be his. She would have to live the rest of her life knowing she was responsible for stealing his dreams. She did not want him under those circumstances.

"What makes you think I'd ever turn my back on the circus?" Her laughter sounded false, brittle.

If he kissed her, if he murmured, *Because of this, Gloriana,* and breached those insignificant inches separating their flesh, she would risk telling him everything.

"The circus is in your blood," he murmured, almost as if talking to himself. Her disappointment cut so severely that she closed her eyes against the pain. "You are a Carlisle woman. Born to be a star. What need have you for a place such as this?"

He lifted himself away with so little effort that only the dissipation of the heat that had warmed her told her of his desertion. Those few inches separating them were as unbridgeable as the rift cleaving the mountain rim. Trembling, brushing at her sleeves to disguise how badly she wanted to pull him back down upon her, she struggled into a sitting position.

"I just thought it might be nice if I could come here instead of going to Florida every time the season ends."

"You told me you loved Florida. You were not forced to winter there."

"No. I kind of got into the habit because my mother loved the sun and walking along the beach. After she died, well, I just never had anywhere else to go."

Blizzard stamped, and with a sudden lunging motion he kicked at the rails of his stall. Crystal grunted in alarm.

"The stallion's antics are making her nervous."

"I'll walk him." She felt the need to escape this place, where so many of her dreams lay dying.

"Nay. 'Tis time that I took another turn at guard duty. I'll ride out on Blizzard to tire him, so Crystal might rest more easily."

He left her side to busy himself with Blizzard's bridle. He was leaving her again, and shame flooded through her when she realized she would do anything to keep him with her.

"Why do you have to take guard duty? I thought you killed the outlaws."

He pressed his hands against Blizzard's bare back and vaulted easily into position. He gathered the reins into one hand, and his long legs tightened masterfully around Blizzard's barrel.

"We dispatched one band, Gloriana. More will come."

He wasn't running away from powerful feelings, she decided, but was merely concerned about doing his job. She was suddenly fiercely glad that she hadn't divulged her secrets to him. "Peter will take care of them."

"I—"

"I know we didn't get around to doing the mirror trick today, but we'll do it first thing tomorrow."

He nodded and then pressed his knees into the stallion's sides, sending Blizzard through the barn door.

She hurried to the door and watched him. He rode with superb skill, equal to that of the finest circus artistes, but there was no element of showmanship, no expectation of accolades, just a man doing his job supremely well.

Blizzard pulled at the bit, eager to run. Dante held him to an easy lope, unwilling to risk the stallion's legs. The sun sat low, nearing the edge of the mountain rim, and already dusk had fingered its way into the valley. He kept Blizzard in the deepest shadows while he studied the land, searching for signs of the intruders.

He found them deep within the shelter of the mountain cleft. Dante could see their campfires glowing, could smell their supper beans and bacon. If they mourned those who had died earlier that day, Dante saw no evidence of it. Ribald laughter trickled through the air, along with the aimless strumming of a guitar. They were bold, these Hash Knife men, and arrogant in their confidence. And well they might be, for no man could approach their camp without exposing himself to view. Naught save eagles and mountain goats could attack them from above.

He heard soft thuds behind him and turned to see Peter Henley arriving to join him in his vigil. Peter peered through the double spyglass he called binoculars, and he swore with a vituperativeness Dante could not help admiring.

"We didn't even make a goddamned impression on them. Here, have a look for yourself."

Dante squinted through the binoculars. It took a moment for his eyes to adjust, and then he found himself consumed with a proprietary rage when he saw one far-off intruder leaning against a boulder with his feet planted on Gloriana's land, looking as if he would never be dislodged. Dante cursed, vowing all manner of tortures, and then cursed again when the watcher started emitting bright flashes of light that all but blinded Dante. 'Twas as if tiny explosions burst from his hands.

"Wonder who he's signaling," Peter mused.

The flashes took on a crude rhythm. Flash. Flash flash. Flash pause flash flash. Dante remembered Gloriana tapping her fingers in the air, claiming that people could send messages without resorting to the written word. "Aha, sending a wire."

"Naw. That ain't no wire."

This matter of wires irritated Dante more than he cared to discuss. He would not admit his lack of understanding to Peter Henley.

Peter gave a short, bitter laugh. "That sumbitch over there is helping himself to the U.S. Army heliograph system. You think they might've taken those damned mirrors with them when they pulled up stakes."

"Mirrors?"

"Yeah, shuttered mirrors, to send Morse code. The Army had the entire Arizona Territory covered at one time, and then abandoned most of the works two, three years back. Pulled out when Geronimo surrendered. Should've stuck around until they wiped out the real problem here in Pleasant Valley."

A second flurry of flashes answered from far up on the northern section of the mountain rim, and then a third set blinked so far away that its flash was little more than the wink of a star.

"'Twould appear they had no difficulty establishing outposts along the northern rim."

"You can thank the Army for that, too. Built a road along the rim to cut the travel time between Fort Apache and Fort Verde. Goddamn trail follows the top of the rim, curves back a few miles to encircle the upper end of the rift, and circles back to the rim on the other side like an upside-down U. The Hash Knife men don't even bother patrolling the south section of the road, on account of there's no way to get past the upper end of the rift without running into their ambush."

Peter studied the flashes of light and swore again beneath his breath.

"You can read this message?" At Peter's curt nod, Dante pressed. "What are they saying?"

Peter's lips moved as he spelled out the message the mirrors conveyed.

"Bragging. Saying this raid went according to plan. They're gonna lay low for a couple days and then wipe out the Canyon Rock Ranch for good."

"We must stop them."

Peter snorted. "Glory's pa was the last man to try driving them out of that camp. They got men posted at both ends of the rift. Any man crossing the valley's an easy target from the bottom. They'd shoot a stranger on sight if you tried approaching from the top. As long as they control the pass, come winter nobody can stop them from sending the sheep through."

"If we sealed the lower portion of the pass, they would be forced to seek another route."

"There ain't no way to seal it. They're not going to sit by their campfires while we go build a fence across the rift."

"An explosive charge might send enough rock tumbling down the side to fill it."

"Yeah. That dynamite in Glory's barn could do the trick." Peter rubbed his chin, and something about the idea served to change his mind. "Naw. You'd have to blow up both sides of the rift to churn up enough rock."

"Is this dynamite not capable of blowing up both sides?"

"Hell, it'd blow up this whole mountain if you got the charges set right. That's the problem. You could use the Army trail to blow the south side. Ain't no way to get over to the north side of the rift without using the road that circles the upper end. You'd never get through the Hash Knife ambush. Can't climb it, either. The rock face is sheer all around."

Dante borrowed the binoculars and verified Peter's opinion.

"I could stand on the accessible side and throw the dynamite across the rift."

Peter snorted his disbelief. "It's a hell of a lot farther than it looks from down here."

"I have a strong arm."

"Yeah, but how accurate can you be? Unless you place that charge just right, it ain't going to do much good. Besides, you can't go around throwing lit dynamite. It could explode in your hand or while it's in the air. Either way you'd end up dead. And if the blast didn't kill you, it'd alert the Hash Knifers to what you're trying to do, and I don't think they'd take kindly to it."

"There must be other options I have not yet considered."

"I don't know why you're so all-fired worried about it. You're leaving. And I mean to hustle Miss Gloriana Carlisle out of here tomorrow whether she wants to go or not."

"She might have other plans."

"She can make all the plans she wants. She won't have much choice, though, if them Hash Knife boys keep launching ambushes from that camp over there."

Gloriana had said time and again that she meant to spend only a brief time on her ranch, so there was no reason why knowing she would have to cut her visit short by a day or two should make him feel so sad. No reason save for knowing the decision would not be hers. Gloriana was well accustomed to burying her desires when circumstances demanded it of her: spending her life in the circus in pursuit of her mother's dreams, not her own; wintering in Florida because she had nowhere else to go; perhaps even marrying Peter, because she could not hope to hold on to this ranch without Peter's support.

It came to Dante then that he had a gift he could give to her, something she had never been given in all her life. He did not require the wealth or power of a king to do it, but only the determination of a man who loved his woman.

He could give Gloriana a choice.

18

Gloriana stirred, brought to half-wakefulness by the determined bird warbling outside her window. She slitted one eye open and groaned. Full dark, which meant no more than an hour or two had passed since Mr. Blue had practically forced her from the barn, promising he would watch over Crystal. *You would think,* she grumbled to herself, *that the danged bird could wait a little, considering dawn breaks godawfully early this time of the year.*

She closed her eye, though she knew it would be futile. She'd never fall asleep again, not with all the worries she had sneaking back into her mind. Crystal. The Hash Knife outlaws. And Dante. Most of all, Dante—and not just because he was out there guarding her land, but because he'd be leaving soon, and sleeping through even one minute of the time she had left with him seemed like such a waste.

She tried to ease from her bed, but exhaustion made her clumsy, and she knocked her knee against the dressing table. "Sorry," she whispered, just in case she'd woken Maud. But since she heard no grunted acknowledgment in return, she probably hadn't made all that much noise. Come to think of it, except for the blasted bird, there wasn't any noise at all. Not even Maud's rhythmic sleeping breathing.

And that was because Maud's bed was empty.

Maud had been sitting on the edge of her bed, twisting an old rope-walking slipper in her hands, when Glory had staggered in from the barn. Her worn cheeks had seemed uncharacteristically flushed. She had dragged her trunk out of the corner, and its lid gapped open, as if Maud had emptied it and then shoved all her clothes back in without bothering to pack them properly. Glory had merely flopped into bed, too tired to ask Maud about her flustered state or whether anything had developed between her and one of Peter's cowhands, who had been particularly attentive to Maud during dinner.

Maud's empty bed gave Glory all the explanation she needed. There weren't many things that led a woman to root through her entire wardrobe and then sneak out in the middle of night. She knew, because she'd fought with that same urge herself, thinking of Dante sleeping alone amidst the skeleton of a house that had been built for love.

Glory looked up and noticed that either her eyes had gotten used to the dark or the danged bird hadn't been rushing the dawn after all. The square of sky framed by the window lightened from black to charcoal and then to velvety gray. Mr. Blue had seemed to think that if Crystal held on to the foal until the sacred azure sky dispelled the darkness, mama and baby would survive. Rubbing the tiredness from her eyes, Glory headed for the barn, praying for a miracle.

She heard Mrs. Blue's humming when she eased through the barn door. The sound filled her with a wistful envy. Mrs. Blue, like Maud, had abandoned her bed in the middle of the night to keep her man company. How wonderful it must feel to have that right. Her mother and father had never shared such simple intimacies. Neither, it seemed, would she, considering that the only man she had any interest in sitting up with would soon be leaving forever.

Mrs. Blue greeted her with a smile and patted the straw next to her.

"I don't want to take your husband's place," Glory whispered. She took a quick look at Crystal and felt relief sweep through her when she saw that the mare's condition showed improvement. Even as she watched, Crystal's ears twitched a welcome, and the mare took a delicate sip from her water bucket. Blizzard's stall stood empty, which meant Dante still prowled the valley.

Mrs. Blue patted the straw again.

Glory supposed that Mr. Blue, like many of the older men with the circus, found it necessary to take a predawn stroll. Not exactly a matter for polite conversation, especially since any conversation with Mrs. Blue was by necessity decidedly one-sided.

She leaned against the bales stacked behind them. Mrs. Blue's humming shifted into something softer, with a hauntingly beautiful melody. Crystal nickered approval.

"I think she's going to be all right," Glory said. Mrs. Blue smiled and nodded.

Glory nestled into the straw. She could understand now why they used it for horse bedding. The stuff was awfully comfortable. Mrs. Blue's soothing melody washed over her. Glory's eyelids drooped shut and a comforting warmth swept through her. But then her chin fell to her chest and she jolted upright, realizing that she'd nearly fallen asleep.

There was still no sign of Mr. Blue.

"Where's your husband?"

Mrs. Blue smiled.

"Maud's not—" Glory clamped her lips shut as an awful suspicion struck her.

Mrs. Blue smiled, dispelling that suspicion, and patted Glory's head in the manner of an adult shushing a child who asked too many precocious questions.

Glory knew she couldn't get any answers from her, anyway, and everyone who could explain what was going on had disappeared. She sighed and settled back against the straw. She'd get to the bottom of it all later, after she'd had a little rest.

Dante gripped Mr. Blue's shoulder while they both stared across the mountain rift. As Peter had said, the chasm that had seemed conquerable from the valley floor yawned impossibly wide when measured at closer range. "Can you do it?"

"A boy with his first bow could place the arrow between the two likeliest boulders," said Mr. Blue. "But I have never tried striking a target with a rope tied to my arrow. I do not know how it will affect the arrow's flight."

"You have to wedge it in there real good," Maud cautioned. "That rope has got to stretch tight—they do call 'em tightropes for a reason. If it sags, I'm a goner."

"I will beg the kachina's blessing for you, old woman."

"Whew, that's a load off my mind,"

"*Can* you do it, Maud?" Dante asked gently.

She bristled at the question, although her indignation didn't quite erase the worry from her eyes. "I got my rope-walking costume on, don't I?"

So that explained her odd manner of dress. She wore an elaborately bejeweled and beribboned gown of an unnaturally intense pink. It bared an alarming portion of Maud's upper reaches and belled from her waist to end just below her knees. Her tight stockings clung to calves so heavily muscled that Dante had not seen their equal, even among the most march-hardened foot soldiers. She wore dainty satin slippers upon her feet; they were so thin and clinging that they flexed like a second skin when she curled her toes.

"I see Bohemians are not the only ones to set such store by their costumes."

His teasing prompted a weak smile from her. "This is my chance to repay Glory for taking me in, making me feel like I'm part of a family. I'd do anything for her."

"Even this? One misstep, Maud, shall send you plunging hundreds—"

She raised her hand to stop him. "This ain't the time to lecture me about weighing my options. Gimme that dynamite."

"Let me and Mr. Blue see to the stringing of your wire first."

"That ain't a wire. That's nothing but a fat old rope."

It seemed Dante would never master the identification of wire. He examined the arrow, tested the knot, and handed the unique missile to Mr. Blue.

"Dante?" Maud quavered.

"Aye?"

"That bundle I propped against that rock over there? I brought the mirror like you asked. I wanted you to know it's there, just in case . . . in case I . . . forget to tell you later."

"I will need help with it, Maud. I am counting upon you, but I will explain what is required of you later—when you return."

She nodded. Maud did not yet know that Dante would ask her to spirit him away. And for good reason. If this daring plan succeeded, Gloriana might be grateful. He thought of those Gloriana kept closest around her, Maud and the horses: all castoffs and misfits who had once performed good services for her. He could not bear it if gratitude alone caused her to add him to her collection, and so he would go.

Mr. Blue set the arrow and took his mark. He drew the bowstring taut and, his lips murmuring a prayer, let the arrow fly. It cut through the air with a whine, and the rope coiled at Mr. Blue's feet hissed as it unwound—then silence.

"Pull." Dante ground the order through a throat gone impossibly dry.

They all three pulled, and none betrayed a doubt for the endless time that passed until a hint of resistance proved the accuracy of Mr. Blue's aim. They pulled harder, and the rope lifted from the ground to the height of their arms. "The tree," Dante called, and they looped the rope around the trunk of a sturdy pine, pulling until they were exhausted and the rope vibrated from the tension they exerted upon it.

"Hold it there," Maud gasped. She grabbed hold of the rope and gave it a tug. Her throat worked; she swallowed—hard—several times, and when she spoke her voice held an unfamiliar tremor. "Good enough. I can walk on that."

When Crystal lipped some oats from her hand, Glory knew the crisis had passed.

Mrs. Blue smiled and left the barn, leaving Glory with the wordless impression that she intended to prepare an enormous breakfast. Glory stayed for a while, scratching around Crystal's ears, crooning her special name and remembering how Dante had pretended disgust with it and yet showed his affection for the horses by using their secret names, too.

He would be exhausted after standing guard all night. She wandered out of the barn, hoping to catch sight of him riding in for breakfast, but only a few of Peter's hands milled around near the ranch house. She blinked and looked again—one of the men sipping coffee was the older fellow she'd assumed Maud had gone off with during the night.

Worry skittered down her spine.

She ran to the ranch house, barely acknowledging the "howdys" and "morning, ma'ams" the cowboys sent her way. She raced through the kitchen and past Mrs. Blue to the bedroom. No Maud. Heart pounding, she pressed her fist against her mouth. The cowboy—she would demand to know if he'd seen Maud, but in a casual way that wouldn't imply that Glory had suspected they'd spent the night together. Oh, the hell with Maud's reputation—she'd ask him flat out if he'd been with her.

But where could they have spent the night? Maud abhorred rocks and insects, so it was unlikely she would have agreed to a tryst out in the open. The Hash Knife cowboys had burnt down the granary. The barn wouldn't have afforded any privacy, since someone had been in there watching over Crystal all night long.

The wagon.

She should've thought of it straight off. Heavens, Maud might have just decided to sleep there, considering her low opinion of the ranch house. Glory charged

back through the house and through the crowd of men.
Their somewhat puzzled "howdys" and "ma'ams" followed her to the wagon. She gripped the latch and flung
open the door.

"Maud?"

Only silence and dust motes drifting in the sunlight
greeted her in return.

Next to the door, the secret panel stood ajar.

Her mirror was gone.

"No." She backed away from the wagon as hurt and
confusion slammed through her.

"Mornin', Miss Glory." She barely registered Peter's
arrival, her thoughts were so aswirl. Maud missing. The
mirror gone. Mr. Blue vanished. Dante still absent,
although the other guards had returned. It was all connected somehow, but how?

"Sure looks like it's gonna shape up to be a fine day,"
said Peter. His cheerfulness penetrated her despair,
making her want to pummel him into silence so she
could think.

Maud, the mirror, Mr. Blue, Dante. She wrapped her
arms around her waist and stared out over the valley.
Nothing. She searched the mountain rim. Nothing.

The rift . . . it was different somehow.

She took a few steps toward the mountain. Such a
minute change in distance couldn't possibly put anything into clearer perspective, but the ripening dawn
somehow did. Golden orange suffused the sky, revealing a thin black line stretching across the rift. And
something, or someone—no more than a tiny glittering
bump at this distance—inched slowly along the line.

Suddenly images flashed through Glory's mind:
Maud sitting on the bed, twisting her old rope-walking
shoe; her trunk in disarray, meaning she'd gone looking
for something packed deep, such as her rope-walking

costume that had caught the light and dazzled the audience in those long-ago days when Maud dared dance across the ropes . . .

"No! Maudie, no!" She screamed the denial.

Peter pulled his horse up next to her. "Miss Glory?" Concern creased his features. He dismounted, walking toward her with his hand held out, like someone approaching a growling dog. "Miss Glory? Are you all right?"

She whirled on him, absurdly reminded of how unpleasant she'd always found it to leave the beach knowing she'd have to spend hours dislodging all the annoying sand that clung to her skin.

Her attention flickered from Peter to his riderless horse standing behind him, doing nothing. She took three running steps, wedged her hands against the horse's rump, and vaulted high into the saddle.

"Miss Glory?"

Surprise propelled the horse forward. Glory hooked her knee around the saddle horn, the way the horse acrobats had taught her, and caught the reins before the horse stumbled over them and killed them both. She settled back into the saddle and crouched low against the horse's neck, urging it across the valley and toward the mountain.

Dante stood as close to the edge as he dared. Maude had begged him to stay there, watching, as if his worried presence would help her cling to the rope. His heart had lurched with every tentative step, with every chance breeze, and he cursed the fool who had ever devised the notion that a woman might hold a pole across her hands and brave a chasm with it. But at last she inched her way back, and with a muffled cry that betrayed her sheer terror, Maud launched herself from the rope into his arms, sending them both staggering backward to safety.

"You placed the dynamite exactly right," he whispered, feeling completely inadequate to still the tremors still quaking through her small form.

"Mmm-hmm," she sobbed into his shoulder.

"You stretched the fuse perfectly to give Mr. Blue a clear shot."

"Mmm-hmm," she sniffled.

"You have proven your oft-stated claim that you are the foremost tightrope artiste in the civilized world. I daresay you could once more challenge the infamous Marietta Ravel."

She leaned back and met his worried gaze with her own tear-filled one, hiccuped, and then clapped a hand over her mouth. "Dante," she mumbled against her palm, "haul me over to that tree. I don't think I can make it under my own steam."

He set her carefully amidst the pine needles and turned away to afford her privacy while she hunched, heaving, near its base.

"I am ready with the fire arrow, *bahana*."

Dante wrenched a sturdy twig from the pine's lowest branch and joined Mr. Blue. He pressed the end of his twig to the flaming tip of the arrow. "I will light the charge on this side once the other catches," he said.

This daring plan would succeed. The fire carried the scent of success.

"Maud," he called, "stand ready to run at my command."

"I . . . I think you're going to have to carry me, Dante."

Mr. Blue placed the arrow. It flew heavenward before curving down in a graceful arch, its tip burning with the fire that would ignite the fuse. Even one so unskilled in the art of bowmanship as Dante could see that its trajectory would carry it to the waiting fuse.

And then the flame gracing its tip flickered out, leaving only a trailing a wisp of smoke.

Dante cursed. Mr. Blue muttered dark words Dante could not understand. The arrow, uncaring that its purpose had been thwarted, buried itself perfectly in the fuse and mocked them with the knowledge that their task had so nearly been completed.

"Try it again."

"Yes, *bahana,* but . . . "

The uncertainty in Mr. Blue worried Dante. "But what, Mr. Blue?"

"That arrow might deflect any others I send near."

"Do your best, my friend."

The next arrow held its flame but bounced away when its tip did indeed strike the already imbedded one. Mr. Blue altered course just a fraction with the next, but it was enough to let the flame burn harmlessly only inches away from the fuse. Again and again he tried, until his quiver stood empty and his shoulders sagged with defeat.

"The old woman, *bahana.* She must go back and light it from that side. We could fashion a longer fuse, to give her time to return before the explosion."

Dante glanced toward Maud and cursed yet again. He had never witnessed such anguish etched into another human's face.

"I'm sorry," she whispered. "I want to do it. I swear I do. But I . . . I looked down, and my legs turned to goddamn rubber. I don't think I can even stand up right now, let alone cross that rope twice more."

Nor could he do it himself. Merely standing at the edge of the rift had all but paralyzed him; he could never force his clumsy, unskilled carcass across that yawning abyss.

The sun drifted higher, casting its unblinking eye upon his defeat. The Hash Knife outlaws would begin stirring soon from their hideout. If only one of them rode out into the valley and chanced to see the line stretched over the rift, the mountain would swarm with killers determined to put a halt to their plan.

The bitter gall of failure flooded him, making him want to kneel at Maud's side and retch into the base of the tree, too. He had come so close, employing every conceivable tool, only to lose by inches. Naught but a finger-snapping wizard could light that dynamite from across the rift.

Ah, but bundled near a rock sat the flame-starting magic mirror of a long-dead, meddling sorcerer. Mirror flashes, according to Peter, were so common here that a few more might not be noticed at all.

The sun settled overhead, so white-hot that the dew clinging to the pine needles evaporated into wisps of steam. Deflecting that blistering beam toward the opposite side of the rift might light the fuse. But exposing the ancient mirror to such intense, unforgiving sun might shatter it, ending forever all hope of returning to his own time.

"Mr. Blue, help Maud and begin making your way down the mountain."

Dante ran to fetch the mirror.

INTERLUDE
Whitehall Palace, London, 1603

John Dee studied his queen.

Seventy years of living had stripped her handsomeness away. Her special white almond paste no longer hid the ravages time had exacted upon her wrinkled countenance, even from a distance. Against the unnatural pallor the false curls of her wig appeared more garishly orange than ever before. He knew she dared not smile lest she bare the ruined teeth that had ever plagued her.

And yet he looked upon her and thought her the most beautiful of women, this brave, indomitable female who dared rule a kingdom alone.

"Gloriana," he whispered. "Faerie queen."

She ignored him as had always been her whim. But this time he could take no offense. She had been sunk in misery ever since the swelling of her fingers had led her physicians to prescribe the removal of her coronation ring. She sat there now, staring into her lap, where she clasped together the sausage-shaped digits that had once awed the world with their deft grace.

"They cut my ring away, John," she said dully, as if he had not been aware of it.

"The physicians feared it impaired your circulation, Majesty."

"How could it? It has been my life's blood for more than forty years. No woman could treasure a wedding ring more."

She began to hum. Dee recognized the tune, penned years earlier by an obscure upstart to poke fun at Elizabeth's prolonged spinsterhood: "Here is my hand, my dear lover, England!" She broke the tune off abruptly.

"I have regrets, John."

He had known her for more than half a century and had never heard her express a single regret. It boded ill that she should choose to do so now.

"Nay, Majesty. 'Tis this accursed January chill that

plunges you into despair now that Christmas is past and winter looms long." He paused and swallowed against the pain that rose in his throat. Winter would not seem long to his queen, for if his charts and readings proved true, she would not live to see another spring. "In fact, my purpose in coming to you today was to urge your immediate withdrawal from this palace. Hie to Richmond House, my lady. Its warmth will soothe the aches from your bones—"

"You need not tell me to beware the intrigue swirling about me here at Whitehall amongst my so-called friends and advisors. They sense my weakness and circle like a pack of wolves round a wounded deer. They vie for the chance to be the first to inform my godson that he might add England's seal to his banner. James Stuart, King of Scotland *and* England—pah." She spit the name and titles like an epithet.

"James is an excellent choice of successor." Dee struggled to hide his amazement and his gratified smile. Elizabeth's advisors waited in vain to hear the very information she had just given him. "Your counselors and the people would accept him—"

"Considering that I neglected to provide an heir of my own body," she snapped.

"This, then, is your regret, Majesty?"

"I should say not! I endured considerable hardship to avoid that very thing, as well you know, John Dee, having provided me with no small measure of assistance."

He wondered if Elizabeth's wits had begun to wander. The stars foretold that a humiliating loss of senses would prove to be the ultimate harbinger of death for this woman who had ruled by wits alone.

"Tell me, then, Majesty, what it is that troubles you,

for I am a doddering old man and have lost any quickness of mind that I might once have claimed."

"There is no profit in recounting them, for all who might deserve an apology are dead." And then, to contradict her statement, she began listing them. "I regret that I doubted Leicester when some whispered his first wife's death was no accident. I regret ordering Essex's execution. I regret withholding from Cecil the knowledge of how highly I treasured his presence as a friend as well as an advisor. And I regret other matters too sundry to recount." Dee made a small murmur of acknowledgment, certain she had exhausted herself upon the matter. "And," Elizabeth continued, "I regret not answering this."

She opened her swollen hand to reveal a dried brown lump studded with the remnants of prickly spines. It lay atop a yellowed scrap of paper, so worn at the creases that Dee knew it had been folded and unfolded, read and reread, times beyond counting.

"The note Dante Trevani sent through the mirror so long ago."

"Aye."

Elizabeth, to Dee's knowledge, had never mentioned Trevani's name to anyone but Dee himself. He had hidden the truth of Trevani's disappearance from his queen for so many years. Perhaps, with the end approaching for them both, he should admit what had happened lest he be forced to atone in the afterworld for his meddling.

"Mayhap, my lady, you might ease your regret in regards to Trevani."

"He is not dead?"

"I do not know. 'Tis possible, but 'tis more probable that he lives still." Dee drew a deep breath, assuredly the most painful one he had ever drawn. "Many years ago, when he would have honored his word, I forced him—"

Elizabeth placed a hand against his arm, shocking him into silence.

"Whose mind wanders now, hmm? I distinctly remember telling you once before that I did not care to be plagued with knowing this man's whereabouts."

"I remember, Majesty."

"It seems we both have regrets, John. And I think they stem from our failure to let Trevani know that no man could have served me better. Let us send a royal response to honor a toothless old man who once dared presume he might marry a queen."

Dee knew he could not tell his aged queen that time might have passed differently for Trevani than for them. Trevani might well claim all his teeth yet, as well as some measure of vitality. The awful possibility occurred to him that hearing from Elizabeth might summon Trevani himself through the mirror. Seeing Trevani still enjoying the full bloom of manhood whilst her own charms had deteriorated would send Elizabeth into an unprecedented rage.

"Knowing what I do of the man, 'twould not surprise me to learn that he felt honor-bound to strive still to reach your side and press you into marriage even at this late date."

Elizabeth blinked and straightened. Her rusty, cackling laugh roused an answering smile in Dee. "Nigh unto sixty-five years since last he saw me, and still he pines, eh, John?"

"One glimpse of your splendor is all that was ever required to bind a man to you, Majesty."

"I shall draw up the letter myself so he knows his suit will be met with no more success than were any of the others." She spoke with the assurance of a woman convinced once more of her desirability. "Fetch your mirror and come back to me. Do it at once, for I mean to order the withdrawal of my household to Richmond House, and I would have this chore disposed of ere then."

John Dee took his leave of his queen, leaving her more happily and busily engaged than she had been for weeks. And as he made his slow way to his chambers, he marveled at the wisdom of the stars. His long-ago meddling and Trevani's chance transmission of the letter had bought Dee's queen a moment's respite from her woes in this, her darkest hour.

It had all been worth it.

19

Gloriana found Mr. Blue working his way down the narrow trail. He carried Maud flung over his shoulder like a sack of flour. Maud craned her neck and sent Glory a feeble smile.

"I'll deal with you later," Glory said, trying her best to sound stern while relief and gratitude at finding Maud safe turned her all mushy.

"Don't go up there, honey. You'll just have to run back down again. Dante's going to blow up the mountain and get rid of those Hash Knife outlaws for you."

Glory didn't wait to ask the hundred questions Maud's comment provoked. She pummeled the sides of her tired mount to urge it past her friends. It seemed to take an eternity to clamber up to the rim. The horse found easier footing atop the summit and obeyed Glory's urging for speed, more speed, as they galloped toward the rift.

She spotted Dante facing the great gash in the mountain, so intent upon studying the opposite side that he paid no heed to her arrival. Her gaze followed the direction of his attention. She saw the rope stretched over the rift. It pointed to a thinner strand. Arrows studded the ground near the strand, which curled up the side of a boulder and buried itself in a cluster of small tubes. Dynamite.

As she watched, Dante hoisted her mirror high above his head.

The wind whipped his sun-bronzed hair. It found the gaps in his shirt and plastered the black cotton against his chest, belling it at the back, but not even that distortion could hide the power of his shoulders, the swell of his biceps as he tilted the mirror toward the sun.

She slid from the horse's back and collapsed into a boneless heap on the ground, certain he meant to deflect the beam upon himself. He was leaving her.

The mirror flashed. Brilliant patches of light skipped over rocks, across a sandy patch. Gloriana shivered; why was he delaying turning the mirror upon himself? He knew as well as she did the risk he ran of shattering the mirror by exposing it to such intense sunlight. As if to confirm her opinion of the sun's dangerous strength, a tuft of scrub grass burst into flame the instant the reflected beam swept over it.

Dante shifted his stance ever so slightly. The mirror's next flash struck a rock clear across the rift. The beam danced across a stone-strewn ledge, and with the next flash a pattern became apparent. He was aiming for the thin strand that led to the dynamite charge.

Gloriana had lived with that mirror, worked with it, used it, and hated it for twenty-four years. She knew the light-bending capabilities of that mirror. To light the fuse from this distance, he would have to hold it steady for such a prolonged period of time that there was no chance the ancient glass could survive the exposure. Which meant it would shatter before he turned it upon himself, and he could never use its magical properties to send him back in time. He would have to abandon his dream of claiming a queen and a kingdom. Dante Trevani intended to give up everything for her, Gloriana Carlisle.

"Dante," she whispered, her heart so full that it kept her in place. She pressed trembling hands against the dirt, determined to rise so that she could stop him. He didn't have to destroy the mirror, not now that he'd proved he loved her enough to do it. She pulled herself upright and impulsively gave a hug of thanks to the brave and noble beast who'd carried her up the mountain to witness this fulfillment of all her dreams.

And then, so slowly that she had to blink to believe what she was seeing, Dante lowered the mirror.

His shoulders shook—no, cold, hard mountains didn't shake. It must have been the wind rippling across his shirt that made it seem as though he trembled and sagged as he turned the mirror into his chest, protecting its reflective face from the sun.

He had made his decision. The mirror survived, and so did his dreams. Hers had never had a chance.

Dante heard a low, muffled sob and knew it wasn't the moaning of the wind through the rift.

It might have come from within himself.

He held the mirror against his breast, so sickened by what he had nearly done that he feared he might drop the ancient looking glass and accidentally bring about the disaster he meant to avert. He heard the sob again, from behind him this time, and he swung a dull glance toward it.

Gloriana, her arms wrapped around the neck of

Peter Henley's exhausted horse, stared at him woodenly with a disbelief that matched his own.

He hadn't heard her arrival at all, he'd been so immersed in the sounds of the wind and his own pounding heartbeat and the echoes in his mind weighing the potential outcomes of the irrevocable action he'd been engaged in. Her expression shifted into its unreadable actress's mask, but there was no hiding the tremor of anger that shook her. He supposed he should count himself lucky that she carried no gun or fistful of daggers, else he might have found himself struck down.

"Bring it here," she said, tipping her chin toward the mirror. "I'll hold it and finish what you really meant to do."

Silently he handed the mirror to her. A sense of inevitability swept through him. This was as it should be. A boulder stood two paces away; he crossed to it and leaned against its solid bulk, shifting once or twice when protrusions gouged through his shirt.

"Quit fidgeting," she said.

"Fidgeting, Gloriana?"

"Fidgeting. Hopping around like a nervous cat. But I guess you're so anxious to get back to Elizabeth that you can't stand still."

"Oh. Elizabeth." He turned away from Gloriana and braced his forearms against the boulder. His position gave him an excellent view of the tightrope, the perfectly placed dynamite. A wasted effort—but he would think of another plan.

The skin at the back of his neck began to prickle and then to burn with so much heat that it felt as if all the rays of the sun had been directed to that very spot.

He clapped his hand over it but found no relief; it seemed the heat meant to bore straight through his palm. He whirled about and found Gloriana standing there, aiming the mirror straight at his heart.

"*This* is what you choose?" he gasped.

"No." A small quiver shook her voice, and tears brimmed in her eyes. "It's what *you* choose. I saw you, Dante. I saw you turn the mirror away so it wouldn't shatter. You made your choice."

"Nay, Gloriana. You saw me turn the mirror away so you might choose your own destiny."

Her hold upon the mirror faltered, but not enough to dislodge the relentless beam. The odor of burning cotton struck his nose at the same time a searing pain brushed his skin. He dove into the dirt, and with a sharp sizzle, the boulder he had been leaning on simply . . . vanished.

She advanced upon him, holding the mirror before her like a shielded knight bearing down upon an enemy.

"What do you mean, choose my own destiny?"

Dante felt tendrils of heat crawl along his belly. "The mirror, Gloriana. Set it down."

"I can't! I love you."

"You . . . you love *me?*"

He sorely regretted his lifelong habit of using words sparingly, but he realized that it would never change. Even now, when he knew words were important, he wanted only to crush her in his embrace and hold on to her forevermore.

"Yes, I love you! So stay still while I make you disappear."

God's blood, but no crossbowman possessed a deadlier aim with his weapon than did Gloriana with her mirror. Dante flopped about with all the desperation of a grounded eel, and still he could not dodge her light bursts. He smelled burning hair. He howled when light sizzled against his leg.

"Gloriana, for God's sake, stop it! I love you, too!"

"You . . . you love *me*?"

"Aye!"

He rose to a crouch. She wavered, the mirror dancing harmlessly. He waddled, ducklike, a bit closer to her. And then resolve crossed her features.

"It'll prove how much I love you if I send you away."

"And 'twould prove how much I love you if I followed you to the circus."

"Well, I don't want to send you away!" She shouted the words with enough force to stir those stubborn boulders from their perches and make the dynamite unnecessary.

"And I do not want to follow you!" he boomed in response.

"What if . . . what if we just stayed here together?"

He swallowed against the fullness in his heart. "'Tis the best option of all, beloved."

He reached toward her, and she slipped her hand into his. With a gentle tug, he brought her down to the ground next to him. He took the mirror from her other hand and placed it face down in the dirt. "I meant to blow up this mountain, Gloriana."

"I know. Maud told me."

"I wanted to make this ranch safe for you. But just before the fuse began to smolder, I realized I was truly forcing my own heart's desire upon you."

She stared at him, uncomprehending.

And suddenly he was sick to death of hiding his true feelings from her, even if it cost him her love. "I wanted that mirror to shatter, Gloriana. I wanted to make it impossible for you to choose to return to the circus."

"Why?"

"A thousand reasons. Because of the way the light fades from your eyes when you think about your job.

Because I cannot bear the actress face and smile that obliterates the Gloriana I love. Because I would willingly throttle any man who dares watch you strut your bosoms in the circus ring."

"Strut my bosoms! Why, I never— Who told you such a thing?"

"Peter explained it to me. He understands all there is to know about circuses and thinks it would be a fine thing to find himself married to a star."

"You would not think it so fine, Dante?"

"I would despise becoming your husband."

She let out a small whimper that pierced his soul. "Ah, Gloriana, as always when I speak of important things, the words come wrong. I would despise being married to Madame Boadecia. I would love nothing more than being married to Gloriana Trevani."

She stared at him, and he hated that the hope he saw rising within her was a tentative, frightened thing.

"Stars shine for any who care to gape upward at them, Gloriana. I want my lady wife to shine only for me. For *me*."

She gave a delicate little sniff. She touched a finger to the corner of her eye and wiped away the tiny tear that clung there like a diamond. And then she hurled herself against him with such force that he fell back against the ground with her lying atop him while she pressed featherlight kisses over his face and neck and the hole she had burned through his shirt.

And then she grew still.

"What about marrying the queen of England and becoming royal consort? Can you turn your back on all that without regret, Dante?"

"My only regret is that we must spend time exploding this mountain when I would far rather cause the earth to shake through gentler pursuits." He claimed her lips with his, tasted her mouth, explored her body, until the thundering of their hearts rivaled any noise the dynamite might create.

They did it together. They stood side by side and directed the sunlight toward the far-off fuse. It seemed to take forever. "Hold steady," Gloriana said softly when he began to curse. He held steady, until a crackling sizzle all but exploded through the mirror. The fuse smoldered, and just as the first finger of flame shot from its edge, the mirror they held crumbled as if it had been fashioned from dried mud.

"Hurry!" He bent to light the fuse for the charge on their side of the mountain. Gloriana bent, too, to capture a bit of paper that fluttered in the breeze. Hand in hand they raced to the horse. Dante mounted first and then pulled Gloriana in front of him so that she might be sheltered within his arms as he goaded the tired horse into motion.

They were well out of danger when they heard a rumble and then a roar behind them. Dante turned to see a geyser of rock spewing into the sky and then falling down upon itself, disappearing into the rift. Though he felt no remorse for his action, he whispered a prayer for the souls of those who would not escape the passage.

Gloriana watched, too, and then she pressed her head against his shoulder.

"Dante, she wrote a letter to you. Elizabeth. It's . . . it's so full of curlicues, I can't read it."

Gloriana handed him a scrap of paper, the one she'd caught drifting in the breeze. Age had yellowed it and faded the bold script of its writer. The edges had been scorched; some of the letter had been burned away, but enough remained to dazzle him with the wonder of it.

Great happiness was mine. I hope you have found

your share. I am not a generous woman, but I pay for value received. Accordingly, I dub thee Sir Dante Alberto Trevani, loyal Knight of the Realm.

Elizabeth R

Gloriana leaned into his arm to stare at him. Trepidation marked her features. "What does it say?"

It said he had been given it all. A title. Respect. The gratitude of a queen. And they were insignificant prattle against knowing that he was loved by Gloriana.

"'Tis nothing," he said. He crumpled the letter into a ball and let it drop into the dirt.

"I don't understand," Gloriana persisted.

He felt a broad, sappy smile curve his lips as he bent to kiss his beloved.

"It means, Gloriana, that thou art stuckest with me for all eternity."

Epilogue

Dante dreaded the first meeting with his daughter.

No man consumed with love for his wife could be expected to welcome the squalling mite whose arrival had rent such screams from Gloriana's throat and racked her slender body with the demands of providing entrance to this world. And yet when he stepped into their room he saw his lady wife resting comfortably and crooning a soft melody, and Dante found there was something oddly appealing about the tiny red-gold head pressed against Gloriana's breast.

Gloriana looked up at him, and Dante all but staggered from the love glowing from her. The child's arrival had intensified rather than diminished the wondrous light of her eyes, and he had not realized until that moment how much he had feared its loss.

Never again.

"Your papa is here," Gloriana murmured, carefully

cupping their daughter's head and turning her so that
Dante might greet her face-to-face.

Newborn babes looked like wrinkle-faced possums.
They did not smile and were as blind as moles, and only
women considered them beautiful. Or so all the cowboys had warned.

They, obviously, had not seen Dante's daughter.

He would have to hurry to Holbrook so he might
purchase one of Mr. Eastman's wondrous photograph
cameras, so all the world might see pictures of his
daughter. Her perfect little lips curled upward in greeting. Her wide eyes wandered around and settled for one
heart-skewering second upon him, promising to bathe
him with her own version of the light his soul would
endlessly crave.

"A Carlisle woman," he breathed, thinking it a fine
thing that he had some part in thus brightening the
world.

"With no small amount of Trevani." Gloriana
pressed a kiss against the curls crowning the baby's
head, and then she smiled up at Dante. "But some of
the Carlisle women's traditions should prevail."

"And what is that, beloved?"

"She should be named after a queen. I thought we
might name her Elizabeth."

Author's Note

Elizabeth Tudor, known to be a shrewd judge of character, endured considerable criticism for her life-long support of Dr. John Dee.

Dee, a mathematical genius, shared an intense interest in astronomy with Copernicus. But while Copernicus was and is revered as the founder of the science of astronomy, Dee's studies led him along the less-respected paths of mysticism and astrology and earned him little but scorn.

Dee recognized the importance and fragility of the written word, and single-handedly amassed what was then England's largest library, containing four thousand volumes, sparking a widespread interest in preserving ancient texts that benefits us to this day.

He earned his doctorate from St. John's College at Cambridge. He was later drummed out of the university, charged with conjuring and practicing sorcery. He was ever after known as Dr. Dee, the great conjurer.

Mary Tudor did briefly confine Dee to the Tower of London, on charges of conjuring and conniving. Some sources acknowledge that Dee was responsible for setting the date for Elizabeth's coronation. Elizabeth and her ladies did frequent Dee's Mortlake estate to consult his magic looking glass. And Dee did urge Elizabeth to beware of the intrigues in Whitehall Palace. Elizabeth abandoned that royal residence and died at Richmond House on March 24, 1603.

John Dee's magic glass was sold at auction from the Horace Walpole estate in 1841. It has since . . . disappeared.

Let HarperMonogram Sweep You Away!

Sooner or Later by Debbie Macomber
Twelve million copies of her books in print. Letty Madden asks a soldier of fortune to help her find her brother in Central America, but Murphy's price is high—one night with the demure postmistress. Letty accepts and Murphy realizes that protecting his heart may prove to be his most difficult mission of all.

A Hidden Magic by Terri Lynn Wilhelm
Ghost romance. When Cicely Honeysett sells Griffin Tyrrell her family's estate, she forgets to tell him about the mischievous ghost that has made Cranwick Abbey his own. At odds with the unwelcoming spirit, Griffin yearns for Cicely—a heavenly creature who will share his bed instead of trying to chase him from it.

Queen of My Heart by Donna Valentino
Time travel romance. Dante Trevani escapes from an unwanted betrothal in Tudor England by traveling through time to 19th-century Arizona and beautiful Gloriana Carlisle. When he realizes his fiancée is destined to be the Queen of England, Dante must choose between returning to the past or staying with the queen of his heart.

Montana Morning by Jill Limber
Debut novel. To find a husband and claim her family's ranch in the Montana Territory, Katherine Holman marries Wes Merrick and saves him from the hangman's noose. Wes refuses to ride off into the sunset, however, and instead tries to turn a marriage of convenience into a match made in heaven.

And in case you missed last month's selections . . .

Chances Are by Robin Lee Hatcher
Over three million copies of her books in print. Her young daughter's illness forces traveling actress Faith Butler to take a job at the Jagged R Ranch working for Drake Rutledge. Passions rise when the beautiful thespian is drawn to her rugged employer and the forbidden pleasure of his touch.

Mystic Moon by Patricia Simpson

"One of the premier writers of supernatural romance."—Romantic Times. A brush with death changes Carter Greyson's life and irrevocably links him to an endangered Indian tribe. Dr. Arielle Scott, who is intrigued by the mysterious Carter, shares this destiny—a destiny that will lead them both to the magic of lasting love.

Just a Miracle by Zita Christian

When dashing Jake Darrow brings his medicine show to Coventry, Montana, pharmacist Brenna McAuley wants nothing to do with him. But it's only a matter of time before Brenna discovers that romance is just what the doctor ordered.

Raven's Bride by Lynn Kerstan

When Glenys Shea robbed the reclusive Earl of Ravensby, she never expected to steal his heart instead of his gold. Now the earl's prisoner, the charming thief must prove her innocence—and her love.

Harper Monogram

Buy 4 or more and receive FREE postage & handling

Escape to Romance
and
WIN A YEAR OF ROMANCE!

Ten lucky winners will receive a free year of romance—*more than 30 free books*. Every book HarperMonogram publishes in 1997 will be delivered directly to your doorstep if you are one of the ten winners drawn at random.

Harper Monogram